THE BOOKS OF ALEXANDREA

THE BOOKS OF ALEXANDREA

Book 2: The Between

JH NADLER

ISBN 978-1-7370098-5-6
Library of Congress Control Number (LCCN) 2022914408

This is a work of fiction. The characters and events portrayed in this book are fictitious.
Any similarity to actual events or persons, living or dead, is coincidental and not intended by the author.

Cover design | Jason Nadler
Cover images licensed from Shutterstock
Cover photo of the Author | Laura Nadler
Illuminated Letters | William Morris, public domain

Printed in United States of America

Published by WorkingCat, Inc
Wading River, NY 11792

Visit **jhnadler.com**

For Laura
For all the moments,
For all the hours,
For all the days,
For all the years.

Table of Contents

Chapter Forty-Three

lex and Abby watched Heather and Rose climb into Heather's car and drive off, tracking the rising cloud of dirt as they disappeared through the field and eventually found the road.

They stood wordlessly for another few minutes, when Abby finally asked, "Do you want to pull some glass later? I'll fire up the kiln."

Alex mulled it over for just a moment. "Sure." *Anything to feel normal.*

Abby didn't move.

Why is she stalling?

"Care to share your plan?"

Can she read my mind?

Alex touched her chest, below Abby's charm. "The way I see it, Matthew knows where I am. I have two choices. I can wait for him to come…"

"Or?"

"I have no idea where Matthew is or where he's keeping Billy. Either he'll come when he's ready, or I make some noise, and make him come."

Abby gently patted Alex on the back. "I like the second one too."

"I thought you might, Abby." Alex said.

Grinning, Abby started towards the barn.

With so much uncertainty ahead, Alex was grateful for Abby's friendship. She thought it should feel strange for her closest friend to have been childhood friends with Peter, her father, but it didn't. The limits to what Abby would willingly do for Alex seemed endless. She'd already died for her, twice. Yet, Abby never asked for reciprocation. Alex tried, but Abby wanted nothing in return.

She never wants anything but to be there for me.

From Alex's earliest memories, a visit from Aunt Abby meant gifts and hours of ceaseless attention. Abby—always in her sleeveless shirts—would forsake her adult friends to spend every moment with

Alex She made playtime with Alex a necessity, as though time spent with her was a sustenance and she craved it to survive the drought between visits; but the gulf between those visits expanded as Alex grew into a teenager. Being doted upon felt smothering and time with Abby was like time with her mother: Alex found she'd rather be alone.

Abby was all but forgotten after Alex's parents died—after Matthew murdered them—until she showed up with Heather to rescue her and her cousins after their exploits at Picnic Rock. It was as though Abby waited until the very instant she was most needed.

Alex's chest warmly swelled just thinking about Abby; *she's my Familiar*. Abby swore herself to protect Alex, before she was even born. Peter asked Abby to be *his* Familiar, but Abby picked *her*. The thought played as a smile across her face: Abby loved her that much.

Alex closed her eyes and breathed in the grassy-scented warm air sweeping through the cornfields. The hypnotic rustling of cornstalks gave her pause. She'd had so few moments of peace that abandoning this one—no matter how appealing learning to pull glass might be—felt like ignoring a gift. The past week had been a whirlwind; an onslaught she still hadn't processed. One day everything would hit her, and that collision would come with the inertia of a locomotive. *A week ago, I couldn't hear someone talk about magic and today I'm a witch. The only witch left in the world.* The thought was like a fantasy she might have pretended as a child.

She opened her eyes and looked up. The sky above was crisp and blue, with only a faint smudging of high clouds. It was peaceful, lacking portents of the storm that must be lingering just below the horizon. How else to explain the buzzing static that drew the hairs on her neck and arms upright? She pulled her long, auburn hair out of its ponytail, and let it spill onto her shoulders. The breeze playfully pushed it back.

She closed her eyes, taking it all in. The sun warmed her face, glowing orange through her closed eyelids. She tried to ignore the waves of whispering as the constant din of incomprehensible voices began drowning out her thoughts. The wash of agitated voices overcame the wind rustling the leaves of corn. She sighed, abandoned the peace, tied up her hair, and headed to the barn.

Chapter Forty-Four

efore she laid her hand on the weathered barn door, Abby's voice cautioned, "Alex, come slowly."

Breath held its place in her lungs. Abby never spoke to her with such authority.

Alex's mind flashed visions of Abby's studio knocked asunder, of damaged equipment, and hundreds of glass beads, frosted with cracks, cast across the floor. The culprit could have been anything, from an errant raccoon, to a vandal, to…. The overwhelming urge to rush in and save Abby from Matthew's vicious attack splashed her like a bucket of ice-water. Rushing in was dangerous so she pulled on the reins of her panic to obey Abby's caution.

Alex stared at the peeling scabs of red paint that freckled the wooden, sun-bleached door. Possible scenarios whirled around Alex's head, drowned out by the whispers, punctuated by her heart kicking the inside of her ribs. Whatever provoked Abby's caution was behind that door. Were her words more than a warning? Had she told Alex— secretly—to prepare for a fight? Or to prepare for something worse... something horrible?

Then, finally she heard Abby's voice, "Alex, come in, *slowly*." She pulled and the door groaned open. Stepping forward, darkness swallowed her vision. She proceeded blindly as the door creaked closed, her eyes laboring to adjust to the darkness. Her mouth suddenly parched.

The light sneaking in illuminated three gray silhouettes. Abby was easy to discern, but the right silhouette was unknown to Alex. The one on the left, however, she knew she recognized. Not even the scars she was beginning to discern could disguise his face. Part of her knew she was responsible for those scars, and that part ached for the anguish she'd caused. She'd burned George. He combusted within her devouring flames. *Did he become a part of me?* Why else would her chest ache so for him?

Abby pleaded, "Alex, please, look at me."

Alex's eyes refused to leave George.

Her stomach and heart were at immediate odds. He forced her to the Library. He tormented her with Abigail's—his sister's—Book. He forced it into her hands, making her experience what Abigail endured as he—her brother—extracted her magic to create it. She burned Abigail's Book; she burned the Library; she burned George. Until this moment, she was certain she'd killed him. Released from that guilt, she ached at the scars covering so much of him. Despite all he'd done, her heart trembled with grief over the physical manifestation of his suffering. Her gut believed he got off lucky, but her heart wanted to comfort him, to ease his suffering, and to heal him.

Alex's gaze shifted slightly to the right. Everything about the man to Abby's left was coiled tight, ready to spring, and yet, he merely stood, his hip tipped like he might rest one foot on a box and tell a story. He smoothed his slick long hair. It was dark, like he dyed it with shoe polish. Except for a few errant hairs, it hadn't known his forehead in some time.

Alex could almost feel the scalpel blade of his studious gaze cutting her skin as it sliced and dissected her. Conclusions read across his face, his expression transforming from shifty-eyed gunslinger to disappointment. His mouth barely moved. "This her?" His voice cracked the silence, like a startling gunshot. She had such anticipation of the guttural words of a spell that when none came it took her a moment to realize he'd spoken.

George's voice was meek by comparison. "Johnny, meet Alex."

Johnny thoughtfully neutralized his expression, converting disappointment to disinterest. "I'm Johnny Cortese. I'm here to see what you can do." He held onto the silence, as though it were a chess piece he hadn't committed to moving. Then he withdrew his hand, "Go on, show me your stuff."

Is this what it's like for witches, men demanding they perform? Alex ignored Johnny's question; his words soaked with condescension. Instead, she asked George, "Where's Billy?"

"Is that that kid you mentioned?" Johnny asked.

George confirmed Johnny's inquiry.

"Where is he, George?" Alex repeated.

"Alex, Jeremiah sent us to—"

"You're talking to me," Johnny ordered like a cracked whip.

Alex faced him, her stomach queasy, palms sweating. She

didn't know who this Johnny was, but everything about him, his appearance, his posture, his tone, threatened her with professional, but violent indifference. Somehow, she managed to keep her tone even when she said, "Come on, Abby. Let's go."

Johnny grabbed Abby's wrist with the accuracy of a striking viper. "Neither of you are goin' anywhere." He pulled Abby closer and growled, "Show me what you can do. Then Jeremiah delivers your kid."

Abby never appeared so frightened before. Uncertainty chopped Alex's response. She knew what he was asking—the same thing Matthew asked—but her magic didn't work on command. She didn't know how to summon or control it. She tensed and replied, "I don't do party tricks."

Johnny rolled his eyes. He looked at George. His expression accused, *I told you so*.

George's expression soured as he stretched the scarred half of his face. Alex's somersaulting gut told her Johnny found nothing funny about her comment. The eye roll wasn't amusement; it was a warning.

As though it fell into his palm, Johnny appeared his Book. He snapped it open. Abby twisted from his grasp, nearly upsetting the Book from his hand. He colored the guttural words with disgust.

The barn lit up in sharp flashes and blinding bolts of light that left neon-orange streaks in Alex's vision once darkness returned. Like hot knives cauterizing her skin, the crackling electrical sparks punched into her, violently throwing her to the ground. Her body vibrated as electricity ricocheted around her insides. Her fingertips throbbed like they might pop.

Abby grappled Johnny to the ground, frantically pulling at his Book to dislodge it from his covetous hands. She snarled and grunted viciously. Johnny yelped at her aggression, her fists softening his grip on his Book as she protected Alex.

George kneeled beside Alex's crumpled form, "Are you okay?"

Alex flashed a poisonous sneer at George; benevolent feelings seared her chest. George disgusted her, yet she found herself accepting his hand as he helped her to her feet.

Abby nearly knocked the Book from Johnny's hands. She pried and kicked while he punched, unable to read from his book.

Abby absorbed his strikes as afterthoughts. She responded to each of his punches with her own. She was rabid, growing frenzied as she broke Johnny's nose and opened a wound in his intent.

George made to escape the barn, beckoning Alex follow. Abby would want her to get to safety, but Alex wouldn't leave her Familiar. Abby kept fighting for control of the Book, but Johnny guarded the tome to the detriment of his face. Seeing an opportunity to help Abby, she threw herself onto the pile. Her hands hunted for the Book, intent on burning it, even if that meant turning Johnny to char.

Johnny grunted for George to help. Alex anticipated he'd stay out of the melee. Yet George's arm slung across her chest and wrenched her from the pile. He dragged her, writhing and kicking to break free. Abby's attention turned to George. She snarled and looked as though she might launch at the boy when her eyes rolled back into her head. Johnny swung his Book, repeatedly knocking consciousness from Abby's skull.

Alex's head screamed, whispers—like fingers clawing the inside of her skull—shrieked in a frenzied panic. Johnny reclaimed his Book and without hesitation, fired at defenseless Abby. Alex's stomach tumultuously twisted like a rag being wrung out. A wave of angry revulsion washed through her with such force she found it difficult to breathe.

Johnny fired again, the sharp, guttural words punctuating each strike like an exclamation point made of knives. For added measure, he struck George, "Get away from the girl, George," he taunted.

George leapt from Alex's side, "We're supposed to *check* if she has magic."

Johnny lowered his Book. Abby was curled on the ground like a bundle of laundry. She stirred, looking hastily for Alex, her apologetic eyes begging for forgiveness. Alex wanted to crawl to her, comfort her, heal her. She didn't move, however; fear froze her joints like rust. This wasn't Matthew provoking her. Johnny Cortese regarded her as dispassionately as he might a discarded candy wrapper.

"What do you think we're doing, you ugly freak?" Johnny sneered at George, as he slicked his hair into place. With a weighted breath, he recentered his steps to face Alex. His eyes snapped to the open page. With a guttural outburst, bolts of lightning struck George. The more George howled, shook, and cowered; the more Johnny cackled.

Alex yearned to make him stop, but given she or Abby were the alternative, she'd allow Johnny's sport of George.

"Show me what you can do!" Johnny screamed. His words startled her, carrying more ferocity than any lightning bolt; as though she'd grown accustomed to the guttural words, the crackling bolts, the yelps, the laughter. His eyes threatened her each time they flinched down to his open pages.

She tried to answer, but aftershocks from her quaking hands reverberated throughout her body, choking her words. Alex's whispers started howling; loud enough that she expected Johnny to see sound waves disrupting the air around her head. She stepped backwards, her heart fluttering like the drumroll at an execution. She thought of Picnic Rock, and her rage splitting the enormous stone. *Why can't that happen now?*

He stared, like a high-noon gunfighter, waiting for her flinch. She was becoming convinced her six-shooters were loaded with blanks. Like spilled wine soaking through a rag, a smirk spread across his face. "The old man must be confused," Johnny said, disdain draining from his tone. "This girl wouldn't even fill a single page, much less a Book." He looked at George. "This is a waste of my time."

A thought crossed his face and his grin widened over clenched teeth, his jaw flexing like he chewed some unseen cud.

Alex concentrated on the emotions roiling within her, the anger, the hatred—they boiled inside. Yet nothing came out. *Am I too afraid? Have too much to lose?* She didn't understand how in one instance her magic unleashed itself and another it remained mute.

Johnny lunged at her, feigning a strike. Alex's body betrayed her and startled. Johnny glared at Alex and bared his teeth, his grin now a grimace. His eyes dropped to the page. Alex's body tried turning her in the hopes that once the door was in view, she'd run. But Alex wouldn't leave Abby.

The harsh edges of his guttural words hurt her ears. The strike knocking the breath from Alex's lungs and her feet from beneath her.

Abby's crumpled form elongated like a compressed spring. In a single motion she was shielding Alex with her own body. A barrage of lightning bolts struck her back like glowing hammers. She grunted, her eyes fixed on Alex, even as tears tumbled down her cheeks.

The expression shifting across Johnny Cortese's face reflected the change in his strategy. He didn't care who he struck. He'd make Alex watch her Familiar die.

"Do something, Alex! You have to—" George's words were swallowed by a scream elicited by an errant bolt.

Abby used the reprieve to fortify her resolve. Her hands held Alex's shoulders. She would not take her eyes off Alex, as though ensuring her last sight as she perished. "Look at me Alex," she whispered. "You can do this. Focus."

Alex couldn't bear this any longer. Nothing was happening. Her head wailed so loudly the sounds around her—Abby's screams, the electrical discharges thudding into Abby's back, the repeating mantra of guttural words—all muted, as though heard through popped eardrums. Her fists clenched. Her nervousness, her fear, evacuated forcefully from her body as though a valve had snapped. Rage flooded her, filled her, threatened to pop her seams. The intensity of the emotion grew, like the heat of a blacksmiths forge; each strike into Abby, each wince, was an action of bellows, until whatever blackened steel her magic solidified into turned first red and then glowed, fiery and white.

Alex intended to emerge from behind Abby's protection. She intended to demand Johnny to stop, threaten him with *or else*, to give him the opportunity to save himself. Suddenly, the boiling within her reached such volatility that she felt momentarily calm and clear-headed. The gravity and balance of each emotion hadn't left her; they were still only because they could do nothing more but explode.

The large water barrel Abby used to cool her tools shot a roiling geyser of steam into the air, the water boiling away. The barn groaned; tools danced from the bench to the ground; glass beads argued against their plastic bins until they escaped, plunking from shelf to shelf before shattering explosively on the ground; the annealer cracked in two, spilling cooled glass objects, their shattered remains spinning across the floor.

"What are you doing?" Abby whispered. Dust cascaded from the loft and ceiling.

Johnny lowered his Book, the grin on his face mutating into fear.

George frantically scanned the room, squealing as the tanks— the ones marked propane, acetylene, oxygen—wobbled and shuffled forward, the steel canisters pinging. "No, no, no," he chanted. "Please

Alex, don't burn me again," he begged.

"Focus, Alex," Abby instructed without ordering, as though Alex could control the flow like re-tightening the screwcap on a shaken bottle of soda.

Johnny surveyed the barn before returning to his page. Alex's words were the splintering of wood, thick timber beams reduced to splinters above their heads, the roof of the whole barn—kneeling.

"Focus it on *him*," Abby urged.

George flipped through his Book, like a hurricane disturbed the pages with random indifference.

The whispers in her head roared. Alex didn't know how to focus something she wasn't even sure how she was doing in the first place. She hadn't wanted to break Picnic Rock. Abby got closer, obscuring everything from her sight. "Alex. Focus everything on that sonofabitch."

Her emotions felt like a gushing fire hydrant. In Abby's eyes Alex saw no accusation nor concern—Abby was prepared to die at her side. Abby willed her to focus. Abby gave her permission to obliterate him without judgement. Alex's anger, her disgust, her hatred hesitated. She could perceive the reach of her emotion, like phantom limbs vining throughout the barn. Alex and Abby's eyes locked. Abby stepped aside—revealing Johnny—who had been torturing Abby's back with his bolts the whole time.

Seeing Johnny, Alex's vision narrowed as though the universe was a singular tunnel with her at one end and him at the other. The sensation that filled the barn focused like sunlight through a magnifying glass.

Johnny's face went wild as every facet of Alex's rage twisted upon him. He must have felt the convergence of her disgust willing his body apart. Dust in the air instantly snapped to the space his body previously occupied. He'd disappeared, but Alex's emotions poured from her.

"He's gone. He got away. Johnny escaped." George pleaded for her to stop.

Every muscle in Alex's body tightened to the point of spasm. Her chest burned, her anger pulsing like fiery blood. She wanted to rip him apart for harming Abby. Not even his departure could salve her rage. Like he'd stepped into another room and Alex still had words for him, but these words were magic and nothing and could stop her from saying her piece.

George closed his Book and hugged it against his waist. He repeated, "Johnny's gone. It's over."

"Don't come any closer," Alex warned. Her wrath swelled into the space around them, knocking over volatile tanks of fuel, swelling dust into the air as beams shattered and the barn roof groaned closer to the floor.

"It's going to be okay, Alex. I won't let him hurt you." Abby put her arms around Alex and drew her close. "He ran away. Let your feelings go. He's gone. It's okay." Abby kept talking. "You don't realize how strong you are. You'll learn control. It's okay."

Alex shot a look at George, daring him to speak. She expected an *I told you so* from him: *Women are too emotional to safely wield magic.* Instead, he fled outside.

Abby cradled Alex's head. "It's okay. You scared him. You are so strong you didn't need to do anything but show him you could. They both ran. It's just us now. You and me."

Alex's anger quelled, like a lump of molten steel falling into ice water. Realizing she was tearing Abby's barn down on their heads, she released a single gasping sob.

Dust settled, the tanks stilled, but the beams still groaned under the weight of the sagging roof.

Tears streamed down Abby's face, which she promptly wiped away.

That the barn hadn't yet fallen on them seemed more a function of opposing forces of collapse. The walls leaned inward, and the roof buckled down. "I'm so sorry, Abby," Alex said.

Abby pulled her along by the arm. "Let's get out of here." The load bearing beams bled waterfalls of dust from their breakpoints. "Those won't hold for long."

Alex's insides threatening to heave up her throat. *This was Abby's barn. She made glass charms here.* She touched her charm, the dark swirls of burned herbs encircling an infinitely black sphere like the negative image of a galaxy. *She made this here. I destroyed the one place that was special to her. I almost killed my family because I burned the roast. I got emotional and magic got away from me.*

Outside, Alex tried telling Abby she was sorry for destroying the barn, that she didn't mean to, when Abby interrupted her. "It's okay. It wasn't your fault. But George needs to explain what he's doing here." Abby turned and looked directly at George, standing awkwardly, opposite them.

At the threat in Abby's tone, George's body went rigid. Daylight revealed the full extent of his burns. Through Alex's disdain, pity welled up. The George she met a few days ago had been handsome: short dark-brown hair framed his face; his large, wide-set brown eyes reminded Alex of a puppy. Had he not been hiding in her bedroom she might have thought him attractive. Instead, she pushed him down a flight of stairs.

Alex's unhealed burns were raw, itchy patches on her arms and legs. She wasn't ready to make them go away, even though she could in any instant she chose. Their presence was a reminder of her pain when the actions of another changed her skin: it was no longer hers alone. She hated Matthew for her burns. *Does George blame me for his?*

She hoped to avoid saying anything he might misconstrue as an apology. She still remembered the feeling, her body transformed by pain, tortured to flame, as other men fed George into her, sacrificing his flesh to evacuate her from the Library. He writhed inside her as she fed on him. She couldn't help but feel pity. Couldn't help but ache for him. The whispers had settled, but each time her eyes fell on George, their volume rose.

Alex broke the long silence, "Start talking."

"Please hear me out," George begged. "Jeremiah sent us. I had no idea he was going to hurt you. You've gotta believe me."

"I don't have to do anything." She approached like a bull spotting a red cloth, watching his growing panic. *I need to know what he knows.* She tried to soften her approach, "I didn't believe Matthew when he told me you survived."

"He told you?"

With three backward steps, Abby extracted herself from the conversation.

"Why didn't they heal you?" Alex regretted the question. It felt insensitive; unsympathetic.

"They did." He looked away, "I know I'm ghastly."

The knee-jerk reaction to contradict him out of politeness would have escaped had she not clamped her mouth shut. But he *was* ghastly. He was also Sara's son. Sara Frost, the witch Matthew killed, the witch who broke Alex's curse, the witch who is the reason she has magic now. She imagined one whisper inside her head belonged to Sara. *Am I feeling her sympathy? I wish she'd tell me what to do with him.* Did he deserve pity or condemnation?

George leaned against a nearby maple tree for support. "Only women can heal," he said apologetically. "They have no choice. They're forced." He looked at his feet.

She almost asked how but didn't want to know. She didn't know who or what most disgusted her.

George spoke softly, looking directly as Alex, "I don't blame you, you know."

"Blame *me*?" Her whispers surged, like a gust of wind, as if they too were annoyed by his assumption and were talking themselves back from striking him.

He shifted his weight against the tree trunk and shook his head. "I should never have given you Abigail's Book."

"That's where you draw the line? Sara was your mother. Abigail, your twin sister. Matthew killed Sara to make a Book, and you did the same to your sister. Showing me her Book is where you went too far?"

Abby grinned.

There was only one reason for their conversation to continue. "I want Billy returned."

George started slowly, "Jeremiah controls the Library. He knows what Matthew is up to. He wants to meet you... about Matthew."

Me? I won't be a pawn in their fight.

"I'm—I'm doing what I have to do to get healed...." He took several trembling breaths. He looked unwell, as though his will was exhausted, his body upright on fumes. "Helping Jeremiah is the only way to save myself." He wet his mouth. "Jeremiah's not just the power behind the Library; he controls everything."

Why is George afraid of him? "Billy is my terms."

George appeared introspective. "He'll do that."

Alex shared a glance with Abby. She was as skeptical as Abby looked. "Don't you need to ask?"

"If that's what it takes for you to agree to meet him." George closed his eyes, deep in concentration as he struggled through a wave of discomfort. "He's powerful, Alex. I don't think there's anything he can't make happen."

Abby made a face. Alex didn't need to ask what Abby was thinking: another trap.

Abby interjected, "Jeremiah negotiates with witches?"

"Circumstances are extenuating." He shifted his weight, grimacing and panting.

He's in agony. Why is he enduring this? "Why does Jeremiah need me? If he's so powerful, why not just kill Matthew? Or me?"

George listened. "He could. If he wanted. He wants to meet the girl who burned his Library."

"Why?"

"He plays a longer game," George protested. "Jeremiah is… old."

"Matthew is old."

"Matthew is maybe three hundred. Jeremiah is… different."

Abby pointed at George, "What's that mean?"

"To most people, the world seems static. Most of the people alive when you're young will be around when you're older. They all grow old together. You know how old I am. I've watched multiple generations be born, grow old, and die. My world isn't static. I've seen change, shifts in belief and culture. Jeremiah comprehends it. He controls it. Like this world is his and he allows us to live in it. Living that long does things to a person we can't begin to understand."

Abby chimed in, "Sounds alienating. Losing everyone over and over. At what point do people like you stop being human?"

George didn't acknowledge Abby, but her words clearly stung, like they reminded him of lives and loves lost. His eyes lingered on her even as he spoke to Alex. "You're different. An anomaly. A woman with real magic. You're not supposed to exist. Not anymore."

"How do I know he won't try taking the Books back?"

George leaned harder against the tree. Excruciating pain animated his expressions. "You don't. But it's not always about Books. It's the Library. It has a power, this collection of all magic, like housing it all in one place made it special. It's ancient. It's hallowed. The story is that it once was a building *here*, like an ancient temple or something, but older than that, grander, and he tore it out of *this* world and hid it *there*. That made the place special. It gave the Library power."

"Then why should I meet with him?"

"I share Matthew's concern: The Library is available to

anyone who knows how to find it. What happens if the wrong people got their hands on it?"

Alex and Abby both laughed. Alex said, "Wrong-er than the people who have it now?"

George braced against the tree like he was preventing the maple from tumbling over. "Jeremiah is too powerful. Jeremiah removed nearly all the magic from the world." George swallowed hard and composed himself. "Take it from Jeremiah."

Alex finished, "To give to Matthew?"

Abby stepped forward. "You're asking her to steal a whole Library. If she can do that, how could Matthew protect one Book? Once all magic is in one Book, it's impossible to protect."

Alex nodded in agreement.

He stared at her, panting. His eyes shiny with tears.

"Why don't you sit down?" Alex couldn't believe the compassion in her voice. *Why am I worried about him?*

"I'm okay," he hissed. He shook like the ground rumbled beneath his feet. "You need to choose a side."

"I don't care about their fight. I only care about one thing."

"Meet him. You'll get Billy back."

"When?"

George opened his mouth and realized she'd agreed. "Tomorrow?"

Alex agreed. *When did Heather say Book Club was meeting? Six?* "Seven tomorrow evening. Where?"

"Jeremiah suggested someplace not personal. Maybe my old house?"

Alex crossed her arms. "That's a little personal to me."

Abby took a step forward, interjecting herself, "What about the fallow farm field? It's just tall grass and ticks."

Alex knew the field well. Winding paths meandered through tall grass between a dead end in her neighborhood to the state park where the stone foundation of Sara's home still stands. "Works for me."

"Our Book Club will be there," Abby said like she was putting down a poker-chip and calling.

"Book Club?" George looked perplexed.

"She means our Coven," Alex clarified. Heather coined the euphemism when discussing magic would twist Alex in pain. "This is to talk, right?" The whispers in Alex's head were roaring. They didn't trust this either.

"Yes."

"Will you be there too?"

George bit down on his initial answer. "Maybe. A few others, too. Can I ask you a question?" George's tone suggested he was no longer discussing business. Alex nodded and he continued, "Matthew never knew where you were. Jeremiah is certain. Why?"

Alex tried to stifle her grin; her mother kept her hidden from Matthew by pairing her coin to her unborn brother's. This also made Alex unable to have magic. Once her mother, Holly, righted them, it made sense Jeremiah could find her. George's confusion amused her. "Maybe you should ask them."

Abby grinned.

George's frame collapsed, spent, against the maple. "A word of advice," he extended a trembling finger in the air. "Don't underestimate Jeremiah. There's a reason he's lived so long."

"See you tomorrow, George," Abby dismissed, grinning beside Alex.

George closed his eyes, relieved to be done. He commandeered his energies and forced himself upright.

Alex expected theatrics, like he would step to the shadows and turn into smoke, pop out of existence, or maybe turn into a thousand roaches and scurry away. Instead, walking on shaky legs, he appeared his Book, and disappeared into the dappling light.

Chapter Forty-Five

lex stared at the barn as she hugged Abby. Even as she healed Abby, Alex felt she owed her Familiar so much. She'd destroyed her barn. Any apology felt too small.

Once they separated, Abby spoke like nothing bothered her. "When you fell into that Oblivion and Matthew thought you were dead, he said something about Jeremiah coming to kill him. Maybe he never told Peter about him?"

"I think I know who Jeremiah is." *The old man in a tweed jacket in the Library; the only one not doing anything. Him and his friend.*

While Abby considered what Peter hadn't known or hadn't told her, Alex's whispers chattered relentlessly. "I hate this!" She banged her fist against the tree. "I want Billy safe at home. We should be chasing after Matthew. Then this Jeremiah shows up. I destroy your barn. The only person I hurt is the one protecting me. How do I deal with all this crap?"

"Is Matthew an option, Alex?" Abby ignored the one thing that most bothered Alex. "Especially if Jeremiah is vying for your attention?"

"Why me?"

Abby made a face.

Alex tried not to get emotional. "I know, but I just got magic *yesterday*." The sentence sounded ridiculous. *How can those words even make sense?* "I had a plan. They'd come to us. Instead, I come when they call."

"Well, they did come to you," Abby drawled. "Everything's changed. Did you see their faces? Whatever George and Johnny were expecting, this wasn't it. Get my meaning? They're afraid of you."

"I don't think Jeremiah's afraid. Not even a little." *He wasn't afraid in the Library.* She could still see him observing her through swirls of fire, as everyone panicked.

"But—"

Alex interrupted; she felt there was something important she needed to say aloud. "I burned George in my fire. It was like eating a piece of him." She pressed her abdomen. "Like magic in the Books I've burned, I think he's a part of me now."

"That's kind of gross, Alex." Abby made a face at her. "I'd keep those details to yourself in the future."

Alex couldn't help but laugh. It felt good. Even the whispers subsided.

"Regardless, *I think* they're afraid of you. That gives you an upper hand."

"I need to ask, Abby," Alex began. "Did my father tell you anything you haven't told me?"

Abby crossed her arms, "I'm not keeping secrets."

"I never said you were." She couldn't help but look at the barn. Offending Abby—however unintentional—was like another beam giving way. *I wish she'd yell at me or say something besides, "It's okay." Why can't she blame me?*

Abby lowered her voice, "I haven't kept anything from you. I told you whatever mattered."

"What's that supposed to mean?"

"You hungry?"

Alex put her hands on her hips, "Don't change the subject, Abby."

"No, no," Abby stammered. "Let's talk over food." She wiggled her fingers. "Eating gives me something to do with my hands."

Alex hadn't felt hungry until Abby mentioned it. *Didn't we just eat a few hours ago, with Heather and Rose?* "Sure."

"Good," Abby said cheerfully. "Every time you glance over at the barn, I get the sense that you're waiting for me to scold you like you're a *bad girl*. What's that going to accomplish? I'm sure you feel bad enough without me adding to it. Come on."

Alex followed Abby into the trailer. Abby filled a large pot with water and placed it on the stove and called Alex over.

"Boil it."

Alex responded with a perplexed expression.

"I'm serious. It's practice. Plus, it'll get food on the table in record time."

Alex leaned over the pot. Myriad small bubbles clung to the bottom. She stared at it, trying to will it to boil. She concentrated. She thought about her anger when Johnny hurt Abby. She tried to recreate the feelings, like he was the water. "It's not working."

"Maybe that's where that *watched pot* adage comes from. Try again. Close your eyes. Don't look at it."

"Abby," Alex warned.

"Try. The barn bothers you enough. You won't damage my trailer."

Alex closed her eyes and leaned against the stove. She felt the warm, wet heat circulating from the pot. Again, she worked through the emotions. *Sara said witches once used a recipe, lists of things that drew on certain emotions. If they could do it, why can't I?* She continued to work through hatred, rage, distrust, all the thoughts in her mind the moment they resolved out of the darkness. She tried to flex muscles, real and imaginary, to will the water hotter.

"You know," Abby said quixotically, "I never realized what a big ass you have. I mean, for a skinny girl it's huge. Maybe we shouldn't have pasta."

Alex was sure Abby lost her mind. "What?"

Abby grinned bashfully, "I'm trying to make you angry. You know, help."

Alex glanced behind herself. "My ass is bony. Not big."

"It was worth a try." Abby shooed Alex from the stove.

Alex settled on the couch at the end of the trailer. Quest, one of Abby's cats, curled up beside her. It regarded her, then tucked its head into its side. Alex looked for Marty, Abby's other gray, green-eyed cat, but with a straight tail. *Probably asleep on my bed.*

Once they were eating, Abby said, "I'm going to tell you everything I remember. Okay?"

Alex nodded.

"Your father and me, we were all growing up. That means growing apart. Friends you have in high school aren't necessarily the friends you have in college or after. The important ones stay. I was nineteen, taking classes at the community college in Ashburn and hating it. Heather and your dad were going to college in Albany. Peter announced he wasn't going back after summer break. It didn't go over well with your grandparents, so he called me. Peter can be stubborn; you don't get him to change his mind by arguing—the more you push, the more he digs in.

"He came over. I still lived with my mom. It was like old times, hanging out and talking on my bed. Your father told me about the girl he was crushing on. They met in class. He never studied, he barely paid attention. He knew the subjects cold. He didn't look like a nerd. During finals, she kept covering her test to keep him from cheating. He stood to hand in his test and whispered to her the ones she got wrong. It was their last day of classes. He waited outside and asked for her number."

"My mom?"

"Holly Lynn Tylerson."

Alex repeated, "Holly Lynn Tylerson." There was something lilting about it, its soft rhyme appealed to her. It felt familiar, like a now-remembered fact she'd forgotten. Like it meant something more, something she'd forgotten. *Tylerson.*

"Your mom said it was a rhyming tongue twister. She joked she only married Peter for his name. She was painfully sarcastic."

"I don't remember her being funny. Only tired."

"Then he told me why school wasn't important. He was studying *outside* of school. Years earlier, he met someone on a trip we took to New York City. We were sixteen or seventeen. I asked what he was studying, and he said *sorcery.*"

Alex nearly choked, spitting sauce across the table. "Sorcery? He just said it like that?"

"Like he'd said *accounting* or *engineering.* I waited for a punchline. He was so earnest I didn't know how to react."

"Did you know about magic?"

Abby shook her head. "Not a lick. I thought the twins were playing a game when they talked about it. A secret game your father and Heather shared. You've been introduced to a unique group of believers, but most women, *most people,*" she corrected, "don't believe magic is real." Abby waited a beat. "He knew I wouldn't believe him, so he showed me the Book Matthew gave him."

Alex took a deep breath.

"Which part got you? Was it *Matthew* or *the Book*?" Abby asked.

"Mom told me he was Matthew's student. It's hearing about that moment, that instant they both came together: My dad showing you the Book Matthew gave him. It's one of those moments that has a lot around it, you know?"

Abby nodded solemnly. "It has *gravity.*"

"That's a good word for it." Alex thought about the recent

moments that existed in a well of gravity.

"Peter, your dad, asked me to help him study. Magic sounded cool so I agreed."

"He showed you magic? You saw him do it?" Maybe Abby could help her.

Abby shook her head. "It's forbidden to use without absolute necessity. At least that's what he told me. It's not like there's some school to learn about it. We spent that summer talking about magic like a Theory and Philosophy class.

"He called Holly Lynn Tylerson that same evening," Abby sang the name. "They went on their first date in August. He went back to college in the fall."

"And that's that?"

"Hardly. As things got serious, Peter told me about this idea he was having. He and Heather were twins, Holly and your uncle Steven were, too. He assumed if he and Holly had kids, they'd be twins. He explained he could use that. He'd figured out how to make a witch."

Alex whispered, "Gravity."

"He kept going back to school, I think more to be with Holly. They lived together on campus. Everyone expected they would get married right after graduation. Only he hadn't told Holly yet. He was afraid."

"She'd think he was crazy."

"Except, she knew about magic. Peter knew Steven, her brother. Through Matthew."

"What?"

"Yeah, small world, huh? Like what are the chances he'd fall for his friend's sister so randomly like that?"

Alex didn't feel like eating anymore. "That wasn't chance."

Abby's face was in contradiction, realizing Alex might be right. "Talk about gravity," she gasped. "Matthew put your parents together, didn't he?" Abby shook her head. "I, um, I'm sorry. I should have seen that. It was just this amazing coincidence back then. My mind is blown."

It was all part of his plan. Matthew left nothing to chance. She didn't want Abby to stop. "Go on."

"What I was getting at, before that mind-fuck?" Abby paused, collecting her thoughts.

"Oh, right. They got engaged before graduation. Heather started dating Eric before the wedding. But me, I belong to another tribe." She winked. "There was the stuff that *made us friends*, but those things couldn't *keep us friends*. Magic did. That, and I was going to be someone's godmother." She nudged Alex.

"*Fairy* godmother," Alex cackled.

Abby's glare melted to a smile. "Peter went to the Library from time to time to study."

Alex growled, "I don't like to think of him *going* there."

"I know. Matthew supplied him with piles of documents. It sounded so dry; treatises on magic and such. It was a lot of theory; he wasn't just reading from *Books*. He started finding things; documents left half-hidden on Matthew's desk. It sounds so fantastical, but our conversations were mundane. It was like a side hustle. His friend, William, helped him. William was like Matthew's personal assistant. Matthew didn't do anything without William, and he really took to your father."

Alex remembered the William from her nightmare. In the moment she was so certain. Now it seemed ridiculous that she even entertained the idea that the older man from four years ago was her missing sixteen-year-old cousin. Just recalling him, she realized what it must have been like for him to be there when Peter died. *They were friends?*

"He'd talk about translating magic back to emotion. It was very controversial, but it referenced another book, which he found. This sort of thing happened a lot. I don't know if Matthew was careless or your father was a snoop, but every few months he'd call me all excited about his latest discovery."

"My father may have been a snoop, but Mathew's not careless." *He worked my father.* "He left those things for my father to find."

"Peter worried about that, too."

"He never saw the coincidences?"

"Maybe he didn't want to."

"Untwinning me wasn't his idea, was it? Matthew played him."

"Alex," Abby chided. "Your father wasn't like that."

"Abby, either he knew, or he was an idiot."

Abby's frame shrunk. "Your father wasn't an idiot."

"Then he worked *with* Matthew and lied to you about it."

"He didn't lie. Not to me. Certainly not to Holly or Heather."

"Call it what you want," Alex whispered. "He did what Matthew wanted."

Abby didn't respond.

"Matthew saw me, Abby, when I was in Sara. Two hundred years ago, Matthew saw me and knew I was there." Alex's head felt ready to burst: She felt eight inches away from a realization. It was just out of her grasp, and she kept knocking it with her fingertips. *What am I not understanding?*

"Matthew still could have kept it a secret from him." Abby's tone suggested she was losing her conviction.

"It's like a feedback loop; Matthew saw me in Sara, so he found the man who'd be my father to make sure I'd be there. If I was there, was it inevitable that all that would happen?" The possibilities introduced were mind-numbing. *Was there a version of events when I wasn't there and had to be sent back?* She looked at Abby, "What if we're missing something. Something outside the loop. Something else that made him choose me. Chance, or some prophecy. What are the chances that he planned the whole thing? How meticulous do you have to be to make sure someone is going to be somewhere you already saw them? No, there's something missing. He used them to make me his tool."

"Or weapon," Abby suggested. "Why else would this Jeremiah come to you, a witch? Unless you're more important than Matthew let on."

Alex grabbed her head like it hurt, "I feel like such a friggin' pawn."

"Except your parents figured out how to keep you safe. Maybe Peter was working with Matthew *and* against him."

"Can we be sure Matthew didn't know that, too?" Alex's face lit up with the answer to her own question, "He didn't. That's why couldn't find me. They beat Matthew at his own game."

"What does that mean to us now?"

Alex shuddered. "Matthew thought they were working *with him,* and they fooled him. Maybe that also means Jeremiah doesn't know everything. Maybe there are pieces about me that confuse him, too. That's why he wants to meet me. That's our advantage."

Abby stroked Alex's hand, watching Alex process her

thoughts. In the most soothing voice Abby could muster, she said, "That's the story, Alex. You know the rest. I can't imagine what's happening in your head. Nothing is your fault. You know that, right?"

Alex wondered if Abby was speaking metaphorically about the barn.

Abby thought a moment. "It's so strange how all these pieces are connected. If George and the other asshole hadn't come today, we'd still be in the barn, pulling glass. Instead, we've figured out something about Jeremiah. You've got to feel good about that."

Alex rubbed her eyes, tears just starting to fall.

"Why are you crying?"

"Because I destroyed your barn and all your beads and equipment. Because I'm terrified about tomorrow. I'm going to meet the *most powerful wizard*—or whatever—*in the world*, and I still don't know how to do magic. Because it's my responsibility to stop these horrible men and I'm the only one who can. I'm all alone—no offense —because I'm the only woman, maybe on the planet, who has magic, so it has to be me."

Abby looked at her feet.

"Every part of me wants to run away."

"So run, Alex."

The immediacy in Abby's voice startled Alex. *She means now.* "I bet that's what they think I'll do. Run. Like a scared little girl. But that's just it. I may be terrified, but when I was stuck inside Sara and Matthew was breaking her fingers to pull her spells out, I couldn't run. And you know what?"

"What?" Abby's voice sounded panicked.

"I lived through it."

Abby nodded.

"They killed Sara. But I lived through it. I don't want to go through that again. But I know I can."

Abby nodded.

"I passed their tests. I burned their Library. I didn't even have magic and dozens of them couldn't stop me."

Abby nodded.

"I thought I was really dying when Matthew burned me. I thought that was the end. But that was just the beginning. I got magic. And the moment I did, Matthew was gone."

Abby nodded.

"What am I terrified of? I've lived through things that killed other women. I shouldn't be the one who's scared. I don't even know what I can do yet. I shouldn't be the one who's afraid. Maybe that's why Jeremiah wants to meet and didn't just try to have me killed. Or that's what Johnny was supposed to do and couldn't. He ran away. I scared him. I'm not the one who should be scared. Not today. Not tomorrow. Not ever."

Chapter Forty-Six

bby wiped down and folded the table against the wall. Outside, the darkness disappeared in flashes of distant lightning. The delayed rumble of thunder might have been a truck barreling down the road, past the barn, past the cornfields, past the rutted drive.

Alex's stomach was a riot of discomfort. Her bloated belly ached like it was distended with an extra serving of nerves and emptiness. If she could—without attracting attention—she might have made herself throw up in the bathroom. Except throwing up was disgusting and as addictive as heroin. At least that's what she'd heard.

Abby threw herself against the couch to mindlessly flip through the channels.

Alex learned what one couple hated about their renovation. How the Vikings buried their dead. Stripes and patterns were sometimes okay to mix. Alien landing strips in the desert. A secret society controlling the world governments made decisions impacting the world geo-political stage using a sacred, solid-platinum, diamond-encrusted, twenty-sided die. At the next commercial break, Abby returned to the renovation show.

Alex paid little attention. Connecting the snippets to try making a coherent storyline exhausted her. She gave Abby a hug. "I'm tired."

Abby stared as though she forgot Alex's name. "You feel it, don't you?"

Alex felt something. Like tomorrow was bound by the motherlode of gravity.

Abby tried to smile. "Just because no one told you the truth doesn't mean they were lying."

We're not thinking the same things. Alex pivoted. "I just wish it wasn't so complicated to figure out."

"Only a newspaper's black and white, Alex. Everything else is complicated."

"Did you just make that up?"

Abby grinned. "No, it's from that joke. Black and white and

read all over."

"What's that?"

"A newspaper." Abby explained the joke.

Alex yawned, "Was that funny before the internet?"

Abby stared. "Sometimes I forget how young you are."

"Or how old you are." Alex tried stifling her grin.

"Go to sleep before I smack you," Abby threatened warmly.

Alex walked through the kitchen, past the pantry and the litter box. She stepped into the bathroom and after washing, just stared at herself in the mirror.

I thought I was so mature. She recalled talking with Heather, just last Saturday, trying to convince her aunt she should go to college. *She was waiting but couldn't tell me why.*

She didn't look any older. Perhaps it was the circles under her eyes or the pinched lines at her brow that made her think age happened not through the passing of years, but with the piling of worries and stresses. *I was a kid last week.*

She held out her glass charm. Abby made it for her a few days ago. It was a beautiful work of art: a clear disk of glass with graceful black swirls around an impossibly dark central sphere. Made with herbs from Heather's garden that Abby burned to ash. The position and changing thickness of the lines created a false perspective that gave the charm depth, making it look—from just the right angle— spherical.

So silly. She tipped the charm, breaking the illusion. *I thought this was special; but it's just a pretty piece of glass.* Alex didn't care. Abby made it for her and that made it extraordinary.

Alex undressed. The burns were worse on her legs and back than on her arms. She inspected her raw, waxy skin. *I bet I could heal them in an instant if I wanted.*

Her mind bridged from her burns to George's. Her stomach turned; she might not need to try to vomit. The responsibility of his pain lain on her shoulders like a mountain of razors, but it wasn't hers alone. Matthew, in a sense, burned them both. He burned her directly. *He probably expected George would die at the Library. Another sacrifice to his cause.* Her whispers meandered about her head like a summer breeze in a meadow. She couldn't blame Matthew for everything. George's suffering was her doing, just like hers was Matthew's. George's burns, his transformed flesh, belonged to her now. She could almost still feel his skin boiling away. The sensation was unlike any other. What right did she have to take something so wonderful from someone and return it so misused?

Outside, thunder grumbled. It was in these quiet moments, alone with her thoughts, when the whispers were most audible. They were always noisy; occasionally hidden in distraction. Now they were nearly all Alex could perceive. She couldn't tease a single voice from the cacophony. *I wish I could hear Sara's whispers.* She knew better, at least that's what she told herself: One voice was Sara's, whispering her grief at what had become of her son. She lamented his burns, but more, his molested mind. Which explained what Alex felt whenever he was present. Sara wanted to save him or spare him. For this, Alex left her burns alone. She thought it was important that when she looked at herself, if any part of Sara was inside her, she might see out those same eyes and know that she, too, was thinking of George.

As Alex stepped into the bedroom, the first close rumble of thunder, sharp and booming, startled Marty from his resting place on her pillow. In a terror of claws and fluffed-out fur, the cat disappeared under the bed.

Rain began pounding the trailer like a drumroll. She felt the vibration without touching the ceiling. She slid into the sheets, the cold cotton relieving her skin of warmth. She shut off the light and closed her eyes, listening to the drumming rain and the mountain-slides of thunder, like Picnic Rock cleaving into darkness and rolling away.

Her head quieted: the incessant whispers hushed like an unruly sleepover in the next room. Alex worried her head would deny her sleep. She'd do anything to distract herself from the past several yesterday's barging into her head. No matter how she tightened her eyes or tried to clear her thoughts, her mind intently showed her its ghastly slideshow of memories.

One by one, blurring and distorting, her memories made her dwell on imagery that haunted her like a green-skinned ghoul creeping under her very skin.

Billy leapt from Picnic Rock, his legs propelling him with certainty, his arms clutching air that would have mass in another week when he and Matthew disappeared together in darkness.

Abby dying, the Coven experiencing the painful realities of their fantasy to send her to Sara.

Imprisoned inside Sara. Locked into her body. Matthew torturing Sara… and her. Losing magic as she vomited one spell up at a time. The pain was exquisite; studied and perfectly administered. Hopelessness tore open her heart and shook it empty until death became more desirable than the secession of pain.

The young man her father had been. All he was seeping away.

Heather, when she believed the spell failed and Abby was dead. Then Alex took the Book, Sara's Book. The ink on those pages distilled from Sara's pain, her pain. She was a witness for the Book's conception. And the cause of its incineration.

The utter despair in Heather's voice; Billy and Rose missing in the fire. The betrayal on Heather's face when Eric told Alex that Matthew had them.

Matthew; George's touch. The twisting in her gut as they disappeared into the Library. The guilty relief when the Book he gave her wasn't Rose's, but Abigail's. Burning George.

Marta falling—disappearing from existence—into Oblivion. Falling herself. Finding herself so utterly, starkly, perfectly alone. The entire universe vanished to emptiness. All that remained of her was a mote of dust that once called itself Alexandrea. The jarring, smothering return of all existence when she tumbled out.

Finding her way to Rose's dream-house, the twisting carnival rooms, the horrors of her cousin's mind. Her cousins tying her up to a post like a witch. Matthew apologizing as his magic bloomed flames to burn her alive.

Waking to her mother's voice. Watching her mother separate Alex's dark coins and flip them around, giving her light. Exposing her to the world. Re-living her nightmare, unable to change the outcome, yet being responsible for it. Her parents dying, again.

Returning to the flames, burning. Latching onto one emotional desire. The millions-years-old boulder breaking in two like a twig.

Embracing her aunt. The idea that Heather should return to her own home flowing into Heather. Heather, giving it voice as though it was all that made sense.

Alex took a deep breath and rolled over, sobbing into her pillow to stanch the pain, to prevent the visions from repeating. This was Abby's bed, and the pillow smelled of comfort. Crying racked her breathing as she fought not to sob aloud, still uncertain how she was even alive, uncrippled by her fear and memory.

Desperation waned. Faded. The empty pit flooded with hope, with trust. Alex had magic now. She survived all these things without it. They were memories and couldn't harm her unless she gave them power to do so. That was the past. Although the future was unknown, Alex found confidence that surviving those traumas portended her overcoming whatever threatened next.

Alex pulled her hair back and rolled over. Rain and thunder. Whisperers drifting off to sleep, and then slowly so did she.

Chapter Forty-Seven

s Alex arose from the deep tomb of sleep, the susurration of a thousand voices—as though discovering her an interloper—hushed to a glassy, whispering sea. Then the birds called to one another as though engaged in a debate of ferocious terms, arguing and wooing. The drips and drops, plinking off corners and drains. The breeze shaking the trees dry. Sunrise wasn't silent like night. It came like power returning to a house after darkness disappointed the party: abrupt, loud, joyful. Brightness poured through the blinds, dressing the bed in stripes.

She slipped out of the bedroom. Abby was at the table with a cup of coffee, reading a book. Abby offered to pour her a cup.

"Maybe in an hour," Alex checked the clock. "I feel all this pent-up energy; all I can think about is going for a run."

"You run? Since when? I mean, I never knew."

Alex thought aloud, "Maybe it's the stress, but I have this urge to just do it." She watched Abby for permission, "You mind?"

Abby raised her coffee mug. "Have a blast. I'm capable of feeding myself."

"Can I run on the property? Or do I need to run on the road?"

Abby grinned, "Do I look like I run?"

Alex caught herself laughing; it seemed rude.

Abby pointed towards the driveway. "Head down the drive. Hang a left or a right at the deer fencing, Before you get to the road, near the deep rut where I worry my truck will get jammed up. Pat, the owner of this property, maintains a gravel path for checking the fence."

"Thanks," Alex gave Abby a quick hug. She practically skipped back to her bedroom to change and tie her hair in a ponytail. She looked in the mirror. *What am I doing?*

She waved to Abby as she left the trailer and gazed down the driveway. The road looked far away. She skipped into a jog, speeding to a run. The crunching gravel soft underfoot. She found it easy to speed up. She couldn't remember the last time she intentionally ran—it happened from time to time when she, Rose, or Billy got on a fitness kick, but it never excited her. Now, her feet hitting the gravel, she couldn't think of anything else she'd rather do. *Easy, or you'll peak early. Find your rhythm. Maintain your speed. Keep enough gas in the tank to sprint at the end.* Thoughts slipped through her mind, coaching her. She'd never had such a practiced experience before, as though running came with a plan or a technique. Near the end of the driveway, she swung to her left, found the deer fencing and raced down the gravel path.

Even the whispers quieted once she found her cadence. Her breathing regulated as if by her footfalls, her motion finding its form. *A little faster; good. Less heel, more ball.* She felt at once free and trapped, light on her feet and weighed down by inevitabilities. Something grabbed at her. A branch? Someone loitering sinisterly. A trick of shadow and light? Each turn gave her a startle that was nothing. As she ran further, faster, the encumbering thoughts washed out in her sweat. Soon, her brain could do nothing but put her next foot forward.

Forty minutes later, she turned the fourth corner for the third time. The driveway was ahead. Her feet quickened, her legs burning as she pushed them even as they begged her to walk. The driveway appeared out of nowhere. She skidded as she cornered through her turn, grateful no car was pulling off the road. Her arms pumped. She raced. She couldn't breathe fast enough. She careened past the dilapidated barn and approached the trailer. Her engine shifted into neutral. She coasted. Her pace slowed. Her momentum burned away.

Out of breath, spent but energized, Alex opened the door to the trailer and grinned at Abby.

Abby's expression soured.

"What?"

"Oh, Alex, you stink. I mean, holy crap. You're disgusting." Abby guarded her mouth and nose with her hands. Alex wasn't sure if Abby was feigning dry heaves. "Get in the shower and burn those clothes. While you're getting de-loused, I'll make you breakfast."

Alex tried not to take offense, but then her stench hit her. Without another word, she raced to the bathroom and jumped into the shower, kicking off only her sneakers.

Chapter Forty-Eight

lex laid out her wet clothes on the towel rack, trying to leave the small room tidy. Her legs, butt to calves, throbbed. The run felt good. The shower even better. Once dressed, Alex returned to the kitchen, her hair towel-dried, her face red from exertion. Scents of soap and clean skin wafted about her, but she was sure her stench stubbornly stained the air. Alex sat and Abby served scrambled eggs with shredded cheddar melted on top.

"I made a fresh pot," Abby motioned to the coffee in the countertop machine. "Thirsty? Want water?"

As though by suggestion, her throat parched. Alex filled her glass at the sink multiple times, drinking so fast the water dribbled down the sides of her mouth, leaving dark spots on her shirt.

"I didn't know you ran," Abby said once Alex returned to the table.

"Neither did I," Alex's eyes narrowed. "Ever get an overwhelming urge to do something?"

"Yes," Abby nodded hyperbolically. "Eat cookies, grab pizza, take a nap. Never, ever go for a run."

Alex cackled, strings of cheese dangling from her fork. "It was like if I didn't, I'd be twisted up all day."

Abby studied her. Her eyes widened.

"What? Tell me."

"There was something about your face, like, for a moment. Probably the sweat-flush," she pointed out Alex's cheeks. They looked sunburnt. "For a second, you almost didn't look like yourself."

"What did I look like?"

Abby leaned back in her seat. "You made an expression; something about the corners of your mouth. Your eyes didn't seem your usual."

Alex wanted to make a joke of it, but the grain of truth clung to her like a barb. Alex considered the first Book she picked up in the Library: *The runner*. Realization kicked her in her gut. There was no other explanation for her sudden desire. She almost decided not to say anything out of fear of embarrassment. "If it happens again, let me know right away, okay?"

Thoughtful reluctance tainted Abby's voice, "Sure."

Alex wanted to dismiss Abby's concern as silly. But she couldn't dismiss what could be true. *That runner, was that her?* That meant the whispers weren't just making noise in her head.

"Any word from Heather about Book Club tonight?" When Abby shook her head, Alex asked, "Can we call her?"

"Good idea. Heather will want to hear you did magic today." Abby squeezed Alex's shoulder.

Alex groaned. "It's not like I can do magic on cue."

"But it comes when you need it. Trust me," Abby's eyes widened, "they'll go nuts when they see you do anything." Abby handed Alex her cellphone. Alex held the phone like it was a rectangular bug. "You're a witch, Alex. An adult. The Book Club will look to you as its leader."

The sudden weight of responsibility smothered Alex.

"I know it sucks, Alex. All the time you're a kid, you want to be an adult. When that happens, you're like, *I don't know what I was expecting, but it wasn't this.*"

Alex, with intense seriousness, said, "The shift happened literally overnight. I thought I'd grow into it, you know, gradually. Like, maybe over four years of college." She shook her head. "These women are all old," she added a noticeable, "-er. They're all old-er than me. Suddenly I'm in charge? Isn't it unfair to Heather?"

Abby took the phone back from Alex, dialed Heather, and pushed it into Alex's hand.

Heather answered on the third ring. "Hey Abby, I was just thinking about you guys."

"Aunt Heather, it's Alex."

Heather's voice softened and lowered in pitch. "I was just wondering how you were doing. You, okay? Your burns almost gone? Done any more magic?"

Alex rolled her eyes. "The burns are getting better. I'm fine, I guess." She wasn't sure how to say what needed to be said.

"It's hard to believe, isn't it? Just a week ago you couldn't talk about magic. It's got to be crazy how much has changed for you."

"It's been crazy all right." It was a lifetime ago she and her cousins left on their hike. "How are *you* doing, Aunt Heather?"

The enthusiasm in Heather's voice neutralized. "Rose slept

with me last night. I don't know whether she needed to be with me, or I needed her. Maybe both. Just knowing she's there, hearing her breathing…. I can't stop thinking about Billy. I wonder where he is and what he's thinking and what's happening to him."

"I miss him, too. That's why I called."

"Right," Heather's excitement returned, "Book Club." She laughed. "Now that you're a witch, do you think we should call it our Coven? I mean, we should *own* that word."

"I kind of like Book Club," Alex mused.

"Listen, I was thinking. Should we meet at Abby's so you—"

"We need to meet at your house. At six." Alex thought she could feel Heather bristle at the shift in their dynamic.

"I've been cleaning. The house is still a wreck. But I guess six's fine."

Alex nodded, realizing Heather couldn't see her.

"I'll let them know." Heather made a noise, a hum like she was holding her place in the conversation. "You should know, Nancy called me last night. Marta didn't come to work. Asked if I knew if she was okay. I couldn't lie, but it wasn't easy to say the words. She took it hard."

"I can't blame her," Alex was unsure if she should add anything else. The pause between them seemed made for Alex to offer some eulogistic statement. She'd just met Marta, but Marta was also the first among her Coven to die.

Heather took an audible breath. "What's so important tonight?"

"Aunt Heather," Alex intoned, her voice a little deeper than usual, "I've arranged a meeting."

Heather's voice softened. "Who with?"

Alex didn't want to say the words. The situation didn't bother her so much until she had to verbalize it. Heather would disagree. She wouldn't be wrong. "We're not meeting with Matthew, if that's what you're thinking. There are other, what do I call them, wizards? Whatever. Other wizard-guys. They don't like what Matthew's doing. They want to meet with me… to talk."

"It sounds like you already met with them."

Alex replied, "Yesterday, right after you left, George—you remember George, Sara's son who was working for Matthew? He was in Abby's barn. He's a mess. I all but killed him."

"Serves him right," Heather muttered.

Alex didn't want to argue. Everyone was friend or foe to Heather. George was... different. *Sara's son.* "He arranged the meeting." Alex abbreviated the event; not telling Heather about Johnny Cortese or destroying the barn. *She'll never agree if she knows.* The thought made Alex second-guess herself: If she withheld information to ensure Heather agreed, didn't that prove *she knew* it was wrong?

Heather breathed over the phone.

"This is important, Heather. It's like they're at war or something. Civil war. Better they fight among themselves, right? For whatever reason, they think I can help them with Matthew."

"Who's *they*?"

"George called him Jeremiah."

"Your dad never said that name. Only Matthew." *How much does she know?* "Alexandrea," Heather hissed, "it sounds like a trap. They're setting you up. You know that, don't you? Tell me you saw that right away and don't trust them."

Alex waited a beat, hoping Heather would say something. She didn't. "No, Heather, I don't trust them. I know it's a trap. It's not ideal, but if we can get Billy back, I have to go. Trap or not."

"Alex," Heather started but held her breath like she was waiting for the other words to queue up. "I want Billy back too, but we should consider the risk."

I can take care of myself, Aunt Heather."

"Can you? Are you certain?"

Alex closed her eyes, thinking about the barn collapsing around her. "I am."

Heather said nothing.

"Besides, I'll have the Coven. Like you said, the more witches, the more you can strengthen my magic."

"Oh." There was a change in Heather's tone.

"I don't want to go alone," Alex explained, "but I don't want to put everyone in harm's way."

"We'll make sure they stay safe." Heather's tone possessed unearned confidence.

Alex mouthed the words, *Really, how?* "It's not that simple, Heather. Matthew is terrible, but I get the impression Jeremiah is worse."

"I'll let everyone know we're meeting at my house at six."
"Thanks. Can Abby and I come earlier? Maybe three?"
"Sure, something up?"
"I really miss you and Rose."

Chapter Forty-Nine

lex ended the call and handed Abby back her phone. She slumped down in her seat and rested her head on her hands. "That was exhausting."

Abby eyeballed her as she cleared away the breakfast dishes.

Alex inquired, "Do you mind if we sit for a minute? I'll help."

Abby slid the stacked plates to the side. She watched Alex, not speaking.

Alex's eyes darted about the room. She sighed out her exasperation, then did it again. Several times she wanted to speak, but each time it was easier to release another sigh.

Rather than wait, Abby said, "Something on your mind."

Alex nodded.

"Out with it," Abby ordered.

"I don't know how to say it."

Abby leaned forward, "Whatever it is, just say it. Did Heather say something that upset you?"

"No," Alex blurted. "It's just, I don't know, it's sort of hard to say without, you know…."

"No, I don't know." Abby incompetently disguised her impatience.

"Crazy. It sounds crazy."

"Crazier than witches? Crazier than dressing up in graduation gowns? Which, if you ask me, are the height of witch fashion. The boxy elegance of a black cloak and all the style of tuxedo pleats in a single garment."

Alex laughed until her eyes teared. "I guess it's not *that* crazy."

"Nothing is crazier than that."

"Letting those witches kill you. For the second time," Alex interjected. "That might be crazier."

Abby's cheeks reddened. "That wasn't crazy."

"Oh, no?" Alex laughed as she said, "That's how you spell crazy."

"I guess," Abby whispered. "It seemed like the thing to do." Her tone became jovial, "All the kids are doing it these days. It's totally the rage."

Alex's voice mocked of authority, "Just because your friends let witches kill them, does that mean you should let witches kill you too?"

Abby guffawed. "You're pretty funny, for a witch. They're not generally known for their sense of humor."

"It's not really me; I'm being fed all the best lines."

Abby laughed then stopped. "I don't get it. Did I miss something?"

Alex's face was still red from laughter but reddened still. "That's what I need to tell you. The crazy thing: I hear voices."

Abby tried to look amused. When Alex didn't respond to it, she inquired, "You're serious?"

"Crazy, huh?"

Abby's laughter evaporated. "You wanna tell me about them?"

"At first, I thought it was the magic. It was like a whisper I couldn't make out. After the Library, after I took all those Books, it got louder."

"Are you sure it's not tinnitus? Ringing in your ears? Maybe something damaged your hearing."

"It's voices. Lots of voices. All talking at once."

"Are they saying something? Telling you something?"

"It's hard to hear, Abby. Sometimes I make out a word, but mostly it's a jumble."

"Are they telling you to hurt yourself?"

"No," Alex professed. "I told you, it's just a lot of noise."

"But they're not telling you to do something? Or hurt anyone?"

"No."

"Are they specific words or is there like a pattern to them?"

Alex shook her head. "They're all talking, but I don't know if they're saying *anything*."

"I guess that's good. Not to be insensitive, but it sounds more annoying than anything else."

"That's why I didn't bring it up before. It's just—it's changing. They're louder, more agitated. Like they can tell something's happening. When George and Johnny came, they got loud. Like they were panicking or trying to warn me... or something."

She pointed to her head. "I feel, I don't know, like I'm not alone in here."

"It sounds like quite a crowd."

"There's more. Sometimes I don't know if what I feel is them or me."

"Whaddya mean?"

"Like this morning. My run. When my face looked different to you. Or just now, on the phone with Heather. I felt like she was wasting my time."

"Was she?"

"Wasting my time? No. That's just it. That's what I'm trying to tell you. It's like maybe one of them thought she was an idiot, and that's why I felt that way. Like one of them wanted to go for a run, that wasn't me. Maybe a little because I went. But the desire to go came from somewhere—or someone—else."

"Where, do you think?"

"The Books. From the Library. You know how I feel, you know, what they went through to make the Book?"

Abby nodded.

"She was a runner."

Abby made a face.

She doesn't believe me. Then realization dawned on her. The reason that made that Book so shocking also confused Abby. "It was brand-new, Abby. Maybe a few days old."

Abby's mouth dropped, "They're still making Books?"

Alex nodded, letting it sink in. "You know how, like on TV when someone gets in trouble because they don't tell someone something that only they know? I didn't want to be that person. I always hate that. It's so stupid."

"I know what you mean, but if they told, there'd be no peril."

"That's not so bad for real life, don't you think?"

Abby laughed. "You told me. What do we do about it?"

Alex shrugged.

"You want to cancel tonight?"

"I can't."

"Why?"

"How would I tell George? Smoke signals? Tie a letter to an owl? Leave crop circles in the field that say we're not coming?"

Abby grinned. "Okay, so logistically, we can't. But should

we? Pretend we had a way to tell them. Would you want to?"

"No," Alex said after a thoughtful pause. "Until Billy is safe at home. The whispers are agitated. I think they want me to go."

"They think something's going to happen?"

"I'm sure. Tonight."

Abby nodded. "Now I know. You don't have to be that TV person. Thank you for trusting me."

Alex beamed. "Completely."

Abby smiled. "Mind if I clean up now?"

"I'll get it," Alex reached for the stack as she stood.

Abby swatted her hands away. "My house, my rules, kiddo. Sit somewhere and relax."

Abby looked out the window in the direction of the barn. Alex hated herself for the look Abby tried to keep from claiming her face. Abby added, "Don't think my glass days are over. That old barn was going to fall apart sooner or later." She raised Alex's face with her hand under her chin. "What I'm trying to say is that you shouldn't take it so hard. It's okay. I'd forgive you if there was something to forgive you for."

"I appreciate that, Abby." *I just can't unknow that it's all my fault.*

Chapter Fifty

bby checked her naked wrist like she wore a watch. Her eyes shot to Alex, who nodded. Abby followed Alex to the truck.

They each felt talked out. Grateful for the silent drive, Alex worked to quiet her tumultuous mind. Even the whispers seemed to grant her solitude. Since she came to live with her aunt and cousins, she hadn't spent more than a few hours away from them and missed them tremendously.

Abby slowed and turned into the driveway, sooner than Alex expected. Pulling alongside Heather's old, yellow car nestled in the tall grasses, Abby sang, "Welcome home."

"I'm not sure where home is lately. It stopped being a place I go and sort of follows me around."

"That's a nice thought," Abby replied, exiting the truck.

The chickens clucked at her from their pen, most ran towards or away from her while the remainder pecked and scratched at the ground, unconvinced Alex's arrival would accompany food.

The garden was alive with nature's presence. In addition to the thick, luscious scents, the air sparkled and dashed with flitting insects and bees. Weeds were gaining hold between the rows. The interruption in Heather's day-to-day rituals over the last week allowed the infiltration of unruliness. The progressive invasion darkened Alex's mood. The weeds were as much Matthew's fault; as if he had sown them himself. It was clear that Billy's absence wounded Heather.

As though innately understanding what troubled her, Abby approached the garden, touching leaves and sampling the plants, as though with simple examination she could determine whether they lacked moisture or mineral. She took note of the weeds. She fastidiously worked the soil to evacuate every strand of root as she collected weeds in her fist. Without looking up, she told Alex, "I'm glad we came. Things needed tending."

The front door opened. Rose raced out, wrapping Alex in a bearhug.

She squeezed Rose back, her heart swelling at the welcome.

"I missed you so much," Rose crowed.

"Me too." Alex closed her eyes, swallowed by Rose's embrace. The other's warmth penetrated Alex's clothes and radiated deep into her flesh. This wasn't just body-heat, but an aura of emotion wafting off Rose in thick waves. Consumed by Rose's desperate embrace, Alex was also sated by the love offered with it.

While still holding Alex, Rose jumped excitedly. Alex resisted at first, but Rose's enthusiasm wore her down. Rose's bright blue eyes beamed. Their reunion wasn't celebrating the conclusion of time apart. Communicated within the waves of energy was the origin of Rose's fervor: Rose witnessed Alex's rebirth from fire. Rose watched Alex confront their menace, Matthew. Rose awed as Alex summoned magic, and for a time, wielded it. Alex's arrival enthralled Rose beyond measure because it heralded her twin brother's return.

Other devils swarmed Alex's head, and the trappings of her meeting with Jeremiah threatened Billy's return like a carrot on the tip of a cattle prod. She yearned to possess Rosemary's certainty. Like she could view the world in reverse, their destinies so fitfully intertwined that there was nothing capable of separating them. To Rose, Billy's return was pre-ordained. If only for the moment, Alex granted herself permission to believe in Rose's conviction, and as she did, her heart soared.

Rosemary and Alex were cousins, but their relationship was more akin to that of sisters or best friends. They had been so close, eager to share one another's company since long before Alex came to live with them. Alex held her as though, while she had ventured down her darker roads, Rose held her lighter heart and was now returning it.

"I missed you, Rose," Alex announced as they jumped together. "I missed feeling like this." Alex self-consciously wondered how Abby judged their antics. She half-suspected her Familiar wasn't looking up specifically to allow Alex her moment of brevity. Abby was grinning wider than Alex had ever seen her smile, as though she'd known no other joy greater than pulling weeds. *Is Abby happy for me or is Rose's joy contagious?*

The more joyful Alex tried to be, the more thoughts of the coming event infiltrated her happiness: Jeremiah, George, Johnny. Would she be facing this trio tonight? Rose's excitement dwindled, almost as though snagged and bled dry by Alex's diminishing mood. Red-faced, Rose stopped jumping, her sparkling eyes examining

Alex's face, as though identifying the thief of her joy. Her head rested on Alex's shoulder. Taller than Rose, Alex embedded her face in her cousin's chestnut hair and inhaled the lavender scent of her shampoo. The scent conjured memories of the dissipating scent-trail a freshly showered Rose imparted to any room she passed through. Before this moment Alex never realized how important or how evocative it was, reminding her in a flood how special Rose was to her.

Alex stepped back to look at her cousin. Sometimes Alex found herself jealous of Rose. Today, Alex saw her beauty objectively. She was glad to be herself. Leaner, stronger, beautiful in her own way. She was a woman capable of surviving the past week, and this gave Alex pride. She worried Rose's smile would abandon her if forced to experience something as traumatic as Matthew breaking Sara's fingers. What might such darkness do to someone so bright? *Maybe I'm not giving her enough credit. I think she's young, naïve, and fragile, but a week ago, who would have thought I could have survived those things? I was young, innocent, and ignorant, too.*

Rose pulled Alex toward the door. "Mom can't wait to see you, but she's got to wait." Her eyes sparkled with excitement. "Abby," she shouted, "Mom's been talking about you all afternoon. She can't wait to hear what's up."

Abby nodded from the garden, her short, dark hair, black muscle shirt, and thick arms looking out of place amidst the myriad insects that flitted about her like fairies. She raised her fistful of weeds like a trophy of war. "Tell her I'll be in soon."

Heather nestled cross-legged on the couch in the living room, a large mug half-filled with coffee in one hand, surrounded by newspaper. Dolly, their tuxedo cat, tucked in atop a square of newsprint which Heather regularly set aside for her.

The room was spotless. Matthew's destruction was only evidenced by absence: The couch lacked a coffee table, the telephone stood atop a stack of books, the buffet lacked its hutch that no longer contained Heather's chinaware and serving ware; all lost, all cleaned up, all thrown away. *Where does she find the energy?*

Rose's whirlwind disturbed Heather's peaceful cocoon. It was a wonder her newspapers didn't spin away. Heather lowered her mug to a coaster on the floor and pushed herself to her feet.

Rose spoke quickly, with nary a pause or a breath between words. "Mom Alex is here Abby's weeding the garden. I'm taking

Alex upstairs, so she can talk to you later,"

"Not so fast," Heather chided Rose with a grin, embracing Alex. She whispered, "I'm so proud of you."

Heather felt almost bird-like, as though if Alex hugged too tight, Heather's ribs might snap. Alex couldn't recall her aunt feeling so fragile before. Recollection suggested Heather was solid. Then, two days ago, while Eric's house burned down, Matthew took Rose and Billy. *He did this to her.* She hated Matthew for the harm he caused to those she loved.

"Rosemary apparently wants to see me," Alex said as her cousin pulled on her wrist. "We'll talk later?"

Heather pointed to the door, "Abby's in the garden?"

Alex nodded. Heather started to the door. Alex observed, "Looks like nothing happened here."

Alex stumbled up the stairs after Rose, who explained, "Mom and me cleaned all night. What a mess. I think she needed something so we wouldn't think about Billy."

Rose's excitement was so distracting from reality that the sound of his name knocked the wind from Alex. There was never a part of her mind that wasn't thinking about Billy, worrying if he was okay, wishing to speed his safe return. His name spoken aloud made his absence real again. She didn't want to think about Matthew; it was Billy she wanted to keep in her mind. *Another reason to hate him.* She blew out a breath, trying to dilute her rising anger.

At the end of the hall, just past the bedroom and bathroom doors, an attic ladder led to Alex's bedroom. Longing for her bedroom's lost sanctuary, wishing she could climb the rungs and reclaim the peace it gave her before all this started, Alex instead followed Rose into her bedroom. Rose pulled the door closed, sighing relief that they were alone. Alex tried not to stare at the empty bed, left haphazardly made as Billy rushed to go on their hike over a week ago. It felt like a hole, a twin-sized bruise on her heart.

Standing in the close confines of the twins' bedroom, engulfed by stale teenage boy funk, a mix of body odor and soap, Alex inhaled deeply, as though capturing it before the last vestiges of Billy disappeared. She wondered how Rose kept up her cheerful façade. *Maybe she doesn't smell it anymore.*

Rose collapsed into her bed, throwing herself against her pillows. Her enthusiasm evaporated like a deflating balloon. Her eyes locked on Alex between the two beds, then slowly drifted to Billy's bed then back to Alex, shiny with sadness.

"I miss him, Alex," Rose whimpered. She chewed on a thought for a moment. "I know Mom's gotta be worried. She says she is, but it's like she's given up already. Like she knows something but won't say. She makes me worry he's not okay."

Alex sat on the edge of Rose's bed. She smoothed a crease in Billy's sheets that he overlooked in his haste. She pulled the sheet to return the crease. Removing it felt like she'd erased something he'd left behind. "He's fine." She realized how untrue it sounded because it was. "He's homesick. He misses us; me and Heather. You most of all," she squeezed Rose's ankle. "He's scared, and he's being told things he doesn't believe, and never will." She took a breath. *Matthew took him; why? As leverage? To hurt me?* Whatever his reasoning, Alex knew, it was his dearest mistake. She would do anything to ensure his safe return.

Rose spoke almost absently. "When we were little, sharing a room was great. We'd whisper all night, trade knocks on the wall. If one of us had a bad dream, we'd crawl in bed together. Being twins made us special and sacred to each other."

Alex didn't speak. Rose continued, "Then we got older. Puberty messed that all up. We go from best friends to resenting each other because we want five minutes of privacy to get dressed. I can't even throw my bra on the ground because there's no telling what he'd do with it."

Alex couldn't help but cackle. "Probably fit it on his head."

"Yeah. He's done that."

Alex rubbed Rose's ankle. Her gaze transitioned from Rose to Billy's empty bed. The three of them would spend the day crammed in this room. The twins taking to their beds with Alex in the middle, a short hop from one to the other, always arms reach away.

Rose broke the silence. "I wished for my own room, like constantly. At least every birthday. Now all I want is to get him back." Rose bit her lip and punched her pillow. "I never wanted it like this."

Alex whispered, "This isn't because you wished it. I bet he wished it, too."

Rose wiped her face, "No way. He loved sharing my room with me."

Alex laughed like she used to. It made her feel lighter. *How is*

Rose doing this?

Then Rose changed the subject. "I heard Mom talking about Book Club. Something tonight?" Her tone suggested something sat uneasily with Rose.

"A meeting."

Rose's face fell once again from happy to sad. "Mom won't tell me much. She's gonna leave me out. Again."

"She wants to keep you safe."

"How am I safe alone? I'm safe with you." Alex's shoulders slumped under the weight of responsibility Rose dumped there. Rose continued, "I was there, Alex. I felt Picnic Rock break under my feet. It didn't just crack; you tore it in two. Like it was nothing."

"It's not that simple," Alex was trying to explain the unexplainable.

"No, Alex, it is simple. He was killing you. He burned you, but you beat him."

Alex didn't know what to say. Rose had a point.

"If Mom wants to keep me safe, I should be where you are. I was at my dad's house, remember?" Rose continued. "I was in my room with Billy. Mom was downstairs. What could have been safer? Matthew still took us and burned the house down. Would that have happened with you there?"

"Well, I ...." Alex tried to argue but found no dispute. She understood what Abby meant regarding responsibility. She would have to speak up for Rose. She'd have to betray the wishes of one of them, regardless of who she supported.

"Didn't have magic then," Rose finished. "But you do now." Rose threw her hands in the air, "I want to be a part of this. When they took the curse off you, I should have been there. I could've helped and then I'd feel like I helped make you special. Instead, I was at my dad's house. Like I was being grounded. I need to say I was there when you win. I know it's a lot, you having to keep me safe, but what's stopping Matthew from taking me again while you're all off playing superhero?"

Alex found that she was nodding. "I'll talk to Heather."

Rose hugged her. "Thanks, Alex." She paused. "What's tonight about, anyway?"

Alex described George's visit. She left out destroying Abby's barn but ended with her demand for Billy's return.

Rose studied Alex, like she was absorbing all her words and digesting them to uncover their deeper meanings. "Do you think George is *good* now?"

The astute question surprised Alex. She fought the immediate desire to respond affirmatively. "I don't think any of us are good or bad. When they think they're right, when the people around them agree, it's harder to see the wrong. When enough people believe something, it's harder to call it a lie."

"You won't help them, right? I mean, Matthew deserves killing, but you're not helping them, right?"

Alex shrugged. "I gave George my condition."

Rose smiled; it didn't look genuine. "Isn't that scary?"

"It is. You saw what Matthew did with a Book."

Rose stared at her; unsure what words could come next.

Alex let a full minute of silence pass between them before changing the subject. She'd needed to ask Rose something. "Rose, how much did you know, you know, before this week?"

"What do you mean, like what?"

"Well, before last week, I knew Heather belonged to a book club. I thought it was just some boring, well, book club. I thought my parents died in a car accident. I didn't know there was magic—I couldn't."

Rose's eyes widened. "When we were kids, Mom talked about magic and witches, but I thought it was fairy tales. She stopped only while she and Dad were splitting up. But she totally stopped when you showed up."

"Showed up?"

"Yeah, don't you remember?" Rose waited for an answer. "You don't, do you?"

Alex shook her head. She remembered the nightmare. She remembered being at Heather's, but not how she got there.

"One day you just came here. Maybe I don't remember it right. You got dropped off or something. Anyway, you were a mess. All in a daze. Mom warned us you were traumatized and said we shouldn't ask you about anything that happened."

"And that was the only time you listened to your mother?"

Rose laughed. "Of course not. Who am I? As soon as we were alone, I asked you. I asked you a bunch of times. But you always grabbed your head and screamed and cried. I thought I'd exploded your brain."

"I couldn't hear it," Alex recalled the crippling migraines she experienced when people spoke about magic around her.

"I know now. Back then I didn't. I thought whatever happened really messed you up. I had these horrible thoughts like maybe you saw your parents dead with broken bones and gore and glass sticking out of their eyeballs. I mean, what else could have made you so messed up?"

"I've been angry that after all these years no one tried to tell me. What else?"

"Before then, Mom told us stories and told us all about herbs and stuff."

"Do you remember? Can you tell me one?"

Rose thought for a minute. "I don't remember the exact wording after *Once upon a time*. It was about a witch. She hid in the woods. One day, two kids came by. They tell her they're starving and lost. The witch helps. She brings them inside. It was winter, and she warms them and makes them all this delicious food. But then a hunter comes and kills her and steals her magic."

"That's not much of a story." Most fairy tales Alex recalled were about evil witches, not about non-magical people looking to make Books.

"Mom told it better," Rose protested. "The way she told it we knew the hunter starved the kids to make them hungry. He got them lost. He made threats and stuff, so they wanted to run away. The thing was, he didn't know where the witch lived. He followed the kids because he knew she'd find the lost kids and try to help. The way Mom told the story, we were afraid for her."

"Interesting. What's that expression, history is written by the winners?"

"Something like that. Sometimes when we'd be watching a story on TV, Mom would tell us what *really* happened." Rose made a face. "It could get boring. Like she had a witch version of everything. Dad hated it even more than we did. He said it was why they split up. He'd yell until she stopped, and for a while she did, but after he moved out, she started again. But it all stopped…."

Alex finished, "When I showed up."

Rose looked at her closed door as though staring through it into the hall. "It'll be different now. You have magic." She giggled,

"You get to do all the chores. You'll wiggle your nose and poof, they're done." She straightened up, as though shedding the joking demeanor. "I don't think Mom will like us hiding up here all day. She's missed you, too."

"You want to head down?"

Rose looked at Billy's side of the room. "When you get Billy back, Alex, promise me something?"

"Anything."

"Don't accept their apologies. Make them regret taking him."

Chapter Fifty-One

lex stalled mid-way down the stairs. She hadn't intended to eavesdrop, but hearing Heather and Abby's hushed tones made what they said more provocative.

"You're missing my point, Heather. She's still a kid."

"She's old enough to make her own decisions."

"Like when she wanted to go to college last week?"

"Now you're being contradictory, Abby. This is different. She has magic. She's powerful. She scared the crap out of you and damaged your barn. She's just scratching the surface."

"She has no one to guide her."

"How am I supposed to do that?"

"Be her voice of reason."

"For the first time, what comes next isn't clear. I know one thing and it scares me. I don't have magic. I don't know what she's capable of. She won't understand the biases and experiences that color my decisions. If I tell her something and she gets hurt, how do I live with that?"

"For sixteen years, you've run Book Club. Some of them are messed-up, broken women. You gave them hope, you helped them believe. Not a one of you has magic. All you knew was one day she'd have a dream and then you'd have to get your brother's Book. All that time, you kept them together."

"It's been like herding cats. Keeping them in line has practically been a full-time job."

"*Exactly.* How is she ready for that? You remember what she said happened after you cast the spell? Matthew almost killed her. Now there's this Jeremiah-guy. Peter never mentioned him. Not once. You feel overwhelmed? Imagine what it's like for her."

"What if she doesn't like me telling her what to do? We never had that kind of relationship. I tried to treat her like an adult. What if I don't know? Do I tell her just how out of my depth I am? What kind of guide am I if I'm even more lost than she is?"

"You owe it to her—to your brother—to try, Heather. She has tremendous power and responsibility and needs someone to navigate her through right and wrong."

"Why not you?"

"You know I can't."

"That stupid oath again." Heather pointing an accusatory finger, "Is that why you're here?"

"She didn't ask, if that's what you mean. She needs you, now more than ever. Don't turn her away."

Heather groaned. "You're right. But my decisions are tainted by my son. She can't trust my instincts about him."

"She wants him back, too. She needs your guidance. Just run Book Club until she's ready."

"She doesn't need me, Abby. She just doesn't know that yet. She's got this, but," Heather said over Abby's *but*, "but, if she needs me, I'll always be there for her."

Alex took the silence as opportunity to announce her arrival. She stomped the next step and in an exaggerated shout, "Hey Heather, you in the living room?"

Behind her, Rose giggled. *You've been there the whole time?* Alex's cheeks flushed knowing what Rose overheard.

Heather and Abby repositioned themselves, breaking the intimacy of their conversation.

Heather called, "Sure, come on down." To Abby, she whispered, "Such sneaks."

Abby responded, "They're *children*."

Alex came in and Abby stood. "I'll leave you to it," she winked at Alex.

Did she know I was listening?

To Heather, Abby asked, "Mind if I trim some herbs?"

"Take whatever you need." As Abby left, Heather asked, "You… kids have a good talk?" She paused before *kids*, as though contemplating a different word.

"Yeah. It was good," Alex sat where Abby had been. The newspapers were neatly stacked. Dolly had wandered off.

Heather reached for her mug and put it down, disappointed at its emptiness. She talked past Alex, "Rosemary, a little privacy."

Rose pouted with her whole body, "Come on, Mom. Can't I stay?"

Heather's face darkened into motherly reproach. Alex knew what came next; Heather would start counting.

Rose turned to Alex for support. Alex's expression was unsupportive. Rose crossed her arms, defeated, and disappeared up the stairs.

Heather raised her voice, "I asked for privacy, Rosemary. That doesn't mean *sit on the stairs and listen*. Go to your room. We'll be only a minute."

Rose huffed and stomped up the stairs.

"Some things never change," Heather turned to Alex, "It's good to see you. I can't imagine what it's been like. You've been amazing, though, you know. We should talk about tonight and how you think we're going to get Billy back." Heather made an odd face. She shook it off. "How are you doing? Are your burns healed?" She pointed at Alex's arms. "You've healed a lot. Another day and I bet they'll be gone."

Heather was trying to do what Abby suggested; Alex found the shift in dynamic fascinating. Heather was trying, and so Alex would try, too. "I've missed you, Aunt Heather. Abby's great. She's made me feel like I'm her family. As nice as she is, it's not home."

Heather's smiling cheeks reddened.

"Once everyone is here," Alex hesitated. "Will we tell them about Marta?" *It's been two days. It feels like an eternity.* "Don't you think some of them will freak?"

Heather started to say, "No one will," but checked herself. "You're right. Losing Marta is a lot to swallow. But if I know Nancy, she already told everyone."

"How will we know if they're running late or not coming?"

"What has you so convinced they won't come? *Book Club*," Heather emphasized her choice of words, "is like a support group for frustrated women who thought they *should have* magic. We're at the action stage. We have purpose. You need us. We *want* to be at your side."

Heather's words brought relief, as though removing some of the weight borne by her shoulders. Alex confessed, "He said we're going to talk. But I don't know what happens after *hello*."

Heather wrung her hands. "Peter prepped me for one thing. He never told me what happens *after*." She paused for a moment, "I'm sorry if that's left a lot on your plate."

"I didn't know I had a plate until now. One day I'm thinking about boys and college, and the next I'm learning about spells and magic." *To think college was the biggest deal a week ago.*

"It sounds crazy when you put it like that," Heather chuckled.

"There's been a lot of crazy lately, Aunt Heather." Alex had something she wanted to ask. Heather sat patiently as though anticipating it. "Heather, last week, when you told me I had to wait for college. Was this why?"

Heather nodded timidly. "I've been waiting since the day you came to live with us."

Alex heard the distant echo of Matthew mocking her mother for having to go through each day anticipating inevitability. It seemed unbearable. "You let me be angry with you rather than letting me get my hopes up. It must have been so hard to know and not say."

Heather's laugh seemed more for emphasis than humor. "It's challenging to live with uncertainty. Sometimes telling people is more selfish than keeping it to yourself. I'm just glad it didn't take another three years to happen."

"I never thought of it that way." She waited. There was one more thing to talk about, "Tonight, I want Rose with us."

Heather repeatedly gestured with her finger, pointing down. "Rose will be where I'll know she's safe: right here."

"Aunt Heather," Alex modulated her voice, trying not sound like she was lecturing her aunt. "The only way either of us will know she's safe is if we have our eyes on her."

A storm of emotion washed across Heather's face. Her expression changed as though she were caught in the ebb and flow of the tide and was yet unable to move with either. Her eyes welled up. "I can't lose her, too."

Alex hugged her aunt. "We'll get him back, Heather. I can't keep Rose safe if I don't know where she is. She has to come. She's sixteen, not six."

Heather said, "Sixteen is so young. She doesn't understand the dangers."

"She watched Matthew burn me alive." Seeing the influence of her words on Heather shored her confidence. "I want Rose at my side tonight. Remember, the only way they get my cooperation is if Billy comes home safe. I'm serious about that."

"I know," Heather sighed after a hesitation. Her body rested against Alex's arms before stiffening. She pushed Alex away. "You're doing that thing again; to make me feel better." They slipped apart. "I let it slide last night when you made me come home."

"I'm sorry, Aunt Heather, I didn't realize I was doing it, this time."

Heather forced a smile. "I understand." Alex wasn't sure either of them believed that. Heather rubbed Alex's arm. "You're learning. I'm learning, too. We'll both do better together, right?"

Alex nodded. "Rose can come?"

Heather analyzed Alex, her eyes beaming, "Yes, but tell me something, Alex, and please, be really, really honest."

"Sure, Aunt Heather."

"How strong is your magic?"

Alex took a slow, long breath. "I don't know." Something was eating at Alex. She decided she trusted her Aunt enough to share it. "At the Library," she said, her voice practically a whisper, "George said that women shouldn't have magic because we're too emotional. Because we could obliterate our family because, maybe we're upset that we burned dinner."

Heather's demeanor changed. "That's fucking bullshit."

"I don't know, Heather. I don't think I meant to break Picnic Rock. I definitely didn't mean to destroy Abby's barn. What if he's right? What if I can't control it? What if I get too emotional?"

"Sweetheart, men like George say things because they're insecure and have tiny penises." She held the first knuckle of her pinky as a guide. They both laughed at the notion. Heather continued, "You need to focus on learning how to use it, not listen to what some asshole says. These men stole their magic. They have no idea how it works. They're saying things to scare you because they're jealous: You don't need to read your magic from a Book." Heather read Alex's face before adding, "And Abby said you *damaged* her barn."

Tears forced their way into Alex's eyes. "It fell down."

Heather mouthed, "Oh." Then she said, "Abby likes to color things positively where you're concerned. I should have realized it was worse than she was letting on. She can't help it." Before Alex could ask Heather to explain, she added, "I'm so sorry I wasn't there for you. Abby said you were amazing. I bet you're going to be even more amazing tonight."

Alex looked away. "I'm scared, Aunt Heather."

"There's nothing wrong with being scared. You'd have to be a little touched in the head if you weren't."

"Really?"

"You don't know what's going to happen. That's scary."

"That's not it. I do know. They think I'm some stupid girl who comes when called and is showing up expecting to get her cousin back and isn't smart enough to see what's really happening. What scares me isn't what happens when I fall into their trap. I know it won't work. I'm scared about what happens next."

Heather asked, "You mean if they catch you?" Alex shook her head. "Then what?"

"I'm scared I won't be able to hold back."

"Maybe they need to learn the hard way that you're not some stupid girl. Maybe it's not so bad if you lose control."

"I don't want to hurt anyone, Aunt Heather. That's what scares me."

"You're protecting the people you love."

"I guess, I mean, I know that. It's just what if I really hurt someone? I mean like, really hurt them. I mean kill them."

"Alex, these are terrible people. If you hurt," she hesitated, "or kill someone, they would probably do the same to you or one of us. This is not simple, Alex. This is complicated and hard to think about. But if it comes to that, remember you acted in self-defense, and believe that whatever you do to them is justified."

"I think George wants to be good. He believed Matthew was good. I didn't mean to hurt him. He's disfigured because of me. He looks so horrible. His burns are my fault."

"Why do you care? He took you to the Library against your will. They killed Marta. Matthew threw you into that thing, that black cloud."

Alex's face downturned. She wet her lips and pulled her hair into a ponytail before letting it fall over her shoulder. "I felt him burning, Heather. I knew what was happening to him," her voice quieting, "and I think I liked it."

Heather didn't respond.

"When I see him, my heart aches. Like I took a piece of him, like I took those Books. He's Sara's son. She's a part of me, so maybe George is, too. I should hate him, but maybe the Sara part of me cares for him." Alex's eyes brimmed with tears.

"Abby told me about the voices."

Alex nearly shouted, "They're whispers, not—"

"Please don't be angry with Abby. She thought I should know."

"I'm not upset about Abby, Aunt Heather. I'm worried you'll think I'm crazy."

"You're not crazy." Heather took a long breath. "Your father told me each one of those Books was the heart of a woman. Their pain, their lives cut short, their unfulfilled wishes and dreams. Their magic. All that is part of you now. To make it even harder, they're trying to talk to you. And Sara Frost is probably one of them. Every time you look at George, she sees her son. He's older than she ever knew him while they lived. I can't imagine what that's like." Heather's eyes focused on an unknown distance, like she was imagining Billy waiting in the doorway. "You carry a tremendous burden, Alex."

"Sometimes I feel like I should stop whining and be glad I have this gift. I mean, I have magic. I'm a real witch." Alex repeated herself in a silly voice, "I'm a real witch." They both laughed. "But then I wonder if it might not be a gift."

"Maybe. Maybe not."

"If Sara makes me feel something for George, how do the others make me feel? What if they make me weak because I care?"

"Compassion is never weakness, Alexandrea."

"What if they make me angry?"

Heather leaned forward and embraced Alex. "I wish I could do that thing you do and make you feel better." Heather paused, her voice somber, "We'll be with you tonight. Tell us what you need. Maybe we can do something with the spells from the other night."

"I appreciate that, but my father cast the summoning spell with his Book. It took nine of you." Heather's expression showed she was mildly insulted.

Heather shook it off. "I'll make sure we bring enough truffle salt this time." They both laughed. "Alex," Heather's voice was metered and serious, "we're witches. All of us—except Abby, but she has her own special reasons for being here—we want to be useful to you. You have magic. When we look back on the day magic returned to women, we get to say we were at Alexandrea Hawthorne's side, helping it happen."

Alex beamed and hugged her aunt. "I love you, Aunt Heather."

"I love you, too, Alex." Heather looked her over. "How are you and Abby getting along? Abby was my closest friend growing up."

"She's great. When I realize she's your age, it feels, I don't know how to explain it, but I know I can trust her."

"I didn't think it would be any other way. The oath she made to be your Familiar, it's serious stuff. She'd die for you."

Alex nodded somberly. "I know. She already has, twice."

"Her loyalty is unbreakable. She'll follow you to hell, warning you the whole way."

Alex laughed. "It's good to know I have a conscience!"

"You have several. Rose, me, the Club, like it or not."

Alex nodded. "Not to change the subject; when is the Club coming?"

Heather picked up her phone to check the time. "Soon enough. Let's eat. We are going to show those men we're not afraid."

Alex tried to smile, but she had plenty of reasons to be afraid.

Chapter Fifty-Two

arrie politely knocked once; the first to arrive. Heather let her in. After they hugged and exchanged pleasantries and apologies, Carrie approached Alex. Seeing her separated from the others, she seemed younger than the rest, maybe only five years older than Alex.

Carrie was a petite woman. Her navy tank top celebrated her muscular arms. Tattoos covered her arms and chest, to her collarbone. There were skulls with words of encouragement and enthusiasm, wrapped in winged hearts; knives cutting steaks; and phrases like "A chef's place is in the kitchen", and "The kitchen's hotter'n Hell so the food's like Heaven". Alex stared at the art. Each time she thought to look away, a new treasure forced her eyes to linger.

"This one's my latest." Carrie slipped her tank top and bra strap down on one arm and pointed at a still scabby image of a sexy witch sitting cross-legged on a broom. Alex didn't know if it was polite to ask Carrie if it was on purpose that the witch bore a resemblance to her. Carrie slid her straps back. Alex noted she was grinning bashfully.

She gave Alex a hug. "Glad I get to see you again," she said, her voice soft and gentle.

Alex couldn't help but smile. Carrie's features might be described as boyish. She was handsome. Short dark hair, intentionally mussed, framed her square face with large blue eyes under bold eyebrows. She understood why Billy liked her. *She's a badass*, he had said.

Carrie noticed Alex's burns at once, touching near them so gently her fingertips barely dented Alex's skin. "Those look angry." She held out her arms and pointed at the repeating stripes on her forearms. "Kitchen tattoos," she offered. "Hot pots oven doors splattering grease. They suck. Pain's a bitch, but you work through it, right?"

"These don't hurt anymore."

"Even better." Carrie stared intensely, for a full minute, like she was spellbound, or stuck finding her next word. Finally, she said,

"I heard; Marta and all. That sucks."

"Yeah."

"How do you feel about tonight? You up for it?"

"I guess." Realizing that might not be the answer the others needed, she followed up with a simple, "I mean, yes."

"Your second answer is better," Carrie gave Alex a gentle punch in the shoulder. "Confident but not excited. I like that. I'm glad I'm the first one here. We have a chance to talk."

Alex got the sense Carrie meant something she wasn't getting. She smiled politely to hide the fact she didn't know how to respond, which widened Carrie's smile.

Carrie rocked on her heels and looked around the room, as though taking inventory of Heather's missing furniture. She glanced at her wrist, perhaps longing for a watch.

"Well," Alex said, "I'm glad you're here. I worried no one would come once they knew about Marta. I thought I might have to do this alone."

"There's no way I'd miss this. You're a witch. You know how hot that is?" Carrie's face reddened. "Sorry, I'm kinda starstruck. You're just so amazing, and I feel so fortunate you're including me." Carrie brightened. "I may not have magic, but I brought some stuff. Left it in my saddlebag. I got a case of pepper spray. I've got your back." The veins running the length of Carrie's arms grew more visible. "What I mean is, you do your thing, and we'll do whatever we can to keep you safe."

"Pepper spray?"

"Yeah." Carry pantomimed spraying a small can and then held her eyes and rocked back and forth like they burned. Alex couldn't help but laugh. "It's not magic, but it'll do in a pinch."

It was Alex's turn to look around the room. She was unsure how to process Carrie right now. Her loyalty carried a weight all its own, and Alex felt she needed to provide some substance of leadership as counterbalance. It seemed a sign of insanity that Carrie came so eagerly. One member of Book Club already lost her life, and in response Carrie brought pepper spray to a magic fight. Was Carrie so confident in her? Alex wished she could hug Carrie, and rather than impart what she felt to the others, take some of Carrie's confidence for herself. Her chest grew warm inside; there was more motivating Carrie tonight than mere confidence in Alex's new abilities, but—

whether she sensed it or imagined it—the notion made her feel special.

"I saw you, Monday night, all burning up. Man, that totally freaked me out. I mean you weren't," she wiggled her fingers in the air, "you were freaking," she waved her hands above her head. "It was intense. My hair caught fire once, so I sort of know what that's like." She made a whoosh sound. "That's why I keep it short now. When it was long, I put it in a bun. I liked when it looked a little messy. I thought it was Victorian and romantic or something. Everyone was staring at me like my head was on fire. I mean, you can't see your head, but your scalp suddenly hurts like hell. Had visions of running through the restaurant on fire. Fortunately, my sous-chef, Ray, great guy, all dreadlocks and everything, throws a bucket of pickles at me. Totally like it was nothing. He barely looked up. I'm soaked and dripping but the fire's out. We just started cooking again. I stunk all night and we were out of pickles." Just when Alex thought she was done, Carrie added, "What I mean is, I know what it's like to be on fire and wanted to tell you that you're freaking crazy to stick with it. Crazy in a brave way, I mean. I respect that, a lot."

"Thanks," Alex replied.

Carrie winked and in an exaggerated girly voice added, "Being on fire is so hot." She giggled.

Someone knocked, distracting them both as they watched Heather answer the door. For a moment they weren't compelled to fill the silence.

Colette walked in, giving Heather a hug. She embraced Rose. When she saw Alex beside Carrie, she excitedly shuffled her feet, her arms in the air, and hurried over.

Colette was nearly Alex's height, her skin luxuriously dark. Her hair was pulled back into a large ball behind her head. At the end of her widespread arms, her wiggling fingernails were painted a coral so neon-bright they looked capable of emitting light. Her large, dark brown eyes looked Alex over as she offered a joyful smile.

Colette squeezed the air out of Alex. She politely hugged Carrie, landing a loud kiss on her cheek. She looked back at Alex. "You're probably sick to your stomach with nerves." She waited a beat before adding, "No wait, that's me." She laughed politely at her own joke, but there was nothing artificial about her joy. "If I were in your shoes, I would have vamoosed hours ago. Some book-guy wants to meet? Sheesh, send me an email or text me. I don't meet in person."

She hissed, "Swipe left." She kept her eyes on Alex, her fingernails slicing the air like orange semaphore flags. "I don't know how you're standing here being all, *Hi, hello*. I'd be in the toilet complaining about my stomach. But I guess that's why you're you." She leaned forward and whispered, "It's because you're here that we're not too cowardly to come. We're all here for you, you know that, right?"

"I do." Alex loosened up. When sarcasm was piled on stress, the load felt lighter.

"Good. I promise I won't run until you run." She turned her back to Alex and looked over her shoulder, cocking her arms and raising one leg in the air. "Just take a good look so you recognize me when I pass you."

Alex couldn't help but laugh. Like breaking a sweat, tension poured out of her with each guffaw. The release felt so good that once her laughter naturally ended, she forced one more, hoping it would continue the purge. It wasn't the same, but Colette had accomplished her mission.

Another knock. Heather opened the door.

Donna entered with June. Donna immediately said, "Nancy's outside finishing her cancer stick. You'd think a nurse would know better."

Donna and June made their rounds. Donna was older, a stout woman, and when she saw Alex the first thing she said was, "Is it possible you got taller?"

Carrie arched her back exaggeratedly looking at the ceiling. "I'm straining my neck next to her."

"She's not that tall," Colette defended, "you're all short."

Donna extended her hand, which Alex clasped for a firm handshake.

June, shaking her head at Donna, gave Alex a polite hug. "Don't mind Donna," June excused, "eighty years as a school-teacher made her allergic to anyone under twenty."

Donna chided June, "It only felt like eighty. Actually, it was only thirty or fifty." She winked at Alex. "It's true. Kids fucking give me hives."

The repartee made Alex feel like each woman tied to her a helium-filled balloon of their own making. Like they knew doubt had been beating her up and were hurling reinforcing love at her. Alex struggled to remember everyone's name and knew the moment when she'd awkwardly substitute a pronoun for an uncertain name was creeping closer. Some she knew. June was the only Asian member of Book Club, a slender woman with dark hair and sharp features. Alex couldn't remember any other details about her until she asked Heather, "Do you have any wine?" and the missing pieces stumbled into place.

"You're in sales," she announced to June, who raised an eyebrow.

"Don't hold it against me," June sneered. "I like to think I don't sell. My recommendations are so convincing that I compel people to buy."

Donna leaned forward, fingers raised, "I'll take two of the crap you're selling."

June apologized, "You can't afford my crap."

"Probably not," Donna replied. "I am retired and on a fixed income."

June's face exaggerated concern as she rested her hand on Donna's shoulder. "My crap does come with flexible payment and financing options. Just because you can't afford my crap now should never leave you waiting to experience how truly crappy it is."

The women were giddy with laughter. Even if it was a defense mechanism for the terror they were trying to hide. As much as they didn't want to be here, they knew she wanted to be here even less.

Donna gave Alex's arm a gentle rub. "We heard what happened with Billy and the fire. I'm so sorry you had to go through that."

Alex took a breath. The fun was over. Business was starting.

"And Marta," Carrie repeated, nodding her head.

"Marta wasn't her fault," Donna said to Carrie.

"Did I say it was?" Carrie's voice barely rose. "Neither was Billy. Or the fire."

"I didn't say that it was," Donna replied.

Colette shook her head. "Seriously? We've been here five minutes and we're fighting? Might as well pack it in and go home."

"I didn't say it was anyone's fault," Carrie murmured.

"Ladies," June held up her hands. "Please. We should toast Marta."

"Marta doesn't need a toast," Nancy shouted from across the room. Alex recognized her as the woman who, a week ago, wore yellow scrubs and helped them when Billy was hurt. Her hair was pulled back into a tight bun, and she was wearing her piercings; Alex could see the rings in her eyebrows, nose, and lip catching the light from a distance. "What Marta deserves is payback."

"Fucking right," Donna shouted, alone in her enthusiasm.

The room fell quiet. Alex dreaded that they would turn back to her. While they were lobbing jokes, it was fun to be the center of attention. Now, she would rather face Jeremiah than be here.

Abby came in from the kitchen burdened with a half-dozen plastic cups. Rose followed with a handful more. "Ladies," Abby boomed, "in honor of Marta."

June helped pass them around. Passing a cup to Alex, she sniffed it and made a face. "Should you be drinking wine? If you're not going to drink it, I'm happy to suffer it down."

Alex rolled her eyes and snatched the cup. June laughed, "I like you, kid."

They held up their plastic cups. A few faces turned to Alex. Heather a-hemmed. "Marta was the first of us to join Book Club," she began.

Donna's face lit up like a teacher rediscovering their red pen, "You weren't the first, Heather?"

Heather bit down on her eulogy. "It wasn't a *club* until the Marta *joined*." When she saw Donna's cheeks blush, she continued, "Marta was dedicated to her work. As I'm sure Nancy can attest, until Book Club began, Marta really had nothing else in her life."

Nancy raised her cup. "She wasn't the only one married to a job." June added, "Here-here!"

Heather continued, "Book Club gave her purpose. For a long time, it was a social distraction, a chance for a handful of us to hang out, bullshit, and enjoy one-another's company. But Marta knew. She believed that this wasn't just some fantasy I had concocted. She helped me wait for Alex. She reminded me when I had doubts. Every time we drifted from our purpose, she guided me back onto track." Heather raised her cup, "To Marta, the first found, the first lost. She will never be forgotten."

Following a round of plastic cups clunked together, Abby, perhaps sensing the group's expectation of Alex said, "I joined Book Club not long after it became a thing. You'd think I would have known Marta better, but I didn't get to know her until her last few days."

Abby swallowed forcefully, blinking rapidly. "You'd think that in seventeen years we'd have the chance to know all there is to know about a person, but it took Alex becoming a witch and, well," she looked apologetically at Alex, "it took dying before Marta and I shared any meaningful conversation." Abby was finding it difficult to look at anyone, as though the only thing holding her tears back was the sight of everyone's feet. "It's shameful. We can know someone so long but not know that they could be special. If we'd only made the effort to talk sooner. I'm just grateful it happened at all. In only a few short days, I got to know so much more than she was a nurse. She really believed in what we're doing. We became friends. Her last act was to save my life. Losing her that way was the greatest expression of love anyone has ever given me. Losing her hurts. She deserves my pain. She deserves to be missed. She deserves for her loss to hurt each of us. She was a hero, and I hope that when the moment calls on me to act, that I can be half as brave and selfless." She looked up at them, her eyes sweeping the room, tears racing across her cheeks. "I hope we all take Marta's lesson and understand where we stand in the order of things." She turned to Alex and raised her cup. "Alexandrea, we ask the biggest sacrifices from you. When I am called upon to step in harm's way for you, I will take Marta's example and will not falter."

Alex watched as each woman turned to her, raised their glass and repeated Abby's oath. She suddenly felt small, dwarfed by the towering professions of loyalty. They were undiminished by her coarse doubt that she was unworthy of their sacrifice.

The whispers were screaming. Like the tidal rush at an ocean beach, they roared in cyclic waves, rising and rising, then crashing in crescendo before rising again. Alex didn't understand why they seemed so agitated; she was surrounded by friends.

As they finished their cups, each of them added theirs to the stack started by Abby. Each went to Alex and embraced her. This was Marta's memorial, yet Alex fearfully felt like she was at her own funeral. Her organs swam and twisted in her abdomen. Like everyone but her knew she was dying. Her skin felt cold and wet, her shirt damp under her arms. Like death was standing behind her. Like she was already gone. Like it was time for her to clasp deaths hand and let it lead her away.

Chapter Fifty-Three

The caravan pulled out of the driveway, snaking its way down the road to the field. One by one they pulled onto the grass at the dead end and got out. The road ended in decay: blacktop failed from cracks, to fist-sized clumps, then to pebbles, until the tall grasses, fluttering in the breeze, tapped against a rusted guardrail beside a drunken *Dead End* sign.

The car doors opening were almost buried by the rising din of whispers in Alex's head, voicing her unspoken apprehension.

She stood on the doorframe to Abby's truck to look over the roof and scan the desolate field. A grin slowly pulled across her face as broad as if her fingers hooked the sides of her mouth. Jeremiah's absence was too good to be true. It offered a momentary reprieve from the tsunami of anxiety of not knowing what came after they saw one another. Should she say hello? At what point would the design of his trap become evident? Could she avoid the snare, and barring that, could she keep everyone else free from it? Each question—each step—gave rise to a hundred more, and the more she tried to find conclusions, the more entangling in her own thoughts she became.

"They're not here yet." June scanned the tall grass with one hand over her eyes. The sun glared like blinding flames above the treetops opposite them.

"Maybe they chickened out?" Even as she asked, Carrie was offering the others cans of pepper spray.

Heather said absently, "They probably want us to sweat."

Carrie sighed, "I was just wishing out loud."

Alex's stomach twisted as though it turned inside-out. She was here: The field, the place and time she awaited all day. She could hear the women walking on the crunching soil and grass, hear their breathing, hear their worry, hear their hearts and minds screaming, *What am I doing here?* and wondering, *Why are we alone?* She assumed that's what her whispers were saying, too. Perhaps they were warning her. Alex meditated on Abby's barn. She didn't know how to summon her magic. She didn't know how to control it. Yet, when she needed it, it came... forcefully. For all her concern, for all her worry—

and theirs—Alex believed she could count on herself. Her magic would erupt. She wondered which she should fear more, Jeremiah, or what her magic would do if she couldn't figure out how to wield it.

Finding this sudden confidence in herself, unwarranted or otherwise, smashed her concern and swept the shattered pieces away. She had uncharted depths of power. The magic of a thousand Books. She might not understand how to summon it at will, but she couldn't doubt it wouldn't come.

Above them, puffy clouds lingered under the unbroken blue dome. It was warm and breezy. As Alex studied the field, her shirt fluttered over her thudding heart. The beat pulsed through her skin, made her fingers tic, roared like abbreviated waves crashing in her ears. *Can I trust what I see?* Her heart told her otherwise. Her whispers added confirmation, intensifying like a sudden gust of wind presaging a summer thunderstorm. *They don't think we're alone.*

Alex marched forward. The grasses crunched beneath her feet and scraped against her body. She'd arrived at the field swollen with dread. The green and golden grasses and wildflowers swayed, bees and insects flew blade to bud to blade, and small birds dove in fast, tight circles, swallowing them up. It was reminiscent of the day she— Sara—crawled from the doorway of her home to die. But that was a memory from a different life, a different time, a different person. Alex now felt abandoned by her fears.

Somewhere ahead she was certain a group of men loitered, camouflaged. Walking forward felt not unlike navigating a minefield. With each step came the potential to discover something dangerous.

The tips of the grasses and weeds tapped her palms. Her heart refused to slow. Everything felt awry. Stepping forward, her foot leaving the ground, came with the anticipation of losing contact altogether and spinning away. *Where are they?* It felt like a mistake to assume them tardy. *Let's see what the girl can do.* Roiling whispers warned her not to trust her eyes. *What if they aren't coming and I'm getting worked up over nothing?*

"Where is she going?" The words came from behind her. "Shouldn't we be with her?"

Alex didn't trouble looking back. Whispers swirled in her head, words outside comprehension, verbal hands clawing at her ears, demanding attention. *Is this the trap? What are they waiting for? What's the game?*

The grasses came to noisy life as the eight other women waded out behind her. It didn't bother her that not everyone was there. Alex didn't slow her progression; her chest clenched her racing heart. The sun glared in her eyes, leaving artefacts that danced in her vision. In that glare, in the streaks of light-beams originating from the sun, Alex thought she might have seen something in the kaleidoscopic display.

"The glare is unbearable," Colette complained from under a shade-giving hand.

"Try after cataract surgery," Donna countered. "I'm a vampire. Sunlight burns my eyes." She huffed. "Getting old is a freaking contact sport. Anyone who doesn't have the balls should bail."

Colette glared at Donna. Alex could almost hear the words she'd never speak. Colette's husband died only a few months ago.

"When was that? The surgery, I mean." That was Nancy. Yellow scrubs, always the healer.

"Six or seven months. The last Monday in January."

"You're not used to the light. I hear that a lot."

"Ladies," Heather chided, "seriously? This, now?"

Alex couldn't ignore their penetrative voices, yet like the whispers, she no longer heard their words. She kept moving forward.

The excruciating glare from the late day sun hurt through her eyes to inside her skull. Squinting, the blinding sunlight blurred.

As a child, told not to look directly at the sun, she'd squinch her eyes and turn the sunlight into rays of light that seemed so solid, she more than once tried to grasp one. Her eyes closed to slits, recreating the rays of her childhood. She looked away, training her gaze on her feet. Her whispers fell away in disappointment. Returning to the light, manipulating the rays through burning eyes, they goaded her on. *Do they want me to blind myself? No one else is here….* Yet, as the women around her muttered endlessly, the whispers guided her. Their din ebbing and flowing as she played with the light. Tears fled her stinging eyes, as she shaped the rays of light into long beams that reached all the way from the sun to her. It was then, blind to the sky and the trees and the field, she saw—perhaps ten or fifteen men— distant in the field. It was like a prismatic vision; they appeared in some light-beams but not others. As she squinted and played with the light, they shifted in and out of existence.

The sun burned dark blue spots that floated before her.

Discovering the men again in a glimpse, the crowd of whispers roared. She tried to focus, the whispers falling silent even before she lost sight of them. She stopped trying and listened. The whispers, the wind, the insects, the trees. She followed their guidance, fine-tuning the beams. Then, following a near-blinding eruption of light, the men appeared.

"There they are," Nancy shouted, pointing. Carrie cried, "Where the hell did they come from?"

The women hurried to Alex's sides, forming a line at her flanks. Rose to her right, Heather beside her. Nancy and Donna beyond Heather. Abby was at her left. Carrie, June, and Colette finished the row.

Across the field, evidenced by heated debate, complete with flailing gesticulations, the twelve men realized they were visible.

Donna asked, "Is it me or were they not there until just now?"

Nancy buzzed, "I have goosebumps. I just witnessed magic, didn't I?"

To Alex, Heather asked, "You did that?"

"I think so," Alex said, the rolls of whispering in her head almost as loud as the evening wind in the grass.

Rose spoke up, "What are they saying?"

"Probably deciding how to murder us," Nancy replied, her tone flat.

"They know I found them," Alex explained.

"Do you think," Carrie hesitated, "it surprised them or pissed them off?"

In the back of Alex's throat, her hammering heart threatened to trigger her gag reflex. Her hands shook, her stomach muscles jittery. She needed the bathroom—which was impossible: She used it three times before they left.

What are they saying? Their arms and mouths moved, engaged in conversation, but whispers, distance, and environment obscured their words. *Is that George?* she thought of one who kept looking in their direction. *Is the one beside him* Jeremiah?

The whispers drove her mad like an incessant swarm of mosquitoes. The men's voices were but stops and fricatives on the breeze. *If they'd shut up,* she thought of the whispers, *I might hear something.* Alex asked, "Can anyone hear them?" No one replied.

They knew she saw them, yet they weren't coming closer. Why? Each occasion she thought she might discern a hint of spoken sound, a sharp consonant or a long vowel, the wind and the whispers, the grasses and the birds, even the insects conspired against her, drowning out anything comprising words.

If she let her breath out as the breeze settled, if she relaxed enough to slow her heart, if she could be still enough, listen closely, pick separate the human from the natural, mute the anticipatory movements of the women around her; perhaps she might hear something…. Her eyes and ears fixed as though the former were laser sights for the latter. She needed to know. *Why aren't they coming? What are they waiting for?* She could move closer, but *they* weren't.

The breeze fell. It was as though the wind found itself exhausted and lay among the grasses to nap. The stillness became so pervasive Alex was almost surprised there was still air to breathe.

The grasses, however, still flowed and swelled like waves on a windswept lake. Blades of grass fluttered. They shined and dulled as they twisted and dipped, rose and fell, creating patterns that would have given body to the wind had there been any.

"What is that?" Heather shushed the others. Leaning, she whispered, "Do you hear it?" Even Alex's whispers held their breath in anticipation.

Alex couldn't hear anything over the grasses, the rush of blades and blooms rubbing against one another. She tried to block it out, to hear over the noisy field, but it was so present and intrusive that she couldn't discern what Heather seemed to hear.

Then a sentence.

"…I'm not worried about the girl…."

Then another.

"…because she hurt you…."

And another.

"…it's in her best interest…."

It wasn't men's voices; it wasn't voices at all: The grass was talking.

Never a voice: A symphony of taps and flutters that all together mimicked speech.

"Are you doing this?" Carrie asked.

Heather shushed her, "Carrie. Listen."

The grasses bent and undulated, almost pulsating, in one direction. Like a stylus in a record groove mimics sound, the field took the sounds of speech and recreating it, carried it across the length of the meadow, each blade imitating a finite aspect, passing it one to the next, a traveling symphony of the spoken words; an echo made from rustling leaves.

And then silence.

The meadow stilled as the grasses and leaves and flowers listened apprehensively for the next words.

Across the field, the men were aware of the patterns recreated by the foliage, visual sound waves like ripples in a windblown puddle, streaking away from them. They were aware their dialog wasn't private.

The grasses tattled, "She's listening? Everyone…, be silent. What are you doing? Watch. Do you see that? She is listening. The boy wasn't kidding. She has magic. We know you're listening, little girl. You should mind your own business. Don't underestimate her. So she has magic. Emotional magic is fickle and weak. She's just a child. A girl. Followed by a bunch of women. Have you ever seen a woman do real magic? She's all they have." The grasses stilled.

The echoing shapes traveled across the field like ripples from a stone thrown in a pond. The sounds arrived with their leafy message "You hear, but you know nothing. Simple spells from a simple girl."

The men started closer. Unlike the wind, Alex's whispers whipped up like a sudden gust. The roar inside her head was deafening. Her ears ached from the volume no one else could hear.

Heather inquired, "Should we meet them?"

"No," was Alex's abrupt reply. "We wait here." *Can they hear my voice quivering?* A sensation twisted inside of her, like something tugging on her heart. "I don't feel good," she said to no one in particular.

Rose looked at her, "What's the matter?" Her expression was a mask of concern concealing disappointment.

She replied, "I'm just, I don't know." She dug her fingertips into her scalp. "The wind left. There's no air. I can't breathe."

Alex. Alex? She couldn't tell who was calling for her.

Rose's hair whipped about her head in a sudden squall. "Is this you?" Rose's gaze shifted to the approaching men. "Or them?"

Alex's stomach clenched like she'd been kicked in the gut; she struggled to breathe, like something hooked into her diaphragm and pulled. This wasn't unlike the feeling when she was trapped inside Sara, and they were summoned. Was someone summoning her?

Alex's knees buckled, dropping her into the grass as though she'd fallen in a hole. The whispers in her head were roaring as though they were being murdered. The terror of the screams gave rise to the hair on Alex's neck. She felt like someone was trying her on, like children fighting over a costume: getting an arm in a sleeve only to have it pulled away by another. Her heart palpitated, like every few seconds it was controlled by a different master.

Alex didn't intend to push Rose's hands away when her cousin began pulling her upright as Alex practically leapt to her feet.

Words formed at the back of Alex's mouth, pressuring their way forward. Even through clenched teeth, a few sounds muscled their way through, bursting through her lips as incomprehensible sounds as if coerced by punches or electrical shocks.

The other women, further from her, heard Alex and felt it opportune to ask their questions. "Shouldn't we be doing something, Alex? Why are we just standing here, Alex? What are we waiting for, Alex?"

Heather and Abby and Rose stared at Alex's wide, terrified eyes. They looked at the approaching men. Heather's hand hovered over Alex's forearm, seeing the white panic in her eyes. "What are they doing to you?"

Alex turned to either side. The wind buffeted her but left the others undisturbed. Her whispers were frenzied. For the first time, one voice rose above the others: *Surrender to me. I'll make it stop. Before it destroys you.*

The singular voice was disarming, like a light shone in her eyes, it blinded her to other sounds. Other voices chattered manically beneath this one, but it was as though they were behind a door, their muted anguish a little more than a buzz. This voice spoke as loud as— if not louder than—her own thoughts, as though hollered directly into her brain.

The twelve men were not more than thirty feet away. They halted.

George stepped past the line; his right hand raised as though offering a greeting. His left hand held a Book. They all carried Books. The trap had sprung. The locks engaged, and all hope of escape evaporated. There'd be no negotiating for Billy, perhaps no negotiating at all. In the wide-open field, there was barely room to move, much less breathe. Alex knew she was trapped. Knew she would soon need to figure this magic thing out. She wanted to be confident. She wanted to know her magic would work. She'd come here with those certainties, but they'd vanished with the air around her. The breath entering her lungs felt as empty as her heart was of hope.

Before her, the men grinned. They held their Books with the same threatening confidence had they been guns. One of them was reading.

Is he doing this to me? She looked at her hands. *Why is nothing happening?* Spikes of fear raced through her, like icy daggers stabbed into her chest, only to quickly melt away in the fires of rage that tensed her arms. Her limbs jittered with the anticipation of turning to run or lurching forward. The others stared. Her body looked like a marionette in the hands of disagreeing puppeteers.

Alex wanted to tell the others what was happening, but was sure if she opened her mouth she'd throw up. Her body quaked; her heart vibrated in her chest. She snatched at Rose's hand. Rose caught hers and squeezed tight, holding it steady.

Individual whispers cried out, louder than the others, voices heard for the first time, perhaps, in centuries. They begged. They demanded.… They threatened. Such fear and anger and rage swelled until they were all muted by the other voice: *They're not going to stop. You are losing control. Give it to me, Alexandrea.* The voice spun dizzyingly around her. Warm confidence wicked through her arm. *Is that Rose?* Hoping to discover the source of Rose's confidence, Alex turned to her cousin, whose grip tightened. *It's because of me, from being beside me.* The circular logic was laughable.

Rose kept a keen eye on Alex, who, despite her growing confidence, was battered by the rave in her skull. Rose said something to Heather, who called to the others, "We need to help her relax."

"How do we do that again?" Donna asked.

Colette huffed at Donna. "How can you not remember? Think of her and think relaxing thoughts."

"Shouldn't we be in groups?" Donna asked.

Carrie growled, "Just fucking do it, Donna."

June protested, "With them staring at us like that?" The group of men, who hadn't yet advanced, or really done anything, seemed to enjoy the disarray of their rivals.

"Come on, ladies," Heather said.

"Hey," Rose shouted, "it's about Alex. Shut up and help her!"

"Rosemary Hawthorne," Heather chided, quickly adding, "nicely said."

The women murmured. Alex ignored their personal placations; the whispers were too disruptive. It didn't matter. The volume grew so loud it was like her head was a pressure cooker dancing on the stove, about to rupture. There was only so much Rosemary could give to her. The rest had to come from within. *I tore apart Abby's barn without trying. It took that man attacking Abby for it to happen.* She looked at the concerned faces around her, their mouths moving like they silently recited prayers. *Do I have to sacrifice their safety to provoke my magic?* She imagined she could see the blue-white strikes of lightning and the women around her dropping to their knees in burning, electrified agony. She hated thinking of their pain just to get her damned magic to work.

The whispers quieted suddenly. *They feel it, too.* The hairs on Alex's neck began to raise and her clothes started clinging to her skin. Freed from the maelstrom in her brain was like being unshackled. Her chest swelled and her breath quickened. It was like watching the ocean rapidly recede; the tsunami would arrive soon. When it came, there'd be no holding it back. *They haven't done anything yet. I can't strike first. I don't know if they're here to fight or not.* Alex looked at her free hand. It tingled. Rose smirked. *She feels it too.* Every time her minds' eye imagined one of her friends struck down, her skin tingled, the anger grew, the whispers growled like rabid, wild things. Something enormous was coming, and the women around her could sense it too.

Abby encouraged, "That a girl, Alex."

Making it grow and maintaining control was like trying to hold the lid still on a rapidly boiling pot. Even if she could trap the steam inside, it was only a matter of time before the heat blistered her skin.

As though sensing her hesitation, a stout man stepped forward. He grasped George's arm, pulling him along. He was significantly older, his round face framed with a shaggy gray head of hair and beard. Tan slacks and, despite the evening warmth, a tweed jacket over a blue buttoned-up shirt. Alex had seen him before: in the Library, amidst her conflagration, as everyone scurried to steal Books to safety from her flames, he observed.

"You're Jeremiah." Even before the name left her lips, the

whispers whipped into such a frenzy it was like speaking from the center of a tornado. Her mouth moved but she wasn't sure any sound came out.

The old man fanned flies from his face. His brown shoes cut through the grasses. He wasn't smiling, nor speaking.

George spoke first. "It's good to see you, Alex. I mean, I'm glad you came. I mean, it's good you did."

Alex's eyes flashed from Jeremiah to George. *He's not going to speak to me. Not unless I make it so he has to.* The pressure of his advance nicked her inflating balloon. It didn't pop, but it required more effort to keep it from deflating.

The other men hadn't budged. Their threat was secondary. Compared to the casual mishmash her Book Club wore, they were all well-dressed. Like their board meeting had been interrupted, or they had a dress code for magic. Their business attire incongruous to the setting.

The wind blustered again, blowing Alex's auburn hair forward and back, stray strands catching in her eyelashes and mouth. Trying to collect it from her face proved futile. The wind troubled no one else.

She studied George and Jeremiah, then the women at her side. *They're waiting for me to do something.* She collected herself, piling all her confidence into a mound to stand upon even as it collapsed.

She broke the silence, "Where's Billy? You said—"

Interrupting Alex with crunching grasses, Jeremiah abruptly turned and departed.

George tried to explain, his words falling from his mouth as though they'd tripped on his lower lip. "Jeremiah thinks you have no value to him."

Alex was apoplectic. She stammered through a few iterations before saying, "You said he," she managed, pointing at Jeremiah, "had you ask *me* to be *here*." She clawed at the hair flying into her face. The wind afforded her no dignity.

Behind them, the men found her amusing. Their smug faces put rust in Alex's joints, seizing her body rigid in anger. Between the wind, and the ever-rising tempest in her head, she worked to reign her attention like a spooked horse.

The air prickled with disgust as the women at her sides raised their hackles. *He asked* me *here!* Relief that the sprung trap was being reset couldn't wash her thoughts of Billy away. She'd come here—

risking everyone's safety—for him. She could not—would not—let this day end without her *requirement* becoming a *demand*. She'd felt her magic building under her skin. It hadn't abated, but as Jeremiah played her emotions, taking her through disappointment and frustration and inadequacy, she could feel the power changing.

She swallowed to wet her parched mouth and pulled hair from her face one final time.

She ran past George and grasped Jeremiah's departing arm, fixing him in place and painting his face with disgust. "We were supposed to trade. My Billy for your *Matthew* problem."

Jeremiah didn't look up from her hand until she released him. He studied her face a moment. "As I understand, Matthew's *your* problem."

She wanted to contradict his statement. His remark felt like a serpent coiled about her wrist, one wrong inflection and its poisoned fangs would strike. He stared indifferently, as though disappointed by the words she had yet to speak. She almost failed to respond. Finally, she forced the words out and told him, "He stole *your* Books from *your* Library."

"Matthew?" The word was abrupt. Her heart sank as he called her a liar. "The Book burning was your doing."

Alex knew she had to return blame to Matthew. "He won't stop there. He wants more. He wants them all."

"He does?" He mocked her with his tone. "How surprising. No one has ever wanted more." He grinned, pitying her. "Little girl, do you think Matthew is the first man to covet my Books? Do you think he'll be the last?" Each word dripped with belittling sarcasm. "Matthew is a flea trapped in an overturned glass. He sees the dog and believes he can reach it."

She took the chance. "He did reach it. Only it wasn't him. It was me." Jeremiah didn't respond. "Help me get Billy back and I'll help you with Matthew."

Jeremiah gestured back at his waiting troops. "You see these men with their Books. Of course, you assume the Books are important." He lowered his tone, his nostrils flaring. "I thought I might let you keep the Books. To see what they do to you." He drilled his finger against her temple as his words slipped, spittle-covered, through clenched teeth, "I can see them wriggling around in your braincase like little worms, devouring you from the inside." He stepped back; his ferocity vanished, hidden beneath a cloak of composure. "Matthew isn't a problem. Or even a distraction. Just another man who believes he can take from me something he cannot begin to comprehend."

Her voice came out high-pitched; she nearly winced. "Then why ask to meet me?"

"Because you'd bring your Coven." Disregarding her coolly, he pivoted about his heel. Marching from her, his left hand rose into the air. "Take her."

George cowered beneath Alex's glare. "It wasn't," he stammered, "I didn't think…. He told me he wanted to talk!"

Alex buzzed. Her heart, previously quieted, exploded in her chest. Had the pounding not rattled her frame the cries inside her skull would have drowned everything else out. Someone screamed. It was disturbing relief from the vocals inside her head. There were men on all sides. Dozens. The trap snapped closed. Any chance of escape lost. Jeremiah had hidden dozens more in the light; she was so proud to discover him she hadn't thought to look for more. Hairs on her arms and neck stood. The inside of her skull felt like a thousand women scratched at it from their graves. Her knees forgot which way they bent and nearly collapsed her to the grass. Each moment drew her gaze to a new advancing Book, cradled by a man, his face painted with disgust. Alex reached for her magic, hoping to find it, but it was like clutching fistfuls of sand. *I fucked this up, didn't I?*

One approaching man stopped feet from her. He was bald with a dark, tightly shaved beard that ran down his throat. He carried no Book. He held out his hands. "Come."

Alex couldn't speak. The squall in her head was unmatched by the storm blowing around them. Her clothes thrashed against her body, she felt buffeted and pushed as though a crowd of spirits shoved past her.

The bald man said, "I am offering you the dignity of walking from here."

Around him, men opened their Books. The wind bent the pages around their fingers.

"Where's your Book?" *I know him. I saw him, in the Library, beside Jeremiah.*

He pulled on his collar. What she had mistaken for a thick beard were dark tattoos inscribed on his skin. They covered him almost completely. Her head roared. She nearly covered her ears; the din was excruciating. Individual cries raised above the storming sea. Then that other voice, *You can't do this any longer. Hand it to me.*

His hand—covered in nonsensical symbols—reached for her, expecting her contrition with a grasp. "Please", she begged, "don't come any closer." Tears spilled from her eyes, pulled out by the wind, pushed out by the screams. If surrender would have offered her peace—offered her friends safety—she would have risked any punishment to escape the torture from within her own skull.

The distant trees swayed and bent. They begin breaking apart.

Alex's stomach reeled. Try as she might, she couldn't look away from him. He was covered in the shapes and symbols she'd only ever seen before in Books.

George shouted over the wind, "You have to believe me Alex, I didn't know…."

Without a word, a shower of sparks from the tattooed man's fingertips sent George collapsing.

The tattooed man threatened, "This is your last chance." As though noticing the storm for the first time, he looked to the sky. Dark, thick clouds racing to obscure the sun. His hand remained extended towards Alex. The voice in her head crying above the others told her, *Take his hand and be done with this.*

Chapter Fifty-Four

he tattooed man's demanding hand reminded her of Charon, the child demanding its coin. The correlation seemed clear. He glanced back and with a nod, June fell to the ground. A deafening static discharge, like the sudden furious crumpling of aluminum foil was simultaneous to the sparks of light that scarred Alex's vision with a deep blue line. Donna cried out, yowling like a wounded puppy. As the others ducked into the grasses, Nancy scurried between the first two wounded, patting out glowing embers on their scorched clothes.

Carrie stood with her pepper spray, but the wind dispersed it. She withstood several blasts of electrical energy, her teeth gritting as she charged towards the nearest attacker. She was struck from multiple directions, crying out as she collapsed and rolled in the grass, whimpering.

As Abby wrapped Alex as though a shell to a turtle, Heather shielded Rose with her body.

"Stop it, Mom," Rose grunted, pushing at her mother.

Heather's voice was wet with fear. "I'm trying to keep you safe."

"I am safe." Rose squeezed from under her mother's embrace. "Look," she pointed at the storming sky, the wind pulling her hair and pressing her clothes flat to her body. "Alex is doing that."

Alex felt the reverberation of the next strike through Abby's body. Abby's knees buckled, but she refused to drop, even on the third and fourth excruciating hit.

The tattooed man wrenched Abby from her, tossing her aside. He glared at Alex as he read from his own skin. Heather howled; bolts of electricity shooting from his fingertips stuck her like a thunderclap. Alex could feel Heather's thrashing pain in her feet, through the ground. When Rose attempted to protect her mother, the strike spun her into the grasses.

It didn't matter how many times her resolve had been pricked. Watching harm come to those she loved was like a thousand knives stabbing her heart. Only they didn't diminish her. The pain was overwhelming, but she fed from it gluttonously. The tsunami was finally rushing forward. She felt swollen on power, barely able to control the energies that swirled inside. Swelling with anger and rage and sorrow and pity, she could feel the emotions transforming, altering from feelings to energies.

Alex realized she was the only one of her Coven still standing.

When offered his hand again, Alex snatched it.

"Don't, Alex," Abby begged, struggling to her feet, her clothes smoldering. "Don't surrender."

With only a glance from the tattooed man, the onslaught ended. The buzzing strikes rang in her ears; slowly replaced by the howling wind and cries from her wounded Coven. Those who could, stood slowly.

Colette and Carrie looked to Alex as they helped one another up, the pain from the marks on their bodies evidenced by their twisted expressions. Alex saw their bewilderment. They hadn't expected magic to be so violent or painful. The others were attending to Donna, who lay still in the grass, not moving.

The tattooed man pulled on Alex to follow him, but she wouldn't budge. The men lowered their Books even as they tightened their circle. The tattooed man failed a second time to pull her into compliance. Behind him, Jeremiah hadn't once looked back as he departed.

"What are you doing Alex?"

What are *you waiting for, Alex?* The voice was louder, closer this time. Even with the roar of whispers, she found it familiar. Her stomach queasy. The wind settled.

Alex turned to prepare Rose for what was coming. Rose, however, glared disappointingly as she braced her mother's wounded frame. Everyone stared at her hand, clutching the tattooed man's hand. They each pulled for control like a never-ending handshake.

Her head grew light, dizzy, as something wriggled inside. As though Jeremiah's words became burrowing worms, feasting on her brain. *It's okay Alex.*

Turning back to the men, the tattooed man gestured with his free hand. "Round them up. They go to the Farm." To Alex, he said, "Come or they die where they stand. At least as Books, they'll live on in some other form. It isn't the end."

Alex, give it to me. I'll bear the weight for you.

Alex recognized the voice. *Sweet child, we've been through too much suffering together. I lived because you were there with me. Let me carry you the remainder of the way.* Tears welled in Alex's eyes. It was Sara's voice, no less real than had she been there. "I don't know if I can. I'm broken. Nothing's working." *They're so scared, Alex. They'd rather die than be forced back to those places. Let me help.* "Help me, Sara." Reminded of the sensation of being trapped within Sara, Alex felt Sara as though the woman slipped into her skin, wearing her like a jacket. She could feel Sara struggling to move her limbs, and as she relinquished control, Sara's movements within her became more fluid.

The tattooed man tugged. Alex's words came thunderous, demanding, confident, and final: "Come here, Book." She pulled him into a face-to-face embrace.

Symbols swam about his flesh, around his mouth, racing up and down his throat.

His ink squirmed. Symbols wiggled, crawled, moved like maggots through flesh. She saw in the squirming shapes whole other patterns of words; she was drawn into them, as though abandoning herself for the endless spiral of words within words within words on and into his flesh. Deeper into his flesh. Her fingers digging into his arms.

She was a lonely woman. Believed she was twenty years and thirty pounds past her prime. Divorced, with two impressionable boys spending a holiday weekend with her ex. They always had fun with him, spoke highly of him, reminded her she wasn't him. Her relationship with her children was about homework and chores and responsibilities and growing up and doing the right thing. His world was amusement parks, movies, desserts, and presents. She grew anxious before they left with him, knowing when they returned, they would resent her rules and requirements. They would fight with her, test her limits with complaints of dictatorship as they returned to real life from their father's fantasy-world. How could she compete with his Never-Never Land? A few too many drinks, a few too many flirty glances, a younger man's insinuating offer to take her home, to help her forget....

It usually ended there. It usually ended with her magic extracted. Made into a Book. This was different. This was horrific. She suffered, excruciatingly transformed, until the only part of her that remained painted the skin of a living Book: they transformed her into this golem.

Alex's head felt split from the screams that came from inside, as though it no longer could contain them. The world spun around her, yet at the center of it, always in focus, the tattooed man. His ink, fine and sharp. Wrinkles on his face like the crease on a once dog-eared page. Flecks of gold amidst an otherwise ordinary grayish-brown iris. Her own reflection in the dark center. The air between them grew hazy with motion and heat.

The tattooed symbols and shapes peeled away, like nervous worms emerging from trembling skin.

He barely made a whimper as she flayed him.

Alex wanted to let go, tried to, but these were someone else's hands now. Her whispers celebrated. Sara had trapped her in her own body, and she was not about to look away as she claimed revenge for them. The bloody symbols of ink and flesh spilled from him, flopping and slapping and slipping to the ground.

The temperature between them soared like the ground beneath them turned molten. He looked upon her like a child receiving a slap, his face pure bewilderment.

He pulled from her hands as the flames spun angrily about them—flames which vanished at their disconnection. He cried out his anguish, the remaining symbols hanging like bloody streamers. His skin and clothes already blackened, like they were as sensitive to her fire as paper. He crumpled to the ground, glowing embers marched across his skin, darkening him. Bolts of lightning fled her fingers, silencing the tattooed man.

"Alex! Alex, please!"

How long have they been calling my name? The moment she heard Abby's voice she realized they'd been calling to her the whole time.

She was flecked with the tattooed man's blood. She wasn't entirely sure what had happened. A vague recollection was all she had, but it fled like a dream. A dream of Sara Frost. Alex looked at her hands and at the remains of the tattooed man. *I did that?*

"I know you're afraid," Abby cried to her. Beside Abby, Heather held Rose. Carrie and Nancy fought to bring Donna back to consciousness. Colette and June. "You've got to let go. Don't hold back. Please, Alex. Stop being afraid."

Alex witnessed the punishment uncooperative women endured as the men recommenced firing their lighting.

She thought the screams in her head were unbearably loud until she realized they were her own. Knots of rage—at seeing her Coven so grossly mistreated—tumbled through her body, tensing her in fitful waves. As though dropping it, hatred spilled from her fingertips. The crackling electricity wasn't like the piteous bolts of light the men shot. The giant, branching strike nearly blinded her; residual lines ghosted her vision like she looked through a cracked globe.

Her mind understood she was still furious, but her roiling hatred had all but vanished, as though fuel for the lightning.

Around her, the smoldering grass was burned in random patterns. Those men who were still standing took a moment to clear their heads of their shock before they lowered their Books and withdrew. Jeremiah was hurriedly returning.

The whispers, at seeing what she'd done, become a mob: a thousand voices demanding use of what she possessed. The thin veil of her skull never felt as flimsy as it did when they bashed their voices against it. She felt dizzy, queasy, turned about. She couldn't help but look at the flayed squiggles and patterns of blood saturating the tattooed man's clothes. She'd done that to him. It made her sick. Her hands trembled. She couldn't make them stop.

"Again, Alex," Abby begged.

It was like her vessel needed to be filled from empty. When, after the second minute, she hadn't done anything more, the men stopped their retreat. They surrounded her and her friends, sneering over their Books, enflamed that although their attacks left Alex's clothes distressed and burned, her skin raw and bloodied, she remained like they'd done nothing. But she had felt it. She felt everything.

You pushed me out. Don't do that again!

Alex was lost to the screams in her head as though the mob had breached the drawbridge and began pillaging the castle. The world tipped and whirled like she was on a carnival ride. She'd lost control of the field. She'd lost control of the fight. She'd lost control of herself.

A series of sparks struck her like successive punches. The breath was knocked from her, but even as she gasped to catch it, the roar in her head was too great to tell whether she'd even been hurt. Her body flailed like she was being pushed about by an unruly crowd, but no hands touched her. She could feel the panicked whispers, feel their agency as they fought against her—over her. Alex hadn't realized how fiercely she'd resisted them until her strength began leaving her. She felt her own hands pried away from her sense of touch. She struggled against them, like holding closed a door battered by a mob. She couldn't hold it for long.

She summoned her anger, not just at him, but at the whispers—the women she'd saved—for their mutiny. She gritted her teeth, trying to hold on just long enough to face Jeremiah when he came to kill her.

The field came suddenly alive. Birds flew from the tall grasses. Great sky-darkening clouds of them; starlings rising in a fearful murmuration, like a blob of liquid stretching into the sky, trying to find the right shape so their message could be understood. The tilt-o-whirl was going too fast, and Alex couldn't help but drop to her knees and plant her hands on the soil. Her legs independently tried to stand, her arms reached and pushed against her desire.

George grabbed her around her waist and pulled her upright. He used his body to hold her steady, fighting against her spasms. His body pressed against hers, her clothes dampened from his soaking perspiration. "Please don't burn me, Alex."

It was only then she saw the flames. Dozens of fires burned throughout the field.

Confusion tormented her mind. She was sick with desperation, watching her own failure as she felt torn apart from the inside. Undone from within.

Alex didn't feel well. Mushrooms of flames erupted and danced and spread. The roar in her head was changing, the siege nearly run its course. The kingdom in collapse as the palace was looted. She'd saved these women; endured their torture and freed them from their Books and this was how they thanked her? By tearing her down and overthrowing her? The whole world narrowed in her vision. What were they doing to her? What did mobs do to deposed rulers? For everything she'd been through, she never expected it to end like this. At the end of Matthew's hammer, perhaps, but never at the hands of the very women she thought she'd saved. No wonder Matthew wanted to make a Book of her. Had he known what would happen? When she could no longer hold on—her very sense of self started slipping away. Until her whole world was swallowed by darkness.

"Help them," she barely heard herself say. "I can't hold back much longer. Help them, George."

*   *   *   *   *

When Heather saw that Alex had shot an explosion of lightning, her stomach made a titanic shift from being stretched with leaden doubt, to rising into her chest, eager to see what her niece would do next.

Rose pushed away from her protective embrace, eager to watch her cousin punish their attackers. With great reluctance, Heather let her go. As though holding her somehow kept her safe.

Instead, Alex fell to her hands and knees. George ran to her and—instead of attacking her—hauled her upright. But Alex wasn't done. Flames erupted through the field. Pillars of fire swirled, sucking in debris and grasses, throwing off fiery soot. The men had been firing at Alex, their terrifying electrical bursts puny compared to the blinding branching storm of electricity Alex had summoned. Heather watched her stoically take everything they pummeled her with, and although her stomach grew acidic at the brutal punishment Alex suffered, she couldn't help but cheer her fortitude. Alex had found her power and the tide of this battle was going to irrevocably change.

And then Alex collapsed.

She went rigid, her back arching, her head tipping back so violently it looked like it was trying to rid itself of her shoulders. She ripped from George's embrace. Her body thrashed and trembled in seizure until she collapsed, disappearing amidst the grasses.

Heather gasped; but instead of withering, the flames grew in the violent wind, rising, spinning like tornados. Abby crawled towards Alex, struck so many times she could no longer stand.

Nancy was the first to run toward Alex, Carrie on her heals. Men fired at them, Carrie tumbled when struck in the small of her back, but she didn't stop. They grabbed Alex from Abby and used their own bodies to still her thrashing form. Heather wanted to be there, too, to cradle Alex's head, to embrace her and heal her, but there was Rose, just past her fingertips. Rose was scanning the field, her face knitted with determination. Heather wanted to hide but wouldn't allow her fear to dictate terms until her daughter—daughters—were safe. Beyond Rose, June was helping Donna to her feet. The older woman still didn't seem quite aware of the situation; asking where they'd left the cars. Colette crowded Heather. Heather knew what she was about to ask, and even with foreknowledge, couldn't find a satisfactory response, "I don't know what we should do."

The flames began dancing through the field, despite Alex's condition. Each time some man thought to attack them, flames set upon him. Each time a man tried to harm one of them, the fire punished them, their clothes and hair alighting. Flames attacked Jeremiah; a wave of his hand and the fiery tornado vanished in a swirl of blackening cinders.

In a moment of clarity, Heather summoned her confidence and called the others. "Get to Alex. She needs our help." She reached for Rose's arm, but her daughter was sprinting ahead. The others followed, even Donna, looking like she was in a three-legged-race with June.

Flames forced the men to give up their attacks. Some gawked at the scene, as though traumatized by what should have been an easy victory. Two others dragged the tattooed man towards Jeremiah. *Are we winning?*

Heather grabbed at Alex, and Alex stared into her face. Her eyes watered and streams of soot-stained tears rolled down her cheeks as the choking smoke closed in around them. "Sweetheart," Heather whispered, "You've done well. It's enough." The sparkling flames reflected in Alex's eyes like a field of stars. "You're going to kill us all."

Alex's eyes fluttered. She stared at Heather. "Who are you?"

Abby gasped.

Colette grabbed George from behind. Carrie leapt at him like a panther, using momentum to pull the much larger George to the ground. Before Heather could tell her otherwise, Rose entered in the fray. Carrie had her hands on George's Book, but he wasn't letting it go. Rose pried at his fingers. She bit them and yanked the Book from his hands. Carrie tried to claim it, but Rose wasn't about to give up her prize.

Beyond them, Jeremiah came upon the tattooed man. His entire charred form opened like a blooming flower as he was consumed by flame.

Heather held onto Alex, whose face was a knot of anger and confusion. Her features knitted tight, as though making multiple expressions at once. Heather cried to Alex, "Can you stop it? Are you okay?"

There was a hint of recognition in Alex's eyes. "You look like Peter," she choked, the smoke burning her eyes as they welled with tears. "I've never felt so much power," she mumbled. "They all want it. They all want to take it for themselves. They don't realize she'll die in the process. If she dies, we all do."

"Who'll die? Who wants the power? Alex, talk to me!" Alex's mouth moved as though she was answering, but at once, her body tightened, the muscles as taut as steel cable. Alex clenched, head to foot, her neck twisted as though she were fitfully shaking it *no*. Even Abby, for all her strength, couldn't hold Alex still.

June screamed. The flaming pillars dropped like napalm, flowing through the tall grasses. Fire surrounded the women. Several men found themselves trapped, surrounded by flame; they sacrificed their flesh for freedom.

With Alex in Abby's arms, worry overcame Heather like ice water running down her back. She'd lost track of her daughter and frantically scanned the field. Everywhere was chaos. Fire. Men running. The grasses wilted and burned, the fire coming closer and closer. Jeremiah was nowhere to be seen. Unable to find her daughter, her dread rose, choking her.

Abby struggled as though wrestling a wild animal. Froth ran from her Alex's lips. Her shirt was splashed with vomit. Urine darkening her jeans. Nancy called to Heather, "She's burning up."

Yeah, we're all going to burn up. As much as Heather thought all was lost, Nancy was still trying to save Alex. Everyone was accounted for, here, at Alex's side. Everyone except Rose.

Where is she? Heather was sick. *What if they have her? They have my daughter now, too? What if she's hurt and needs me? What if she's dying, alone, and wondering why I'm not there with her?* She would find her daughter, regardless the cost.

Then Heather saw her daughter and gasped, "No."

Rosemary stood, no more than a dozen feet away, surrounded

by flames. George was beside her, screaming and begging as the flames closed in on them.

"Rose," Heather screamed twice, attempting to let her daughter know she was there, if unable to save her. She would have left Alex but any time someone stood above the grasses they were immediately struck as one of the few remaining men fired at them. She'd never been so terrified; Rose was trapped, about to be burned alive and there was nothing she could do. Rose was going to die, and her last sight would be her mother nursing Alex. Rose looked back, her lips moving. *Is she calling to me?* Heather wished there was some apology she could make for not being able to save her daughter. Only the expression tormenting Rose's face wasn't fear; Heather had never seen her daughter look so determined before.

Then Heather saw the Book: George's Book in Rose's hands. Open in her hands. Her eyes fixed upon it. Her mouth moving. Rose was reading.

Rose gesticulated with her hand as she commanded incomprehensible words. The flames died in a final roar, leaving nothing more than dark smoke rising into the sky from the blackened battlefield.

With the angry flames extinguished, the field fell into dead silence. Heather cried out, "Rosemary, what have you done?"

Rose flipped the pages as though looking for a lost note. Then read. Combinations of sounds so guttural and foreign expelled from her mouth as sparks flew from her fingertips, striking at each of the remaining men, driving them back or dropping them to their knees. Rose turned to Heather and grinned. Then she drove forward, strike after strike leaping from her fingertips as she embraced her offensive.

Abby shouted to Heather. "Nancy says she's dying."

Heather fought to tear her eyes from her daughter. *She is amazing.* She touched her niece's feverish forehead. It felt like flames still burned inside her. "We've got to get her home."

Abby looked about them. Heather followed her gaze. Rose maintained an aggressive pursuit, firing shocking bolts off her fingertips, even as the remaining men fled to the trees or disappeared into daylight, hiding like they came. They fled her daughter. But Heather still despaired as Rose got further away. *Where's that man? Where's Jeremiah?* The flame-ravaged field was otherwise empty. Only they remained.

Leaving Alex in more capable hands, Heather ran to Rose, kicking up soot as she raced between the remains of smoldering grass. Rose panicked at the expression on her mother's face and with another utterance, disappeared the Book from her hands.

88

Chapter Fifty-Five

ars skidded into the driveway at the Hawthorne house. They stopped wherever there was room: the lawn, the driveway, everywhere but the garden. Even before engines shut, doors were opening. Carrie raced, nearly tripping. June and Colette left Donna and ran. Everyone converged on Abby's truck. Then they waited, unable to look at one another, unwilling to look at the truck. They didn't want anyone confirming what they all feared. The front doors opened. Neither Heather nor Abby made eye contact with any of the others or each other. The back doors creaked open. Rose looked up. She held Alex, who was limp and unconscious, covered in vomit and stinking of piss. The seizures had stopped.

Nancy leaned in to examine Alex.

"I've been holding her," Rose cried out tearfully. "It's not working," she apologized. Abby pried her arms from Alex to pull her from the car.

Under her breath, Heather muttered, "It's the Book. It gave you magic—men's magic—but maybe it took your real powers away."

Rose glared but held back her argument.

Nancy shouted at Heather, "We need to get her in an ice bath and get her fever down."

Heather helped Rose from the car. Her tone was direct, "Go to the bathroom. Start filling the tub. Only cold." Rose started for the house. Heather shouted after her, "Get ice. Dump it in the tub. All of it."

Abby cradled Alex's body like a giant, gangly babe. Her head and arms lulling about, devoid of muscle-tone, swaying with each step Abby made towards the house. She looked fake; she looked dead.

Heather hadn't moved. She stood as though her toes had grown roots. She was terrified to leave this spot, terrified to discover her niece was dead. Donna struggled from Colette's car. A pained grunt broke Heather's meditation and she took the older woman's elbow and helped her to her feet. Donna wasn't about to allow her drama to compete with the moment, so she uncharacteristically accepted the assistance.

Carrie opened the trunk. She glared into it. "Get the fuck out." She slapped at George's hand as he reached for her help. Without looking up, she shouted, "Heather, where do you want me to put this trash?"

Isn't this kidnapping or something? Do I want him in the house? Heather had to take control of the situation and herself. "Maybe, let's take him to the cellar. Tie him up." She pointed to the shed near the garden, a little red shack of rotting wood and broken shingles held together with rusted nails. "June, there's rope and stuff in the shed. Take anything you can use to tie him securely."

June ran to the shed.

Colette joined Carrie. Flashing a can of pepper spray, she warned George, "Don't try anything."

George kept his hands glued to his sides. His shoulders hunched, his eyes laser-focused on his feet, he shuffled alongside his accusers. Obediently following them into the cellar.

The steps creaked into the dark, dank underbelly of the house. The heat of the day broke at the second step, as though wading into a pool of cold air. In the immediate vicinity of the stairs, the basement was tidy. A washer and dryer stood at the foot of a red area-rug. Shelving units held laundry essentials and pantry staples. A few clothes hung; wooden pins holding them to cotton line.

Beyond the circle cast by the florescent work-lights was a place where abandoned things collected. Piles of odds and ends stacked on relics of furniture. This was the place she brought George, as far from the circle of light and the things that were a part of her life as possible. Heather pulled a pull-chain, illuminating a bare bulb. To her right, the filthy boiler knelt like an ancient beast felled with pipes that knotted at the ceiling and dripped perspiration. A muddled rush of water shook one of the pipes; the tub was filling. Carrie freed a child's chair from its burden of old primers and schoolbooks, dragging it alongside a gnarled column. George sat. Colette and Carrie tied him to the column with a deliberate knot of rope and electrical cord.

*   *   *   *   *

Abby stood awkwardly, one knee on the toilet to give Nancy room to attend to Alex, who was sprawled in the large, white tub. Water gushed from the spout. Water pressure wasn't a problem; it splashed and splattered onto the floor. Rose was stomping upstairs from the kitchen with ice trays in hand. Nancy pulled off Alex's shoes and socks. Then she wriggled Alex out of her piss-soaked jeans. She slipped off Alex's vomit-stained shirt, leaving only her bra and underwear.

Nancy took Alex's glass charm in her hand. "Can this come off?"

Abby gently pushed her way to Alex's side and opened the clasp. She held it like a memento-mori. Taking it felt like stealing a jewel from the dead. *I'm going to give it back to her. She'll need it.*

Nancy folded towels and placed them beside Alex's hips and behind her head. Positioning her, so her limp form was unlikely to slide beneath the water.

Rose stepped in, a tray of ice in each hand. She held out the trays to Abby, her eyes asking what to do. Abby deferred to Nancy, who said, "Dump them right on her. We've got to bring the fever down. She's raging hot."

Rose twisted the ice trays. Two dozen cubes fell on Alex's stomach and chest. Rose stood over her cousin, staring at the unconscious body. "I thought it would look like more. That's not enough, is it?"

"Is there more ice?" Nancy asked.

"We only have the two trays." Rose looked at the plastic trays in her hands. "I'll refill them."

Nancy gave her a nod and Rose disappeared back to the kitchen.

Nancy gave Abby a whimpering sigh. "Rose shouldn't have to see this. Alex should be in a hospital. She's dying. Cooking her brain. They have machines to do this." She sensed Abby's unspoken question. "If we're going to treat her, we've got to do it right."

"I'll get ice."

"We need a lot."

"Tell me exactly how much. The gas station in town has those barbecue bags."

"As much as you can carry. Nothing will be too much. Get back quick."

Abby reached into the tub and cradled Alex's cheek in her palm. She anticipated something the touch wasn't giving her. It felt strange. *It's like it's not even her.* Abby's chest might have been filled with cement, it so weighed on her. It strained her shoulders and her neck as though they held up the rest of her.

"If you're in there kiddo, be okay. I'll be right back. Don't go anywhere." Turning from Alex took all the effort Abby could muster. She knew she had to go but her body ached to remain. She took the stairs two at a time, wincing at the bruises and burns covering her back. Downstairs, Rose—balancing water-filled ice trays on her way to the freezer—gave her an inquisitive look. Abby told her, "I'm getting ice from the gas station. If your mom asks, I'll be back in ten."

When Abby returned carrying several sleeves of ice piled in her arms, most of the women were sitting around the kitchen table, looking exhausted and defeated. Abby climbed the stairs and saw Nancy, Heather, and Rose crowded into the bathroom. Nancy was sitting on the toilet, Rose and Heather were soaking wet from taking turns hugging Alex. When Heather saw Abby, she pulled away from the tub. Rubbing her face, her hands substituted one type of wetness for another. "Nothing's working."

"She's burning up," Nancy's voice trembled. "Dump the ice on her."

Abby unceremoniously dropped all but one of the bags at her feet. She rabidly tore it open and then the five smaller bags it contained. She was on the second outer bag before Heather and Rose and Nancy joined in, opening bags and piling the tub with ice.

When they finished, Alex was buried up to her collarbone under piles of melting ice.

Nancy plunged her hand into the water. She made a noise indicating it was cold. She pressed her palm to Alex's forehead, shaking her own head. "It's out of our hands now. The fever needs to come down. The water is cold enough to be harmful, but she's burning up." She turned to Heather, "It's an acceptable risk. There's not much else we can do."

Heather took a breath, trying not to cry. "Be honest, Nancy. Are we doing more harm here? Should she be in a hospital?"

Nancy shook her head. "Hospital's too far; we'd have to take her out of the ice. Maybe once she's out of danger we can think about it. Right now, she's better off right where she is." She splashed water onto Alex's forehead and throat. She slid a handful of ice around Alex's face, stirring the bath to keep the coldest water against Alex's body.

Abby couldn't believe how quickly the ice was melting. It was like Alex was a furnace. *If it weren't for the ice, would the water boil?*

After several minutes, Abby looked at her wrist. "It's closing in on ten. You're all exhausted. I'll stay with Alex. You folks go downstairs, get something to eat, think about getting some sleep." For the first time she felt overwhelmed by exhaustion. "Is everyone still here?"

Heather thought before nodding. She hugged Abby. "Only because I know she's in the best hands."

Nancy said, "Shout to me if anything changes. If she moves, sinks, shivers, mumbles, farts; that's something. Okay?"

Abby nodded, "Anything changes, and I'll scream bloody murder."

Nancy, her head low, shuffled into the hall. Heather asked Rose to come. Rose hesitated, "Just a minute, Mom."

Rose knelt beside the tub, running her fingers in the water between the piles of ice that occasionally collapsed as they melted from underneath. She touched Alex's face, running her fingers against her cheek, clearing the hair matted to her face, letting it join the rest that floated about the water.

"You better be okay," she told her cousin. "There's so much I want to show you."

Rose gave Alex a hug and left to join her mother.

*   *   *   *   *

Heather was waiting at the bottom of the stairs. "Not now, but we need to talk, Rosemary," Heather meant to be firm, but Rose's face suggested she thought she was being scolded.

Rose's tone was at risk of drowning in sarcasm. "What about, Mom? Why not now?"

"You know what about," Heather looked upstairs. "You used a Book back there."

"Mom, I…."

Heather interrupted, "I saw you."

"Come on, Mom," Rose dismissed her concern. "Someone had to do something. The only one with real magic couldn't. Everything was crazy. You would have done the same thing. If you could."

Heather shook her head. "No, I wouldn't." *Did my daughter just insult me?*

Rose made a face that Heather felt like slapping off, "You just keep telling yourself that." She motioned up the stairs. "It's because of *me* she's even alive. It's because of *me* you're all even alive."

"I know that," Heather said, "but it's a Book. You don't know what you've done. Using it is a horrible thing." *This is getting out of control. I should be asking if she's okay. The Book will bring her trouble.*

Before Heather could say anything else, Rose added, "The Book is safe and secure. You don't have to worry about it anymore." She turned and walked away, leaving Heather alone.

Chapter Fifty-Six

lex's eyes opened. Her body suffered the ache of a deep chill, like she had been shivering for hours. She splashed and slid in a panic before realizing she was in the tub, the water cool. Resting against the outside of the tub, unaffected by the noise, Abby lightly snored in the dark. A small night-light beside the sink, reflecting off the medicine cabinet mirror, provided enough light for Alex to see.

Alex stood, a hand bracing the wall for balance. Water dripped off her body, plinking into the tub. Aside from Abby's snores, the house was silent. Her head, however, wasn't. The whispers were quieter; the whispers that nearly killed her.

Her hands squeegeed the water from her body. She examined her bra strap. The fabric was unusual. She admired the design. A small rose adorned the fabric between the cups. She ran her hands across her underwear. They felt waterlogged and small. Perhaps they'd shrunk. She noticed many scorch marks on her flank. Older burns marred her arms and legs. *No time for these now.*

She knelt beside Abby and placed a hand on her shoulder. Abby stirred, either from the touch or the moisture wicking into her sleeveless shirt but didn't wake. Alex was certain Abby would now continue to slumber.

She dripped into the hall, leaving wet polka-dots surrounding her damp footprints. Peering into the bedrooms, to ensure everyone was asleep before taking the stairs, leaving wet footprints on the wooden treads, Alex made her way to the living room. The moonlight formed a rectangle around a sleeping form on the couch, covered in a red and white quilt. Alex examined it. This wasn't the one she remembered. That quilt would be much older and was better made. Alex rested her hand on their head to ensure they continued to sleep.

She whispered to herself, "Where did they put him?" He wasn't in any room thus far. She turned to the kitchen and discovered the basement stairs. The door was open. The juxtaposition between the spaces made it seem unusual for this door to be open: clean, tidy kitchen and musty, exposed wood basement.

The stair treads and floor felt coarse to her bare feet, her wet hair dripping, leaving tiny dust puddles sticking to her feet and ankles. It was perilously dark. She found a switch and shaded her eyes from the sudden illumination. She looked around, whispering, "Where are you, boy?"

Slumped in a chair, ropes and electrical wires knotted preposterously about him and a thick wooden column, George slept.

Alex stealthily approached and knelt at his side. She examined his tortured skin. Seeing him like this, scarred and tortured by burns, Alex's eyes teared and her lip quivered. Her heart broke for him. *It shouldn't have been like this.* She slid her arms around him. She held him for several minutes.

He stirred, awoken perhaps by her clasp, her dampness, perhaps by what he felt. He groaned. He saw her and rested his head against her, his shoulders flexing as he strained against his bindings to return her embrace.

She held his warmth against her naked skin, feeling him sob at the pain she was releasing. She whispered his name in his ear. She ran her fingers down his scalp, his neck, his back in a caress. He hadn't earned this, but she could not allow him to languish any longer. She fiddled with the ropes. The knots relaxed and fell loose. Finding his freedom, he embraced the opportunity to wriggle his arms free and hold her too.

His pain abated. He was breathing deeper, more relaxed. Although he'd received all the possible benefit of her embrace, she wasn't ready to let him go. She missed George, the idea of him, at least.

He slid from her grasp to look at her. His face needed time to heal; his scars rearranged to healthy flesh, lacked hair and pigment. That would come. He was boyishly handsome, his wide-set brown eyes thanked her like some puppy. He leaned forward, his lips touching hers. She withdrew, his kiss perhaps slipped from her cheek. He kissed her again, his hands pulling at her, caressing her, groping to her face where he held her, kissing her repeatedly, then kissing her cheek, her throat, her collarbone.

Alex's voice broke its whisper. At the risk of awaking the others, she demanded, "What are you doing?"

George sat upright. "I love you," he said to her, matter-of-factly.

"Is that what this was?" She stared and tried to understand what he was thinking. It disturbed her.

"Alex, you came down here, dressed like this, and healed me. I could feel it, you made me feel it, your love for me. Let me show you mine for you."

She laughed, pulling away from him. "You love her?" she said, grinning. Alex stood. She felt more aware of her state of undress than before. Shaking her head, she said to George, "You have me confused for someone else. I understand why you might." He attempted to interrupt her, to tell her he didn't, but she spoke over him. "I find it confusing, too. But it makes perfect sense. It wasn't her love you felt. It was mine. My love for you"

"But you're Alex."

"No. I'm your mother."

He looked at her as though her words took turns slapping him.

"I look like Alex," she noted herself again, "I guess for now I *am* Alex. I'm not sure why she'd dress like this. I'd never imagine having so little on, even for a bath. I just woke and…."

"You think you're Sara?"

"George, I *am* Sara Frost."

"Did you lose your memory? They wouldn't let me near you. You were in bad shape."

"The poor girl," Alex confided, "every Book holds a part of a woman. It's what gives the Books their magic; the women in them."

George's eyes widened. "She's had a lot of books."

"And they were all inside her, fighting her. Terrified. They don't understand they're dead. They don't understand. They're a part of her. They tried to take over to save themselves. When she was at the field today—that was today, right?"

George muttered, "Technically, yesterday."

"I guess she and I are connected. She and I were the same when Matthew took my magic, *and* she's had my Book. She doesn't have control over them. They were desperate. It was madness. They were killing her. They would have if I hadn't taken over." She looked away. "I still hear them, like whispers. They're subdued…." She looked at George, "But they don't like you."

"Then why heal me?"

Alex nodded. "Because I'm your mother. I still love you."

"But—"

"Even though," she interrupted, "you did such horrible things. How could you? Abigail?"

George whimpered. Tears welled in his eyes. "I had to," he whined. "Matthew said if I didn't, he would. Better I do it." He couldn't look at her. She wished he would read the disbelief on her face. "I didn't know better. It was horrible. I didn't want to hurt her, but it doesn't work unless there's pain."

"I know what you did," Alex replied. "You gave Alex her Book, remember? Abigail knows the truth. She doesn't believe you."

He cried, "I'm sorry, Mama. I'm sorry." His head shook back and forth as he apologized, "I am sorry. Abigail, I'm sorry. I'm so sorry."

Alex shushed him and settled on a knee to embrace him again. "There, there, my little man," she soothed, rubbing his back.

His sobbing subsided. His breathing normalized. He sighed. "Are you making me feel better? Is that why I loved you?" he said. "I feel how much you love me. In spite of everything."

"I lost you when you were a baby. I never got to see what you might have become. Who you became is not who you'd be if nothing happened to me." She stared at him, "You deserve more than the life you got."

"All I've known is Matthew and Willie, his friend. They raised me, taught me, told me about what happened to you. I don't know you. I'm sorry."

The words stabbed her heart even though his tone told her they weren't intended to hurt. Alex whispered, "That's all in the past. I know who you are. I told you to help them, to help the women in the field. And you did your best."

"I didn't want to burn again. You, or Alex, said to help. I thought if I helped, she—you'd protect me."

"You've lived so long under Matthew's thumb. He corrupted your heart, fed you women to keep you young. He cheated you out of life to make you believe you were living. You've amassed a debt, child. It's time you settle your balance."

"Mama, I believed in him. The coins kept time away. They taught me things, showed me things I shouldn't have seen. He made me believe I was special: His plan wouldn't work without me."

"For false praise you trusted a man who murders women? You never questioned if that was wrong?"

"Oh Mama, it was horrible. But there's an end to it. He needs one more woman. One. And then it'll be over; for good. He swears. He needs Alex. Once she's emptied the Library, he will make one Book, the true Book. He'll balance the scales."

Alex was silent. There was no arguing with someone who can't see the lie they speak.

"He'll keep the world safe, its single guardian. All the magic, in one place, under his protection."

"And when he dies? Or would he try to live forever?"

Now George was quiet.

"It's always *one more coin*, isn't it?"

"Matthew said sometimes doing right requires sacrificing the innocent."

"You never thought to stand against the man who had you murder your own sister?"

"What should I do? What do you want me to do, Mama?"

"You have a choice. A side to pick. It must be your decision."

"You and Alex or Matthew? Or Jeremiah."

Alex didn't respond.

"You think I *have* a choice? Matthew will kill me if I—"

"Like he's trying to kill Alex? Like he killed me? Like he made you kill Abigail?"

His eyes welled. He sobbed again.

"There, there, my baby boy." She held him. She wouldn't let go, not until he believed he was making the choice on his own. "There's another boy. He's lost. Find him. Bring him to Matthew. He needs the boy to lure Alex to the Library. Or you can bring him to me. Bring him back to Alex and his family. This is your choice, George. Do you understand?"

George nodded. "Billy."

"That's right. Find Billy."

George said, "I'll do what you want."

Alex released him. "How can I be sure you're not saying what you think I want to hear?"

George took a thoughtful breath. "I know what kind of man Matthew is."

"So do I."

"Do you?"

Alex nodded. "I've looked into his eyes as he ripped mine out.

I know exactly who he is." She turned away. "For the first time, you're free to make up your own mind, under no pressure from anyone else. Show the world who you are, George."

"Mama?"

Alex didn't look back as she walked to the stairs, shut the lights, and left George in darkness. "Don't say it, George. You don't love me. You felt what I gave to you and thought it was your own." She climbed the stairs.

Chapter Fifty-Seven

lex made her way back to the bathroom. She stepped past Abby and climbed into the tub, the filth on her feet clouding the water. She pulled out the stopper; water gurgled through the waste pipes below.

She rested her hand on Abby's shoulder. Abby looked up. Seeing Alex, she leapt to her feet and gave Alex a tearful hug. "You're okay! I was afraid you weren't coming out the other end of this."

Alex nodded. "I'm better but feeling awful. I'll be confused today, but you'll help me get through that, right?"

Abby wiped tears from her eyes, "Anything, kiddo."

Alex smiled. "I should put on some dry clothes, right?"

Abby coughed, "You should put on any clothes."

Abby stood aside and held Alex at the elbow as she stepped out of the tub. Leaning into the hall, Alex gestured across the hall to Rosemary's bedroom. She asked, "Should I go there?"

"Don't kid around, Alex." Abby assumed she was misunderstanding something. "You didn't take all your clothes. They're still upstairs."

Alex noticed the ladder at the end of the hall. "Up that ladder?"

Abby studied her. "You're more than a little confused. You seem, I don't know, different."

"Come up with me?"

"I think you can get dressed by yourself."

Alex took a long, deliberate breath. "Abby, I need you upstairs."

Abby followed Alex up, into her bedroom. Alex froze at the top of the stairs; Abby flipped the switch, filling the room with light.

Alex began opening drawers. She took several shirts from one drawer and placed them on the bed. Then a bunch of socks. When she opened her underwear drawer, she paused. "These are so small," she held up a pair of pale blue underwear. Then she grabbed a bra and held it up like it might snap her fingers. She examined the one she wore, trying to match the parts with the one in her hands. "How does this work?"

Abby made her put the bra down on the bed. "What's wrong with you... Alex?"

Alex took another disconcerted breath. "Help me get dressed. I'll tell you everything."

"Help you?" Abby asked, the two words sounding unrelated. She handed Alex a shirt.

Alex took it and began fumbling with her bra. Abby demonstrated by reaching behind her own back. Then Abby turned around. Alex followed suit.

Once dressed, Alex sat on the bed and patted it with her hand for Abby to join her.

Abby sat but didn't say anything at first. She studied Alex. "You're not yourself." She tilted her head as though changing her perspective. "Everything's wrong." Alex waited; she could almost feel Abby coming to it on her own. "Like you're not really here. It's the way you hold yourself, your expressions." Abby gasped. "Is this like before? One of the whispers?" She didn't blink; didn't take her eyes from Alex as though reading every expression. "You are, aren't you? Is Alex... in there? Who are you?" Abby's questions became more frantic. "Is Alex okay? Did you hurt her?"

"Abby, Alex needs your help."

Abby stood as though discovering a spider racing towards her.

"Abby, you're the only one I can trust. We've met. Twice, and—"

"What the—" Abby interrupted, but Alex interrupted her before she could utter an obscenity.

"Let me finish, *please*."

Abby nodded. "I should sit down." She grabbed the chair from Alex's desk and turned it around, throwing herself into it.

Alex waited until she was certain Abby wasn't speaking. "We've met. Peter trusted you with his life, so I know I can trust you with mine."

"Peter?" Abby asked slowly, as though there were room for confusion.

"You asked if this was the whispers. Did Alex mention hearing talking or whispering? In her head?"

Abby shivered despite the growing heat in the attic. "*Alex* told me *she* was hearing whispers, but they weren't telling *her* to hurt *herself*. Are the whispers telling *Alex* to hurt *herself* now?"

"No," Alex replied gently. "Each Book Alex took and—what would you call it—absorbed? Each Book contained a piece of the woman it came from. That's how the magic works when it's writ down." She hesitated. "Make sense so far?"

"No. But I'm following."

"She's absorbed a lot of Books. A lot. The whispers were one voice each from hundreds and hundreds of women. A small part of each one inside her. Still following?"

"Are you one of those voices?"

"The symbols on the pages in the magic Books? That's not writing. That is the woman. Alive, spread thinly across the pages. Alex freed them. She broke their bond with the Book and took them inside her. Once they're inside her, they think they're alive. They don't realize how long they weren't. They understand—on some level—that they're not trapped in the Book anymore. They feel for the first time in—in some cases, thousands of years. But they don't understand. They don't understand what's happened. Years in the Book was like a slumber, being half awoken whenever the Books were used and then put back to sleep. Like Sleeping Beauty, over and over. Suddenly they're awake and don't understand. They think they're trapped."

Abby had barely breathed. She whispered, "That sounds horrific."

"When Alex met Jeremiah on the field yesterday, some of those women recognized him. A few recognized that Book fellow with the marks on his face. They were terrified. They don't understand they're in Alex. They sense her, but she makes little sense to them. They feel their magic and they want to use it, but Alex restricts them."

Abby was nodding.

"Sometimes she lets a little squeak out. I felt it before at the barn. I felt it again in the field. She was letting some of it out. They felt it too. The power. But they don't trust her, not with the last vestiges of what they were. They fought Alex. They each tried to take her over. Fighting so many of them weakened her, which made them more eager for control."

"Which one of them are you?"

"My connection with Alex is different. She fought so hard, but they were killing her. They didn't mean to, but they hurt Alex. When she got too weak, I stepped in. I took over for her. I held them back.

She was still fighting. But it was too much. She blacked out."

"She didn't black out; she had a seizure. We thought she was going to die. You almost killed her." Abby took a breath. "Please, tell me who you are."

"Sara. Sara Frost."

Abby's eyes widened. "The witch from the old house?"

"Yes."

"The one I keep dying to summon?"

Alex giggled, extending her hand. "It's a pleasure to make your acquaintance."

Abby shook her head. "It really isn't a pleasure, Sara. How do we get Alex back? Or," she paused, her voice rising a little, "is this the part where you tell me you aren't giving Alex back to us? Because I don't want to hurt her, but I will beat you out of her if I have to."

"Oh, no. One painful life was enough."

Abby bit her lips. "So how do we get her back? She and I have a connection, too. I feel it slipping."

"She's so weak. I barely sense her. Once she's strong enough I will give control back to Alex."

"Why can't you do that now?"

"Too soon and it could get messy."

"Explain," Abby demanded.

"They're all in here, waiting. I'm placating them. It's temporary at best. If we encounter Jeremiah, I won't be able to hold them back. Same if I give up control before she's strong enough. They would destroy us both."

Abby nodded. "What do we need to do?"

"This is my room, right?"

"Um, yes, but you've been living with me—Alex I mean—for a few days."

"Can you take me there without arousing suspicion?"

"Maybe in the evening. Your—Alex's aunt, thought you— she, was dying last night. Leaving now will hurt her, a lot."

"Which one's her aunt?"

"Oh sheesh. You really weren't paying attention in there, were you?"

"I wish it worked that way. We don't experience your world the same way you do. The living and the dead see things different. Inside Alex, it's like a world within a world."

"Fine. I'll give you a hand with the who's-who. Once we get to my place, what happens?"

"Once she's ready, we'll try to wake her. If it works, she should be fine."

"If it doesn't work?"

"If it doesn't work," Alex shrugged. "She'll be trapped inside her own body until whoever takes charge gets killed."

"And then?"

"Then? Then nothing. Then she's dead."

"How do you know all this?"

Alex shrugged. "The universe whispers to the dead. Sometimes it tells us a secret."

Abby bristled. "You're got to find another way. I don't like this, Sara."

"Me neither. I can keep control for the time being. I hear the whispers. For now, they're mostly quiet. If they feel threatened, I may not be able to hold on to her."

"We're not out of the woods yet, I guess." Abby sighed. "What next, Sara?"

"We wait until we're at your home. Call me Alex so no one overhears."

"I'd feel more comfortable if they knew."

"They can't. None of them. One of them has used a Book. There's no telling how that might corrupt her."

"Wait, what? Rose is dangerous?"

Alex shrugged. "Women aren't supposed to read from Books. The power, the woman inside the spells; there's no telling what it could do to her."

Abby heard the battle between certainty and speculation in Sara's statement. "But you don't know for certain, do you?"

"I'd rather not take any chances."

"I'll keep an eye on her."

"You should also know about my son."

"George? He's in the basement."

She shook her head. "Not anymore."

"Gone? How? When?"

"I let him go."

Abby's eyes narrowed. "You didn't just wake up."

Alex shook her head.

"Why would you do that, *Alex*?"

"He told me everything we need."

"Like?"

"Our enemies are divided. This is a war with three fronts."

"War? Did he know it was you?"

"Yes."

"You just let Matthew and Jeremiah know she's weak."

"Not weak," Alex replied, "compromised; for the time being."

"Only if they see it that way."

"George needs to find his way. He needs redemption. Alex wants that, too."

"How can you know that?"

"We've shared each other's lives. In her heart, she aches for George, just as I do." Alex looked away. "I put a thought in his head to find the boy."

"Billy?"

Alex nodded. "Alex is obsessed with finding him. It distracts her." She collapsed back on the bed. "I'm exhausted. Let me sleep a while."

Abby gave her ankle a shake. "I need to let the others know you're alive. Heather or Rose may pop up to see you."

Alex groaned. "How will I know who is which?"

"Which witch is which, you mean?" Abby laughed at her joke; Alex didn't. "Heather is my age; Rose is a little younger than Alex. Pretty as heck. She's the one who read the Book."

Alex got comfortable. "Should be easy to tell them apart."

"Oh," Abby startled with recollection. She retrieved Alex's charm from her pocket and held it out. "This is really important to Alex. She never takes it off. I held it for safe keeping today. You should wear it."

Alex accepted the glass charm from Abby and inspected it. She wondered at it, the clarity of the glass, the swirls of the carbonized herbs creating the illusion of circles around a perfectly dark sphere at the center. "You made this? It's stunning."

Abby nodded proudly.

"Is that…." Alex pointed at the dark central sphere.

Abby nodded. "It is."

Alex gasped with wonder, tears filling her eyes. "Peter…. You didn't give it all to Charon. You saved a little piece for your daughter."

Abby nodded proudly.

As Alex fixed the clasp around her neck, she said to Abby, "He had to have known this could have saved him. Does Alex know?"

"I never told her. I wanted to, but for whatever reason I didn't or couldn't. It never felt like the right time."

Alex pressed the charm against her chest. "She deserves to know she carries a piece of her father near to her heart."

Chapter Fifty-Eight

bby quietly turned off the light and left Alex to sleep, as she climbed down the ladder. Even in the dark hallway, she noticed Alex's drying footprints in the hall. *If Heather sees these, she'll figure it out.* Abby took a towel from the bathroom and wiped down the floors.

In Heather's room, she found Heather sprawled on her bed, still in yesterday's clothes. She gently rocked Heather's shoulder. "I brought Alex to bed," she whispered. "She seems, um, better."

Heather mumbled incoherently, her eyelids barely parting. Abby repeated herself, "Alex woke up and asked to go to bed." Abby felt terrible telling Heather a lie, even a partial lie. Her head felt like a shaken snow globe, a blizzard of confusion obscuring the important issue at the center. Her absolute loyalty was to Alex. This looked and sounded like Alex, but it didn't *feel* like Alex. Yet, her compulsion was to help Sara. Giving up Sara's secret—however terrible lying to Heather felt—might cause Alex harm. Lying to Heather *was* helping Alex.

Heather opened her eyes, one at a time. "Wait, what?" The momentary confusion passed, and the events of the previous day crashed upon her with all the subtlety of a tsunami. "Alex is better?"

Abby nodded. "She's in bed. She woke up and couldn't wait to go back to sleep."

Heather smiled, "Sounds like my girl."

Abby knew Heather couldn't know, but something about Heather's statement—*sounds like*—provoked the need to correct any confusion. Before she could rationalize her way out of it, Abby found her mouth making excuses for Sara, "She seems out of it, so if in the morning, if she's, I don't know, confused, I mean, it should pass. She seemed confused, I guess, waking up at home when she remembered being in the field, and, well, you know, just in case she is still like that, go easy on her."

"Of course," Heather agreed. "I need to see her." She started crawling off the bed.

Abby wasn't sure this was in Alex-Sara's best interest. "Don't wake her."

"I thought I was going to lose her. She scared me half to death. I'm not going to wake her; I'm going to beat the crap out of her." She winked at Abby and started past. "Nancy's asleep downstairs. She should know. I'll call everyone tomorrow. No sense waking them. Tell Nancy to stay for breakfast. I'll make something celebratory." She hesitated, "And tell Rosemary. She'll want to know. She was devastated."

Downstairs, Abby found Nancy asleep on the couch. She took Nancy's hand and whispered, "Alex is better."

Nancy didn't open her eyes until she finished speaking, "That's good. Were her reflexes normal or delayed?"

Abby stammered. "I, I didn't know to check her reflexes. They were fine. Perfectly reflexive."

Nancy sat up. "She's out of the tub?"

"Heather's with her. She woke me. Alex, not Heather. Alex woke me. We talked a few minutes. She wanted to go to sleep. She's exhausted. Then I told Heather. That's why she's with Alex now."

"Sounds about right. Everyone assumes people are sleeping when a seizure knocks them out, but they wake up exhausted, like they were running a marathon."

"Well, like I said, Heather's with her now."

"While she's up I should give her a once over."

No, no, no! How do I stop the whole world from going to see her? She won't know who Nancy is. I didn't tell her about Nancy, did I? "Maybe wait until the morning. If Heather senses something isn't right, she'll get you, and she knows Alex better than anyone. Plus, she needs to sleep. And so do you. Like you said, a marathon."

Nancy yawned. "As long as you say she's fine. You know her as well as anyone, right? There isn't much to do unless she needs a hospital, and Heather will freak if she's slurring her speech or can't remember names."

Abby played out a scenario in her head. It ended with Nancy assuming Alex was brain damaged. Her relief that Nancy wasn't going upstairs was choked by the worry that something might be wrong with Alex that only Nancy could diagnose. *Did I just screw this whole thing up?* Abby's head swam so torturously, she felt like she might throw up. *If Nancy thinks it's okay to wait, it's okay.* Abby cringed, hoping Heather didn't overreact when Alex doesn't remember something. "Get a good night's sleep."

Nancy lay back down. "It'll be tough. I've been dreaming of flaming tornadoes and being struck by lightning. I don't suppose you know how that got into my subconscious or why I'm processing it?" She winked.

"It was really a rough day."

Nancy groaned. "That it was. I never imagined anything like that. Magic sucks. You get some sleep, too, Abby."

"Oh, and Heather invited you to stay for breakfast. That work for you?"

Nancy nodded.

Between Nancy and the stairs, Abby glanced at the basement entrance. Her head swam, worried George hadn't left the house yet. She was tempted to check. So many things could go wrong. *What if he's there and puts up a fight? What if someone finds out I knew he was gone? Maybe he'll find Billy. That's what Alex wants.* Should she tell Heather or let Heather find out on her own? *Maybe Heather finding out on her own is better than me making up some story about why I checked and found him gone.* She took the stairs up to Rosemary's bedroom.

As Abby walked in, Rosemary complained, "I've heard you talking all night."

Abby felt her blood go cold. *All night?* Fearfully, she sat on the bed next to Rosemary's darkened frame.

"I'm so glad Alex is better," she slapped Abby's thigh. Beside Rose, Dolly stretched and yawned, baring her teeth before looking at Rose and yowling. Rose pushed her away. "She's been like this all night, bitching at me."

"I'm sorry I woke you, but I guess I was going to wake you to tell you anyways."

"No," Rose replied, "it's fine. It was better this way."

"Glad you think so."

Rose lay her head against her pillow.

Abby took a breath, "I'm going to find someplace to sleep. See you in the morning."

Rose pointed at the bed behind Abby. "Sleep there; Billy's."

Abby drawled, "It wouldn't feel right."

"It's okay," Rose declared. "We're going to get my brother and bring him home. You're just keeping it warm."

"You sure? Heather won't like it."

Rose shook her head. "It's not like he's using it. If you don't want to sleep there, fine, go somewhere else. Otherwise, lie down and please, shut up. I need to sleep. I'm so tired my bones ache."

Abby sat on Billy's bed and ran her hand over the comforter and sheets. Perhaps if she just slept on it and didn't disrupt the sheets, she could sleep and not commit any faux pas.

Heather came down the ladder and peeked in the room. "She's out of it. She was all, *Is that you, Aunt Heather?* It was so sweet. Like she was a little kid." Heather's smile deflated when she saw Abby on the bed. "Oh, you're sleeping there?"

Abby stammered, "If you'd rather I didn't, I can find someplace else." She felt terrible, like Heather caught her sleeping in someone else's grave.

Heather faltered, "I guess it's fine." Abby could tell from her tone she didn't mean it at all.

"I'll just sleep on the floor next to Alex's bed," Abby countered, with no passive-aggressive intention.

"No, no. Billy's bed is fine. He'd want that."

Rose groaned. "Now that we've got that out of the way, do you both mind shutting up so some of us can sleep?"

"Rosemary Hawthorne," Heather chided, but in a more pleasant tone added, "Goodnight." She half turned to the door, then whispered to Abby, "I'll check on our guest."

Abby stood up in a panic. *She means George. If I try to convince her not to, how'll it look when he's gone?* "Can't you wait 'till morning?"

Heather shook her head. "I'm up and my mind is racing. Now that she's fine I need to settle it down and make sure everything's in its place."

"I'll come with you." Abby stammered. "Just in case."

"Come on," Rose complained. "Go, stay, I don't care, just please shut up already. Let me sleep."

Abby and Heather stifled their laughter as they crept out of the bedroom and made their way downstairs.

As they passed Nancy, she asked, "That you, Heather?" Heather answered in the affirmative. Nancy asked, "How is she?"

"She seems good, Nancy. Tired. Exhausted, but in good spirits. She's a trooper."

"Good to hear," Nancy rolled over.

Abby followed Heather down the stairs to the basement and followed her through the darkness to the light switch. The light hurt their eyes. Heather gasped, which Abby was expecting.

The chair sat beside the thick post, coils of rope and electrical cords formed a loose loop around them, draping off the seat and onto the floor.

Abby saw the dried patterns left from Alex's dripping bare feet. She hoped Heather missed them. She picked up the rope, pretending to examine it while kicking the dust with her feet.

Heather spun around. She grabbed Abby's wrist, "Grab something. He's hiding."

Abby's heart pounded, even knowing full well he was gone. She went through the motions, hunting around the basement, peering into dark places. Terrified she overplayed her part and Heather would see through her. Fearful she wasn't taking it seriously enough to be believable. She wanted this game to end. She tried to sound just the right level of disappointed, "He's gone, Heather. We were distracted with Alex. He must have seen an opportunity."

"We don't know he's gone."

"Would you stay?"

Heather nodded, "Long enough to slit the throats of the people who tied me up in their basement."

Abby didn't know what to say. Perhaps her fear at Heather finding her out read differently to Heather, who asked, "You sure he's really gone?"

Abby scanned the perimeter of the basement. "He's not down here."

"What about upstairs?"

Abby wasn't sure, but she started talking anyway, "We were both in Alex's room. He's not there. Yours and Rose's bedrooms check out. Bathroom, too."

"Kitchen?"

Wearily, Abby replied, "Let's go look."

"Shouldn't we take something, a weapon? If he's in the kitchen, he might grab one of my knives."

Abby climbed the stairs. *What will it take to convince her?* "There are plenty of weapons upstairs. Chairs and plates and other knives."

They climbed up to the main floor and through patchworks of moonlight, looked around the house. The kitchen door was unlocked. Abby asked Heather, "You leave this unlocked tonight?"

"I never locked my doors before last week. Now I've been checking them twice before I can sleep. I'm sure I locked that door."

Abby nodded. "There's your answer: He's gone."

Heather cursed.

Abby felt baptized by relief. Her lies washed away because the story she told matched the truth closely enough. Abby practiced her volume—the last thing she wanted was for everyone to wake and make a bigger deal out of this—and said, "If you think about it, Heather, it's for the best. What would we do with him? Torture information out of him?"

Heather slouched, defeated. "No. I've been fretting about that. What was I going to do if he wouldn't cooperate? I'm actually relieved he's not under my roof anymore."

Heather looked deep in thought. "I won't be able to sleep until I'm certain he's not here."

Abby didn't want to keep arguing the point. Her body begged for sleep, but there'd be time once she'd accompanied Heather through every room and around the perimeter of the house at least once.

Chapter Fifty-Nine

ose glared from the bed across the room. Abby just opened her eyes to the morning light and couldn't imagine what she'd done to receive such scorn. She asked, "What?"

Rose scowled, "You snore like a truck driver."

Abby rolled her eyes. "Sorry if I kept you up."

"Not really. Just thought you should know." Rose dismissed her, returning to thumbing through her Book.

Abby did a double-take. "What's gotten into you?"

Rose shrugged. "I had crazy dreams last night. You know when you're sleeping but dreaming you're awake and can't sleep. It really felt like I couldn't sleep, so instead of tossing and turning, I climbed up on the roof and spent the night capturing stars in a jar." She looked around. "You don't see any jar with stars?"

Abby pretended to scout the room. "No jar."

"Good," Rose replied with dramatic relief as she fell back against her pillow. "Everyone was so mad at me for turning the sky black." She looked at Abby, "I did leave the moon."

"That's very considerate."

"I know," Rose exaggerated. "That's what I said."

Abby glanced around the room, disoriented in a new location. She looked at her bare wrist. "What time is it?"

Rose pointed at the clock on her nightstand. "Just after nine. Mom's downstairs making French toast."

"How do you know?"

Rose touched a finger to her nose and then her ear. Abby sniffed and listened. She could hear the battered bread sizzling in the pan and smell the vanilla custard. Her mouth watered.

"I know," Rose's eyes went wide. "Smells so good. If we wait until she calls us down, we won't have to set the table, either."

Abby stood, still dressed from yesterday. Rose pointed at her, "Don't say I didn't warn you, and don't you dare tell her I'm awake. I'm always setting the table. I hate it. If I take out large plates, she wanted small plates. If I take out small plates, she wanted bowls. I think she does it on purpose."

Abby shook her head. "Life's rough."

"That's what I'm saying."

Abby smiled. She liked Rose. She also liked that it was Alex who stayed at her house. "I'm going up to check on Alex."

Rose informed, "Sleeping beauty always—lately anyway—waits until we've started eating. Then she doesn't have to help clean up, either."

That doesn't sound like Alex. "Seriously?"

"Sometimes. At least once in a while. Could be I have her confused with me." Rose giggled. She dismissed Abby, returning to her Book. She wasn't reading it, just turning the pages, caressing the cover, like she was soothing a fussy baby.

Abby was sure her eyelids clinked audibly. *Has Rose always been like this?* She started for the door. "If you're not down once food is ready, I promise that I will eat everything, and you know I can." She hovered, waiting for Rose's acknowledgement before leaving.

Abby climbed the ladder and found Alex sitting upright in bed. "Morning."

Alex startled. "I didn't hear you come up."

"No one has ever accused me of subtlety before." Abby sat on the edge of Alex's bed and looked around the room. It was a finished attic space, a single cupola over the bed let in copious golden morning light from windows that faced the cardinal directions, with a ceiling that sloped down to the floor. Furniture encircled the limits of usable space. In a few places Alex had hung some large pieces of fabric to hide the empty attic. At Alex's age, she would have done anything for a space this private and "cool".

"What's that smell?" Alex took a long breath. "It smells good."

Abby explained French toast.

"Oh, I know that." Alex made a face. "That's too sweet for breakfast. That's after-dinner food; dessert."

"Well, it's Alex's favorite, so eat it and like it."

"Was she peculiar?"

Abby nodded. "She likes this thing called coffee. Takes it sweet with lots of cream. It'll wake you up a little."

"I know coffee. Can't I not feel like eating something?"

"Not pretending to be Alex and definitely not around French toast. Slip-up and you'll wind up at the hospital. We can't afford any mistakes."

"I'll do my best."

Abby allowed Alex's words to linger, hoping they'd age better than they did. She felt unsettled. "I'd rather tell Heather the truth." When Alex shook her head, Abby explained, "Heather knows about Sara. She trusts me when it comes to Alex. I'll vouch for you. It'll be okay."

Alex's expression didn't change. Abby wasn't sure what that meant, except that she didn't like it: Alex was as easy to read as a headline.

"I'm imploring you. You can't tell her."

Why? She never felt comfortable questioning Alex's judgement before. Alex told her about the whispers. She never explicitly said not to tell Heather. Had she, the oath would never have allowed Abby to tell Heather. This was different. Alex said no. But this wasn't Alex. Yet, in her gut, the feelings were there: The giddy joy of agreement. The satisfaction of carrying out an order. It felt like trying to juice a carrot with her bare hands, but she managed to ask, "Are you sure?"

Alex nodded. "If I slip up, I'll tell them. That way it looks like you didn't know."

Abby watched Alex, who watched her in return. She felt cornered, unable to respond any further. Then Alex added, "You're protecting Alex. The fewer people who know the truth the better. You're keeping us both safe. We can't risk fracturing their allegiance. Not now."

She has a point. Heather could overreact. Rose even more so. That would be bad. Abby started to leave. *But she told George. How is that okay and this isn't?* She turned to ask Alex only to find Alex heading for the ladder. Alex waited for her. She was Alex. The way she looked, anyway. Something was off about her posture, about the look on her face, but Abby could dismiss that. In fact, the more willing she was to accept it, the better she felt. *Here goes.*

Alex followed Abby downstairs. Abby explained again that Rose was the younger one and Nancy the only other person there. As they entered the kitchen, she caught Alex staring at Nancy's piercings. As Alex leaned closer, Abby seized her by the waistband and gave a tug.

"You seem much better," Nancy held her coffee mug in two

hands. She blew off the steam. She then mouthed to Abby, "I know."

Abby's stomach somersaulted. *She knows?* She tried to judge Nancy's expression and saw the opened basement door. *She means she knows George's gone.*

"I feel a little better," Alex sighed. Abby directed her to her seat.

"Alex," Heather sang from the stove. "Come here so I can give you a hug." She nodded to the group at the table. "We were really worried about you."

Alex jumped up and walked right over to Heather, arms out for the embrace.

Heather eyeballed Abby as if to say, *Who is this girl?*

Heather took a moment away from the stove to embrace her niece. She pulled away. "I don't want anything to burn. I made your favorite to celebrate you're better."

"Thanks, Heather," Alex answered. She continued to stand, hovering over her aunt.

Abby walked over to Alex and whispered, "You can sit down now. *Aunt* Heather doesn't need help."

Alex took her seat.

Abby asked of Heather, "Anything I can do to help?"

Heather nodded. "Tell my daughter Nancy was kind enough to set the table."

Abby was about to call upstairs when Rose appeared, "I heard, I heard." Dolly followed at her heel. Rose gave her cousin a long hug. Dolly snaked between their feet, making a sound that wasn't quite a purr, not quite a trill.

As they were finishing breakfast, Abby interrupted the final bites. "With everything that's happened since yesterday, I was thinking, Alex has been through a lot. I think she needs, what is it called, convalescence? You know, when they sent people away to heal? Maybe it'll be good if Alex comes back to my place. It's secluded and she can rest. Maybe this evening?" Abby winced at the sound of her awful excuse.

Heather looked up from her plate, surprised. "Oh. I thought Alex could move back here. I mean, doesn't that make sense?"

Rose and Heather looked to Alex for a reply; Alex looked at Abby, who answered, "Well, sure, but she has so much of her stuff at my house. Maybe tomorrow?"

"I don't want to get involved in family matters," Nancy interjected, "but it's best Alex stays put and keeps her stress to a minimum."

Heather held out her hand, offering Nancy's statement in lieu of her own.

Alex mumbled, "I thought it would be wise if I were away. My distance would keep everyone safe. A night or two at Abby's to clear my head and make sure things are where they need to be. I have given everyone quite a scare, after all; I'm sure you could all use a break from me."

Heather looked at her queerly. "By all means. When you're not here, I don't even know you exist. So sure, when you leave, I'll be thinking to myself, *Why was I so tense before*? Then I'll say to myself, *Self, you know, I have no idea. It's like you were worrying about someone and they disappeared.* It'll be wonderfully relaxing."

Rose cackled, spooning extra syrup into her mouth. She looked at Alex, "Better you than me." Dolly was curled up on her lap, not quite sleeping, her tail a fit of agitation.

"Besides," Heather mumbled, looking out the window, kneading her hands. "We have a lot to figure out. Billy is still missing."

Abby stood, then fell into her seat. "You're blaming Alex for that?"

"That's not how it was intended," Heather tried to lower her voice.

"That's how it sounded, Mom," Rose muttered under her breath.

Heather glared at her daughter.

Abby placed her fork down with a clank. Alex was sliding a piece of French toast around the maple syrup, trying not to get involved. "Two days, tops," Abby's tone was unrelenting. She wasn't asking. "This is why Alex needs to be away. To clear her head. One day, two max. Then she'll be in the right frame of mind to get Billy."

Heather wordlessly took her plate to the sink. Abby was certain she was furious.

Rose gave Alex's arm a gentle rub before putting Dolly on the floor. Rose walked over to her mother. "Mom," Rose comforted her mother who was washing syrup off plates before putting them into the dishwasher. "We'll get Billy back."

"Stop saying that," Heather shouted, tears running down her face. "You don't know that."

"Yes, I do Mom," Rose touched Heather's shoulder, "because I'll do it."

Heather threw the plate down in the sink, smashing it. She screamed at her daughter, "You are not using that Book again!"

Rose backed off as Heather retrieved shards of plate from the sink, crying as she looked at them. To Rose, she said, "That Book is dangerous. Where is it? Where do you have it hidden?" She dropped the shards in the trash and with wet hands grabbed at and turned Rose about as though inspecting her body for signs of the Book. "Is it in your room?"

Behind them, Dolly paced the floor, yowling.

Rose pulled away. "No Mom, it isn't in my *room*. Search all you want. You'll never find it. I *will* get Billy back. Not you. Not Alex. Look at her." She repeated herself, pointing at Alex, "Look at her, Mom. She's broken. This almost killed her. You want that? You want to lose Billy *and* Alex? We almost died yesterday, but you know what? We didn't. We won. They ran. And you know how, Mom? Me. I cast spells at them. I showed them what it was like. Me, Mom, me. I saved us."

Heather turned to Nancy, tears streaming down her face, and spoke in rapid-fire, "I'm sorry you had to see this. Thank you for all your help. Don't feel you have to clean up before you leave." Sobbing, Heather stomped upstairs and slammed her bedroom door.

Rose turned to the others at the table. "Don't say a word," she warned. "Not about my brother, not about my Book."

Abby stood. "I'm not telling you what to do Rose," she collected the plates. "I'll clean up breakfast. Figure out what you need to do to calm down."

"That sounds a lot like telling me."

"Rosemary," Alex started in a tone reeking of lecture.

Rose turned around twice before storming out of the house, slamming the door behind her. Dolly turned as she reached the door, hopped up into a windowsill, and yowled out the window as she watched Rose stomp around to the back of the house.

Nancy blew out a breath. "Wow," she muttered, shaking her head at Rose's departure. "Rose seems so different. Is that because of the Book or because it gives her magic?"

Abby rolled her eyes.

Nancy studied Alex. "I have to work tonight," she stated matter-of-factly. "But I'm not leaving until I'm certain everyone's okay."

"I've got this," Abby scolded. "I'll take care of things."

Nancy bit down on her reactionary rebuttal. Recomposing herself, she said, "Maybe getting Alex out of here for a day or two is a good idea."

Alex said, "They're like this because of me."

Nancy placed her hands on Alex's. "Don't blame yourself." She motioned at Alex's plate, "you couldn't even eat breakfast."

Abby could feel Alex's tension. She spoke as if making a statement to the room, rather than the people in it. "We're defeating ourselves."

Nancy blew air out her lips. "Why is Heather so upset over Rose's Book? Rose saved us, but it's like it went to her head."

Alex looked up. "Think of it this way. When magic comes out of a woman and is put in a Book, it's not the magic that ends up on the page, but the women. Each spell looks like shapes and symbols, but they're not. Every time you read it, you reconstruct the broken bits of that woman and channel her through yourself to make her make that spell for you. The reader doesn't cast the spell, that woman does. Rose knows what's happening."

Nancy gasped. "How do you know all this?"

"I have a lot of Books inside me now, Nancy," Alex confided. "I know the pain each one of them endured coming back to life for a moment each time someone used them."

Abby stared at Alex. Sara was speaking from experience. She'd helped Peter use Sara's Book. Had he known?

Alex volunteered, "Once she's had time to calm down, I will talk to her."

Chapter Sixty

nce they cleaned up breakfast, the dishes dried and put away, Nancy, Abby, and Alex said their cautious goodbyes. Nancy took some convincing but walked out to her car. Alex took Abby's hands in hers. "I'm going to find Rosemary. I think it might be good if *Alex* talks to her."

"You want me to come?" Abby could feel she didn't.

Alex forced a smile. "Maybe talk to Heather."

Abby groaned. "I was afraid you'd say that. What do I say to her?"

"Maybe because Alex is weak, Rose having a Book might not be the worst thing. In the short-term, anyway." She looked out the window. When she turned back to Abby, her words came soft as she said, "Peter wasn't the first to read my Book. The things I was made to do." She looked away, refusing to cry. "Waking up, feeling my magic after years asleep, made me want more. I wanted my Book to be used. My desire to live fed their desire to use me. Rose is feeling that. She feels the power of absolute mastery over another. It's twisting Rose. Makes her think she is the one who is powerful."

"Couldn't you take it away? You know, magically?"

"There's a lot of power in her now. I don't know how much magic I can summon without these annoying whispers becoming too strong. There's too much to go wrong. You're not willing to sacrifice Rose or Alex, are you?"

"No. Of course not."

"Because if it goes wrong, that's what happens."

Abby didn't want to give up that easily. "But she got the Book yesterday. How can she be strong so soon? Doesn't she have to read the whole thing to know what it does?"

Alex rubbed the tabletop, "Read one spell and know the whole Book. The Book isn't neutral, the reader briefly gives something to the Book while the spell is being cast. The Book guides them. It controls them through the spell. It's very personal, almost symbiotic." Alex shuddered.

"Why do they need the Book, then, if they know it?"

"They always need the Book to cast the spell. They know the page, not the magic."

"Like a downloadable table of contents?"

Alex thought a moment. "Sure, whatever you said sounds close enough."

Abby drummed her fingers on the table. "Good luck. Rose can be stubborn, but she's a good kid."

Alex walked outside looking for Rose.

* * * * *

Rose left the house in a huff and found herself unable to go anywhere. She argued, the breeze taking her mothers' side. She walked through the garden, anger freeing her feet from caution. So what if some herbs got stepped on or broken? Heather had more.

She came upon the rosemary patch, a scraggle of three plants, woody from wintering over multiple years. She took one of the fronds in her palms and pulled. The small pine-like leaves popped off in her aggression. She loved milking the rosemary for its sticky oils and was usually more careful.

The sensation that she wasn't alone snuck up on her; she turned as Alex cleared her throat.

Alex stood at the edge of the garden, her eyes spotting Rose as they willfully traversed the garden several times. *Why is she looking at the garden like she's missed it? She's only been at Abby's a couple of days.*

Alex wasn't speaking, so neither was Rose. She pressed her palms to her face and inhaled deeply.

"I've always loved that smell," Alex said wistfully. "It's one of my favorites, too."

"Who said it's my favorite?" Rose taunted. "Maybe I'm touching it because my namesake gives me special powers and I want to fill up before mother forbids it."

"Namesake?"

"Rosemary?" Rose eyed her cousin.

"Oh. Right." Alex touched her head, as though her excuse.

"Who names their kid for a plant?" Rose shook her head,

grinning. "I guess my mom and her mom. Heather. Rosemary. *Rosemary.* Stupid name. I mean, look at this. It's all gangly and ugly. All it does is smell good." She sniffed her palms again.

Alex listened, hands at her sides. "It's medicinal. It's good in food. It's very strong. The more you cut it up and damage it, the more powerful it becomes."

What does she know from medicinal? Mom was so afraid of triggering her head she never talked like that. She joked, "Who are you and what've you done with my cousin?"

"What?" For a second, Alex appeared panicked.

What if her head's really messed up? Rose tried changing the subject without it looking obvious. "I mean, if you have to name me after a plant, how about Foxglove or Deadly Nightshade? I'd be a superhero in the making."

"Rosemary makes everything else better than it would be by itself."

Rose understood Alex wasn't talking about the plants anymore. It took the argument out of her. Some of it anyway. She ambled towards Alex. "I don't know what the big deal is. It's not like I'm on drugs. Can't she see it's good that I have my Book? I can protect us now." Even as she said the words, she began to understand her mother's problem and gave it voice, "She's jealous. She didn't get the Book. I did."

"She's scared. Your brother is missing. She never thought she'd have to comprehend that pain. She can't bear to lose her other child. No mother should know what that's like. Now you have a Book. You're the one who stands between us and danger. She doesn't know how to protect you."

"What's to protect?" Rose looked at her hands. "I shot lightning from my fingers. I hurt men who were trying to kill us." *I did everything you were supposed to be able to do.* The desire to voice the stinging remark was so strong Rose felt like she needed both hands to hold it down.

"You saved us."

"I know!" Rose crumpled the remaining rosemary in her hands, letting the debris fall to the ground before smelling her palms one more time. "She doesn't understand. It's like she doesn't want to. The Book is strength. It's power. It's why they've been killing us for centuries and why all we do is die. A woman died to make that Book.

That idiot George has been using it for—I dunno—years, and that's okay? When I use it, when we turn the tables on them, that's when my mother freaks out."

Alex was making a face. Something Rose said curdled her stomach. Her demeanor changed. Her tone lowered. She spoke like she was sharing a secret or making a threat. "You know why."

Rose found herself taking a step backwards defensively. Her lip curled in disgust towards Alex. *How dare my cousin talk to me like this. How many Books does she have inside her?* "Was it the same for you?" Rose asked. "I sensed her wake up as I read from the page. It was horribly creepy. She just woke up and moved through me. I felt her like I was her. It was amazing what we could do."

"You mean it was amazing what *she* could do. You made her do it. Don't take credit, too."

"You're saying it's different for you? You take the Books inside you and-and-and, what? What's so special about you that it's okay when you do it but not me?"

"When you feel her wake, you're okay with that?"

Rose objected, "She and I are like one now. Like you and all the others."

Agitation decorated Alex's expression. "It's not the same and you know it."

Rose could feel how Alex's obstinance had broken her hold on her anger. She could no longer hold the hate down. "That's right. I know it. When it mattered, I didn't piss my pants and pass out." Rose pretended to swoon.

"I wish it were that simple, Rosemary."

"Actually, it is. I have my Book. Everyone thought you were special. Everyone thought you were the only one. You're just like her: jealous." Rose turned to stomp off. *Why am I leaving?* She turned back to Alex. "I believed in you. I thought you were going to be this amazing witch and save the world. When you couldn't handle the pressure I thought, *Maybe it's too much on her. I don't know if I could be strong enough.* And then I had to be. And I *was*." She glared at Alex, wishing she didn't need the Book to cast spells, that beams would just shoot out of her eyes to prove how angry she was. "And what's worse isn't that you failed. What's worse is that you come out here and talk down to me because I didn't." She was so angry that rather than laser-beams, tears fell from her eyes.

"If it makes you feel better to think that's why I'm out here, you do that," Alex replied, her voice shaking. She was rattled, and Rose couldn't tell if she was angry or upset. "I didn't come out here to talk you out of using the Book."

"It sure sounds like it."

Alex closed her eyes and pressed her fingers to her forehead like she was massaging away a migraine. She was practically panting. Twice, she looked at Rose, ready to resume her lecture, and twice she took her head in her hands. She practically bowed to whatever was hurting her.

At first Rose figured she was faking for dramatic effect. When it continued longer than even Alex's sense of drama would have allowed, Rose put her arm around her cousin. Alex wriggled from the embrace and pushed her away. She glared at Rose, the veins in her neck bulging. Through clenched teeth, she forged ahead. "The Book gives you... power. Makes you cocky. Makes you a target...." She gasped, her eyes wide. "Rosemary, I can't hold them back. There are too many."

Rose tried to catch Alex as she crumped to the ground. Alex's throat clenched in agony as it choked her screams down to rabid growls. Her eyes swam in tumult. Her face shifted as the muscles cramped, changing her appearance. Rose wanted this to be a game and for a moment, just froze, waiting for the *Gotcha*! But Alex wasn't kidding. She labored to breathe. Rose cried, "What can I do, Alex? Tell me what I should do?"

"I can't," Alex panted. She raised her hand like she was going to touch Rose's chest. "No," was all she said.

Like a cartoon hammer hitting her square in the chest, Rose half thought the explosion of light was from the injury—like seeing stars—but it came first. Then the garden was facing the wrong way. The sky was on its side. Alex stood over her, her face in a fit.

"Help me, Rose. Save her. Save Alex."

The words would have left Rose stunned if not for the lightning that followed them. Alex yelled over the crackling that felt like knives penetrating Rose's body, wriggling inside her, jarring her muscles and arching her back in pain.

And then it was over. Alex was hunched over at the edge of the garden, her body soaked in sweat. "I'm going to be sick," she murmured. "I don't have control."

Rose pushed to her feet. She couldn't dust herself off with the Book in her hands. She turned to a page, demanding, "Who are you?"

"Don't Rose. Let me explain."

"Don't what, exactly? Protect myself?" She lowered her newly appeared Book, her thumb keeping track of the page. "Who are you?"

"Sara. Please, Rose. I can't keep fighting them."

As Alex's expression shifted, Rose looked at the page her thumb held. Her mouth snapped open. Her lips and tongue forcefully shifted into positions. She exhaled, and together they formed the words, guttural and coarse. The sparks she fired at Alex were nothing like the branching electricity she'd endured, but it dropped Alex to her knees.

Watching Alex writhe in pain shouldn't have felt good, but it re-balanced the scales. She'd been slapped, so slapping back felt twice as satisfying. She fired again. And again. She needn't read the whole spell each time, just repeating the last few words—shapes—runes, and the entire spell was conjured anew.

Alex clawed at the ground, her eyes fiery with hatred. She glared *through* Rose. She sneered, her expression saying things more hateful and hurtful than her mouth was ever capable. Alex raised her hand and Rose shot sparks from her fingertips again and again until— for a moment—Alex connected them with a jagged line of light. Rose felt her insides heat up, her fingers felt like they were on the verge of boiling and popping off. She collapsed to the dirt. Taking a breath only once Alex's torture stopped. She felt sick. Her body trembled.

"I'm sorry, Rose," Alex whispered. "I can't…."

"Who are you?" Rose repeated, her chant rising in ferocity like a growing hurricane. "Who are you and where's Alex?"

Rose could feel it. Like a nudge. Her fingers pushed the pages aside. Another. Another. She pushed herself upright, crumbs of dirt and finger-stains of mud painting the page. She read. This wasn't a bolt of lightning. This wasn't some slap to make her feel better. Rose could feel the gravity of the shapes on this page, the weight of the ugly words formed as her eyes scanned the page and her breath gave them life. This was power.

Alex grabbed her shirt and pulled at it. "You're not just killing me," Alex mewled. "You're killing Alex."

Alex growled and writhed in the garden as she struggled to her feet. She was like a wounded animal, ferocious, trading fear for rage.

Through gritted teeth, she forced out, "I'm Sara Frost."

And then Rose stopped. The spell was complete.

Alex collapsed to the ground in a heap. Her eyes rolled in her head like she searched for something she couldn't find. She growled and convulsed. And was still.

What have I done? Rose looked at her Book. Although the symbols on the page were nonsensical, something in her head understood this was a killing spell.

Rose dropped at Alex's side.

"Alex," Rose sang desperately. "Al-lex, wa-ake up."

Rose looked at the Book she'd abandoned in the garden, crushing a young thyme plant. *I only wanted her to stop. She would have killed me.* She collected the Book and held it to her chest. *The Book made me do it. It was protecting me. Mom won't understand. She'll blame me. She won't believe Alex could hurt me. She'll demand I give her my Book. She'll take it.* With a thought—she wasn't quite sure how she made it happen—a swirl of mist allowed her to hide her Book away.

Rose wiped her face. Her stomach swam. She felt like she did when she knew her mother was about to discover the bad thing she'd done and could only wait for her mother's wrath. But a hundred times worse. She wanted to throw up, if only to give the sensation room as it grew.

"Please don't be dead, Alex. Please be okay." She touched Alex's throat. The pulse was weak. She'd never felt such relief. Alex wasn't dead. Despite the spell, Alex wasn't dead. *Who did I kill?*

"Alex," she shouted into the others ear, "Alex, wake up!"

Rose rolled Alex over, crushing the row of thyme. "Alex? Alex!"

She was lying. That was Matthew. I took care of him. It wasn't Alex. Whoever that parasite was is gone. It wasn't Sara. Right? She wouldn't try to hurt me. I did the right thing. If something happened to Alex, it's because of what they did to her. Doubt seeped through Rose's body like acid burning a line through her insides. Alex had told her about the old witch. Her eyes welled up. She looked back at the house, wishing her mother would just sense something was wrong and come out to save her from it, tell her it would be okay; tell her she hadn't just killed her cousin.

Chapter Sixty-One

ose shook Alex's body. She didn't understand why Alex wasn't coming to. Whoever, or whatever was inside of her was dead, only Alex wasn't waking up. *Was that Alex? Was the spell too strong? Maybe Alex was already dead when Matthew, or Sara, or whoever, took her over. Can that even happen?*

Rose wiped tears she didn't realize were falling from her face and peered at the house. Her hands trembled. Everything was horribly wrong, and it was her fault. Her mother warned her about using that Book. *What does she know? She's never used a Book before. No woman has. I'm the first. Whoever that was attacked me. I was defending myself. But she'll never believe* that *part. I'll never hear the end of this. Even if it's not my fault, she'll believe it was. She'll blame my Book. She'll blame me for using it for the rest of my life. Oh, crap, what did I do? Alex can't be dead.*

Rose realized Heather would demand she relinquish her Book, not realizing how desperately they needed it now. *She'll take it away from me and then realize it's the only way to get Billy home. I bet she'll use it herself.*

She remembered Alex's description of her father: a soulless zombie, an empty but living corpse. Alex was unresponsive. *Did I do that to her?* She cried into her hands.

Rose had a thought; the Book got her into this trouble, perhaps it would get her out of it. She appeared her Book. Just touching it soothed her. There was power here, resources and solutions. She stared at the illuminated pages, running her hands over the symbols and shapes. She couldn't forget opening it for the first time in the field. Then, flames and screams and sparks all around; she freed the Book first from George's hands and then from Carrie's, opening it to a random page.

Even with chaos and war happening around her, the Book stood apart. The exquisite pages, colorful illuminations, elaborate borders, elegant shaped calligraphic symbology; whatever was writ appeared foreign and undecipherable. It was beautiful, perfect. The worn and old pages embossed with thick, crisp dark ink.

In each of those shapes there was more text, as though the shape or letter was not ink but the darkness of space below. In that space, smaller symbols and designs swirled around. And in those, even more. She felt herself transported, sucked into the Book, down through the infinite characters, each symbol containing within itself an entire Book, until she lost count, lost her will, obsessed only with finding the next within the next, until she found the last.

Only then, once she could no longer distinguish herself from the Book, there she was, standing in the field, holding it. Staring at the page, the swirls, the symbols, the shapes made no sense to her, but she somehow comprehended this wasn't the page she wanted. She brushed it aside, then another and another. Then, there it was. How she understood she couldn't say. It felt right. The page gave her a feeling that locked perfectly with the sensation of desire she had. Like puzzle pieces snapping together, this page transfixed her. She examined the first shape: enlarged, set in a box lined with flowers, inked in red. Her throat closed. Her mouth and lips tensed, as though suffering a cramp. As she exhaled, the tensed passage created sound. Her eyes slipped across the page and at each new symbol, her mouth twisted, her tongue danced, and the noises emanating from her were as foreign as the shapes she inexplicably uttered.

The spell was brief. As she read, the power awakened, drawing through her, pulling to her center and rushing down her arms to her extended hand, where it left her in a bright explosion of light. Repeating the last phrase—if that group of symbols constituted a phrase—was enough to repeat the entire spell, if done in quick enough succession. How did she know? She just did.

This time, there was no falling in, no discovery. It was almost disappointing. She opened the Book and turned page after page until her desire was quenched. This was what she wanted, as though her emotion fell into sync with the indecipherable magic described by the page.

Alex was as good as dead. Could her effort make things worse? Her stomach was sick, her breath acidic from the churning vitriol. The Book comforted her, made her feel it wouldn't—couldn't—do harm. She thought to wait, to think it through, but realized Heather was bound to spy her from a window, discover Alex prone in the garden, and whatever she hoped to accomplish would be forestalled until she convinced her mother to let her try.

Eyes locking on the first shape, her lips pursed, and she was underway. This spell was long, written across multiple pages. She tried to rush, pushing her eyes a little faster, but couldn't. The spell took what it took. Without evidence, she sensed Heather's judgement. She knew Heather was watching. She knew whatever Heather would think she saw, she would misunderstand. She half expected Heather to grab her, wrestle her to the ground and pry the Book from her fingers, leaving the spell half-cast. Leaving the spell to dissipate, leaving Alex however she was. Rose steeled her body; resentful Heather would even try. Alex—or Sara—attacked her. She got what she deserved. Now she was helping save Alex and her ignorant mother was going to try stopping her? It disgusted her that her mother would even think to try.

The spell was so long she failed to notice the energy filling her, only feeling full. She felt like a water balloon, filling and swelling to accommodate the rush of power. It grew so large and strong she feared it would exceed the limits of her body. When she uttered the last shape, tension left her face and throat. She leaned forward and placing her hand on Alex's forehead, gave purchase to the magic. The energy rushed from her so rapidly it was pulled, ripped from her. Knocked back by the recoil, she neither fell nor took her palm from Alex's forehead.

She waited for Alex to come around. *How long should a resurrection take?* Rose kept glancing at the house, expecting her mother's scowling face half-hidden behind the reflection of every window. *Maybe Alex isn't dead.* She dreaded learning such a spell could be harmful if that were the case, like giving someone anti-venom when they hadn't suffered a snakebite.

Alex's eyes fluttered open. She stared at Rose. Rose stared back, waiting for her cousin to say—or do—anything. At this point, Rose would joyfully accepted Alex's admonishment, just to have her back. But as the moment stretched to a minute and then another, Alex hadn't moved.

Rose curiously touched a fingertip to Alex's open eyeball. Not even a blink. Her hands trembled as though freezing as she closed Alex's eyes again. She couldn't endure another minute under her cousin's deathly gaze.

It did something. Her eyes opened. Why didn't it work? Why isn't Alex better? Rose fumed through frustrated tears and returned to the Book. *Is there another spell? A better one?* She tried to match her emotion with the feelings the Book gave her. *This one.* It seemed pointless, given Alex's state, but what did she have to lose? What did Alex have to lose? It took nothing for Rose to cast one more spell, one to give Alex protection: she would keep her safe.

Rose cast the final spell. Touching Alex, it rushed out of her like a sense of relief that everything would be okay. Somehow Rose knew it wouldn't be.

Rose waited to hear her mother start screaming at her: *How dare you use the Book? Didn't I warn you what would happen? Now look what you've done!*

Rose didn't put the Book away. She felt oddly calm. She'd done all she could. Whatever happened to Alex was no longer her concern. She'd done her part. She'd saved them all from whatever took Alex over. She alone had discovered the hidden monster and defeated it.

The door slammed open, and two sets of footfalls raced around to the garden. Rose held her Book against her chest. In her head, she imagined turning to them as they raced to the aid of their false messiah, and she'd tell them how she—again—saved them all. She turned. Heather's face was ravaged with concern. She looked haggard and old, as though seeing what her daughter had done sucked out nearly all the life left in her. Her mother's expression—Abby's expression—the loss, the fear, the desolation, reached into Rose and ripped out her courage. She hadn't realized she started shouting. "It's not my fault. I didn't do it. It wasn't even Alex!"

They didn't even notice her—Rose—standing there. Their eyes unacknowledging. There was Alex and no one else. Nothing else existed. Nothing else mattered.

Abby threw herself into the dirt, flattening plants and wrapping her arms around Alex's living corpse, howling in anguish like a mother animal finding her cubs mauled and half-devoured.

Heather was barely a step behind when inexplicably she noticed Rose. She was torn, however, between Rose and Alex. Her eyes abandoned the body and she stared at her daughter.

Rose would have taken contempt. Hatred. Resentment. For the first time, she wanted her mother's ire. Instead, Heather stared at her like she no longer mattered. Like she wasn't even sure if Rose was there.

Heather's voice sounded empty, devoid of emotion, leaving her question pure and unsullied, "What did you do?"

"It wasn't Alex. She, she; I protected us. She attacked me. It was… someone, someone bad." Rose thought to show her mother the scorch marks on her clothes, but there were too many to find one.

"So, you did… what?"

As Rose spoke, Abby looked up, Alex's limp form dangled from her arms, "I killed the thing inside her."

Abby's whole form, the magnitude of her, crumbled as defeat shrunk her. Her arms loosened, and Alex's body slid from her embrace. "You killed Sara," Abby wailed. "You murdered Sara. She was protecting Alex."

Both Rose and Heather answered in unison, "You knew?" and, "What?"

Abby clutched the limp form, hugging and releasing, hugging and releasing, rocking her. She steadied Alex's wobbling head, wiping hair and smearing soil from her face. She straightened Alex's neck, holding her to her chest. "We put so much on her; she's just a child," Abby shouted, tears flowing from her eyes. "All those Books, all those women. She was always fighting them back. It was too much. We asked too much from her."

"What are you talking about?" Heather questioned Abby, her own eyes streaming with tears, her hands trembling with anger and fear and loss.

Rose seethed, "You knew she wasn't Alex, and you said *nothing*?"

"Sara saw Alex losing. In the field. She was dying. We put too much on her. Sara took over to protect her. Alex would have died."

Heather asked, "You don't mean the old witch?"

"The first Book," Abby buried her head in Alex's hair.

"You knew she wasn't Alex? Why didn't you tell me? How could you keep that a secret?" Heather's voice rose until she was screaming. She seethed, "Don't tell me it was your fucking oath!"

Abby shook her head. "She... it was so confusing. Alex was back, alive, but it wasn't Alex, it was Sara. If anyone knew it wasn't her, if anything happened…. She was so fragile; Alex was dying. No one could know. She wanted to give Alex time to get strong and help her back. You see? You understand why I couldn't say a word?"

"That's why you wanted to take Alex home," Heather lashed

out at Abby, her face twisted in disgust. "You lied to me. You made me think that was my da-niece."

Rose snapped, "Your daughter? You almost called Alex your daughter?"

Heather reached for Rose, trying to embrace her. "Of course not, Rosemary. You're my daughter, but you're all my kids. I raised her."

Rose pulled away. "For four years. Four. She's not your kid," Rose accused. "She attacked me." She glared at Abby, trying to maintain her anger at the pitiful sight. "Sara wasn't strong enough either. She said she couldn't control herself and attacked me. *She tried to kill me.*"

"I'm sorry Rose, please come here," Heather cried, her arms outstretched. Rose saw only desperation in the awaiting embrace. Heather wanted to hold her, control her, stifle her.

Rose backed away. "No, Mom. You don't get to kiss my forehead and make it all better."

Heather reached, trying to force Rose into an embrace, but Rose maintained her distance.

"Where are you going?" Heather watched her backing away. Unsure whether to pursue.

The question put an answer in her head. *Why didn't I think this before?* "Where do you think? I'm going to do what we should have done from the start. You could've fixed all this, made it right before it went wrong. But I get it. I see you now, Mom. You're weak. You had a Book in your hands, and you wasted it on *her*." She witnessed in Heather's expression a pain unlike anything she experienced before. For a moment, Rose regretted her words. She never realized she had such power to hurt her mother so deeply.

Heather could barely speak. She swallowed and her words barely came as a hiss, "What are you going to do?"

"I'm going to get my brother back. You know, Mom, your *son*?"

"No Rose," Heather whimpered. "Please don't go. Not alone."

Rose knew what her mother had said, but it felt like a restriction. "Don't think you can stop me, Heather," Rose said, abandoning *Mom.*

"You can't go, Rose. Not now," she considered Alex and Abby, sobbing and heaving. "You can't. Please don't. I can't lose you, too. You can't go."

Heather looked so weak. Disgusting mucus ran down her mother's face. *Would she be this upset if that Alex-Sara thing had killed me? Heather is pathetic.* Finally, there was someone capable of saving Billy, someone willing to endure the risks, and Heather was too weak to endorse it. Rose imagined she could have knocked her mother over with a flick of her finger, much less a spell.

"You can't go, Rose. Not now. Not yet."

Rose opened the Book, immune to the sorrow in her mother's voice. She warned Heather, "Tell me again I can't leave." She thumbed to a page and placed her finger on the big shape in the box, marking her place.

"You'd hurt me?"

"Tell me, Heather, tell me you want Billy back. Tell me you care as much about Billy, *your son*, as you do for her!"

Heather tried to speak. She looked on her daughter who, standing not ten feet away, prepared to cast a spell from a Book. Heather turned away and collapsed into the dirt beside Abby, reaching out to embrace them both.

Rose looked at her mother, the turmoil in the garden, their bodies, the broken and uprooting plants, and turned away in disgust.

Her eyes welled. *They've all turned against me. They hate me. My cousin, my mother, everyone. The only person I have left is my brother. My twin brother.* Just thinking of him made her feel his spirit filling an empty place inside her. She looked at the Book and let the words flow through her. A configuration of mist appeared, and she stepped into it.

She found herself atop the devastated hillside. Before her, Picnic Rock had torn up the ground, folded the grass back in rolls, pushed scrub pines and shrubs over, destroyed everything, leaving a scar of deep brown soil, like a wound.

He's not under there. I'd feel it. I know I would. Wouldn't I?

This was the place she'd lost Billy. The place he leapt from twice. After Picnic Rock, his trail was cold. She'd left her mother to find her brother and now realized she didn't know what to do next.

Although it wasn't there, Rose could see it. A house. Picnic Rock had crushed one of its corners. It was a small house on the outside, made of multitudinous rooms, a sprawling manse secreted within.

Billy sometimes comes here, she thought, finding it sad that she thought it was creepy when she learned he'd visited her in her dreams. What she wouldn't give now for him to visit. She'd ruined everything. She'd murdered Alex, left her home, and devastated her mother. There was no going back. No one would ever want her again knowing what she'd done.

Rose walked to the front door, and despite knowing it was locked tight, grasped the ornate handle and pressed the thumb lever. Her house always let her in. She opened the door, and she was home.

Chapter Sixty-Two

bby shifted her weight, telegraphing to Heather she was about to move. As Heather gave room, Abby stood, raising Alex from the dirt. Her limbs and head dangled and wobbled.

"Take her inside," Heather mumbled. "Put her to bed."

Abby couldn't look at Heather. She looked only at Alex, cradled in her arms, like she carried the entirety of the universe. Her heart was torn out, evacuated from her chest leaving only a jagged hole, sensitive only to the breezes that blew through it.

Heather approached with caution and reverence, wordlessly communicating she'd come to help. Abby paused to allow Heather a moment. Heather stifled a sob, tears falling freely. She took Alex's arms and folded them across her chest. She stroked Alex's forehead. Using the same hand to cover her mouth as she sobbed again. Although Abby understood the pain Heather was feeling, losing her three children, she felt nothing. Everything she felt was gone, taken the moment Alex was taken from her. Heather backed away, allowing Abby to continue on her way. Then Heather dropped to her knees and bawled. Abby didn't pause or look back as Heather cursed herself, her daughter, and her brother.

Abby reached Alex's ladder and shifted Alex as gently as possible to insure she'd not get jostled, as Abby climbed the perilous ladder. Alex was like breath in her arms; Abby barely felt the weight of her.

She rested Alex onto her bed, positioning her body as though merely asleep. She stepped back, her eyes never leaving their purchase. Reality hit her like a landslide. She felt buried, unable to breathe, suffocating in darkness. She existed in a void, absent even the memory of joy. Her hands trembled as she touched Alex's body, picking off leaves and grains of soil. Everything felt wrong. She tugged the shoulder of her sleeveless t-shirt to wipe perspiration from her forehead. She felt responsible to clean her, but the burden was too much. She'd endure any utility of her own body in service of Alex if only to bring her back, but she knew—she could feel—Alex was gone.

For the first time, Abby looked away. She collapsed to the

floor beside the bed and sobbed. She cried, wailing. She hit the floor with her fists. Eventually, the desire to cry leeched out of her, like she only had so much inside and had spent it all. She looked at her palms, compelled to wipe them on her shirt. She clasped Alex's arm, held it, hoping for the slightest hint of consciousness, knowing there'd be none.

Heather came up shortly thereafter, taking the treads on the ladder slower than usual, her steps deliberate and heavy. She stared at the body on the bed, and then at Abby kneeling beside it. She lowered herself to her knees and put one arm around Abby's waist. She rested her head on Abby's shoulder.

Perhaps an eternity passed. It was forever to each of them, their knees aching on the hardwood, their bodies cried to exhaustion.

Abby spoke, perhaps to Heather, perhaps to Alex, perhaps to herself. Her voice was like a wrecking ball to the silence that had smothered the attic. "What's the point? To any of this? She was just a child, and we pinned all our hopes on her. We did this to her."

"She never asked *why*," Heather finally spoke after a moment's reflection. "She just understood."

"Waking up all those years ago, watching the life drain out of Peter, my heart broke. He," Abby studied Heather, "and you were… are my best friends. My only friends. Watching him fade to nothing was the most horrible thing I ever thought I would endure. Until today. I believed it was for a reason—a damn important reason—that his sacrifice was noble. A damn fool your brother was. We're idiots, pretending we can make a difference."

Heather's voice was barely a whisper. "You were there? When he…." Her expression softened, her eyes never losing their intensity. "You are so strong, Abby. You kept going."

Abby lay her head on the bed, still holding Alex's arm. She could feel a pulse through skin, but nothing else. Heather rested against Abby's lowered shoulder, trying to maintain contact.

"Peter was eighteen minutes older. My big brother. He guided me. He explained everything. Everything I thought I understood, everything I did was because he laid it out for me. I was lost when he, you know, stopped being Peter, but I still had his instructions. It was like I still had him. Like a treasure map to find parts of him. Now I'm lost. I failed him. I failed her. My kids. Maybe he didn't know what he was doing. Maybe I confused his certainty with truth."

Abby took a breath, long and slow, and released it as a sigh. "I'm all cried out. I never imagined I'd find the bottom of that well, but here we are."

Abby let her hand slip from Alex's arm. She turned and embraced Heather.

The bottom of that well gave out and she found tears anew once Heather started sobbing into her shoulder, lamenting the loss of her family.

"You're all I have now, Abby," Heather whimpered. "Everyone is gone. I ruined everything."

It was Abby's turn to be the strong one. She brushed her hand down the back of Heather's head. "Rosemary is out there. She's all alone."

Heather growled, "Don't say her name."

"Heather, listen to me. Until we know otherwise, there's hope Billy's alive. Your daughter is intent on bringing him home. That's all Alex wanted."

Heather's face squirmed as though forcefully regurgitating the words, "She killed Alexandrea."

Part of Abby wanted to wallow and to pull Heather down with her. *Who cares if we both drown in sorrow*? Except Abby realized she cared. "She has a pulse. She's breathing. Maybe she's like Peter." Abby took a moment to let that sink in. "Sara said she was saving Alex." Abby chose not to repeat what Sara said about the dangers if Alex wasn't strong enough. "When Sara took over, Alex was still in there. Maybe she still is. Maybe she'll wake up a minute from now."

Heather couldn't stifle a tearful, snotty laugh, "That would be so like Alex. *Aunt Heather, why are you crying? I'm hungry*."

Abby laughed. Heather knew her niece. "Rosemary is all alone, and whether or not you agree with her use of that Book—"

"That Book…. It's trouble," Heather interrupted. "I thought I was careful. Look where it got me. It's like a *monkey's paw*. It's cursed. Everything we wish for comes true but perverted and horrible."

"Whether or not you agree," Abby repeated, "Rose is doing what we imagined Alex would do. You saw her in the field yesterday. She was a fuckin' badass. She saved everyone."

"She did, didn't she?"

"Imagine what those assholes were thinking when some pretty

girl started handing them their asses. She was amazing." They both laughed. Abby waited for Heather to look her in the face. "What are the chances Rose wasn't terrified? That Book could have done anything to her. She snatched it from George and read from it. Women aren't supposed to be able to read from Books. That was real bravery."

"She didn't seem scared," Heather confessed. "I've never been as confident about anything in my whole life as she always seems to be." Heather looked at Alex. "She really was amazing. Is amazing."

"Now, imagine how she feels. We've abandoned her. You raised her right; she knows she's doing the right thing the wrong way. Look at how angry that conflict is making her. She chose the one option too scary for the rest of us to consider. What if the only road to the end involves us all doing it the wrong way? What if the right way ended with Alex? If Rose succeeds, will it matter in the end?"

"Shouldn't we be better than them?"

"Maybe we can't. If we set things right, fix the injustice, does it matter?"

"I don't know, Abby. I really don't know. I know I should." She motioned to Alex. "But," was all she needed to say.

"We can't fix her. Rose said she was defending herself."

"Is this what defending herself looks like?" Heather shook her head. "She isn't in control of the magic."

"Alex was always worrying about what George told her. That bullshit about some woman killing her family because she ruined dinner." She gestured to the bed. "If this were Rose, if Alex lost control trying to save us, would you turn your back on her so quickly?" Abby stared at Heather. When Heather failed to respond, she resumed, "All I'm saying is that if there's any way we can help Rose, we have to do it. If she fails, that's our fault."

Heather slipped from Abby's embrace and stood, her knees aching from kneeling. "What about you?"

"As long as there's life in her, I'll be at her side."

"The oath won't ever let you leave?"

"I don't know, Heather. It's more sacred than an oath."

"What do we do then? What's… next?"

"Find Rosemary. Help her. Whatever it takes. The stakes are too high to not take every chance. Then, let me know. Tell me what you need. I…," she stared at Alex. "I want to help, but I can't abandon her."

"But you just said if Rose fails, it's our fault. I can't, Abby. Not alone."

"I know what I said." Abby gestured to Alex's body, "Look at her, Heather. I can't leave her. Not like this. Not without her say-so." She swallowed, hoping the words she was thinking would fail to come out. "Maybe, when you and Rose are back, I'll know that Alex is gone. Or I'll make myself believe that helping Rose is all Alex would want."

"How do I do this, Abby? I don't know where Rose is. I don't know what to do."

"Who knows Rose better than you? If you really, really don't know, then we've lost, Heather. Maybe without Alex, everything is lost. You know if she could, she'd tell you to find Rose."

"That's not fair, Abby."

Abby stroked Alex's arm. "Neither is this, Heather." Abby watched Heather disappear down the ladder.

Chapter Sixty-Three

ose's dream-house was always familiar; however, with each visit, her mood subtilty altered the layout. The rooms, their completeness, their décor, were always familiar enough. Walking from one room to another, the anticipation of discovery was always new. Each doorway became a new possibility, a representation of experience and emotion. It was a dream. A safe place when she was scared. Today it felt more real. Billy sometimes visited her, and she'd hoped to find him here. She wandered room to room, becoming less confident he'd be in the next. She ventured deep into the house, into previously undiscovered places. Normally, such finds would thrill her. Today, however, the spaces seemed smaller, the doorways narrower, the décor uneasy with corrosive colors and edges.

This room, where today Rose felt least threatened, most at sanctuary, was decorated with yellow wallpaper. Creeping yellow-green vines formed an unrecognizable pattern encaging the four walls and the inexplicably wallpapered ceiling. Water stains delineated the corners and edges, the thick vinyl peeling in places.

A hulking four-poster bed made of white wicker held court in the center of the room, draped with large, swooping bunches of gossamer pink tulle that kissed the floor. The dresser, the desk, the vanity, and the mirrors were all the same style of white wicker; vines of wood tortured into feminine-looking curves. Cut-outs of half-moons gave the furniture a cheerfulness. The longer Rose stared, however, the more they formed sinister, grinning faces.

Rose crept along the walls, running her fingers over the wallpaper. There were no longer windows or doors. The forest of twisted vines consumed however she'd entered. Even the floor, which she recalled being planks of hardwood, disappeared as vines wrapped from floor to wall to ceiling.

This didn't frighten Rose. Not the forest, not the scowling wicker faces on the bed and dresser and desk and chair and mirror. *This is my house. Nothing here will hurt me, and if it tries, I have my Book to protect me. I'm not afraid. Not of scary faces. Not of a forest growing in a room without doors. Not of Matthew or Jeremiah.*

Nothing. Except of what she'd done to Alex.

Rose retreated to the bed. The four posts and the dingy pink netting looked torn by unkind fingers. All she needed to do was pull the damp, moldy comforter up to her chin and all feeling would go away.

She welcomed that. She felt too much. She remembered the twisted expression that distorted Alex's face but not her smile. *She almost killed me.*

She peeled back the sodden comforter. The sheets were heavy with mildew and polka dotted with mold. The smell was sweet and earthy, like her mothers' garden soil. She sat on the bed and slipped her feet between the sheets. She was safe. The bed was warm and moist, almost hot. The mattress was spongy beneath her. Gently, she pulled up the comforter.

"Rosemary?"

A settling creak of the wall faintly spoke her name, conjured echoes of her mother. She pictured her mother, standing in the garden, raging over something. She stilled so the crunching leaves and grinding soil wouldn't drown out her name if spoken again. There was nothing but the hushed breeze and low grumbling of a hungry belly. She placed her hand on her stomach, but her hand on the bed felt it, too. She pulled the comforter over her head, covering herself like a corpse.

"Rosemary? Where are you?"

The settling house called to her again. *She'd never come here.*

Roots stretched through the ground, tangling around her. Worms and other wet bugs snuggled beside her. The forest buried all but her face, leaving her safe and contented in her bed.

"Rosemary? This place scares me."

What's scary about this place? The sod weighed on her chest. It rose and fell with her breath. Like a drain-plug had been pulled, she felt emptied of something. Something that had torn at her insides evidenced by scraps hanging in the evacuated space. Whatever once tormented her was gone; absorbed into the ground, feeding the growing vines.

"Rosemary, I'm sorry. Please forgive me. It's all up to you now. I need you. Billy needs you. We need you to use your Book so we can be a family again. Just the three of us. We need you to show us how."

How long have I been here? She didn't know. She recalled once being at some other house with some other people. *When was that? Was that me?*

"You were so brave. You were amazing. You saved everyone, Rosemary. Everyone."

Rosemary?

The girl in the ground closed her eyes. Leaves blew over her face, which slipped into the soil, swallowed whole by the damp earth.

"Rosemary, please. Are you here? I don't know where else to look. This place gives me the willies. Please, let me find you and I'll do anything you say. We'll get Billy together."

Billy? The shape of that name tickled her insides. There was something, like a tag around the toe of that name. *Is Billy someone special? Someone important?* She didn't think she knew, and then it came to her. *My brother; my twin.*

Rose lurched upright, soil and worms, beetles and dirt, leaves and roots falling from her clothes. She tried to listen for her mother's voice and found herself inextricably tangled in the bed curtains. She tugged, the tulle tearing from the frame, the fabric vining around her.

"Rosemary? Are you here?"

It was fainter than last time. *Is that really Mom? She's looking for me? Why? To yell at me more. To tell me to come home and accept responsibility?*

"Please, Rosemary, I need you. I came to help. You don't have to do it alone. Rosemary, please. Speak to me."

Her mother called. "Mom?" Responding was involuntary.

"Oh, Rose, I hear you, where are you?"

Knowing her mother knew where she was awakened a desperation she didn't know was sleeping. All the times she was frightened and wanted her mother piled on her until that need was all she knew, the clutching ache to feel her mother's touch. "I'm in here, Mom."

"In where?"

"In my bedroom." Rose said it before she realized it. She looked at the forest, at the vines and weeds snaring her. "It's a forest now, but it was my bedroom. I came through a door. It's gone." Just knowing her mother was coming lightened the crushing weight of believing she had chosen Alex over her.

"Rose, every time I go through a door, it's like I forget which room I came from. Where are you? Help me find you."

Rose stretched against the snares and the vines, pulling closer to the impenetrable forest to bang on it with her fist. "I'm in here."

The wall banged back. "I'm on the other side of the wall. Where's the door?"

"I told you. There isn't one."

Heather was silent.

The possibility she'd been abandoned again sneered from the back of her mind. "Mom? Where'd you go?"

"There's got to be a door. How is there no door? How'd you get in there?"

"I don't know, Mom."

"How is that even possible, Rosemary? Did you crawl through a mouse-hole?"

"No." The fear in her own voice brought Rose to tears. She came here because of what she did to Alex. Because she didn't know what else to do. The room did the rest. It promised eternal rest from her troubles. "I came through a door, Mommy, but it's gone now." She took a trembling breath. "It was a bedroom, but now it's a forest." She shuddered, looking back to the bed, she saw only the hole she emerged from. It was a grave.

"Does that happen to you often, when you're here?"

"Please help me, Mamma. I'm scared. It wants to keep me here. The vines are pulling. They want me in a grave, Mamma. Hurry," Rose screamed. "Hurry, I don't want to go back in the grave."

Heather banged the wall again, much harder.

This used to be wallpaper. Rose pushed her hands through the tight knit of vines and trees and hoped she'd find the wall, but the space was too constricting for her hand. She took hold of the furthest thing she reached, and pulled.

The tree peeled from the forest. It wouldn't break or tear. It separated with the sound of a tremendous gust of wind. It hung loose, curling like an entwining vine as it came to rest on the floor. This was no tree; she had pulled away the wallpaper. She reached through the forest and pounded her fists on the plaster, each strike a reply to her mother's.

Behind her, the vines grew.

Just as the plaster began giving way under her fist, her heart raced, and the vines tightened around her calves.

Working ferociously, Rose dug her fingers into the crack, disassembling the wall, creating a hole into the dry, dusty cavity between the rooms. Her hands trembled, her whole body loose and exposed, the vines taking firm hold of her thighs. They squeezed, wrapping around her, tightening until her feet were numb.

The vines twisted about her waist and hips as, through the dark hole, she spied the first cracks of light. She dislodged enough plaster for her fingertips to pass through. The very tips of her fingers met the very tips of her mother's. The moment they touched, Heather's hands snatched her fingertips like a sprung trap, pinching her first knuckle.

She expected her mother to release her, so they might pull more plaster, might enlarge the hole, but Heather didn't. Heather was pulling Rose through a hole no bigger than two, maybe three of her fingers.

"Mommy. I won't fit, Mom. It's too small."

"Come on, baby, push. Come on, push through. Push." Heather groaned as she pulled.

The vines wrapped around her torso, her shoulders. The vines found her throat.

The dry, chalky plaster scraped her skin. As her mother pulled her hand, parts of the wall broke away as the hole enlarged. It was too small; the vines crept up her body. In her mother's grasp, only her fingertips felt safe.

Her mother's hands took claim on her hand, and then her arm. Her head pressed against the wall, her neck threatening to break.

"Mom, please, you're hurting me," Rose yelped.

Heather was unrelenting, as though breaking Rose's neck was the whole point of the endeavor. Rose rolled her head around the hole as her shoulder disappeared into it. Plaster pushed in her eyes and her mouth as her head burst into the wall. Heather tugged savagely, one foot leveraging against the wall. She grunted and groaned, pulling Rose through the hole. Rose spilled to the ground. Knotted around her throat, twisted and wrapped around her waist and her feet, were lengths of pink gauzy tulle, torn from the bed.

Heather dropped to her daughter's side, cleaning the fabric away from her face, wiping plaster dust from her eyes and mouth, holding her, panting in relief.

"How'd you find me?" Rose asked as Heather freed her from the twisted fabric. Rose looked up at the hole in the wall. It still wasn't large enough for her to have passed through.

Heather panted and rubbed tears from her eyes, "I didn't know you'd be here. I hoped." A silver thread undulated from Heather's chest, weaving through the warren maze, presumably ending at her sleeping body.

"I didn't mean to hurt Alex. You have to believe me."

Heather embraced her again, holding Rose's head to her chest. "Oh, my sweet baby," she rocked her. "I'm here because you're here." She picked bits of plaster from Rose's hair. "You have a Book. You will get Billy back. Abby helped me realize I can't let you do it alone."

"I could, you know, do it alone. You didn't have to come."

"I know you could, Rosemary. But you shouldn't have to." She licked her fingertips and wiped her daughter's face. When Rose opened her eyes, Heather looked into them. "When you're ready, tell me what you need me to do. Tell me how I can help you, and we'll get your brother."

Rose clutched her mother. "I'm glad you're here, Mom."

Heather's reply, as she scanned the house, sounded stilted and devoid of emotion. "So am I, Rosemary. So am I."

Chapter Sixty-Four

as that a sound? Someone moving? There. In the darkness. What is that?

Shuffling fabric or feet padding across the floor. Stalking. Or creeping. Disrupting perfect silence. There. Moving. Closer.

A heartbeat, pounding. Darkness. The sound crept closer. Touch. Warm. Fabric. Sheets. Darkness. Movement. Closer.

Something knocked into something that rattled, eliciting a curse.

Where was *she*? A grave? A cell? A bedroom. A bedroom in an attic. *Her* bedroom. Everything flooded back. Screams. The field. Flames. Cries for help. The whispers revolting. Book. George. Heather. Abby. Jeremiah.

"Excuse me," the voice was deep and lyrical and heavily accented. The woman continued, "Can you please tell me, where has the baby gone?"

Baby?

"I don't think she hears you," replied another voice. It was higher in pitch, speaking in a faster cadence. "Perhaps she doesn't know."

"What kind of thing is that to say, Lesedi? Of course she knows; she is the mother. Why else would she be in the room where the baby should be?"

"That's precisely what I'm saying, Banhi. Look on her, what woman looks like this, four days following birth?"

"Are we in the wrong place?" It was Banhi, her voice coarse and gravelly.

"Perhaps, but Kholwa insists this is the right place for finding the baby."

The deep, lush voice replied, "Don't blame me if we are lost. We all felt the heart-star when it was born. We followed it here to bless the newborn. *All of us.* If we're lost, it isn't my fault alone."

Lesedi replied, "So why is it not here?" Her tone changed, "Lady, do you know where a baby might have gone?" After a pause,

Lesedi added, "She does not answer. Look on her, the body is empty."

"I have an idea," Banhi said in her gravelly voice.

There was movement, and as Kholwa said, "I do not like this idea," three glowing disks sliced the darkness.

One of the glowing coins approached Alex. "It does seem you are dead. And not dead. Your heart-star burns bright. But outside of the world of the dead, you do not rouse." Banhi's voice was intimate and husky.

Alex tried to speak; air stalled in her throat.

"Something happened to her," Lesedi proposed. "She does not *look* dead."

"Perhaps," Kholwa suggested, "she is caught on the Between; not dead, not alive, not anything."

"I hate to think such things," Banhi said, louder now that she wasn't speaking to Alex. "That's bad magic. Murder."

Lesedi sounded perturbed, "No. The heart-star wouldn't be so bright. It would be gone, no? Who would kill but leave the heart-star?"

Khowla suggested, "Maybe one who hoped to lure the likes of us."

Lesedi laughed. "Big effort for three little women. Maybe there is a reason they do it to *her*."

Banhi said, "Do we leave her and search for the baby? Do we help?"

"How do you ask such things, Banhi?" Lesedi said, "Would you suggest we leave someone trapped on the Between?"

Alex heard the smile in Banhi's voice, "Of course not. I wanted to not be the one to suggest we help her." After a moment, she said, "Over there, Kholwa, and there, Lesedi."

Like singular stars in the darkness, the three coins shifted through the murk. Footsteps and fabric shifted about Alex.

As though a switch had flipped, Alex's lungs burned as she gasped for air. The room suddenly flooded with light. She looked at the three women, their coins bright, trailing fine, silver threads that disappeared at the edges of darkness where the roof in her bedroom sloped beyond the furniture.

Alex sat bolt upright and asked, "What's happening to me?"

She matched appearance with voice, each as distinctive as the other, as they spoke.

"Oh, sweet child," this was Lesedi. A tall, slender woman.

Hair pulled tight into a giant pom-pom atop her head. She smiled at Alex, more in pity than joy. "You are but a dream now. Even to us."

"Why do you say these things?" Banhi's gravelly voice went with her older face. Stout and stooped, her face wrinkled joyfully. Long hair, parted deftly in the center, hung in gray waves past her breasts. "Your body is alive, but you cannot return to it. It is in the living world. Only in dreams, Lesedi means, can you live."

Alex slid to the edge of the bed as Kholwa spoke behind her. Alex looked upon her own body, still prone on the bed, arms folded over her chest, a silver thread floating to where she stood, tethered to the glowing coin in her chest.

"I don't mean to ignore your troubles, but can you help us find the baby?" Kholwa was wearing a necklace of what looked like brown stones cut into slender disks to show their concentric rings. Her skin was lighter than Banhi's, her lips large and impossibly red, her eyes big and dark. Black hair bloomed around her head. "It was born about four days prior to today. We followed the heart-star here."

How long ago was I in the field? Not enough time seemed to pass for her to be wherever here was. These strangers told her she was dead and immediately went back to looking for some baby. Just waking here would have been confusing enough, but encountering these women severed those memories and left her feeling untethered, as though she'd been lost in time until this moment. Alex shook the fogginess from her head. "Heart-star? You mean this?" She held her hand over her coin.

The three nodded.

"Four days ago? A baby?" Alex tried to piece together why they thought they might find a baby here.

"Yes," Lesedi said, holding her hands a short distance apart, "it would be a small baby."

Kholwa laughed. "All babies are small, Lesedi," she mocked. She turned to Alex, "Perhaps you haven't seen it because of your condition?"

"Thursday was four days ago," Alex counted on her fingers, not certain what day today was. She tapped her chest as she spoke, "That's when my mother flipped my coin."

"Flipped?" Banhi's voice rose high in pitch, a sign of her incredulousness. "What is this flipped?"

In spite of the accusation in Banhi's tone, Alex couldn't help but adore the older woman. She tried to explain. "I have two." She cupped her hands together. "They face this way now, but four days ago they were opposite." She demonstrated by awkwardly reversing her hands.

"That is not natural," Banhi accused. "That makes them disappear? Flipping them …," she trailed off in contemplation.

Kholwa finished, "Would make her be born."

Lesedi shook her head. "This is not possible. She is too old to be born four days ago."

"No," Banhi corrected, "*appear* to be born." She gestured at Alex, "This is the baby we came to gift."

"To gift?" Alex was confused.

"A baby was born," Lesedi said, "and a girl."

"A witch," Banhi's eyes widened as she smiled.

"We come when that happens," Lesedi continued. "Not always us, but this time it was us three. Tomorrow it may be me and two others, or sometimes—"

"She understands, Lesedi," Kholwa interrupted. "You need not explain all possible variables." She turned to Alex, "There are some of us upholding the tradition, gifting the new babies."

Lesedi glared at Khowla before continuing. "We come to give the baby a gift each. Mine is joy."

"Mine is wisdom," Banhi grinned.

"Mine is health," Kholwa finished.

"You come for every baby?" Alex asked.

Kholwa nodded. "Every child deserves these gifts. There are fewer who still believe. Even fewer willing to try."

"The good that it does," Lesedi scowled. "Long ago, witches were in demand for gifts. Kings would beg our kind to gift their princesses. Always it was beauty and grace. Useless gifts." She posed, mocking poise.

Banhi groaned in agreement. "Why not strength and compassion or confidence and intelligence? No," she rubbed her forehead, "better a pretty girl than a strong-willed, confident woman." She scoffed.

"Since you are our baby," Lesedi asked, "what gifts might you like? I have never before gifted a child who could tell me."

Alex slowly formulated her sentence; fearful the wrong words would leave her like the butt of a joke she'd heard about a man on a deserted island finding a genie in a bottle. "To not be... on the Between... and wake up in the world... alive."

All three women hushed, looking from one to the other in surprise, as though shocked this would be her request.

Lesedi leaned forward. "Let me look on you closely, child." She smiled, her bottom lip rubbing her large teeth. "Do you see that?" She jumped back as though startled.

"What did you see, Lesedi?" Kholwa asked.

"Look, Kholwa, at her." Lesedi replied.

As Kholwa leaned closer to Alex, Banhi gasped. "I see it too."

Kholwa's mouth was agape in study, "What do you see?" Then added, "Oh no. This cannot be. How is this possible?"

Alex worried, "What? What do I have? What do you see?" The examination left her fearful of some on-the-Between-lurking parasite or hideous deformation.

Lesedi edged forward again, touching Alex reluctantly on her shoulder. "It is your aura child. It is blacker than tar on a moonless midnight."

"What does that even mean? A black aura?" Alex looked to each for an explanation.

Kholwa explained, "Your aura should be white or blue or pink: any color. It is the energy put out by the emotions that dominate who you are. You, child, have one that is black."

"Is that bad?" Alex panicked.

Banhi answered, "It is not what we like to see."

Lesedi drew her hand from Alex's shoulder and rubbed her palm against her jeans. "Color of the aura can change for many things. Like, you could grow into an angry person. But black is no absence. Black is all color, muddied together. This, this is what happens when one body has many, many souls."

"What horrible things have you done, child?" Lesedi hissed.

The women all backed away; suddenly fearful Alex might have lured them to feast on their souls.

Alex shrugged at Lesedi's inquiry. "Nothing. The last thing I remember we—"

Lesedi interrupted, "Who is this we? You and your souls?"

"Me and my cousin and Aunt. And my friends," Alex almost said *Book Club*, but avoided explaining that novelty. "*We* went to the field," she pointed as though confident of the direction, "to meet with

Jeremiah."

All three women recoiled from Alex. Banhi whispered, "Maybe this is a different man she tells of. Otherwise, how is she here?"

Matter-of-factly, Alex replied, "Why? He asked me to go and then tried to force me to surrender to him."

"Then how are you here?" Lesedi shivered, "What did you do for him in return for these souls? What deal did you strike?"

"I, I don't remember, but I didn't surrender or make a deal. The voices," Alex was trying to recall, "they got so loud. I saw the fires, but then nothing until just now."

Banhi asked, "Voices? When did they come to you?"

"Before. Five or six days ago. This other man, Matthew, sent me to their Library. When I touched his Books—"

"What?" Kholwa shook her head incredulously. "You met Jeremiah? You went to the Library? How are you alive, child?" She squinted at Alex, "Who are you…, really?"

Banhi's voice quieted, "No woman visits the Library, except inside their Book." She looked at Alex, "How did it turn out that you are not still there?"

Lesedi pointed at Alex, "You are telling us a story. It is not a truthful thing. How could it happen?"

Alex wasn't sure how to answer. "Matthew tested me to determine if I had magic."

"Ma-a-a-gic?" Banhi laughed as she spoke. "What woman nowadays has magic?"

Alex's voice softened. "I do."

All three women simultaneously motioned to speak.

Finally, Kholwa asked, "So, *magic girl*, what happened at the Library? And better, how did you leave?"

Banhi hissed at her, "Do not encourage her. She is false."

"When I touch a Book, I—me and the Book—become fire. I burned a lot of Books," Alex answered matter-of-factly. "They sent me away to spare the rest."

The three women looked at one another. They whispered and gestured before coming to a consensus.

Lesedi spoke first. "Perhaps the Books explain the voices; the voices explain the aura. Nothing explains how you are yet living." She looked like she was counting columns of hashmarks. "This is still mostly good."

Banhi continued, "If we believe this story, for each Book you burned you took that magic inside. The magic is the woman attached to the spell. Take the spell, take the woman."

She stepped closer to Alex. "It is not unlike a hologram," Banhi held her hands up to demonstrate.

"A what?" Kholwa put her hands on her hips. "What are you trying to say?"

Banhi turned to Kholwa and continued. "I may be an old woman, but that does not mean I am a dumb woman. I attended university. I studied physics. I held a job in research. When my sister died in childbirth, I returned home to be with my parents. I took my niece as my daughter. I saw what happened to women, dying in childbirth for stupid reasons, so I stayed and became a doula."

The others looked at one another in surprise and Kholwa said, "We did not know, Banhi. We thought you were always a midwife."

Banhi laughed, "You never asked." She then turned back to Alex. "In a hologram, each piece contains information for the whole. This is why you can see it from different perspectives. I think this is the same for that little piece of spirit. That little spell has all the information for the whole, so inside of you, all the Books means all the women." She nodded; the words she spoke sounded truthful enough.

Alex wasn't sure she understood, but the explanation made sense. She remembered her father nodding to Sara, certain he didn't understand what she had said. *He didn't know, but it made sense.* "How do I stop them? I hear them all the time." She listened, but found silence, "Except right now."

"Child, we cannot take them away from you," Kholwa said sincerely.

Lesedi nodded, "They only think they are alive inside you; however, they are not. They speak their worries and their fears, their hatred and their love. You, child, simply must not listen. You must tell them to shut their mouths. You must show them who is in charge of this body."

Alex pouted. "I wish it were that easy."

Kholwa nodded. "It is like that girl behind you in the classroom, telling you your clothes are ugly and you are a filthy girl because she does not like you. You must tell her no and not listen to what she thinks even though she does not shut up."

"Yes," Banhi agreed, "you must learn to not care what they think even when you hear it. A good lesson for all of life."

"But how?" Alex looked to each of them. "They get so loud, it's like they're shouting in my brain. I get lost in the noise."

Lesedi nodded. "Of course, it is not easy. When you tell someone that you will not be listening, who really are you telling?"

Alex wanted an answer that could help. So far, they didn't have answers. "Myself?"

"Child," Banhi replied, "you are a wonderful, powerful woman. You have nothing but doubt inside, as do we all. Am I good enough, smart enough, strong enough? Always asking. Always doubting. Only the ignorant are certain of who they are. Only the people who think they know everything, because they believe everything to be little and small, do not doubt. They tell you that you are dumb, they tell you that you will die; what do they know? Who are they to have lived your life, to understand who you are? They are a voice, and yet when you listen, someone who does not know tells you who you are. You must ask yourself, *Who am I?* Are you who you try to be or who they tell you that you are?"

Alex took a deep breath. None of this was easy. None of what they said was a simple answer. She hoped she understood. She'd spent all this time *trying to listen* to the whispers. The voices would always be there, sowing doubt, fear, worry; trying to tell her what to do, whatever they thought. If she listened, she could not be who she wanted to be, only who they told her she was. It sounded crazy— obscenely crazy—but just the doubt in her thought made Alex consider what Banhi meant.

"On that note," Kholwa said, "who are you? Seriously. What is your name, child?"

Alex laughed. "Alex. It's short for Alexandrea. Alexandrea Hawthorne."

They took turns introducing themselves. Banhi mentioned her education again, repeating that she was a midwife now. Kholwa was also a midwife, and Lesedi explained that she worked as an advocate, trying to negotiate settlements to allow women to break arranged marriages, and educate the people in her city so they understood that menstruation huts were not signs of people who wanted to live civilized lives. The other two looked at her incredulously. Lesedi nodded proudly. "If I say silly things, men will always underestimate me. Plus," she half-grinned, "it is a gift to make another laugh."

"Before," Kholwa began, "you said you met Jeremiah. Was this another man? A less dangerous one?"

"No," Alex replied, "It was Jeremiah."

Lesedi gasped, covering her mouth with her hands. "Yet you live."

"Oh," Banhi remarked, "but look at her, on the Between."

Kholwa pointed her finger at Alex, "You are lucky to be alive. That man, he is the bogeyman."

"The devil," Banhi hissed. "All the demons in one. He is the curse, the plague, each of the four horsemen and their steeds."

Lesedi added, "He is the dark center of the universe, Baba Yaga, the breath under the bed."

"Every people have memory of him," Banhi said. "He has walked this soil since the first days. Every people fear him."

Jeremiah didn't seem as bad or as dangerous as they implied. Alex added, "There's Matthew, too. He and Jeremiah don't like one another."

"You mean they are at odds?" Kholwa played with her stone necklace. "Any man who opposes Jeremiah is an ally. Do you fight alongside him?"

Alex shook her head. "He's only ever tried to kill me. He wants what Jeremiah has, and somehow, I'm the key for him to get that. He's not a good person, either."

Banhi nodded thoughtfully. "Child, do not be so quick to assign a person as good or bad. Ask instead, *Are they useful?* Can they serve your purpose? Even an evil man may be useful until a mutual enemy is vanquished."

Alex hadn't thought about Matthew this way before. "That's an interesting thought." She looked to each of them, waiting for one of them to speak next. "I am sorry if this is really ignorant of me, but you all speak such wonderful English."

Banhi's eyes widened. "We're speaking English?"

Reluctantly, Alex replied, "Yes."

Lesedi cackled, "I'm speaking *English*! Listen to me, in *English*. Listen to the way I make the sound of the *English*."

Kholwa rolled her eyes. She pointed at the silver thread emanating from her coin—heart-star as she called it—and said, "We are in the after-life. The world of dreams. On the Between. Here is the Babble. All languages are one. To my ear, your Zulu is remarkable."

"I know a little English," Lesedi offered. "Really. I speak true. Listen," as she began, her voice changed. It became less confident, punctuated by a thick Afrikaans accent, "Would that you can tell me where to find the room of bath?" Her thick, almost impenetrable accent vanished at the end of the sentence. "I also know how to ask to find the library."

Alex tried not to laugh; it was more than she could say in any other language. A shortcoming she suddenly found embarrassing. "Better than I could do if I couldn't speak English."

"Except here you speak every language." Lesedi frowned. "Jeremiah and this Matthew. You must be a brave woman to face two men, to make flame of their Books, and take their magic away."

Alex shrugged. "I never thought of it that way, it's just what happened."

"Happened?" Kholwa blinked. "Child, no one willingly stands before the stampede. Even if they do not know what is coming, the rumbling earth makes even the idiot seek shelter."

"They came after me," Alex said, trying to offer context. "Matthew needed me to have magic and Jeremiah, he," she hesitated. *What does he want?* "Maybe he wanted to see why Matthew was interested in me."

"It is the noblest of fights," Banhi said. "We wish you success from all women."

"You could help," Alex said cautiously.

Kholwa sighed. "In my home, those are the people who need me most. Many women have faced lesser men than Jeremiah and failed, and not for the want of alliances. This is the sad state of the world. Men control the rules and change them once we figure out what they are."

"None of you will help?" Asked Alex.

"We want to," Banhi whispered. "We have all learned from the past. The cost is too great. Always we fight this battle. We think we step forward, but wherever we walk, the mud that holds us is the same."

Alex felt abandoned. She hoped she didn't sound like she was begging. "I need help," Alex told them. "A teacher or a mentor. Someone to show me how magic works."

Lesedi shrugged. "None of us have seen magic. No woman knows magic. Who are we to teach you? All we have are the platitudes, the stories we pass down and tell each generation: Magic is magic. It is emotion."

Banhi agreed. "I think if you control the way you feel then you control the magic. It is physics. What can burn, what can freeze, what can flood, what can dry. You cannot make anything happen that couldn't truly happen."

Lesedi grinned, "Except here." She whispered to Alex, "I love it here so much."

Banhi agreed. "Yes, in the afterlife, in the dreams, everything is possible. Magic is imagination, not emotion." She paused, her face losing her smile. "We are so weak now, there is no magic left in women, so we come here. We dream. Only, we don't know well enough to make it happen. We've forgotten what is possible when we sleep. It is a trick."

"Sadly," Kholwa acknowledged, "these are two worlds. Enchantments are for dreams."

"We should be going," Banhi said to the others. "We need to give Alex our gifts and be on our way."

"Do you have to go so soon?" Alex wondered out loud.

Kholwa explained, "It isn't safe for us to be here, traveling the land of the dead and dreams. But it is tradition. Many travel each night, to give a newborn our blessing. We leave our bodies behind. There are things, bad feelings, bad dreams, which wander this place, seeking out those who have stayed too long or strayed too far." She nodded at Alex, "You have felt one, when your dreams go dark."

Lesedi nodded in agreement. "I travel every few nights, sometimes with Banhi and Kholwa. In life, we have never met, so we only know each other from these dreams. Like we now know you."

Banhi smiled, "We need to give you your gift now, to help you wake from on the Between."

Lesedi scowled at Banhi, "That is but one gift, is it not?"

"But it is mine," Banhi answered. She stepped forward and wrapped her arms around Alex. In Alex's ear, Banhi's gravelly voice soothed into a whisper. "You, child, will wake up. Like a swim up a deep hole, your first breath will be what matters most. Voices are the water that drowns you, so pull yourself out and listen no more."

When Banhi stepped back, Kholwa stepped forward and

placed her hand on Alex's forehead. "You are already too wise for wisdom, too pretty for beauty. We are witches, and what little magic we have is too weak. What can I give you? There is nothing you truly need, I think, so let me wish you… well."

Lesedi took Alex's hands once Kholwa had stepped away. She smiled awkwardly. "I am sorry, Alex. Normally I place my hands onto a baby, and they are much smaller than you. Joy to a child can be found in everything. As we grow older, it is harder to come by, found in fleeting moments and memories. I hope you find joy, child. Your road ahead will not be easy. When you stop, when you choose to look for it, my wish for you is to find joy."

As Lesedi stepped back, she paused and, excusing herself, clasped the charm that hung about Alex's neck. She studied it. "This person must have been important to you."

"Abby is an amazing friend. She made it for me." Alex answered.

Lesedi gestured at the charm, "Not who made it. Who is inside."

"What do you mean?" Alex asked.

Lesedi tapped her finger above the dark center. "Here," she said, "a fragment of someone's heart-star."

Banhi barged forward. "Are you sure?"

Lesedi showed her. Kholwa came closer.

Finally, Banhi explained, "Someone loved you so much, child, they gave you a piece of themselves, so you are never alone." She smiled, her eyes misty. "That is not metaphoric. This is unimaginable love."

Alex placed her hand over the charm. She never thought about it, but it made sense: the dark center was just as dark as the hole in her chest when her coins were flipped. Did Abby give a part of herself and that's why she didn't have magic? Was that her mother? She watched her father give both halves of his coin to Charon, so it couldn't be him. She couldn't wait to ask Abby. *It's not that kind of charm*, she'd said to her. Now Alex understood what she'd meant. She felt stunned by the revelation, filled by the proposition of love.

Lesedi leaned forward and cupped Alex's cheek. "Are you okay, child? That is a revelation burdened by much weight."

"Weight?" Khowla made a face. "What I don't understand is why someone would give such a gift."

Banhi stepped before Khowla, answering her but also addressing Alex. "Someone gave her a piece of themselves. I do not know why one does this, only that it is a sacrifice. They gave up a piece of themselves. The girl is never alone."

Khowla shook her head. "How is it a gift? Is it not like cutting off a finger as a gift?"

Lesedi cackled. "Cutting off a finger? Have you never given someone a lock of your hair?"

Khowla shook her finger. "A lock of hair is no heart-star."

"Neither is a finger," Banhi shook her head. "Khowla, you have an odd sense of gifts." She addressed Alex. "Can you imagine who might give you such a thing?"

Alex paused before answering. The realization that not only couldn't she say—because she couldn't narrow her answer down to a single person—gave her pause. "I don't know. My mother. Abby, my Familiar. I don't know who."

"Familiar?" Lesedi asked as though clarifying which color wire would diffuse the bomb. "You have a Familiar?"

Alex nodded. "She swore her oath before I was born." Alex looked at the charm. "Maybe this is Abby's heart-star. Is this part of the oath?"

"A willing Familiar?" Banhi shivered. "Some people are Familiars against their will. Who are you child that someone willingly be your Familiar *and* give you their heart-star?"

Alex nodded at Lesedi. "This is a lot of weight." She never felt so loved.

Banhi reminded them, "We must go."

Alex wished they could tell her more. They had explained so much, but she wanted more.

The three women said their goodbyes. "See you again, child," Kholwa said as they began following their silver threads into the darker corners of her bedroom, their light fading as one by one, the three women vanished.

Alex looked upon her form sleeping upon the bed. She'd seen herself like this once before, when she returned from Sara. She remembered Sara in the field, her hand extended. *Give it to me. I'll carry the weight for you.* The memory tugged on her heart. As much as she longed for the home that was her own body, she was apprehensive to return. The endless screeching cries in her head were their own agony. They didn't use a hammer, but the voices beat her nearly to death. Had it not been for Sara…. The voices managed to take the sanctuary of her own body and make it a dungeon. *Everyone wants to take something from me. Being afraid won't stop them.*

She thought of everyone at the field. She'd convinced Heather to allow Rose to come. What happened to them? Alex had recollections of the fire, of the tattooed man, but they were fever dreams. Like being trapped in an elevator filling with murky water as it descended into a flooded basement, dread bubbled into Alex's heart. How many from the Book Club were still alive? She worried about them all. Mostly about Heather and Abby, but especially Rose. If anything happened to them, she didn't know if she could forgive herself.

She sat on the bed and slid herself into alignment. She soon felt the difference between having life and being alive. Sensation returned in her limbs, first as pins and needles, as though her limbs were asleep. As her sleeping nerves awoke, Alex experienced a completeness that was absent while she was separated from her body.

She lay back and felt herself fit. She closed her eyes and sighed.

Chapter Sixty-Five

he overwhelming rush of noise was like being honked at by an angry mob of speeding trucks. Alex clasped her head to keep it from exploding. She'd grown accustomed to the silence on the Between. Rejoining her physical form reminded her how bad the whispers had become. Calling them whispers was a matter of habit now. It was more like a hurricane of screams.

Gritting her teeth, the noise was so loud, Alex was unaware of anything else. She took a deep breath. *This is the breath Banhi told me matters most.* She blew it out through pursed lips.

"Okay," she repeated aloud to herself, "time to stop listening. Stop listening." She kept repeating it, focusing on the sound of her own voice, trying to ignore the raging din inside her head.

She stopped speaking to them, about them, she just started saying things at random to keep her voice going. "The sky is blue, trains run on tracks," she even began reciting multiplication tables and repeating Beatles lyrics. Anything that came to mind, she spoke aloud.

"Why won't you stop? Why won't you shut up? I can't do it if you're all fighting with me. I can't do it if…," she let the notion go. She took a moment to release the desperate tension from her voice. "You need to be quiet. I will do this. I will succeed because you won't control me. I will get us through this because you all trust in me."

She kept talking, listening to her own voice, her own words growing louder than the cacophony. "You're afraid. You're afraid of Jeremiah. You're afraid because you have no control. Have faith in me. I found you. I took you from the Books. I've lived your pain. I will keep you safe. I will protect you. I know what happened. To each and every one of you. I am just beginning."

She wasn't sure the whispers were listening. She couldn't hear herself thinking, much less the words she spoke, but she wouldn't stop. "I'm here for a reason. I'm here to stop Jeremiah. I'm here to protect you. I can't do it with you fighting me. I also can't do it alone. I have all of you. You're all with me. Together we can be so much stronger than any one of us ever imagined."

The next breath she took, the next breath she exhaled as words, left her disoriented. The voices hadn't left her but had changed. They were still speaking, but for the first time they were speaking to her. They were listening.

She moved, as a test. The rustle of her hand dragging across the sheets. Her own breathing. Her heart beating. The whispers weren't gone, but they were, for the first time, silent.

Alex opened her eyes. The little available light was excruciating. As she tolerated it, her surroundings resolved. Her bedroom. Beside her, sitting on the floor with her head resting on her arm upon the bed, Abby slept. *How did Abby sleep through that? Didn't that happen here? No. That was all on the Between.*

She touched Abby's head, stroked her short hair, and whispered her friend's name.

Abby awoke with a start. She squinted at Alex, trying to wipe the mirage from her crusty eyes. "Hi."

I hoped she'd be more excited. "Hi Abby."

"And who are you today?"

Alex flinched at the accusation in her tone. "It's me, Abby: Alex."

Abby exploded into motion, bounding onto the bed, grabbing Alex in a bearhug, and rocking her side to side. "You're awake! I knew it wasn't forever. I knew you'd wake up!"

Normally, Alex would resist this sort of overbearing, smothering hug, but the warmth radiating from Abby was so much more than body heat. It was love. It was joy. Abby poured happiness into her.

Abby released her, like a bear realizing it should be gentler with its errant hiker. "Sorry. I didn't mean to shake you like that. Are you okay?"

"I'm fine," Alex laughed.

Abby made a doubtful face. "What's the last thing you remember?"

"I was in the field. We, um…. It's foggy. They were hiding in the sunbeams. We heard them speak with the grass. But then," the recollections came disjointed and twisted, as though seen through someone else's vivid retelling. "They attacked us, didn't they? But then… flashes of things." She examined her clothes, the dirt around her on the bed. "How did I get back here?"

"You don't remember anything?"

"The last thing I remember...," Alex concentrated. Her recollection was like one of Escher's buildings, all folded over upon itself. "I remember the tattooed man. I called him *Book*. That wasn't me. It was like when I was in Sara. Some else's words kept coming out of me. I saw fires. I don't remember starting them. Nothing after that. I was *not* feeling good. The voices, the screams in my head made me sick." She fell quiet. "Sara was there. She was trying to help me. Or am I crazy?"

"You had a seizure at the field. There *were* flaming tornadoes. It was impressive."

"Did I hear that right?"

Abby repeated herself syllable by syllable, "Flay-ming tor-nay-does."

Alex took Abby's silence to ask, "Is everyone okay?" She was afraid to hear the answer.

"About that," Abby cautioned, "should we talk about this later?"

Alex felt sick. What was Abby not telling her? Why hadn't she called to Rose and Heather? Unless.... She beat the thought from her brain. They had to be okay. Had to be. "I need to know." Abby's concern was written in her expression. "I'm better. Seriously. I promise." She swallowed. "Did everyone make it home? Is Rose okay? Please, tell me everything."

"Everything? The field was two days ago."

"I've been unconscious two days?" Alex looked at her clothes. She wouldn't have chosen them. Her head spun with scenarios that involved other people changing her. Rather than feeling concerned about the violation, she found herself wondering about the desperate levels of necessity that resulted in her outfit. Someone went out of their way to find the most ill-fitting clothes she owned.

Abby struggled, "Not really."

"What aren't you telling me?"

Abby retold the story of the field. When she got to the point where Alex collapsed, she studied Alex's face, "Then Rose took George's Book."

"Okay?"

"And she opened it."

"And...?"

"She started reading from it."

"What?"

"I know. Heather was ripping pissed, but Rose started shooting lightning from her fingers and put out the fires. She bought us time to carry you to the car and escape."

"Wow." Alex looked away from Abby. *At least someone did something right. I'm lucky Rose was there.*

"Yeah," Abby agreed, "wow."

"Rose saved the day. Is she okay?"

Abby nodded.

"And I've been unconscious ever since?"

Abby pointed downstairs, "Oh, and we tied George up in the basement."

"George is here?" She didn't mean her tone to sound so excited. She only wanted to speak with him.

"No, not anymore," Abby used her hands to slow Alex from trying to leave the bed. "You let him go."

"When?"

"It wasn't really you."

"But you said—"

"It was Sara."

"What?"

Abby smoothed the bedsheets. She stared intensely at Alex, as though her eyes might leave a mark. She started with, "Looking back, I realize that when you woke up, you'd already been up for some time," and ended with "We thought she killed you, too. Rose took it especially hard." Abby told her everything up until this moment: Rose was gone and Heather—having nearly disowned her in a fit of rage— was now looking for her.

Alex felt bloated by the update. She wasn't sure if she felt sick or just wished she did. She unpacked what Abby just told her: Sara died at Rose's hands. She wanted to dwell on the sensation in her heart and gut. She knew she shouldn't. She'd been out of the mix for two days and now everything was amiss. *Sara wouldn't want me to mourn. Sara was a fighter.* The more she tried to think past the pain, the more her heart ached. She had wondered what happened to Sara and learned Sara was here and gone in the same breath. She had been a whisper in her head all that time. Although she'd been one of thousands, the void in Alex's chest was cavernous.

Alex considered what the three witches told her: not to

consider someone—or in this case something—good or bad, only useful. *Having a second witch with magic qualifies as useful.* "Where's Heather now? She should know I'm back."

"She's in her room. She's dream-walking, to find Rose."

"I could help."

Abby stammered. Her face twisted each time the words parked on her tongue, refusing to be moved.

Finally, Alex said, "Maybe I should sit this one out."

Abby agreed. "At least until we're sure you're better. Heather and Rose have some fence-mending. It got bad. Rose threatened to, well, I don't know what's going on in Rose's head, but she dared us to stop her. She had the Book open."

"She thought she'd killed me. She was probably scared and angry and confused." Alex knew how hurting George made her feel. *What's going on in Rose's mind? She took a life; that's got to mess her up. Was she acting under the influence of the Book?* She didn't want to accept that Rose was capable of murder. Her thoughts shifted to Sara. What had been inside her was and wasn't Sara: it was the part of her that was her magic, as Banhi said, like a hologram, a part but with information of the whole. *I thought Sara was dead. Why does knowing she is hurt so much more?*

It felt disrespectful, but Alex wondered what happened to Sara's magic. Did it die with her? There wasn't time to dwell on that now. How long before Jeremiah returned? Matthew? She had to get ready. She'd have time to grieve when this was over. Then, she'd cry for everyone she'd lost. She said to Abby, "Anything else I should know? I'm starving."

Abby laughed. "That's what Heather said you'd say." Abby continued after they laughed, "I think we should take it slow, until we know you're truly well."

"There is a lot I need to do," Alex brushed dirt off the sheets. "While I was... dead, I dreamt I was visited by three wise women: three witches. They thought I was a baby. That I was born when my coin was flipped."

"Three witches?"

"It sounds crazy. They were like real fairy godmothers, coming to give a newborn their blessings. They said I was *on the Between*, not alive, not dead. They guided me back."

"You dreamed this? Or *dreamed* it?" She stretched the second utterance.

"I traveled on my thread." Finally having a coin was a thrill. Doing something with it…. She half wished there was time to experiment with astral projection and dream walking.

Abby nodded. "Oh. Got it."

"I am better, Abby. Better than ever."

"You think you are," Abby cautioned, "but Sara said that all the women inside you, all those voices, they're killing you."

Hearing it put so bluntly, Alex was beginning to understand how close she'd come to not returning. It was easy to be glib and dismiss it, but understanding she nearly died weighed heavy on her. The experiences these women had were so horrible, and she thought collecting them was akin to saving them. They needed to know she knew they were there. They needed to know she would protect them. *With my life.* "We don't have to worry about them anymore." Alex reflected, "The three witches taught me what I needed to do. They're still in there like a rowdy party, but it's different. We have an understanding now."

"I'd still feel better if you took it slow. Voices or no voices."

Alex looked down, "I understand, but—"

"Each step, we all trusted that you were ready," Abby interrupted, "and each time, something happened to you. I can't go through that again."

"I was always there."

"I mean in the field. You had a seizure. You were burning up. You were dying."

"I understand, Abby. You need to see for yourself that I'm better."

"I need convincing."

Alex sat upright, "I get it. You need action."

Abby hesitated, "Don't push it."

"Could we at least eat?"

Abby guffawed and accompanied Alex towards the ladder like she might fall over and shatter. She wanted to tell Abby to give her some space but began to realize Abby did this as much for her as herself.

Heather's door was closed. Alex wouldn't disturb her until she had found Rose.

In the kitchen, Alex took bowls and mugs from the cabinets

for coffee and oatmeal. Outside, the sun was beginning the day.

About an hour later, when they finished nursing their second and third cups of coffee, Alex stood to clean up. Abby tried to take control of the process when they heard Heather's bedroom door open. "We're down here," Alex shouted.

Heather screamed and buzzed down the steps, missing a few as she skidded down on her heels. She turned into the kitchen and froze, her eyes glossy with tears. A smile slowly drew across her face and showed no signs of stopping until she was practically grimacing. "Oh, Alex," she mouthed as she raced to give her niece a crushing hug.

"I can't believe you're up and about." Heather said to Abby, "She's okay being up?" Abby half-nodded, half-shrugged. "I am so relieved." To Alex, she said, "It's so good to have you back." To Abby she asked, "It is our Alex, right?"

"I'm fine, Aunt Heather. And it is me," Alex told her.

They traded questions and answers until Heather was satisfied that Alex was actually Alex and well.

Abby interrupted a moment of silence. "How'd it go, Heather? You find Rose? She okay?"

Heather nodded. "She went right to... her dream-house."

"Was she still angry with you?" Alex asked.

Heather looked at Alex with a smile. When she looked at Abby, the expression evaporated. Twice she did this before telling Abby, "I wish I paid more attention in college psych. She was so conflicted and grief-stricken she literally walled herself into a bedroom. I had to claw her out. She's waiting. I told her we will look for Billy. Together." As she spoke, her tone shifted. Alex wasn't sure what that shift intoned; it was almost as though she doubted the endeavors' success. Heather pointed at Alex, "Except you're better. Maybe Rose should come home. Maybe seeing you is more important for her right now."

Alex didn't need to think it over. "That's not a good idea."

Heather and Abby looked at her with surprise.

Alex continued, "Aunt Heather, I was supposed to be the one to save the day. You told me I was the only one who could do this. I mean, everyone supported me and all I did was fail."

Heather started to say, "I wouldn't say fail—"

"No, Aunt Heather," Alex interrupted, "I failed. Every time.

Then Rose does the one thing she's been told never to do, and the tide turns. She's able to do the things I was supposed to." She watched for Heather's reaction. "What does bringing me into things now say to Rose?"

"We need your help." Heather answered.

"Do you? Alex asked. "When you tell Rose I'm fine but you're going with her, you're telling her you have as much faith in her as you ever had in me. If you believed I could do it alone, why won't you believe in her?"

Heather looked slapped. "I never thought of it like that."

"You had a Book, Aunt Heather," Alex explained. "You didn't think you could use it any other way. When I look at Books, I burn them up. Maybe not all women can read them. Maybe only Rose."

Abby interjected, "Peter said women can't read Books. Not shouldn't: Can't"

Heather defended, "Peter gave me instructions. You saw; he covered every page. He told me never to look at the first shape of each spell."

"Sounds to me more like *they don't want us to know we can.*" Alex remembered how she felt like she was falling into the symbols in Sara's Book. "I can't imagine what it was like for Rose. How scary it must have been picking up that Book. Not knowing what would happen. "She has magic now. Don't take that away from her; not ever."

Heather nodded sheepishly. "I can tell her you're okay? I suspect it'll make her feel better to know she didn't kill you."

"That's a good idea." She gestured at Abby, "Abby and I need to do something. Afterwards, we'll connect with you and Rose. Hopefully you'll have a lead on Billy."

Abby looked concerned. "You sure that's a good idea?"

"What?" Alex asked.

Abby stated, "Rose."

"We're both witches. Just like I had the voices causing me problems, she has the Book. I know from the voices Rose gets her magic from the woman in the Book. I can't say it won't have an agenda or try to influence her. Look what the voices did to me. Now's not the time to take her glory or her Book." Alex took a moment. "I've had this power for almost a week, and today is the first time I can hear my own thoughts. It took almost dying to learn what they're about.

The Books are alive. They're the most powerful part of the woman. It wants to keep living." She paused. "Do you know where to find Rose?"

Heather nodded. "She told me to meet her by Sara's house; the old foundation."

"She has good memories of that place." Alex reminisced.

"At least someone has good memories of that place," Abby joked. "I got killed there. Twice."

"You're never going to let that go, are you?" Heather said laughing.

Abby mocked indignation, "I should let go your poisoning me? That stuff tasted disgusting."

Heather couldn't find the humor Abby was trying to inject into the conversation. Alex saw the growing awkwardness. "Get to Rose. Until we know what that Book will or won't do to her, pay attention to everything she says." Alex could hear Sara's warning, *Don't lose yourself to me.*

Heather nodded like she had no choice but to agree.

Alex hugged Heather. "Be safe, Aunt Heather. Trust in Rose. We'll see you soon."

Heather sighed obviously. "You don't know how grateful I am that you're okay." She smiled. "If I didn't know you better, I'd say you sound like you have a plan."

Alex nodded and looked at Abby. "I'm making it up as I go. Sara once said that death and dreams aren't so different. Before I can move forward, I need to go back to the beginning. I think none of us were told the full truth. I intend to find out what the truth is." She turned to Heather, "We're going to my old house. It's time I had a talk with my mom."

Chapter Sixty-Six

An hour earlier, they dropped Heather at the side of the road near the path to Sara's house. Alex could tell that leaving Heather left Abby apprehensive. "Heather is right," Alex told her as they watched Heather disappear into the woods. "If Rose saw me, there's no telling how she might react." Abby frowned, not in agreement.

For the remainder of the drive, Alex tried to find the right words to ask about her charm: *Is there a reason you kept who this is a secret?*

"Abby, can I ask you something?"

Abby replied, "You don't need permission to ask a question. Sort of defeats the purpose."

Alex nodded with exaggeration. "I see your point."

When Alex didn't continue, Abby asked, "What's up?"

Alex held the glass charm out from her neck, stumbling on the words to jumpstart the question when Abby interrupted, "That's Peter. That's your dad in there."

"My dad?"

Abby couldn't resist, "Peter *is* your father's name."

The truth out, Abby's posture relaxed.

Alex's dozen questions evaporated. All she could do was hold the charm. She held it out as far as the delicate silver chain allowed. She stared at the small, black center. *That's my dad? He saved a piece of himself to give me?* The sacrifice overwhelmed her. She had to remind herself to breathe again. *It was more important to him that I have this, than for him to live.* All her doubts about her father's loyalty evaporated. She couldn't take her eyes off the dark center, as pure and black as her coin—her heart-star—before her mother flipped them. *Did Mom know? Did she give up their life together for me to have this?* Alex's eyes welled; she never felt so loved before.

Abby spoke quietly, almost apologetically, "I should have told you, but I didn't know how. Peter told me never to tell you. I swore. Until you asked, I just…, I wanted to…."

Alex took several attempts to evict the words from her mouth.

"When... did he give it to you?"

"When he visited Sara."

"Abby, I saw. I *was* Sara. He never gave you anything. By the time you, um, you know, revived, he was gone. How did he give you anything? When?"

"I had no idea what to expect. I wasn't sure at first, this small, dark little thing. He told me he was going to try to leave you something. When I discovered it in my pocket after I came to, I put the pieces together, so to speak."

"He could have lived. Wasn't this little piece enough?"

Abby shook her head, tears falling from her eyes. "I don't know. He said I'd find it and I found it. It wasn't my place to ask."

Alex recalled the moment her father knelt at Abby's side. She thought she saw him slip something into her pocket. *He did it right in front of me.*

"For the longest time, I resented having to keep it. It's so small and insignificant. I kept track of it all this time. You know how easy it is to misplace something so tiny?"

Alex tried to imagine what it would have been like keeping tabs on such an insignificant bauble for nearly nineteen years. *How often did she think about it? Did she always keep it in its special container by the kiln? I would have lost it at least once a week. Was seeing it every day a constant reminder of losing her best friend?* She stared in awe of Abby's loyalty.

"Don't get me wrong, Alex," Abby voice was moist with tears. "I'm not stupid. I knew that maybe if I gave it back to him, maybe he'd be normal again. It's such a tiny piece, but maybe that's all you need: just a tiny sliver of your coin. He seemed so valiant, talking about sacrifice before it happened. It didn't seem like much when he told me, like, *I'm going to give you this thing*, and then I have it and he's gone and if I give it to him and that's not what he wanted there was no undoing that. He worked so hard for this. He wasn't sure he could, so I was excited at first; you know, *wow, he did it*, but once I realized the cost, well, he asked too much of me."

Alex nodded somberly; both their faces wet with tears. "I'm sorry, Abby." Abby wiped her face with the back of her hand, snorting. Alex struggled to grasp how difficult being entrusted to this insignificant thing of extreme magnitude was for Abby.

"You have it now." Abby rubbed Alex's shoulder. "He was

my best friend. I held onto the one thing that maybe could have saved him because he said to. Because I had one solemn duty. Because it was more important you have it than he did. It was horrible, every time I went over to your house and saw him. Holly once confessed to me she wished he could be normal again. I pretended I didn't know. I hated myself for lying to her, and I hated him for making me have to."

"Why did he want me to have it? What's so important?"

"I wish I knew," Abby sobbed. "I've been asking myself that for nineteen years."

"Abby?"

Abby pouted, "What?"

Alex reached across the front seat and rested her hand on Abby's arm. "No one gives you enough credit."

"What do you mean?"

"You're the best of all of us."

"Stop it."

"No Abby. Where would I be without you?"

Abby shrugged. "Blissfully unaware of all of this."

"And what good would that do?"

Abby looked away. She slowed the truck and pulled off the road. "Alex, I've seen how the past few days has damaged you. Your seizure, Sara, your burns from Matthew trying to kill you—"

Alex interrupted, "He wasn't exactly trying to kill me, but I get your point."

"That's a messed-up way to see if someone has magic."

Alex shrugged. "It worked."

"What I'm trying to say, Alex," Abby's raised voice prevented interruption, "is that I signed on to this. I thought I knew what I was getting myself into. My life for yours. Protect and serve you."

"Abby, I don't want you to feel that—"

Abby interrupted, "All I do is drive you around and feed you. If I were a real Familiar, I mean, doing my duty properly, this would all be easier for you. You've suffered so much."

Alex looked out the front windshield. She watched the trees that lined the road, the leaves barely moving in the still air. Almost absently, she said, "It has been mostly awful. Experiencing Sara's life, what those men—what Matthew—did to her. What he did to me. Every time I take a Book; the pain." She sighed. "I feel like such a baby complaining about someone else's torment. They died from it.

What am I complaining about?"

Abby tried to console her, but Alex interrupted her attempt. "Losing Billy, Marta, Sara, almost Rose. When does the cost get too high? It's easy to think I'm in too deep to turn back, but what if I'm just getting started?" She turned to Abby. "These men are so certain they're right, they almost convinced me, like, enough to doubt what I was thinking and feeling. They got me second-guessing myself. What they did to me, though, is a drop in a drop in a drop in the ocean. There are hundreds of thousands of Books, millions. If I give up, it'll be my fault when another Book's made and every one after that. It has to end, Abby. It must fucking end. That's what we're doing. Isn't it? Making sure no one experiences this pain again? How could this be easy? It can't be. It shouldn't be. None of us know what we've really signed on for, only the danger of giving up."

"It shouldn't be easy," Abby breathed. "It just shouldn't be so hard. I carried that piece of your father's coin for almost twenty years. I kept it from his wife and his sister—my best friend—for your whole life." She rubbed her watery eyes. "What if he was wrong? Or w-what if he was testing me? What if I was supposed to give it back and I failed?"

Alex stared into her lap. "Best friends don't test each other. What he made you do was harder than anything I've ever had to do."

Abby had nothing more to add. She fought back her tears and wiped her face. She snorted and wiped her nose with her wrist and tried to straighten herself out. Putting the truck back into drive, she muttered, "We've already wasted enough time."

"Abby? Please, listen to me?"

Abby raised an eyebrow. She would not speak any more.

"Thank you. You were asked to do impossible things, and you'll probably be asked to keep doing them. You never ask why. You never say no; not to me." She held out the charm. "Because of you, I have this. My father. Right here, always with me. I can't imagine how that hurt you. But because of you, I know how much he loved me." She shook the charm to draw attention to it. It felt heavier knowing what it really was. "He loved me this much, Abby, this much."

Chapter Sixty-Seven

he fluttering of queasy butterflies arrived at the same time the landmarks leading to her parent's house became familiar. The houses, the trees and shrubs had matured. There were places along the road, little niches, where she remembered playing as a child, finding special pebbles or floating paper boats, places she'd ride her bicycle, places as unique as the moments their sight helped recall. *Was that me?* Each memory seemed so long ago; recollections of a carefree girl escaping her house to be outside and away from her parents. *Not my parents: my father.* The thought that she wanted so much to be away from him buried her alive in guilt.

Alex held her charm, ashamed for things she had and hadn't done. As a child, she never saw her father as a living being. She wished she could whisper to the small black spot, like a prayer, that he might hear. She'd unburden her heart and he'd know she was so sorry for being a stupid kid. Her actions were nothing but selfish, unempathetic, juvenile curiosity, but some of the things she did—because he couldn't talk back—seemed in retrospect to be marinated with malice.

This house held many memories for Alex. Most were good, like holidays and family moments. But it didn't matter how many wonderful moments she shared with her mother: autumn days collecting colorful leaves or winters drinking hot cocoa after shoveling out and building snow-forts. The darkness Matthew brought to the house overshadowed them all.

Recalling pleasant memories of that house didn't dilute her growing anxiety. It was her home, at least it was, once. She was there—twice—to watch her parents' lives end. She fled; her life threatened. She left everyone behind. Abandoned Charissa. The past still echoed there. She anticipated stepping inside the house and being bombarded by those echoes, tormented by them. Alex hoped that she could also bring with her all the memories that made it a home. She wondered which possessed the greatest power.

Several times Alex looked over at Abby, wondering how her experiences were playing in her head. Abby was unreadable, focused on the road, hands tight on the wheel. *Abby isn't excited about coming here either. What memories are Abby dragging along?* She reasoned if Abby wasn't sharing, this was a question better left unasked.

She wished the trip was longer, that Abby would take the least direct route. It felt like they were approaching a large hole—being drawn to it—and would inevitably fall in.

Four years ago; also, four days. Time rattled Alex's head like loose screws. Four days ago, she witnessed her parents' murders four years earlier. Saw the version of herself from four years ago. However fresh the memory seemed, she knew its taste was off.

She wondered what she'd encounter when she arrived. Did another family move in? If not, why? Did the house possess recollections of zombies and witches and spells that made people explode to dust? Was it the taint of death? *Maybe I'll get there and find another family has moved in and I'll explain that I used to live here and maybe they'll say there was always a draft they couldn't seal and I'll know it wasn't a draft.*

Abby turned like she was ditching the truck. Alex screamed at Abby, preparing for impact as saplings and shrubs clawed the sides and undercarriage of the vehicle, but then the house appeared at the end of an overgrown gravel driveway.

Alex's chest tightened. Memory and fantasy were frequent bedfellows until proof peeled back the covers. There it was. Evidence her memories were real. It was exactly as she remembered, yet not at all. Although she'd seen it just days ago, the truth of that time—four years—had done the house no courtesy. Paint curled from the wood clapboard siding, cracked windowpanes fell from the frames. Rot crept through the lower boards and the eves and the soffits and the fascia. It was as though the corruption imprisoned within the house was weeping through to the exterior. Weeds and vines climbed the house, intent on strangulation. What once was her safe place now appeared like a wounded animal in the final moments of struggle. Soon it would collapse, and nature would consume whatever remained.

Abby pulled onto the overgrown lawn and drove right up to the porch: a sign of a welcome guest. When Alex was a child, Abby visited frequently. When she became a teenager, she saw Abby with increasing infrequency. Alex didn't know why Abby stopped coming. She thought to ask but what she saw in Abby's expression numbed her tongue. Abby drove within inches of the porch. Alex felt like she was coming home: *7756672 County Road B, drive right up to the house.*

On the porch, the storm door hung to one side; the front door open. Alex had not passed this way when she last left this house. In fact, she didn't use any door the last two times she left. *Is there some silly superstition or rule I should know about re-entering a house I haven't actually left?*

Abby put her truck into park. Her eyes on the house, she said to Alex, "I'll wait here." Alex wasn't sure if Abby made a statement or asked a question.

This house was not abandoned by a family packing their belongings and stealing away. Inside, she expected to see dishes in the dishrack from the breakfast she'd made each of her parents: The last meal they'd eat. Time was frozen inside. Yet it wasn't. Wildlife would have exploited the pantry. Food would have rotted away. The nerves in her skin squirmed uncomfortably. Time hadn't aged her memory the way it had aged the house. Everything that happened here four years ago happened so recently—for her—that the scab hadn't yet set on the oozing memory. "I'd prefer if you came with me. The last two times I was here, Matthew murdered my parents."

Abby's eyes welled with tears. "Okay," she mumbled. "That's why I thought I should wait outside."

Alex reached across the car. "I need you with me, Abby. My mom, Holly," she tried to make a little light of the situation, "knew you too."

Abby nodded and opened her door. "You'll tell me if you need me to die?"

Alex was unsure if Abby meant it as a joke. "You don't need to die." Her reply possessed the intended sarcasm.

Alex opened her door, the creaking called out unnecessarily in this solemn, quiet place.

They walked to the porch and navigated the rotting decking, the piles of leaves from four autumns slowly decaying against the house. Stickers around the door and on windows warned of overdue taxes and leans against the property. They were sun bleached and ravaged by the elements: the abandoned house remained unclaimed and unwanted.

Alex pushed the front door wider, shoving aside piles of leaves and detritus that the years blew in. She and Abby crossed the threshold.

She'd stood here just days ago with her mother. Yet that experience—and the room it occurred in—didn't match what she saw. It was like the house called her a liar. Alex felt like she stood in two rooms. The room that was and the room that is. Her recollection of the living room, the life that was there, and then the room with piles of leaves and animal fur and feathers and fecal matter. It smelled sweetly pungent of rot. Upended pieces of furniture looked swamped from a tide of leaves. Someone will always right an upended chair—if someone is there. Dust chalked the furniture in their locations, evidencing a strange fission between the crisis that battered them and then the years they slumbered in these new situations.

Alex walked to the stairs. Her feet careful as she stepped on leaves in case something was nesting in them. Dust-choked light filtered through filth-clouded windows. Their intrusion awoke insects that now flew in frenzied circles. The dust was thick enough to engrave.

Climbing the staircase, in spite of her best efforts, Alex's feet played the treads. Every movement brought forth a creak or a groan, like the stairs offered only uncertainty in their ability to support her weight. With each step she pushed through her desire to abandon this quest. Her memory haunted this place. Made her fear discovering she abandoned her parents too soon. She would have known any ghosts yet lingering here. At the top of the stairs, at the end of the hall, was her room. And in that room, she dreaded what she was about to discover. She knew too well what she'd left behind.

Abby found the first step spongy. "Maybe I should wait here."

Statement or question? Alex pounded her foot on a step. The board held but its crack reverberated through the quiet house. "It'll hold. Come with me." Alex feared being alone with whatever remained in her bedroom. Perhaps this was why Abby desired to remain behind. Alex worried her anxiety made her selfish.

At the top of the stairs, Alex peered into her parent's bedroom. She had been the last person to occupy this space—that she was aware of. At the end of the hall, a hole gaped in the wall opposite her bedroom, below the small window, where the wallboard was shattered. Matthew had been thrown here; a result of his spell gone wrong as Alex pulled him out of her father. *Was he trying to obliterate me, or did I somehow alter the spell?* Given what she thought she knew of Matthew, Alex couldn't be sure.

The door to her bedroom leaned precariously, torn from its hinges years earlier. A solitary pair of sneakers stood just inside the doorway, a coating of dust and filth made them one with the floor. Alex stared; the moment her father stood in them and then didn't, replayed in her vision like a transparent overlay. She turned back to Abby. This was one relic she would never explain. *Abby will recognize the shoes and know.* Saying the words out loud, *This is where my father turned to dust*, felt cruel and unnecessary. Sneakers aside, the room was vacant. She entered. Following, Abby gave them a wide berth. *She knows exactly what happened.*

Her bedroom felt smaller than even her most recent recollection. She considered how many people occupied it at once and wondered if there was some way the space could have shrunk. She didn't want to replay the events over in her mind but found herself trying to make sense of the movement and action.

She stood before her bed. Charissa was curled in the corner, a huddled mass of fright, if only in Alex's memory. She hadn't given sufficient thought to what became of the only other witness to that night. Guilt crept into her skin. *Is Charissa alive?* She wondered if somewhere in the Library there was a Book with her name on the spine. *Maybe Matthew and George took her.* Her mind betrayed her with visions of Matthew feeding on Marta's coin, only it was Charissa's. Perhaps, Alex hoped, Charissa awoke alone and stunned and frightened and dazed—then returned home. Maybe after years of therapy she came to believe her childhood trauma was little more than a bad dream from the time when her friend and friend's family all went missing. Alex preferred this story. There was no police tape or evidence to disprove that Charissa never left this place of her own accord. *Maybe I'll never know. Perhaps that's the better truth for me.*

The bed's white satin comforter was time-turned dull yellow. The room felt alien: the books, the clothes, the belongings, all felt like artifacts from another life. Her wounded dresser and the clothes spilling from it were covered in dust, muting the vibrant colors of blouses that once brought her joy.

She stood in her own room, in what had been her own private and personal space and felt an interloper. Her fourteen-year-old self, frozen in time: a window to whom she was once. To her eighteen-year-old self, those four years felt an eternity. This was a girl's room: a teenager clinging to childhood. Had Alex no other purpose here, she might have opened a few drawers to conduct an archeological examination of her younger self, to learn who that girl might have been. Her clothes, her books, her toys, her dreams, everything that had been her remained here, abandoned when she fled. She became someone new that day.

"This room doesn't feel like you," Abby broke the silence. "Not anymore, anyway."

"It was my mom's ideal of me."

Abby nodded. She looked somber, as though aware she was trespassing on hallowed ground, walking on an unmarked grave.

Alex paused. Her mother died in this room. Alex saw her in memory, collapsing to the ground and standing, the silver thread connecting her two forms. Yet, no bodies—or evidence of them— remained here. The room disturbed her, but not just for that. The objects that had been moved and broken seemed possessed of some kinetic energy, awaiting the return of the mover or breaker. These objects, like the room, seemed weighed by disappointment at being abandoned for so long. Yet they failed to recognize she had returned.

Alex pointed to the bed. "I was sitting here. My friend, Charissa, was here," she pointed. "Matthew came up the stairs, and he killed my mom right there." She pointed to the middle of the room, a foot or two from the bed. It felt odd to say the words, like they made the event banal.

Abby looked to where Alex was now pointing. Evidence of scorched flooring peeked from beneath the dust, marking where her mother fell. Her gaze drifted back to the hallway and the destroyed wallboard.

"He broke his neck there. Matthew." Alex mimicked his stance, lowering her head until it jutted from between her shoulders.

Abby's gaze returned to the shoes, like she saw a ghost standing in them.

Alex took a preparatory breath. "Matthew was inside him. What would you call it? Possessing him? For a minute, I thought my father was trying to kill me."

Abby broke her venerable gaze. She didn't need to speak what was in her eyes: *Your father could never hurt you.*

"I know," Alex answered the unspoken.

Abby looked about her feet. She made an expression at her footprints in the dust. She seemed aware what it was, and it was everywhere. Abby groaned.

Part of Alex wanted to leave this room as she found it, but she found it a tomb. She took the filthy comforter and peeled it from the bed, revealing clean, white sheets. They smelled of must and moisture and time. Alex sat. In one action, she made the tomb hers again.

She motioned for Abby to sit next to her.

Abby sat, "What now?"

Alex pointed at the wall to her right. "Last time, this wall was mist. I went through, twice. Once to Heather. The other, back to Picnic Rock." She paused in thought. "You know, Billy called it Sacrifice Stone."

"I heard that before. It goes way back."

Alex made a face, "I never expected to be the one sacrificed on it."

Abby didn't respond. Her expression fell like Alex's joke brought her shame.

Alex motioned at the spot where she had last seen Charissa. She said to no one, "I wish I knew what happened to her."

"Charissa?"

Alex's heart thudded. Abby's awkward silence suggested a hesitance. "What is it, Abby?"

"Charissa's fine."

Although she remained seated, Alex nearly jumped off the bed. "How do you know?"

"Pat, the farmer I rent from?"

"You mentioned Pat. I wasn't sure if Pat was a Patrick or a Patricia."

Abby laughed. "The farm has been in *her* family for generations. When I was looking for a place, your mom introduced us."

"My mom knew Pat, too?"

"Through her brother."

"My Uncle Steven? What are you trying to tell me, Abby?"

"Steven, Pat…, Charissa."

Alex felt her breath sucked away.

"You didn't know?"

She shook her head.

"Wasn't her last name the same as your mom's maiden name; Tylerson?"

Alex had to remind herself to breathe. Her mother never told her. Charissa just showed up one day. *Why didn't she tell me?* "My mom went out food-shopping and brought Charissa home. I pictured Charissa sitting with the lettuce and my mom deciding to buy me a friend."

Abby guffawed. The humor abandoned her expression and she blurted out, "I got here not long after…, you know. I found Charissa. She was shaken up, really freaked out. She didn't understand what happened. I brought her home."

"I've wondered about her so much. Why didn't you ever tell me?"

"You couldn't know magic. You were convinced your parents died in a car accident. What was I going to tell you?"

Alex had nothing to say. Charissa, the girl with the phone who did all the things she wasn't allowed to do was her cousin. Finally, it made some sense why she was allowed to be friends with *this* one girl.

"You wanna meet her?"

"Now?"

Abby bit back her grin, "No. When we get back to my place."

"Wait, Charissa, my cousin, has been living on your farm all this time?"

"Technically I live on her farm, but yeah."

"And you never told me because…?"

Abby shrugged. "You never asked. Steven wanted her kept safe. But it was important to him that you two know one another. She didn't know who you were, either."

"Does she now?"

"No idea you are cousins. You're the girl whose family disappeared. I don't know what Steven told her, but I don't think she remembers."

Alex looked around the room as though Charissa might have left her shadow. Her cousin? Her mother's twin's daughter. "Does she have a brother?"

"No."

"Did Steven, you know," Alex motioned with her hands over her waist.

"No, no twin. They didn't have a backup plan. At least if they did, Charissa wasn't it."

Alex took a deep, long breath. "Crap. I never thought I'd see her again. I figured Matthew and company took her."

Abby looked to the door. "I took care of things."

Alex realized Abby wasn't just talking about Charissa. She looked at the floor. She hadn't the heart to ask a question she didn't want the answer to. She'd rather pretend the bodies disappeared on their own.

"Let's not get distracted," Abby looked around the room. "You came here with a purpose."

She doesn't like being here. One realization begot others. *Abby carried my mom out of here, herself. All this place reminds her of is death.* Alex was tempted to ask where her mother was buried.

"What's next?"

Alex couldn't explain how she was so sure. "Summoning my mother."

Abby whispered, "Tell me what you need me to do."

"I told you, no more dying."

"Dying is how I usually help at this stage."

Alex gave her a reassuring hug. "You didn't die to summon Sara," Alex explained. "My mom sort of explained that the time loops could only be triggered by death. That's how I got back here from Picnic Rock."

Abby's expression suggested she hadn't known why she had to die.

"I need you to protect me while I visit my mother."

Abby nodded, suddenly alive, revitalized by purpose.

Alex felt she owed Abby an explanation as to how she knew what she was doing. "I wish I could explain what I'm doing here so it makes sense. Magic isn't just a part of me. When it's put in a Book, it's removed from the world: It's a finite resource. When I take those spells, I returned them to the world. The spell becomes a part of me and a part of everything else. I think it's the connection between the two that somehow makes it all work."

Abby half-nodded, raising a perplexed eyebrow.

At least she's honest when she doesn't understand. "It's also the whispers," Alex added.

"I thought you didn't hear them anymore."

"It's less them telling me and more how we interact. It's like a gut feeling; intuition. Like I tap into, I guess, whatever they knew."

With a grin, Abby replied, "Sounds like bullshit to me."

Alex laughed. Almost to herself, she replied, "May very well be, until proven otherwise. I don't have much of a track record." After a moment's silence, she added, "I guess it's time to try."

Abby looked at her with no small surprise. "Try? We came all this way for try?"

"There's a lot I'm doing for the first time." Alex stood but motioned for Abby to remain seated. She needed to bring the mist. She needed to find her mother. She closed her eyes.

Alex pictured Holly's face in her mind. The last time she saw her mother—days or years ago—was in this room: simultaneous moments separated only by her sense of time. She thought about their final conversation, her mother flipping her coin and telling her about her magic. Alex felt the chasm open, the empty feeling of longing. She missed Holly tremendously. She wanted desperately to see her mother one more time.

Abby gasped, "You're doing it."

Alex opened her eyes. The wall before her roiled with mist; a thick, dark gray undulating fog: the result when two places are brought together. In this case, the real world and the dream realm. Alex's coin glowed. The bright light was still such a novelty, she couldn't help but grin. She turned to Abby, "Be right back."

Alex stepped into the mist, leaving Abby to guard Alex's catatonic form, the silver thread extending from her chest disappearing into the mist.

Chapter Sixty-Eight

lex remembered her lessons from Sara; movement was an illusion. *Does that mean I create the distance in my head?*

Regardless of how that distance was governed, it had to be traversed. *If I knew where to find her, would it be shorter?* She walked.

After a few moments, an idea danced through her head. No one was here to judge her if she failed. She'd done this several times in dreams, and while she never accomplished it with intention, it seemed worth the attempt.

Alex leaned forward, allowing her weight to tip her balance. Leaning more until she could no longer maintain herself vertically, her arms pinwheeled as she lost her balance. Her body shuddered in preparation of impact. Her downward momentum translated into forward motion. She moved slowly forward, not touching the ground: it was more like missing the ground than actual flight. She arched back and extended her arms as poor airfoils, as she flew awkwardly higher.

Alex squealed with glee; she'd never intentionally flown in dreams. Her body existed in a state of constant panic, as though it kept reaching for and missing something solid to lean upon. She wobbled in the air as her limbs kept instinctually trying to connect with the ground. She soared, moving faster and faster, gaining confidence the longer she didn't crash and die.

She was in the dream space; on the Between. Wasn't anything possible here? The ground rushed past her. Arching her back, she carried herself higher. She looked down on the landscape whizzing past. Her stomach nearly dropped at the distance, treetops far below her. Looking into the sky gave her a similar fright. She kept her eyes on the horizon, trying her hardest to ignore the way her body felt in constant freefall. She cautiously soared, uncertain when flight might fail her.

Her heart pounded. The height was frightening, the speed terrifying, but the action of flight was spectacularly exhilarating. What held her up? However she tenuously hung in the air, concern never leaving her that some invisible support might snap and cause her to fall.

Taking rapid but short glances down, she sought familiar landmarks: streets and houses she knew. She was all too aware that in dreams, memories weren't recollections but projections. *Maybe if I think about my house hard enough, I'll think it into being and get there sooner.*

Soon, she spied a house that possessed enough familiarity to the house where she left her body. They weren't identical: rooflines and windows and dimensions were dissimilar enough to create doubt, and yet, Alex was certain this was her house. *It's amazing how quick we believe things in dreams.*

She kept her eyes on the house and flew closer. She couldn't get used to the sensation. She felt her weight in the way she moved through the air. Her arms trembled, trying to find the breeze that was keeping her aloft as she swooped lower. The closer her proximity to the ground, the faster everything whizzed by. She twisted around trees, circling over the vast yard, over the driveway and somehow managed to navigate a loop. Although she couldn't feel it holding her aloft, wind blew in her face, messing her hair. She wished she could fly in wakefulness. She felt light and powerful. She swooped down to the lawn, putting her feet to the ground. Unable to slow, she crashed in a rolling tumble onto the grass.

She climbed to her feet, dusting herself off. She cackled. *That was amazing. That was, wow.* Words failed her, earthbound again. Even if all sensation here was an illusion, there was ground beneath her feet. She did her best to tuck her grin away and walk to the front door.

Standing inside the storm door, her mother smiled. "That was quite an entrance. It's good to see you, Alexandrea."

Alex approached the door. "It's good to see you, too, Mom." Seeing her mother, however, did little to quell the raw vacancy in her heart. This felt too temporary to salve that wound.

Alex reached to open the door, unsure why her mother hadn't. However, Holly gripped it closed.

"Alexandrea, you shouldn't have come."

Alex felt like she'd been slapped. "Mom, I had to."

"They'd expect you to do something like this. It's too dangerous for you to be here."

"I know."

"You know? Then why?" Holly looked pitying on her daughter. "You should be hiding, not going to the most obvious place."

"Where can I hide?" Alex asked. She tapped her coin. "They can find me now."

Holly looked at her with a mark of disappointment. "You never turned them back?" Holly motioned with her hands as though holding the coins, separating them, then reversing them.

"I didn't know that was possible." Alex bit her lip. "I never thought to even try." Alex felt the weight of her mother's disappointment. It tugged on all the raw spots in her chest. It was so obvious now. How could she *not* think to turn them back?

"It makes you invisible to them," she said. "But prevents you from having magic."

"Then why would I?"

"To hide, Alexandrea."

"Hide? Why?"

Holly gave her that look again: disappointment. She and Peter thrust this burden on her, and she took it unflinchingly. She fought the rising resentment that her mother would judge her after everything they put her through.

"I need you, Mom." She tapped her chest over her coin. "I didn't know they could be flipped back. There's so much I don't know about what you and Dad did, how Matthew was involved, or what you expected me to do."

Holly pushed the door open. "No sense having this conversation outside," she held the door. "If they know you're here, I might as well try to answer your questions before you have to go."

Stepping inside, Alex looked around her mother's house. It wasn't the home she grew up in, but a resemblance of it. Rooms seemed larger, the furniture spoke to styles, but nothing was the same. The house made Alex feel something. Like the rooms were different, but only like some uncanny valley. The couch whispered of afternoons snuggled on blankets. The kitchen remembered meals together. She perceived memories everywhere, like subtle shadows seen with the corners of her eyes. Warm, heartfelt ones were about her. The bittersweet, the passionate ones were about Peter. They radiated from all over the house. Alex blushed, knowing most were from times before she was born. Moments of passion shared while

Peter was still truly alive. When they were still hopeful of their future together.

Alex hadn't come to a house at all. Everything around her was her mother's memory, her mother's emotion. Things lacking emotional resonance were absent. Yet, in spite of the weight of loss and sacrifice, Alex felt nothing but love. She wanted to hug her mother. Everywhere she looked, she took in her mother's memories of moments they shared.

"Can I get you something to eat or drink?"

Alex felt jarred back to reality by her mother's question. "Just a glass of water," Alex replied. She wished she had time to eat. She recalled Sara's ghost stew and wondered what her mother's cooking would taste like.

Her mother handed her a large, orange glass, circumscribed with ridges and cut ovals. She recognized it as one her parents owned before she was born. She saw it in an old photograph taken when her parents weren't much older than she was now. Alex took a sip: tasted like water.

"I've missed you, Mom."

Holly's face softened. "Four years is a long time to miss someone." For a moment, her eye sparkled. "For you it's been, what, a week?"

Alex made a face. "Yeah, four days since your murder. Good times."

Holly ignored her daughters' sarcasm. "Let's go to your room." Holly started towards the stairs. Alex emptied the glass and placed it on the counter beside the sink. Holly gave her that look again. Alex put the glass in the sink. "There's a dishwasher," Holly told her.

Alex wasn't sure her mother wasn't joking. "It's not really dirty, is it?"

Holly motioned to the dishwasher. "Did Heather have a stroke? Does she let you leave your dishes all over the place?"

Alex almost didn't care what her mother was saying. She loved that her mother was saying anything. Holly's voice blossomed into joy inside her.

As they reached the top of the stairs, Peter stepped from their bedroom. A version of her father she'd never seen before, older than when he visited Sara, a smile bloomed across his face at the sight of them. "I love you so much," he effused.

"Come on, Alex," Holly said, her tone painted by her reddening cheeks.

"But I," Alex stumbled over the words as she tried to express her desire to share a word with her sentient father.

Holly pulled Alex aside to allow Peter to pass. "That's not your father," Holly explained. To Peter, she ordered, "Hon, go to your room."

Peter turned around and nodded with a glint in his eye as though Holly had complimented his style. He paused at the doorway. "I love you so much," he said as Holly closed the door behind him.

Alex waited for Holly to explain herself, as Holly seemed to be waiting for the moment to pass.

Before Alex could form the words, pointing to the closed door, Holly offered her explanation. "This is all imagined. The dishes, the furniture, the house. Even your father. He's not here. He's gone." She watched Alex, perhaps for a sign that the explanation was sufficient. Alex could feel her questions surfacing through her facial expressions. "I chose this. This home, these memories. I wanted it to be familiar. Not just for me, but in the expectation that you'd come." She touched her daughters' arm. "I could have had anything. Memories of a vacation or a from a travelogue, but I chose this. For me. For you. But this sort of life—afterlife—is lonely. That memory of Peter keeps me company. It's just enough."

Alex didn't know how to process what her mother had said. Her emotions were conflicted. Her mother imprisoning herself inside a memory—when she could be anywhere—because she wanted familiarity for Alex felt like a guilt trip seasoned with martyrdom. Alex hoped her mother hadn't intended it that way.

Holly motioned to the next doorway. "It may seem like torture, but there's comfort in familiarity. Perhaps one day I'll move on from these memories, but for now I need the sense of security this brings. The universe whispers to me and being here helps me ignore it." She turned away.

Alex stared at the closed door that separated her from the automaton that resembled her father. This counterfeit version felt more real than the broken man Alex knew her whole life. His facial expressions and his voice might have been preselected by her mother, but this fake person was so much more real. The glint of an epiphany sparked for Alex and although she could never express it verbally, she fathomed how much her mother lost when she was born. That this imagination—to Alex—was a better version of her father, yet was so much less to Holly, barely touched on the depths of her mother's grief.

Alex followed her mother into her old bedroom. She hesitated, unused to seeing the glowing thread snaking away from her. It traced her motions: down the hall, down the stairs, through the living room, out the front door. She imagined it existing for miles and miles, rising and settling to the ground from her flight, twisting this way and that until at last, it crossed the threshold of the mist into the living world, connecting with her body. *What happens if someone cuts it? Can it break?* Alex worried about the miles and miles of this delicate, undulating, sparkling thing. *If I move too much, could I accidentally get it knotted up?* She imagined getting tangled in her own thread. Was she like a balloon, lost to the wind and sky if snapped?

This was the only room so far unchanged. The bed, the furniture, even the books and stuffed animals were identical to the last time she saw the room undamaged. Holly sat on the bed right where she left Abby and motioned for Alex to sit beside her.

Alex sat beside her mother; the mattress forcing them against one another.

In Holly's eyes, Alex saw something she wasn't sure how to interpret: she felt her mother pitying her. Holly drew her arms around Alex with a crushing hug. She pressed her face into Alex's hair and greedily drew a breath.

"Oh, how I've missed you."

"I've missed you, too, Mom." The words seemed insufficient. Held in her mother's arms, Alex could feel the reinforcements on her heart release, opening wounds still so tender and raw. She clutched at her mother, realizing that whether it was four days or four years, the duration didn't matter, it was the finality of the loss: Her mother was dead and, even sitting here, holding her, aware of her scent, of her warmth, she would never have the luxury to take her for granted ever again. Every meeting, every embrace, every shared word was weighted with finality.

As Holly released her, she said, "It's been a tough week, I gather."

Alex nodded. Part of her wanted to fall into her mother's arms again, to get her mother to tell her it would all be all right, but Alex would not make the dead lie.

Alex mumbled, "It never occurred to me I could turn my coins back. What else don't I know?"

Holly looked away from Alex. "I've had a lot of time to reflect here, and I... I think your father knew."

"Knew?"

"When you're dead, the universe tells you secrets. Never when you need them, of course."

"What secrets?" Alex remembered Sara telling her she learned unknowable things.

"I think he sacrificed himself not for us, but for Matthew."

"No, Mom, that's not true."

Holly looked up; her head still held low. "Are you sure?"

Alex nearly blurted out the truth. The charm rested against her chest. *Can I tell her? How will she take knowing Abby had a way to bring Peter back?* Part of her worried that the dead were no longer their own. *Will she want it? Was it meant for her?* Alex began doubting her father's reasoning. *Maybe I was supposed to give this to her.* "It doesn't matter, Mom. Please, if they know I'm here, there isn't much time. What should I know?" She watched Holly's eyes. Alex was unsure if she was questioning her or doubting her. "Mom, you did this—thing—to me. You made me different. Matthew wants it and now I think Jeremiah wants it, too."

"Who?" The urgency in her mother's voice shocked Alex.

"Jeremiah."

Holly blanched. "You know him?"

Alex nodded.

"How close has he come to you?"

"We've met."

Holly gasped. Her words were a hiss, "How are you alive?"

Why does everyone ask me that? Alex struggled not to answer; it took energy to reframe her thoughts. "What aren't you telling me?"

Holly closed her eyes. "Matthew didn't tell us about Jeremiah. Not at first."

"You sound like you were, I don't know, what, friendly?"

"To a degree. Matthew was your father's teacher. He convinced your father," she held out her hand to Alex, "to take the coin from our son. We were well underway when Peter told me the truth... *a truth*: Matthew was using us."

"You told me you figured this out and hid me from Matthew,

so I'd be safe."

"We hid you from Jeremiah, too."

Alex rested a hand on her mother's arm. "What did you think would happen? Matthew's plan involves killing me." She watched her mother's face for any reaction. "You knew? Was I a sacrificial lamb all along?"

Holly's face processed, as though she took her initial response and stomped the life out of it. "Whatever our reasoning, Alex, we didn't know enough. The complications weren't apparent. We never intended it to be like this for you." She motioned to Alex's coin. "Go back. Flip them dark. Run. Hide." Her tone suggested she meant right this second.

Alex slid off the bed. She looked at the silver filament that drifted from the glowing coin in her chest, disappearing through the bedroom door. She turned to her mother. She'd consider what her mother was asking, once Billy was safe at home. "I can't do that, Mom. Not yet. I feel like you're not telling me something. What aren't you telling me?"

"Sweetheart, I wish I could make you understand. I know things that aren't for the living to know. Concepts; realities too great to comprehend with mere words. If you were dead, I could share them with you, but the language you use can't contain their scope. You can't defeat Jeremiah. He's not like you."

"I know he's not. He's a thousand years old."

"No, Alex."

"Two thousand? Three?"

"More. Eternal. He's not just immortal; *he is*." She grunted. "That's what I mean, words don't work. That's why Matthew's already failed. He's just a man. He assumed he could conquer Jeremiah by taking the magic away. He assumed that would leave him powerless. But Jeremiah…, he *is* the magic."

"You're telling me I'm doomed to fail? Just when I see a chance?"

Holly looked up, almost surprised. "You see a chance?" Holly shook her head again. "You don't see a chance. That light at the end of the tunnel is the train, Alexandrea. You're all dead at the end. You, Rosemary, Heather, even Abby. He's seeing to it. One at a time, like a lazy circle," she slowly drew her finger in the air, "slowly closing and tightening."

Alex didn't want to believe the doom her mother forecast. Was it worth fighting if she could just flip her coin and go into hiding? What was the point of a normal life if she knew the truth? Could she not pay attention to what she knew existed? She'd seem crazier than Eric ever accused Heather of being.

"No one wants to believe," Holly's tone was calm and even, "that the road they're taking leads to damnation. That the sunny morning will turn into a stormy afternoon. That they'll take a drive and never come home." She reached out and cupped Alex's cheek. "Go home. Flip your coins. Hide."

Alex backed from her mother. She wanted to tell her she was wrong. She wanted to scream it. Holly basically told her all her suffering had been for nothing. Everyone's suffering. Giving up now disgusted her. She wanted to fight. The pain was always there, lurking behind every emotion, every feeling. Not just her suffering, but that of all those other women. Those women deserved better than someone who hid themselves away. And then there was Billy. He was out there, somewhere. Who else could save him but her?

Alex didn't even realize she was walking towards the door when her mother asked, "Where are you going, Alex?"

Alex looked back at her mother, framed in the doorway, looking so small as she slipped from the bed. Alex walked back and just held her. "I love you, Mom."

After a moment, Holly patted her back. "You need to go, Alexandrea. You and Abby are in danger."

"From Jeremiah or Matthew?"

Holly warned, "Jeremiah's people. They're close."

Alex slipped from her mother's embrace.

"They have spells, Alex, ways to mute magic."

Alex recalled Sara being unable to cast a spell when Matthew came to her. "How do you know? Why are you telling me this *now*?"

Holly collapsed onto the bed. "Dying isn't like dreaming. We only go to the same place. Dying is becoming a part of this place, and with that, having access to its secrets. You can't argue with the universe."

Alex didn't want to, but she nodded. Her mother still had something to say, but all Alex could think of was Abby. She was all alone. She had no idea what was coming, and she'd die before she let anyone touch Alex's body.

"The universe has a dark heart, Alex. It wants you dead. That's how this ends. He'll kill everyone if he has to. Everyone who knows you exist. Just to erase all memory of you."

Alex took in her mother's words. She held up a hand to offer her goodbye, turned and left.

Chapter Sixty-Nine

lex left her mother and began following her silver thread to Abby and where her corporeal form awaited: the actual house.

Could she trust Holly? Was her mother telling her the truth? She couldn't take any chances. Abby was in danger. Her thread sparked and shimmered as she ran. It never gave slack, it always appeared just as taut whether she moved towards or away from it.

What was happening to her Familiar? Would she know—sense—if Abby were attacked? No matter how fast she ran, it never seemed fast enough. She leapt into the air. Flying was still an awkward endeavor. Her silver thread disappeared into the distance. She half anticipated watching the tether collapse to the ground, severing her from her body.

Why am I thinking like this? Worrying about things that haven't happened? Her mother's words stuck in her head like thorns. Abby was in her bedroom with her body, unaware someone was coming to kill them.

Alex's head swam with worry. Was she taking her mother too literally? Was Holly trying to motivate her or scare her? Or, was Holly telling a truth too painful to believe? Did it matter? Abby was in danger. It seemed pointless to analyze warnings from the dead.

Was it just Abby who was endangered? Would Jeremiah send people after Rose and Heather, too? What about the rest of the Book Club? Perhaps even Lesedi, Banhi, and Kholwa? Why stop there?

As Alex navigated the skies, looking for the terminus of her thread, her heart soured with doubt. Rose and Heather were off on their own. *Can Rose protect both Heather and herself?* What would happen when she got back and found that Rose was missing, too?

She recognized her head was spiraling out of control, taking avenues of *what ifs* that had no logical tributaries to the roads she was on. Her overreactions obscured the true danger with imagined ones.

Below her, only her miniscule shadow wasn't blurred as she rocketed back to Abby. *Why did I leave her? What did I learn that was worth the danger?* She was doubting herself. Her coin could be flipped back.

Floating in the sky up ahead, she saw it: a boil of mist with her thread emanating from within.

Alex hit the mist and felt like she'd momentarily fallen into the spin-cycle of a washer. The sickening twisting of reality and restriction of being body-bound; the universal laws of physics vengefully returning.

Her field of view shifted savagely. One moment she was staring at the wall she'd come from. The next, she tumbled hard to her back, her breath knocked from her. Rapid pop-pop-cracks of explosive spells stung her ears. Abby smothered her with her own body.

What's happening? Alex struggled under Abby's weight; slaps of flesh as spells struck Abby, the darkly acrid scent of burning cloth and flesh.

Abby grunted with concussive blows. She struggled to breathe, panting, whispering, "Come on Alex. Get the fuck back."

Glancing over Abby's shoulder, Alex saw two men entering the bedroom, Books in hand, kicking up billows of dust. One tumbled across the room, tripping on her father's sneakers.

Alex's stomach became a deepening well of fear, her concern for Abby and herself hollowing her out. She was trapped, pinned, vulnerable. Her friend and protector took the brunt, but for how long? They'd kill Abby. Alex's heart threatened to crack through her ribs. She wondered if Abby felt it, like an animal banging its cage. The whispers were reaching a crescendo. Alex focused on the room, ignoring the roar. They would not control her—ever again.

Searing pain radiated through her leg, like a fierce punch that became a stab that became an electrical spider web that twitched the surrounding muscles, beating a yelp from her lungs. The site burned, a twisting pain like raw skin exposed to salt. The sudden intensity made Alex question how many more she could endure. How many had Abby already suffered? Were she not pinned beneath Abby, her instinct was to thrash and crawl for cover.

The two men crashed atop them, crushing Alex at the bottom of the pile. Abby's bare shoulder pressed hard against Alex's face, forming a seal on her mouth. Desperate to breathe, Alex nearly bit as Abby lashed at the two men grabbing her. She refused to be pried from Alex. One man's guttural words came in a monotonous drone as he continued casting spells. The other used fists.

They were relentless to Abby. They beat her violently, as though they were prepared to force their way through. Together they pried Abby up, freeing Alex's breath. She gasped for air as Abby's groans and grunts sounded less like resilience and more like resignation; she was losing her steam, weakening, battered like a doll.

Abby needed her help. She had just clawed out from beneath Abby when hands seized her waist and threw her onto the bed and—holding her by a fistful of hair—thrust her face into the filthy comforter. Billowing dust powdering her nose and muddied throat. It was like gravel in her eyes. Abby grunted and cursed. Alex swung her arms uselessly behind her, receiving punches to the ribs for her efforts. The fabric muffled her pained cries. Grit and dirt forced into her eyes and nose and mouth. Each breath drew into her mouth the filthy, foul-tasting fabric.

The old dresser cracked when Abby was thrown across the room. The broken drawer-front ripped off in her hands. She collapsed to the ground, the wound of old clothes spilling out atop her.

The hand mashed Alex's face harder into the mattress. Heat from her nose spilled across her face.

"You're not casting any spells today, girl."

Alex felt that odd sensation she experienced when Matthew arrived at Sara's. She felt Sara try to cast a spell, but even the last witch, experience and all, could not overcome Matthew's trick.

Her attacker flipped her onto her back and crushed her ribs with a knee.

Just feet away, Abby fought maniacally. Her angry fists bloodied his nose. She kept Alex in her sights as she struck hard. Crashing to the floor, he appeared his Book. He practically screamed his spells, spitting his words. Abby cried out like a wounded puppy at the onslaught, screaming for him to stop, but he continued wantonly.

Held down on the bed by a knee to the chest, Alex was helpless to do anything but witness Abby's cries and whimpers, the sizzle of burning flesh mocked by his guttural threats as she convulsed in agony.

Abby strained to look at her, her eyes bulging from the effort. She crawled through the dust towards Alex, the unrelenting strikes battering her. She only cared about protecting Alex.

"I got her," said the man holding Alex against the bed, his

hairy forearm pressed against her throat. His face was doughy and pockmarked. Small, rat-like brown eyes glared at Alex, inches from hers. "Kill the bitch so we can get outta here."

"I'm trying," came the breathy reply, as though fatigued by vocal repetition. "She won't die." He screamed to Abby, "Sit the fuck still."

Abby pulled herself closer. A crack of light struck, and Abby collapsed. Alex gasped, but before she could think Abby was dead, her Familiar found another reserve to inch closer. "Stop," Alex's voice was reduced to a squelched whisper. There was nothing more painful than watching Abby suffer for her relentless dedication.

From the hallway—like a third man waiting, bored—fingers drummed on the wall.

"Alex," Abby groaned, tears running down her face as she pulled herself closer to the bed. She reached for the man holding Alex.

Alex couldn't reach to touch her hand. *I'm watching her die and I can't even touch her. I can't save her. I can't do anything. And it's all my fault.*

"Get her off me," the rat-eyed attacker yelled. He kicked Abby in the forehead, knocking her head into the desk. His forearm loosened from Alex's neck. She wasn't thinking about breathing as she clawed her fingernails across his face. The frenetic tapping—drumming— from the hallway became banging.

Abby's eyes were still spinning in her head as she sprung from the floor, bellyflopping onto the bed, grabbing and pulling the man as she slid off, like a killer whale dragging a seal from the ice.

"Get her off me," Rat-Eyes screamed again. He glanced to the door: *He hears it, too.*

Alex beat her fists against his stocky frame; his sweat-soaked shirt left her knuckles wet. With a kick, Alex knocked him away by inches. It gave her room to scurry to the wall. The drumming was maddening. It fell into a rapid pattern, as though many somethings struck at once. The bright snap of glass cracking accompanied it. Alex's head swarmed, the whispers weren't shouting or screaming. Whatever they were doing vibrated her brain within her skull.

With her rat-eyed assailant momentarily distracted by whatever was happening in the hall, Alex focused her anger. She tried to cast a spell. The maelstrom of emotion was like a wet piece of ice: She couldn't hold it, couldn't pull the one thread that would unravel whatever was holding everything back. This is what it felt to be muted. They did this to her. Her feelings didn't matter. Voices in her head called to her. There were too many to peel apart meaning, but it was clear they were trying to help.

Rat Eyes inched closer to Alex, his hands extended defensively. He growled, "End her already!" He lurched and Alex flinched. A white shock of pain frosted her sight. A shattering crack, like her nose broke, echoed in her skull. Her hands instinctively protected her face. He grabbed her shirt at the collar, snagging some skin beneath it, and pulled her from the wall.

Instead of fighting, she launched herself blindly into him, screaming gibberish anger. She punched and kicked. She let loose a stream of obscenities about things he did with his mother. He writhed from her berserker punches. He withdrew from her onslaught.

"What the fuck?" he screamed. Her head vibrated.

Abby shouted, but it was lost to the cries from the men. Something was wrong with Alex's ears. They buzzed. The other man slammed his Book into furniture, again and again, as though he'd forgotten Abby and was satisfied hitting anything now.

The air thickened about her. It vibrated. It swelled and swirled past her. A thousand small objects circled her close enough to touch. Even half-blinded by tears, Alex saw the entire room had become a tempest of wasps, hornets, and bees. She couldn't see more than a few feet through the churning cloud. She nearly froze as honeybees danced about her clothes and entangled through her hair. Shiny black hornets decorated her assailant, their bulbous abdomens wriggling as they stung.

Alex slipped off the bed. "Abby," she shouted as she wrapped her arms around her friend. Bees hurriedly gave way for her embrace. Abby's hands weakly clasped her. *Please don't die, Abby.*

Abby's head collapsed against Alex's shoulder. Her body trembled in Alex's arms. "I'm sorry, Alex. I tried."

"Move," Rat Eyes shouted, retreating toward the hall.

Alex pulled her close, trying to find within herself the love she needed to give her friend.

Abby pressed against her. "Is this you?"

"I don't know. Yes."

"I thought you cast the spell!" one man accused the other. Rat Eyes confirmed, "You saw me do it." They were screaming, squirming, swatting at their own bodies, tripping over sneakers and spilled clothes and one another, thrashing into the hall which surged with bees.

Abby tried to wrap her arms around Alex. "It's okay," Alex shouted over the buzzing din. She needed Abby to stop protecting her and accept her healing.

The room blackened with swarm as the bees converged around the doorway. Walls and floor writhed. The men swatted and shouted and screamed as they fought their way through the hall.

Alex felt the anger, the fear, the twisting in her gut. How was this happening? In her head, the voices screamed. No, this was different. The voices chanted. Alex realized: the men *had* muted her magic, but not *theirs*.

Alex didn't care the men were still in the house; they were gone from the room. Her body ached like every inch was broken. She reluctantly touched her face, half-expecting the shift of broken bones. It was tender and sticky, but nothing moved. Her hair still crawled with honeybees. Beside her, Abby was covered with congealing blood. *What should I do?* She pictured the bees stinging their attackers into anaphylaxis. *They tried to kill Abby. Bees are not enough.*

Alex took Abby's face in her hands. "Can you move?"

"I think so."

"I need you to get outside. Can you do that?"

"I think so."

Alex got to her feet. Every surface she touched was fuzzy with honeybees. She took Abby's hands and pulled her upright.

Other bees concentrated in the hallway. Alex crossed the bedroom and entered the hall.

Alex and Abby slipped untouched through the swarm and descended the stairs; bees danced on the walls and the ceiling, coating the house with a living, moving, buzzing carpet. When she reached the front door, Alex pulled it open, pushing aside a mat of rotting leaves. The bees, disenchanted, exited the door like a giant, lurching shadow, and dispersed.

The departing bees revealed the men. One lay at the bottom of the stairs, like he'd collapsed or tumbled down, his Book inches from his hand. His breathing was rapid but shallow, his exposed skin a mountain range of welts. She might have pitied his situation were it not for the throbbing of her face and what they'd done to Abby. Rat-face pulled on the railing, climbing to the higher ground at the top of the stairs. He leaned against the wall, one foot on the landing, the other on the next step.

Sharply, Alex ordered, "Get out."

Rat-Eyes sneered, "Not without you."

Alex didn't need to think. She collected the other man's Book. She flipped it open and dug her fingers into the pages. The symbols printed on the page fell away; the heat rising.

Yellow and orange flames snapped around her as she suffered alongside the woman beaten for these spells; the Book turning to ash in her hands. The dying flames still played about her as she approached the stairs. "Give me your Book and I'll heal you both."

Abby shouted, "Alex, watch!"

In the moment her eyes flashed to Abby, Rat-Eyes appeared his Book. He opened it; finding the page. She watched the spell contort his mouth.

"Out, Abby!" Alex didn't take her eyes from the top of the stairs. Abby didn't move. Alex ordered, "Out of the house, Abby!"

The lightning strike came like a string of sparks hurled directly at her. Reflexively, Alex's hands protected her face. Her palm burned, but instead of raw flesh, she held a molten puddle of light in her hand. She held out the thrashing energy for Rat-Eyes to see before throwing it to the ground. The energy sparked to flame across the floor and the leaf-litter piled against the wall.

He looked down at her, his ratty eyes wide with fear.

Alex understood the change in dynamics. Working with her whispers instead of constantly fighting them felt like the moment a motor engaged, gears snapping together, and the whole mechanism lurching into synchronized movement. It felt good. It made her feel, for the first time, strong. She glared at the top of the stairs. Alex shouted, "Why lightning? Don't you know anything else?"

Rat-Eyes was no one. He was king of the stairs. His apprehension that Alex stood between him and the exit was demonstrated by his darting eyes and panicked expression. What had seemed like a great idea moments ago, now clearly had him questioning what he'd gotten himself into. Jeremiah sent them because either the pathetic girl would fail, or she'd have to take their lives. She didn't want to hurt anyone, much less kill them. *They don't matter to him. Jeremiah sent them to see how far I'm willing to go.*

"He sent you here to die," she told him. "He wants to see if I'm capable of killing you."

They know nothing about me. But he *does.* Realization soured her stomach. They deserved punishment. Her hands wanted to pound sense into them. Pity swirled about her disgust. She was nothing but a task to them: get me this girl. They invaded her home. Tried to kill Abby. These men didn't deserve leniency. Whether it was her emotion, finally unbound, or that of her whispers, she didn't care. She was filled with a confused anger. Their actions were driven by another. They didn't think twice about what that entailed. Her pity wasn't for them. It was for what had to be done. *They will learn who I am.* Her skin prickled, as though pressure increased within her. *Jeremiah is right.* In discovering who she was, Jeremiah was allowing her to learn, too. This wasn't what she wanted. It was what she had to do. What she had to become if she would ever stand a chance.

"Alex, what are you doing?"

The house fell silent as Alex turned to her Familiar. "Get out of the house, Abby. I need you safe."

Abby pointed out the open door. "I can't protect you from out there. I can handle myself," Abby protested.

Abby's petulance prickled Alex. Perhaps more than anything the two men could do. Of everyone, she should listen. She wanted to holler at her Familiar, *How dare you defy me?* She realized it wasn't what Abby said, but that she'd said it in front of these men. The realization was like reigns in her hands. Pulling back on her anger, like she'd opened a shaken soda bottle only a little, Alex felt the pressure release—the tiniest bit—and Abby skidded out the doorway.

More sparks sizzled from the top of the stairs while she was distracted with Abby. This time she held the lightning in her hands, sparking and crackling against her skin. She held it tight, feeling its angry heat. Opening her empty palms, only dissipating sparks of static remained.

"It's not natural," Rat-Eyes cried at her. "Women shouldn't have magic. It's dangerous."

"I know," Alex replied. "We get emotional."

Her anger broke the rational chains that bound it. There were no words that would bring Rat Eyes peacefully down the stairs. Her very existence disgusted him—and that knowledge was the catalyst that fed her rage. Fed the angry rage of all her whispers.

Dust bloomed off the floor. Wood beams throughout the house cleared their throats. The house trembled. Her anger towards these men inflated under her skin like she might explode. These men might have come because they were told, but ignorance wasn't innocence. Her muscles tensed. Her teeth clenched. Dust rained from the ceiling as nails emerged from under paint, the wallboards cracking and crumbling.

Am I doing that? The house lurched, shifting on its foundation. *Yup*, Alex grinned. *He knows it, too.*

A breeze pushed the blooms of dust around the house. Wind whipped flaming leaves into a dervish. The walls and ceiling gaped in ghastly cracks, like mouths opening to feed. Decomposing plaster danced and spun in the wind like fairy-dust. Windows shattered. Wood studs splintered. The staircase gave way, the top half releasing the landing and swinging into the basement with a crash, pulling the other man's body as it all momentarily disappeared into a blooming explosion of dust.

At the top of the stairs, leaning over the broken crevasse, still clutching his Book, Rat-Eyes wrapped his arm around the doorframe to her parent's room. Alex held out her hand and demanded the Book one last time. Over the wind and the flames and the groans of the protesting house, she shouted, "Give me the Book and I'll let you leave."

He shook his head. The wind sprinkling him with sparks and dust and ash. The shaking structure thrashed him from side to side; he screamed at Alex, "Make it stop. Make it stop!"

At once, the dust and ash stilled. It hung in midair, then gently settled. The entire house groaned to rest, the walls leaning. It was like Abby's barn.

"The Book," her hand, like Charon's, demanded payment.

He held it out, reaching from his perch at the top of the missing stairs. "Here." His arm exaggerated his intent. He laughed as the Book clattered into the broken bowels of the basement, its covers twisting backwards, its pages fluttering like butterfly wings disappearing into darkness.

Above her, Rat-Eyes continued to laugh. He glared, his swollen face a motley of welts, his swollen lips almost a purple-blue. He pointed at the ruins of the staircase in the basement, at the Book. "Go fuck yourself."

Alex bridled her rage, fingernails practically drawing blood from her palms. She wanted to crush him in that hallway. Inevitably, she'd get the Book. Only he was controlling how she obtained it. He might be losing this battle, but he controlled the battlefield.

He craned over the pit, perhaps looking for a route to the main floor. Alex stepped back to allow him to climb down, although she hadn't yet decided what to do once he reached her floor. He adjusted his footing and stepped to the splintered cliff of the hallway. His eyes went wide as the flooring collapsed and he pinwheeled into the piles of splintered wood and bent nails below.

Alex cringed at the extended avalanche of wood and debris that fell atop him. She wished she could be certain she wasn't responsible for that. The rubble hid his crumpled body, inches from his Book. Perhaps he was beside his compatriot, lost when the stairs collapsed.

Instinct pushed her dangerously close to the chasm's edge to see if she could help, but Alex hesitated. *Why?* The Book was below, amidst a dangerous pile of rubble. Crackling, snapping flames chatted behind her back. Leaves smoldered throughout, as the dusty kitchen curtains crawled with flame. Billowing gray smoke curled over the counters, crossed the ceiling, racing into the stairwell like an upside-down waterfall. Alex expected to feel angst at the destruction she'd wrought. Watching flames devour her home made her realized she didn't want this house abandoned again.

She peered into the debris pile below. Trapped by shattered beams and flooring, the pages tried turning as heat curled their browning edges. *Should I let it burn? What happens when a Book is destroyed? What happens to the woman? Is she aware as she dies a second time?*

Flames roared in the kitchen, pumping murky smoke to the ceiling where it moved with animalistic intent to the upper floor.

Small fires crackled upstairs; excessive heat brought by the smoke causing the dry, brittle things to burn.

She reached out. Willing the Book to her, like a hero in some movie. Alex wanted it to just spring from its resting place and leap to her hand, but it just lay there.

From the pile, Rat Eyes staggered to his feet. He regarded the Book, then Alex, then grinned. He hadn't yet noticed the glowing coin in his chest or the sparking cord connecting him to the corpse at his feet. He edged forward, his sneer threatening wordlessly, that as soon as he pulled himself clear of the collapse, she was done for. His startled pause broke his anger. It was only then, looking down, that he discovered the reality of his condition.

Instinctively, Alex knew the small child emerged behind her from the flames. She turned to greet the child. It's cherubic face intelligently scanned the room with large, dark eyes, its pudgy bare feet crunching on plaster dust and other litter. It looked upon Alex as if it found her a curiosity it had never seen before. It judged her height as if unable to comprehend how someone so new to the world could already be so tall.

Rat Eyes kicked and hauled himself from the cellar. His eyes fixed beyond Alex. With a swirl of rustling fabrics, the child held out its hand, demanding of payment.

He clamored to his feet and regarded the pit as the second man rose from his grave to greet the conveyor of the dead.

Alex threatened, "Don't come up without the Book."

He looked at Alex, at the Book, at Rat Eyes. With a look of contempt, he climbed out. It wasn't just an act of defiance. Their actions told Alex she was not a threat. That she didn't matter. It seemed trivial, almost egotistical that she make them get the Book for her, but it was the only way to get them to acknowledge she had won. And Alex wanted a win.

She positioned herself between them and the child. "No one passes me without the Book. Charon wants payment. So do I." Her heart pounded like someone was kicking their way out of her chest. *Does magic affect the dead?*

Rat Eyes ensnared his coin in his fist. His snide smile was proof she wasn't being taken seriously. The rising tide of voices in her head sensed her anger and her frustration and her resentment.

Behind her, the child's impatience grew.

She demanded, "Give me the Book." Rat Eyes retreated two steps.

With a shared glance that multiplied their meager confidence, both men offered their coins to Charon.

Alex had witnessed what happens when someone interferes with Charon's payment. The Book was just feet below.

"Look where this got you," she cried at them. "Jeremiah sacrificed you. He knows what I can do. Was it worth your life? I only want the Book. Give it and I'll let you pass."

One man glanced back at the Book.

"That's right," Alex motioned with her hand. "That's all I'm asking. Give it to me and be on your way."

Rat Eyes tried to force past. Her fury for his utter disregard threw him into the kitchen.

Apparently, magic does affect the dead.

Stealing her attention from his shocked expression, a commotion erupted behind her.

Bones tore through the child's skin, ripping the cherubic creature apart as it lurched and grew, the skeletal monster emerging. The multitudinous cloths wrapped about the child faded and fell to rags—same as the flesh and viscera—turning ancient as they dangled. Her heart dropped into the bowl of her hips, witnessing the towering horror billowing up like a volcano's erupting ash cloud.

"It's not fair," she screamed at it. Ribbons of flesh swayed as it lumbered towards her. Huge, clawed hands covetously snatching the air, intent on her glowing coins. Alex knew what came next: it would rip her coins from her chest.

Against better judgement, despite her trembling legs and the fear threatening to loose her bowels, Alex stood her ground. Churning smoke and crackling flames swirled as wind again raced through the house. Flames did nothing to burnish the bleached skeleton. Ribbons of flesh sizzled as fire slipped through and around the bones.

She couldn't believe they were going to win. Again, she would lose. It wasn't fair. The skeletal terror threatened closer. All she had to do was step aside, let them pass, then claim the Book. She thought fear had frozen her legs but realized it was something greater that anchored her now.

Alex's fury emerged from her thrust hands as sparks of lightning. Bolts struck ribs; charges crackled between the bones. She threw more, striking its skull; electricity giving its dark eye-sockets the illusion that it glared right through her with luminous eyes.

The creature thrashed its bony talons and crept into her growing lightning storm.

Why lightning?

Doubt grew like a thornbush in her throat, spike-studded vines curled about her as the monstrosity shrugged off her attack. Panic bloomed acid in her stomach. A cold sweat dampened her body. She was moments from being torn apart. Everything she'd been though; all the sacrifices, would be in vain. The thought infuriated her. Lightning burst from her hands, the energy encasing Charon. Lightning raced through it, sparking between bones, lighting the creature's indifference to her magic. Her frantic eyes looked for anything to throw at the creature; it seemed immune to magic. The only things within reach were pillows from the couch. Even as her brain prepared her body to be torn apart, she couldn't help but laugh at the imagery of a pillow-fight solving this problem.

The bubble of laughter and the shiver of fear translated through her fingertips. Lightning was replaced by the booming of concussive thunder. Reverberations rumbled down her arms, deep under her skin and exploded from her hands. It pushed against her palms, rolling across the room like an approaching summer storm. It exploded in and around the skeletal cage. Charon's form contracted as thunder rumbled violently through the air, rattling its bones.

Then it stood, unabated. All she could think was how much she regretted not climbing to the basement to retrieve the Book herself.

Charon towered over her. It was over. It was too late. It had only to swoop its arm and rip her beating heart and coin from her chest. As though acknowledging her with dramatic flourish, Charon raised a taloned claw into the air.

Protectively, Alex clutched her coin. *Maybe?* In an instant, she'd pulled the two halves apart. She snapped them back together; the glowing disk returned to the darkest black.

Charon's aggressive advance faltered. The creature looked through her; all its aggression lost. Its clawed hand lowered to within a breath of her. Its size collapsed under the weight of its disappointment.

The expectation of dismemberment clung to her like sweat. The bony skull scanned the room, confused. It was as though Alex had vanished from its sight.

Alex was fearful she would throw up if she opened her mouth to breathe. The threat of death loomed so close she anticipated its resumption, but it quickly became clear to her—and only her—that without her glowing coins attracting it, this creature lacked purpose. She stood practically under the monstrosity, close enough to plink its ribcage with her finger.

She could taste its dry emptiness on her tongue. Waves of its presence washed over her. A moment more, and she would have followed it to the afterlife. Instead, she felt sick. She felt thrilled. She swallowed to push her rising stomach contents down. She took a deep breath and faced the men.

"I will not ask again." She demanded, "Get me the Book or you will not pass." Her tense body encouraged her words to belie her unabated terror.

Both men looked from her to the looming skeleton behind her. It scanned the room as though blind. As though it might find her lurking in a cabinet or hiding beneath the table.

Desperate to convince them, she urged, "What are you waiting for? Don't test me." She considered the worst thing she could do to them now. "If I send Charon away, you're lost here. Don't force me to be so cruel." Alex panned her gaze between them. The flames and heat from the fires seemed to pause; expectation draining air from the room.

Rat Eyes slunk away. Witnessing this act, the other turned and together they retreated to the basement.

Alex was reluctant to turn around, knowing the hulking form was right behind her. She could feel its presence. Smell it. *How long will it keep searching for me?* The fire roared everywhere.

A moment later they pulled themselves from the basement. They approached. When they were still out of her reach, they reverentially proffered the Book.

Alex placed her hands on the cover. For a moment, the three of them held it. Their hands withdrew.

"Thank you." She stepped aside. She had won the battle. She controlled the battlefield. She had won. Victory wasn't as savory as she imagined.

Rat Eyes stared at Charon but spoke to Alex, "Does he know?"

He took a step, followed by the other man. Charon seemed to melt; tatters of flesh re-knit as the skeleton became encased with the visage of the cherubic child. It held its hand out again.

"You can cheat death?" It was a statement and a question. It demanded a response.

Alex hoped there was more power in her silence.

Around her, the smoke grew thicker, the air scorching hot.

"He doesn't, does he?" The second man stepped forward. The

child accepted the glowing coin unsympathetically. It acknowledged the glow in its palm. The man regarded Alex, saddened—perhaps—that no one mourned his passing. He then stepped past the child and disappeared.

Rat Eyes waited a moment longer. His expression confused Alex. She half expected their battle to resume. Her magic worked, but her coins were now dark. Turning them around meant facing the Reaper again.

"He'll destroy you. Either to possess that ability for himself or make sure no one has what he can't have." He held out his coin to the child. "You don't stand a chance. You get that, don't you?"

Alex had no need to answer. She got what she wanted, and they, what they deserved.

Charon inspected the coin and with the same awkward expression, the slightest headshake as though disappointed, it allowed him to pass. Before moving on, Rat-Eyes stared a moment, almost like he had something to say. Then he turned and disappeared.

The child looked at Alex with eyes that didn't understand what they saw. Then it, too, turned, disappearing into the mist. As the mist disappeared, raging, boiling flames replaced it.

Alex opened the Book.

Her flames joined those consuming the house. She felt herself roiling about, filling the air, rising upward. For a moment she felt the house within her.

Her flames pressed towards the front door. Everything she touched brightened with flames. The door frame, the door, the siding cladding the house, and the porch roof.

Alex stepped from the conflagration. She made her way down the front steps, departing the suffocating smoke and heat for fresh air. Behind her, flames engulfed the house. Fire roared out the upper-story windows and black smoke billowed from invisible gaps between boards. Abby and her truck waited at a safe distance. Her hand contained a clot of bloody wipes, her face badly bruised but bloodless. Seeing Alex, Abby clasped her hands together. Once close enough, Abby grabbed her in a bearhug.

"Holy shit, Alex." Abby wiped tears from her eyes. She regarded the house; it listed ever so slightly. "Was that all you; the house? That was too close, Alex. I was freaking-out out here. I mean, what if you needed me? But you told me to get out. I didn't know what to do."

"I didn't want you in danger."

"Um," Abby exaggerated, "a little late, I think."

Alex saw the singe marks and raised welts on Abby's arms and face. Her battered clothes showed she likely had many more. "I didn't want you in any *more* danger." She took Abby in an embrace. "It's okay. I took care of things."

Abby shook her head as they separated. Looking back at the house, she blew a breath out between pursed lips. "I've never seen anything like that. What happened?"

Abby's bruises and marks were almost healed. Alex jokingly wished that she could heal clothing as well.

Alex walked towards Abby's truck. She'd been trying to consider how her spells changed. If asked, she'd be hard pressed to replicate the thunder or the wind. She'd felt anger shake the house without knowing how she was doing it. "It's hard to explain." The roar of the house almost drowned her out. "I think when they're written down, a spell does a thing and that's that. When it's emotional, different emotions do different things in different degrees. Every little thing affects every other little thing. I think maybe it's never the same twice."

"Bees, Alex? Seriously? Why not spiders or, or cockroaches? Death by slugs? I've never been so grossed and freaked out. I didn't want to inhale."

Alex pulled open the passenger door. "I don't know why bees, Abby. Of all the things, I wasn't expecting that."

It was the whispers. She addressed them; *Thank you.*

Abby tittered. "Neither were they." She shrugged. "Birds might have been cool, too. Remember that for next time." Abby waited for Alex to laugh. "You had to see what you looked like covered in those bees. You know when, in Greek mythology, the gods come and visit? I bet they look like that."

Alex hesitated outside the open truck door. Abby always had faith in her, but now that she'd proven herself, Abby's enthusiasm felt reverential. It felt uncomfortable.

Alex climbed into the truck. Abby into the driver's seat.

When asked, Alex told Abby about Charon and the trick with her coins. Even as Abby nodded enthusiastically, pining for more, Alex kept thinking about how afraid she'd been that something truly bad—irreversibly bad—would happen to Abby. She finished the story but mused on the fact that although she watched the two men depart with Charon, their bodies were still in the basement, burning. Her victory felt hollow.

"If you want to talk about it, Alex," Abby said with genuine care, "you know what I'm getting at."

Alex nodded as she looked from Abby's truck to the car parked in the middle of the driveway. "No one gets it," she complained, "drive right up to the house."

Abby laughed. "Where to?"

"We need to meet up with Heather and Rose when they're done."

Abby nodded. "Home then?"

"I'm sure Quest and Marty miss you."

"That was nice," Abby smiled. "I meant Heather's, but my place is fine, too."

Alex reached across the seat and pat Abby on the shoulder.

As Abby turned the truck around, Alex watched her house, in a smoking ball of flames, collapse into its foundation.

Chapter Seventy

lex awoke Tuesday morning rested and refreshed. It was good to be back in Abby's trailer. The seclusion and limited space felt cocooning. She had expected her dreams to be fraught with anguish, but she slept darkly: not a single dream.

She lay in bed, not sure what to think about yesterday. She'd done magic. She nearly understood it, too, and that alone was thrilling: The way her emotions reached a boiling point and emerged from her in physical form and how, as the spell left her, it took the intensity of feeling with it. The ultimate catharsis. The real trick, however, was maintaining her anger while releasing magic. It was like anger was the fuel creating the magic, and each spell left her... less angry.

Then, there were the other things that made her not want to consider yesterday: Sara. Had it been anyone else, learning that someone maintained control of her unconscious body, would have been an incredible violation. But this was Sara Frost; turnabout seemed fair play. Only Sara was now dead. Deader than Matthew left her. Murdered—however accidentally—by Rose. Alex didn't yet know which one of them suffered the greater tragedy. Both left her hollowed out by grief.

Her mind churned through unwanted thoughts, feelings, and memories. She met her mother: an opportunity she never expected to have. Yet, it only intensified her sense of loss. Her mother never felt so far away. Alex didn't dare drift in the sea of uneasy what ifs.

Two men died yesterday. They weren't the first deaths she'd witnessed. Her mother. Sara. Her father. Marta. Others. They should all have been worse than this. It didn't seem right that these two men weighed on her more than any of the others. She fought them for her life, and although she wasn't directly responsible, they did die because of her. She didn't debate whether they deserved their ends; that was Charon's realm. What weighed on her, like a sweater made of tacks, was that this was a warning shot. Jeremiah gave her a taste of what was to come. Eventually, he would force her to take a life. Maybe, to save the life of someone she loved, she would have to sacrifice that of another. Was that something she could live with? Would there come a day when the memory of such acts wouldn't define who she was? Those two men represented an unknown quantity yet to come. It was like being haunted by ghosts from the future, punishing her for things she'd yet to do.

But now, it was over. That was yesterday. If she could forget, would she? Alex welcomed the new day by crying into her pillow, letting her tears wash the pain, the fear, and the anxiety out of her so she'd be strong enough to get out of bed and cheerfully greet Abby for breakfast, pretending nothing bothered her.

Once dressed, Alex found Abby lounging on her couch, Marty resting on her feet and Quest curled on her lap. Alex could tell from Abby's smile that she sensed her dismay. Whatever she knew, she said nothing.

"Small problem, kiddo. I don't feel like cooking."

"That's okay. It's breakfast. I'll cook." Alex tried to sound like it was okay. She realized she overdid it.

"I was thinking the diner. Have someone else do the cooking and the cleaning."

"That has merit."

"That has French toast, too." Abby's eyes widened. "If that's what you want."

Alex smiled.

"That's better."

"What's better?"

Abby tipped her head side to side. "I can see the weight you carry, Alex."

"It's okay," Alex replied unconvincingly.

"Is it the magic? Does having it do something to you? Does using it make you feel different?"

Alex hadn't thought about it before. "No," her tone afloat with surprise. "It's like thinking, or, I guess, feeling. It just sort of happens around me. Through me. I mean, I guess it can get exhausting, like being really happy, or sad, or angry too long. Carrying emotion is work. But," she thought of what she wanted to say, "the weight you see is different."

"You've seen things people aren't supposed to see."

Dead bodies twisted in debris. "I guess."

"I can't relate, exactly. I know how I felt with Peter. I know how I felt after my parents died. That stuff sticks with you. Pain is like tar; you get it on yourself and it takes forever to get it off. A little bit each day. It doesn't come off on its own, either. You have to work at it. Work through it. And when it finally comes off, you're a little raw from all the scrubbing."

"I'm working on it. It's all so new to me."

"Death always is. Every time." Abby pulled her legs out from under the cats. "Point I'm trying to make is, when you want to or need to talk about it, it's not a burden or anything. I'm happy to listen; even if I have nothing useful to contribute."

Alex hugged her. "Thanks, Abby."

Chapter Seventy-One

Breakfast at the diner was everything Alex hoped it would be. Their waiter was a funny, older woman who cracked sarcastic jokes and called them names like "doll" and "sweetie". The coffee was never-ending, and Alex's French toast was nearly as thick as it was wide—crispy on the outside and creamy on the inside. Alex wished she was still hungry, so she could ask for another meal to keep the experience going.

Abby's phone rang. She still hadn't changed the loud, thrashing ringtone. As soon as Abby answered, "Hi Heather," her realities crashed into the diner. She was no longer a kid putting too much syrup on her breakfast.

Abby cupped the phone with her hand and asked for the check. She handed Alex the phone and got up to pay. Before putting the phone to her ear, Alex tried to decide if Heather reaching out was a good or bad thing. She was supposed to be looking for Billy. For a moment, her heart swelled with anticipation.

"Hi, Aunt Heather," Alex couldn't hide the joy in her voice. "Did you find—"

Heather didn't seem to care that she interrupted her niece. "You need to come home, right now." Heather's tone reminded Alex of times she'd done something wrong.

"What's wrong? What happened? Did you find Billy? Is Rose okay?" Alex walked to the door and waited for Abby, unsure of what good her litany of concern would accomplish besides delay Heather's reply.

"There's someone here, Alex. She says she knows you."

Alex couldn't for the life of her guess who might be there. Someone Heather didn't know. "Who is it?"

"Her name is," Heather said something that sounded like *Bonnie*.

Alex clarified, "Banhi? Banhi is there? Older woman, wavy gray hair?"

"You know her? When the hell did you meet her?"

Alex explained as she and Abby walked out to the truck and

started towards Heather's.

Heather hissed, "Can I trust her?"

The question took Alex off-guard. She second-guessed her warm feelings towards Banhi, Lesidi, and Khowla. *After what they did for me, what does Heather know that makes her not sure if she can trust them?* Maybe Heather wasn't questioning but asking for confirmation. "Yes. They saved my life."

Alex could almost hear her processing. "Alex, I'm concerned. She said she needs your help, but you're nowhere to be found. I just called you. You're right there. It sounds shady. Why can't she find you? Who is she, Alex? What have you got yourself involved in?"

No explanation was simple. Everything she thought to say required clarification. Once they were face-to-face, it'd be easier for Alex to just show Heather her coin was dark again. "We'll be there in a few minutes."

"Good." Heather said nothing else. She breathed loudly into the receiver, like she was trying to remember her line. Alex waited for Heather to remember all the unanswered questions she was avoiding. Then Heather began explaining things. "We came back a few minutes ago. Found that woman rummaging through your room, like a ghost." Heather huffed. "Did she think you lurk in dark corners? She was stalking around your bedroom. Calling your name. Alex, it freaked me out. Hearing someone talking upstairs that wasn't you. Rose took her Book out, ready for battle." Heather's voice lowered to a whisper. "I don't know what would have happened if I didn't stop her. She might have killed her. She's fragile right now.

"That woman, she's here in a dream-state. I don't know how long she can stay. She keeps muttering about, how did she put it, *on the Between.* Do you know what that means?"

Alex nodded, realizing Heather wouldn't see her acknowledgement. She said, "It's okay, Heather. It's what she calls that *other* place. You're not alive, you're not dead, you're *in between.*"

"Then why not say that?" Heather groaned. "Listen to me. I'm nervous and scared and lashing out at a stranger who saved you."

"I know you don't mean it." Banhi wasn't physically there. She was travelling on a silver thread. Her body was somewhere else, just like when the three visited her previously. Alex's stomach spun. *What is so important that Banhi would come looking for me?* She wanted to keep Heather talking, wanted the location of every piece in play so she could make informed decisions once she arrived.

"Did you have any luck; I mean with Billy? Any leads?" It shocked Alex they were already back. It'd barely been a day. *Why would they already be back if they hadn't found Billy? Or learned that they never would.* Alex's stomach crept around her abdomen. She didn't want to know what French toast and coffee tasted like in reverse. Alex didn't want to think that Billy was dead, but with each moment of silence, the thought pried its way into her head. Recollections of Billy, broken and bloodied below Picnic Rock, taunted her. *He can't be dead.* But until Heather confirmed otherwise, it felt like he might be.

Frantic for a response, Alex tried to ask another question. She failed at making her words not sound accusatory. "How'd you even know where to look?"

Heather's tone responded directly to Alex's. "I know people, Alex. It's like he vanished off the face of the planet. No one knows where Matthew is." Alex thought she heard something more, but it could have been her own guilt vocalizing as Heather in her head: *What did you do to them?*

Abby pulled into Heather's driveway.

"We're here, Heather." Alex looked at the phone. *Hopefully Heather hung up because she saw us pull in.*

Abby tugged Alex's sleeve, "Tell me what you need me to do."

The question froze Alex. *How do I plan for this?* Abby's expectant face begged Alex to tell her *something.* Alex considered what she knew like building blocks. *They saved my life. I owe them that. They know what I can do. That means no one else can help. It's on the Between. Maybe it has something to do with Billy. And if it doesn't, maybe I can learn more than Heather. Maybe there's someone they know who I can ask.* She worried she was building a tower on false assumptions. At least it was a plan. And as long as Billy was at the center of it, it felt like the right thing to do. The only thing.

Alex explained her thinking to Abby, adding, "So when I tell Heather I'm going, I need you to keep her from convincing me otherwise."

Abby nodded and jumped from the truck.

Heather met them at the front door. "That woman won't leave your bedroom. I keep asking her to come downstairs. I keep offering her something to eat. I know she can't eat. She must think I'm an idiot."

Alex placed her hands on Heather's shoulders. "Slow down, Aunt Heather. Take a breath."

Rose came out from the kitchen. Upon seeing Alex, she smiled. "Hey."

Alex held her breath a beat. All day she wondered what she would feel when she again saw Rose. Here she was: She killed someone. *Where's her head right now?* Alex was still trying to convince herself that the two men at her parents' house were responsible for their own deaths. Rose murdered Sara. *Sara.* That had to weigh on Rose heavily. It weighed on Alex. She hadn't processed enough to know how she felt about it: Part of her loved Sara. Part of her *was* Sara. Alex worried there might be unexplored emotions on both sides; feelings that would remain benign until some inopportune moment. "I'm so glad you're here, Rose."

"Are you?" Rose asked lifting her eyebrows.

Alex looked at her. *Is she trying to get a rise out of me? Start a fight so she can argue it wasn't her fault?* Alex felt a part of herself that wanted to hear those words uttered, so she could yell back, *"Then who was it, Rose? Who, besides you, killed Sara?"* Instead, Alex exhaled to release her rising tension. Then she crossed the room to embrace her cousin. "I am, Rose."

She pulled away from Alex. "I didn't realize it was Sara, I thought—"

Alex interrupted. She couldn't hear Rose say it wasn't her fault. "It doesn't matter, Rose." The words felt false. She was diminishing Sara's death to let Rose move on. "One day, maybe we'll want to talk about it. Right now, we're both here, and that's a very good thing. We need each other." She thought about who Rose was and added, "I can't do this alone."

Rose flashed a smile on her face. "I can help. I've been using the Book. I'm getting really good at it."

Before Alex could answer, Banhi shouted from upstairs, "Alexandrea, is that you?"

Alex looked around the room, so Heather, Rose, and Abby understood she was including them. "Come on," she told them. "Let's see what's wrong."

Rose caught Alex's arm. "Can we trust her?"

Alex didn't think Rose was asking for her opinion, like Heather had. She wanted a concrete answer. Rather than summarize what they had done, she told Rose, "We have to trust her." She didn't know what else to say that Rose might misunderstand or misinterpret, so she added, "They're good people." Alex couldn't help but grin. "They're like my fairy godmothers." Thinking about the threesome warmed her heart.

Alex headed upstairs with Heather, Rose, and Abby following. When she climbed the ladder and entered her bedroom, a glowing coin materialized out of a dark corner and Banhi approached her, her silver thread trailing behind her like a sparkling filament of light.

She was wearing a similar wrap to the one she wore last time, only this one was emerald green with yellow and black trim.

"Oh, I am grateful I find you again, dear girl. I come to beg you for help, but you were disappeared. I fear you died. I come here, to the last place we meet, hoping your heart-star might be reborn."

Banhi's voice didn't match the woman Alex knew. It was her voice, but the words coming from her weren't spoken with her previous graceful fluidity. *She's not on the Between. She is speaking English here. Her words aren't being translated by dreams.*

Banhi examined Alex and the three women flanking her. All their coins were glowing, save for Alex, whose coin was an infinitely dark spot on her chest.

"What darkness is this?" Banhi gasped as she pointed at Alex's blackness. "What happened to you?" She poked Alex in the chest. "How do you live?" She looked past Alex to the three women behind her. To them she asked, "Is this normal?"

Abby nodded. "You get used to it."

Banhi turned to Alex. "It's like a miracle. We find you on the Between, yet you live. You met Jeremiah, yet you live. You have no life, yet you live." She leaned closer and whispered, "Who are you, *really*?"

"It's a long story," Alex replied. "I can hide my heart-star."

Abby heartily laughed, "She's not kidding. It *is* a long story."

"What?" Banhi asked.

Alex explained, "It was like this—hidden—before. That's why you thought I'd been born. And why you can't find me now."

"Sorry to interrupt," Heather said from beside Alex, "but you came to ask for her help?" She looked from Alex to Banhi, her eyes insane with curiosity. "Ask her already."

Alex wordlessly asked Abby to manage Heather. Beside her, Rose watched, her face in intense concentration, like she was preparing for a shootout.

Banhi's wrinkled face slackened with concern. Banhi half-smiled, as though that were all the joy she had left to share. "It is horrible, this that is happening. It may be too late now," she said to Alex. "It has been a half hour since I left. He is killing us all."

Alex's spirit sank. Her mother's words, spoken by Banhi made her nauseous. These women saved her just days ago; was Jeremiah punishing them for it? "You're sure it's *him*?"

Banhi crossed her arms. "I wouldn't accuse the devil unless it could be none other."

When she asked them for help, they refused her. Now they were asking. Except, this was because of her. Of all the options she might have, Alex only saw her obligation. "What can I do?"

"Jeremiah is murdering people? You're not prepared to face him." Heather grabbed Alex at the elbow. "You're not going with her." Her tone was motherly and absolute.

"He is not there," Banhi clarified. "He sends these shadows. Shades."

Rose asked, "Shadows doesn't sound so dangerous. How is that bad?"

"Shades," Abby said, matter-of-factly, "are old souls that lose their desire to be. If a person clings too strongly to the things they had in life, they suffer as time passes. They cling to things that no longer exist. They lose their humanity because nothing is left that's important to them. They fade, lose their recollection of life."

Rose rephrased her criticism. "That doesn't sound dangerous at all."

"Shades are what's left when the dead give up." Abby's tone changed, insinuating she was making an important point. "They're filled with regret, sadness, disappointment, and sometimes even anger. They are the empty space where the person used to exist, a tatter of emotions and memories. Peter, once told me they could be controlled, put into service. It bothered him. You promise them things they don't realize they can never have. You prey on their sadness and desire. When you have nothing, an empty promise is everything. It's like you offer them the thing that will plug the hole their essence drained from, and they think it fills them up again. Nothing fills them but what you put in. What goes in makes them something very different. When you wander through a shade in a dream, unhappy things happen. Peter told me that after one time I had a really upsetting nightmare."

"How do you know this, Abby?" Alex was more than a little concerned. "And why am I hearing it for the first time?"

Abby shrugged. "I guess I know more than I realize. Your father told me a lot of things I'm sure I've forgotten. When I heard her say the word, it popped right into my head, the whole conversation. I can see it in my mind like it was yesterday. We were in the basement at his house, just him and me. He held his hand under the light to make a shadow, then he placed his other hand in the shadow and moved them like they were one hand."

"Did you forget or, maybe, did he make you?" Alex asked.

"I hope not," Abby replied. "That would be, I don't know, cruel. Why wouldn't he trust me to remember? I mean, what context would I have to tell you about them before right now?" Abby's expression showed she wrestled with the possibility that Peter messed with her memory.

Banhi gestured at Abby. "She is right. The shades are what that evil man sent. We need your help." She looked from Alex to Heather. "Please do not deny us her aid. If it were one of your friends or children…," Banhi's face wrinkled at the distaste of the words she nearly said. "Please," she pleaded.

To Alex, all Heather said was, "Are you?"

"They need me." Alex answered softly.

"How can you leave us right now?" Heather accused.

Alex took a breath, resentful for Heather's guilt. "Please don't do this." She motioned to Banhi, "She saved my life." Heather was unconvinced. "Heather, I'll be on the Between. Someone might know about Billy." Heather's eyes widened. Alex was unsure what Heather's fearful expression meant except that she knew something she wasn't sharing. Alex's stomach bubbled caustically. *She knows Billy is dead. She's not telling us, so we have hope.* Her room felt claustrophobic. She wanted to cry. She wanted to give up. *If Billy is dead, if Heather knows, then what's the point?* Heather must have noticed because she did her best to mute her expression. Alex waited for her aunt to say anything, both standing silent.

Rose spoke up, "I'll go with you."

Heather looked conflicted as she realized there was no way to keep Rose, too, if she wanted to go. The look on Heather's face pained Alex, like she was losing them both.

"No, Rose," Heather said, her eyes begging Alex to agree. "This is something Alex needs to do herself."

By keeping Rose home, Alex realized, Heather wouldn't begrudge her going. "I need you here, Rose. To protect Heather and Abby. We're all in danger. If Jeremiah comes to harm them, he'll be surprised finding you here."

Rose's eyes narrowed, "We're *all* in danger?" There was excitement in her growing grin.

Banhi breathed impatiently behind Alex. Alex said, "My mother warned me. No one who knows me is safe. He doesn't know about you and your Book." Alex knew her assumption was cavernous, but Rose needed to believe she was being deputized.

Rose nodded, her stance widened, her back straightened. "They'll be safe."

"Thanks," Alex said to her. Then to Abby and Heather, she said "I'll be back as soon as I can."

Abby called after her as she walked towards Banhi, "Something besides bees."

Alex turned back and smiled; Heather and Rose looked confused. Then she turned to Banhi, "Show me the way."

Banhi froze, her hands in the air as though showing Alex an invisible loaf of bread. "How? You have no heart-star." She gestured at her sparking thread. "How is it you travel on the Between?"

Alex opened her mouth and hesitated. *How do I explain what I don't understand?* "Trust me."

Banhi started talking to herself as she walked to the patch of mist where her thread originated. "Find the girl, but the girl is not alive. She has no heart-star. How does she travel with a dark heart? Listen to me. Travel? How does she live? I understand none of this."

Alex stepped into the mist beside Banhi; the older woman shrieked. "What is this? Your body is not allowed on the Between, why do you not leave it behind? I've never seen such things." Banhi's eyes darted between Alex and her dark heart and the open darkness of the unimagined dream-space. "This is not a good omen, Alex. You bring your body here. How?"

Alex couldn't answer. She'd never given it much thought, but learning she was doing something which violated the laws of nature gave her pause. She felt like she'd left something important in her room and was drawn to return for it. Instead, she pointed onward with her chin.

As the two walked through the utter darkness of unimagined dream-space, Alex asked, "Banhi, where are we going? Someplace in India?"

"It's night in India. We dream. We travel on the Between. We meet. Just one night each month. All dreaming of one place. The same place. Markets for trading ideas and places to sit and talk. From all over the world we are. We never meet except on the Between." She hesitated. "It's a place I like to call Yes-where, because it is the opposite of no-where." Banhi hurried along, nearly breathless as she strode as rapidly as she could. "Anything can happen here," Banhi continued. "This is the place of the dream. Anything you imagine or desire can be made and happen. We come and talk, practice magic, we do wonderful things."

"Magic? You have magic?"

"Only here. But not the elemental spells of the real world. Here, it is not magic, but imagination." She touched her forehead, "This is the limit of our ability."

Alex thought about her mother's house, Rose's house: imagined places, forever changeable, unreal. Her mind worked through the details of what this could mean.

Banhi continued, "For as long as I know, for my mother and my mother's mother, this has been done. Tonight, he sent the shadows. We fought; we defeated it. Then another and another came, stronger. Each time, they know the trick that defeated the last."

Anticipation for what she was heading towards grew inside Alex like a hive that teemed and shook but never revealed what was inside. She kept telling herself that in this place, where ideas were shared, she would find someone who knew about Billy. She'd use her magic, like she had at her mother's house, calling on all the voices to make her more powerful. She could nearly imagine giving her victory speech, and a hand would raise, "I know. I know where your Billy is." Her hopefulness was all she had to tamp down her fear, but Heather's expression weakened it. *Heather doesn't know anything. Heather is just afraid.*

In the distance, Alex saw what looked like a small market town that might exist in a movie, but the structures were unusual, looking otherworldly and futuristic. Colors and shapes made her eyes buzz. No rules of architecture or physics were consulted for the construction of this place.

As Banhi spoke, Alex saw all was not well in the market. "Kholwa said to me as it began, *Get the girl*. Then the horrors."

"Kholwa is here?"

"Lesedi, too. Or were. Some maybe fled to be awake. But it happened fast, the shadows broke many threads."

"What? You can cut the threads?" *I knew it.* What that meant was terrifying.

"I never thought it to be true until I saw tonight. But these shadows, none have a heart-star." She looked at Alex apologetically. "I mean to say none of them are real. They are like nightmares." She paused. "Horrible things hide on the Between. We remember our fear of them from when we were small and easier prey."

Alex watched her face; Banhi studied hers as well. Alex saw the distant buildings in greater clarity. They were creations of imagination. Cantilevered ceilings, swooping walls and curving, impossible windows. In the center of this created town, a large explosion of flame erupted in a small mushroom of fire and smoke; screams and the growl of collapsing structures followed.

Alex grabbed Banhi's arm. "Come on," she shouted.

Banhi let out a shriek as Alex pulled her and she looked up to see Alex, flying.

Chapter Seventy-Two

anhi's surprise was mutual. Alex had leapt on a whim, shocked—because her coin was dark—when she didn't fall. She felt like some cartoon animal pinwheeling in the air, suffering the panic of losing the ground. Confidence slapped her startlement, and she leveled off. Some things were magic and other things were of imagination. She'd flown in her dreams, but it now felt almost as natural as walking... for a toddler. In dreams, it seemed, anything was possible.

Carrying Banhi didn't add any sense of weight. Nor a change in aerodynamics or control. She had Banhi's hand in hers, but there was no strain to the grasp.

Approaching the edge of town, they came in slow. Alex tried to rotate her body, but she could not seem to position her feet beneath her. Their landing was less graceful than Alex preferred as they crashed and rolled on the hard-packed ground.

Alex cringed in expectation that the older woman would cry out from grievous injuries. Banhi jumped to her feet, "*What was that*? You *must* teach me to do *that*!" The excitement made her face glow, but the joy was short-lived. The blowing wind carried in its warmth the sounds of women's screams.

Realization washed over her like dirty ice water. *What have I gotten myself into?* What was she going to do that they couldn't? *They have magic here. If I can fly....* She was drowning in the paralyzing panic of nightmares. Though she hadn't yet seen any of these *not a man*, her skin crawled. Her panic was like a shadow lingering at her shoulders, whispering doom into her ears. *I came because they need me.* Although it was like breaking rusted joints, Alex forced herself to turn towards the cries.

A canyon of fanciful buildings stretched before her. In the distance, three women raced towards them, their silver threads sparking and undulating in their wake. The three wore different clothes; one an ochre-colored sari, another a navy blue niqab—only her dark eyes visible—and the third wore jeans and a red beaded tunic. Their clothes fluttered behind them. Their hands waved in the air.

They shouted warnings. Their panicked gestures twisted Alex's concern: these women were terrified.

But nothing was giving chase.

"There is one," Banhi gasped.

Alex saw nothing. Just ripples, like heat rising. It reminded Alex of how she appeared to herself in her dreams when she was cursed. The dimmer, distorted air shifted her view of the buildings like looking through a glass of water. As it moved, the ground reverberated.

The three women offered breathless warnings as they raced closer. There was still nothing in the road behind them. Just a shadow. Then, her eyes seemed to adjust; her chest tightened with the realization that the shadow took the shape of a giant man. And it was coming closer. And it wasn't alone.

The seedlings of fear, planted when she first saw the running women, bloomed into knotty, thorny plants as they approached. The shadows were of monstrous proportions, perhaps fifteen or twenty feet tall. They were whisps of smoke to the eye, yet their lumbering movements shuddered the ground.

Neither of these shades had a coin. Alex glanced at her own dark heart. *Can shadows hurt?* Alex suffered nightmares before and always awoke unharmed; she didn't understand how this was different.

Alex watched Banhi dig her heels into the hard-packed ground and did the same. The passing women didn't slow. They ran haggardly. Sweat staining their clothes. Shouting at Alex and Banhi. Waving them away.

Perhaps finding Banhi and Alex between them and their prey, the shadows paused pursuit.

Alex felt like a golf ball was caught in her throat. She swallowed it down. Sweat trickled down her back. Her heart banged against her ribs like someone trapped in a coffin. Her skin tingled with electrical fear. "Come on, ladies," she whispered to her voices.

As though collecting kindling, one shade ensnared the three silver threads trailing behind the women. The fine strings sparked like steel-struck flint where touched. It seemed in violation of reality that something nearly invisible was able to grasp the threads. Disturbed vibrations racing along their irritated lengths.

Alex was sick. The sickly sweet of maple syrup swelled at the back of her throat. *I'm about to watch people die.* Helplessness chilled her skin, raising goosebumps everywhere. Thoughts of anger fled her mind, like water draining from a tub. She did her best to stopper its retreat and with gritted teeth, thrust out her hands, expectant of some version of electricity. It felt wrong. Nothing happened. The women screamed, no longer able to run, begging for their lives.

Banhi stared expectantly at Alex. Before them, the threads sparked madly as one giant shadow strained to tear them apart. Banhi made a face that Alex read as disappointment. It felt too small a punishment for her failure. Banhi closed her eyes in deep concentration. She clasped her chest. Her hands tugged the fabric of her wrap, pulling it taut until it snapped from her grasp. Her hands parted to reveal a small emerald flame. She threw it at the shade with the threads.

Banhi's colorful fire struck, splashing against the shade like napalm. The burning shape darkening. Sunlight broke through the shadow wherever the fire rapidly died away. As the last flames disappeared, the threads snapped free, buzzing and sparking electrically.

With a massive wave, the second shade sent Banhi tumbling like a pile of leaves in a gale.

Alex cried after Banhi, watching her body crash into a bright orange wall. *Did she just die because of me?* Banhi moved, not uninjured, but the bearings knocked from of her. Whatever relief Alex expected to feel was poisoned with guilt that her failure nearly killed Banhi.

She turned to the shade with all her rage. Nothing happened. *Where'd my magic go? Why can't I cast a spell here?*

The three women raced past. One of them shouting to Alex, "Run or they will kill you next."

The shade grabbed at Alex. She thought she could jump away, but the monstrosity's size meant its hand was everywhere she went. She could barely make out the thing as it pressed firmly around her. Alex shivered; heat sucked from her body. She fought, but it held her solidly, yet she had nothing to leverage against. Her feet lost the ground. It squeezed air from of her, like water from a wrung towel. She hadn't the lungs to scream. She found herself thinking about Abby and Rose and Heather. How long would they wait for her return before accepting that she never would?

A second ball of green flame burst against this shade. Heat from the emerald fire was like opening the door to Abby's kiln: suddenly blazing hot. She slipped from its distracted grasp. Falling hard to the ground, Alex wasted no time in scurrying away.

Alex's panic-blindness evaporated. From the height of the shadow's grasp, she'd caught a glimpse of the next street and the next. Those were no different. Shades. Snapped threads. Lifeless bodies littering the roadway. No tricks of light and shadow. Real nightmares. The carnage sickened her. A single dry-heave broke her transfixed gaze. Her mouth tasted of syrup.

Banhi screamed. Cornered by the shade, she repeatedly threw emerald fire at it. The flames hit the shade but burned away harmlessly. It closed in on Banhi. She flattened against the orange wall. Alex watched, her heart like the drumroll announcing the impending execution. Banhi's expression showed she knew it was over. The shade collected her sparking thread, menacing her. Muting Banhi's emerald wrap to gray.

Her hands trembling, Alex grasped her dark coin. Banhi screamed, suffering the swift unraveling of her thread. Alex didn't want to take her eyes from Banhi, but her hands were suddenly incapable of working unsupervised. She fumbled with the edges. Banhi's thread sparked and jumped, showering the ground in a fit of sparks. It felt like abandoning the woman, but she tore her eyes away to look at her coin.

Banhi screamed.

The coins pulled apart. Alex turned them about.

They snapped back together.

Alex hadn't noticed any difference when she'd turned her coins dark but flipping them back around was like flicking a switch in a dark room to find someone had wired up hundreds of bare bulbs. Her hands trembled, this time with power. This time, with magic.

She pushed her hands forward, her fists clenched.

Nothing happened. No lightning, no thunder; nothing flew from her hands. She was about to give them a shake, like her flashlight went dark when, within the shade, a miniscule spark illuminated.

The shade whipped around to her. The small spark in its center swelled. Banhi's thread fell to the ground, sparking rabidly where it had been damaged. It charged Alex.

Banhi cried out as sunlight splashed across her face. Alex

panicked as she tried to release her emotions through her hands; it was like she'd forgotten how. Nothing worked.

The shade was upon her, its darkness overflowing with light. Anticipating the stone-cold grasp, she was instead greeted by a chilly breeze that mussed her hair as the spark dissolved the shadow.

Banhi's mouth formed a gaping "O". She collapsed against the wall, clutching her chest in relief. She shouted, "You did that?" Her widening eyes caught sight of Alex's glowing coin. She motioned to her own and gave Alex an excited thumbs-up.

Alex adored this spunky, old woman. She helped steady Banhi to her feet.

"That was *amazing*. How did you do that?"

Alex wasn't sure how to answer. Disappointment deflated her voice. "I thought I was going to shoot lightning."

"You shoot lightning?" Banhi asked in awe.

Alex looked at her hands. "It's like magic is different here."

"Child," Banhi offered, "everything is different here."

Chapter Seventy-Three

hey raced deeper into the market. The cries of anguish and pain and destruction echoed from everywhere. Alex hoped Banhi failed to notice how nervous she was.

They raced through a narrow, confusing maze of streets; some throughways were as narrow as alleys. With no need for vehicles or delivery trucks, the width of roads became as unusual as the structures. They twisted and turned in a way that gave Alex haunted reminders of the layout to Rose's house; there needn't be any useful design to places of dreams. Alex supposed that in less harrowed times, she'd lollygag down the lanes, gazing in wide-eyed wonder at the sights around her. Instead, buildings made of soap bubbles or marbles or matchsticks threatened to blind her attention with their uniquity. The tension of angles and cantilevered levels bore a weight that caused Alex to duck despite being them well above her. The tight corridors and narrow turns were rife with blind corners and choke points. They ran into what appeared to be dead ends only to emerge out arterial streets that seemed to come into existence as if summoned by their disappointment.

Alex anticipated an ambush or fresh horror around every corner. They climbed around rubble from a collapsed wall made of feathers. Alex pretended not to notice a bloodied handprint or a splash of blood on the ground. Gleaming edifices that would have captured her imagination any other day blinded her with the way their sparkling eccentricities shattered sunlight. They passed bodies. Some women looked like they slept, covered in dirt. Others looked like savaged ragdolls, abandoned by a bored dog. Alex tried to refocus her eyes on anything else, but Banhi always checked; guiltily relieved when it wasn't someone she knew.

Alex trembled at the sights. Her stomach churned, molten and acidic. She'd never seen a war zone, but if she ever wanted to understand the dichotomy of creation and destruction, this place was a masterclass. The spectacle of giant peacock plume overhangs and buildings made of towering soap bubbles stood beside other broken and shattered dreams. Danger lurked everywhere. Partially collapsed structures supported as if by a thought. Destroyed and unstable heaps continued their decay in fits and explosive lurches long after their destruction seemed complete. And that was just the inanimate objects. The unmistakable cries of the dying were unlike the constant shrieks of fear.

Even brief silences offered no respite. In the moments when everything hushed and went still, broken glass crunching underfoot called out their position.

Turning a corner, Alex found herself face to face with a new shade. She backpedaled, crashing into a counter, spilling a stack of glass tablets that fell like a race of dominoes, each one dropping in turn, shattering to the ground.

This shade mutely roared, exposing mats of cloth and flesh and gore twisted around nearly invisible, gnashing teeth.

Alex held her hands out and clenched her fists. The spark appeared, but the shadow darkened as though creating a chrysalis around the it. Like a flame swallowed, it blinked out.

Now I understand. Banhi said they learned the attacks. Each is good only once.

The shadow rushed at Alex. It had but steps to cover between them. It was upon her before she had time to think. Lightning came as spots of light. Burning a shadow made no sense to her, yet Banhi's trick worked. The hungry mouth opening, washing her in cold stench, as though she'd opened a freezer. Cringing at the expectation of a shadow-mauling, she waved her hands. The shadows collapsed as wet puddles; air changed to water. Dry soil sucked them away, leaving the ground dark and muddy. All that remained were the scraps once caught in its teeth.

Alex wiped the spray from her face. She was no closer at understanding how magic worked, but she'd had some intent in mind in the moment. For a change, what she intended and what she accomplished were the same. She nodded for Banhi to follow.

The further into the market they proceeded, past stalls made of knots of iridescent thread or crocheted from colorful wool, the worse the destruction. There was something about the carnage that reminded her of a ransacked playroom. The buildings were so fantastical that even their ruins seemed playful. As though pointing out how serious this was, a trio of women clamored over the rubble of interlocking plastic blocks. Two others, battered and broken, hadn't the strength to follow. Alex tried to help them. One woman's eyes fluttered. The others closed. Both their coins fading until they vanished. Their threads disintegrating in a cascade of sparking light turning to dust.

Alex couldn't even look Banhi in the eyes. All this death, because three women had helped her. Not even the weight of responsibility could smother her anger.

There were so many to help, so much loss, so much pain, and always Banhi's fear the next victim might be Kholwa or Lesedi or someone else she knew. Alex was new to death; the shattering of life left her cold.

When she found herself worrying about Heather and Abby and Rose, she kept convincing herself that shades were a thing of dreams. They wouldn't have to face anything like this.

Every encounter with shades she faced, her anger, her disgust, her heartache, grew. One she unfolded like it was covered with a blanket, another she turned into a single thread that unspooled in a giant knotty heap. Dispensing the shades became easy. Imagining new ways to accomplish the task wasn't. She wanted nothing more than to destroy them for the pain they caused. She wanted to lash out, to reel the raw power of lightning from her fingertips. What it required was nuance and concentration. More imagination than emotion. A thought, birthed from deep in her mind as opposed to stammering rage. Staying in the moment made her cold and sick. Forced her to ignore pain and death. Compassion prevented her from immediately finding the loose thread that solved the riddle of the next shade, and the next, and the next.

They reached the market center, a large, open square with an ornate tiled fountain. Its circling base depicting the eight phases of the moon, repeated thirteen times. The base was immense, a hundred feet across or more. A shallow layer of water splashed and burbled, sprayed by myriad sculptural creatures bathing, and squirting, and pouring water. Nymphs washed, fish spat, women overturned urns; each a different scene as though a dozen groups frolicked. Alex held her breath at its magnificence. The water played through each scene, splashing one to the next, tying together all the vignettes, so a small fish spat a stream into an urn which poured into a bowl which was sipped by a ram and on and on. In the center, rising to a towering peak, was the tallest structure she'd yet seen: a narrow mountain twisted into an ornate spire, the likes of which she'd only seen in photographs of gothic cathedrals. Only this gigantic spike was overrun with a menagerie of mythological creatures. It seemed they were climbing up, the rivulets of water cascading over them like muscles twitching at their effort.

Alex lost herself in the view. Her eyes made out a unicorn, a dragon, a flying horse, a flaming bird, and at least several dozen others she had never seen before; animals whose biology made no sense as claw and fur and feather and scale intermingled, as though stuck together at random. She recognized creatures from astrology, rams and crabs and fish and scorpions. Snakes twisted upon one another, others paired and devouring their twin. She stared in awe as water sprayed in majestic arcs from all around them, following unnatural paths winding and twisting and falling. Everywhere her eyes fell, some magnificent new creature seemed to flex—through a trick of flowing water and sunlight—as though its stillness was the illusion. Someone had imagined this: wanting something beautiful couldn't make it real. It had to be imagined to be created.

The fountain demanded the tribute of her vision before allowing her to view anything else. When she observed the entire square, she despaired. Bodies were strewn everywhere. Some were dead, many nearly so. Hundreds of white, wooden chairs lay strewn, knocked askew, and broken. Stains of blood and smudges of burn marred most surfaces.

Banhi followed close behind. Woman huddled about the fountain base, sipping the water, cleaning their wounds. Some creatures Alex—from a distance—assumed were centaurs, were— from a closer vantage—bodies tossed and broken atop sculptures.

Throughout the square, dozens of shimmering threads crisscrossed this way and that. Then one would collapse to dust. Indifferent to the surrounding chaos, the fountain proudly sparkled and burbled, spraying water in a hundred different arcs.

Banhi, her hands and emerald wrap dusty and blood-stained, collapsed into Alex's arms. She sobbed as Alex held her. "We are too late," she whimpered.

Alex fought to keep her eyes dry, but the whimpers of the dying were too great to bear. "We can still help some of them." Alex helped Banhi to survey the square. "I can heal these women. Can't I?"

Alex realized the rumble of voices came not from her whispers but from a surge of women feeding into the square from all directions.

They streamed from every street and alley. Banhi desperately hunted through the crowd, looking for familiar faces.

Why are they all coming here?

Banhi's head bobbed, anxiously trying to see past the approaching throngs. She hunted with increasing urgency. "Where could they *be*?"

Alex recalled Kholwa and Lesedi's appearance well enough, but there were too many to make out just two. Here, amidst the filling square, she felt the foreigner. Most women around her were Indian and Middle Eastern and Asian, and their clothes touched the gamut of what Alex might and might not expect: from dungarees and blouses, to saris to burkas, to some clothes as fanciful and imagined as the surrounding buildings once were.

Every one of them, however, came wearing their shock, soiled by dirt, scratched and abraded, smeared with blood. Some came silently. Some mumbling to themselves. Some moaned in unbearable pain.

There are so many. She guessed thousands.

"Maybe they are safe at home," Banhi wringed Alex's shoulder. "Maybe they are not dead but somewhere smart and safe, no? What do you think? Can you find them better than me?"

"Find who?"

Banhi's face melted to joy at the sight of Lesedi behind Alex. "Who are you looking for?" Lesedi added, "I can help."

Banhi burst out in an embrace. "Where have you been? Is Kholwa with you?"

Lesedi lowered her voice, "If I am with you and Kholwa is not here, how could she be with me?"

Before Banhi could scold her or laugh at her joke, Lesedi wiped the tears from her face. She nodded to Alex that she was okay, dirt smudged on her dark skin, her hair loose and looking mad. "You found her. Now this can end. Kholwa will be along."

Banhi nodded. "You know where she is?"

"Of course I know, Banhi." Lesedi answered.

A deep voice asked, "Know what?" It was Kholwa, squeezing through the crowd to join them. Her jeans were torn at the knee, caked with dust and mud, and splattered with dark browns of dried blood. She had tucked her necklace beneath her blouse. The shapes of the stones showed as rubbings of dirt on the fabric.

Alex troubled to smile at the three women having their bittersweet reunion. There was much she wanted to say, to ask, but was an outsider among these three friends. They were so happy she was here, confusing her as savior when she knew she was the reason suffering haunted them.

Banhi embraced Kholwa. "I am glad to know you are alive."

Kholwa nodded. "I should hope so." Before Alex could think their joy strange considering the hellscape they reunited in, she noticed such joy was not unusual. Coming together, finding friends still alive even when others were not, offered—if briefly—enough comfort to triumph over grief.

Lesedi held out her hand to Alex. "Thank you for coming." Alex embraced Lesedi, who said, "I thought Americans only shake hands."

Banhi grinned at Alex. "This one isn't an American. This one is a witch."

Kholwa asked Banhi, "Where had she gone?" She turned to Alex, "It was like you were born then unborn."

Banhi explained—in exaggerated and fantastical terms—how Alex's coins were turned around and dark.

Lesedi squinted in wonder, "But still alive?" She turned Alex around, gasping as though surprised anew with each push and pull. "Where is your spider silk?" Alex was the only woman in the square lacking a silver thread.

Banhi answered for her. "When she is one of the dead, she travels," her voice deepened, "like the dead."

Alex couldn't help but touch the glowing spot on her chest. *Is that what I am when this is dark? One of the dead?*

Even Kholwa seemed impressed. "She does not seem dead."

Lesedi, her skin marred with burns, hugged Alex again. She tried to pull her uncooperative hair taught. She managed to tame it like a loose cloud that listed to one side. "I am so grateful you would come for us," she told Alex. "Who could want to do this?"

Kholwa scolded her for asking a stupid question. "It was the breath under the bed. Who else destroys us?"

Banhi rested her hand on Alex's shoulder. "This woman saved us all."

Alex shook her head. "Don't say that."

"What? You did." Banhi said puzzled.

Alex looked around doubtfully. Everyone congregating in one location set her ill at ease. *I haven't seen any shades since we got here.*

Banhi's old face wrinkled in joy. "They would be fools to stay when they have such an enemy as you to contend with." She motioned with her arms as though throwing imaginary spells. "To watch you is amazing." She turned to the others. "Do you know this girl can fly!"

Lesedi nodded, "Her legs are long. I bet she is very fast."

"No, Lesedi," Banhi held her arms out, "*fly*."

Alex tried to ignore their enthusiasm and looked about as the crowd coalesced into small, cohesive groups of women familiar with one another. Many nursed injuries. They helped one another, tended to the many wounded. Even here, in dreams, people cried out in pain. Sometimes magic healed, but not always. The survivors kept looking in expectation. No one else was coming.

"I should try to help," Alex told them.

Banhi's eyes went wide. "No," she hissed. "Let no one know you are here."

Lesedi agreed, "You are unknown to the world. Best to remain that way."

Kholwa rubbed Alex's shoulder. "You have helped. The shadow-men are gone. No other heart-stars will be lost today."

"What happens," Alex asked, "when your coin, I mean heart-star, is darkened here?"

Lesedi replied, matter-of-factly, "You die." She paused. "Well, not you. But the others. The ones with the darkened heart-star. They die."

Banhi nodded. "In the morning, their body will be found, cold and quiet."

Kholwa added, "They will say the woman died quietly in her sleep." She looked around. "We know. We all know. It was not quiet or sleep."

Alex asked, "It happens often?"

Lesedi replied, "Imagination is magic. One can make very big magic happen here." She pointed at the gigantic fountain, "Big magic, big risk. Easy to make things go boom."

Kholwa laughed with Lesedi as though they shared a secret. Then she said to Alex, "In your own dream, all is your own making, so it is safe. Here, on the Between, creation is shared. It is not my dream or your dream or hers or hers," she pointed at the crowd for emphasis. "It is ours. It is shared, like the awake world."

Banhi stepped closer. "Some of the time, a woman, she is noticed to be a witch. In the world. Maybe someone can pay another to find her here, silence her behavior. A desperate woman can be a dangerous friend to have. There is no safe place for a witch when man is hunting her."

Lesedi put a hand on Alex's shoulder. "It is normal that it is safe. Today," she sighed, "is not like normal."

"No," Kholwa interjected, "they sent horrors to kill us. This is a nightmare. Who would do this?"

Banhi and Lesedi made similar faces.

Alex appreciated the knowledge they shared. She wanted to know more. "They'll kill a witch and not make a Book?" It surprised Alex. The men she'd met were covetous of magic.

Lesedi mused, "I think it is nice to go as a Book. Are you dead if part of you lives?" As she spoke, she opened her hands like a book, holding them on either side of her face and giving a slight grin.

Kholwa elbowed her, looking around in hope no one saw her friend's pantomime. She hissed at Lesedi, "How do you say such things? Better as a Book? Give no man your magic is better. As a Book? You are mad."

Lesedi became defensive. "I am trying to make sense of it."

"You? Make sense?" Kholwa laughed as she added, "Why start now?"

Lesedi looked hurt. Kholwa poked her in the arm. "Do not be stung by my bad jokes, my friend."

Alex heeded their warning not to interfere. She didn't know why so many women remained when they could leave. "What happens if you get hurt here?"

Banhi shrugged. "You wake up after this. You are lucky to wake up."

"Then why heal? Why not just leave?" Alex questioned.

Lesedi leaned closer to Alex to whisper. "That achy foot that you never hurt, that stiff neck you never wrenched. All unhealed wounds from this place."

Alex nodded. "I can heal all of them—"

Before she finished, Kholwa grabbed her, "Shh, child. Only us three know of you. If the world knew you were a witch for real, how many of these women will accept payment for that information?"

"But they're hurt," Alex protested.

Lesedi nodded, "I know. You want to do right. You are here because we sent for you because we were scared." She looked at the other two. "We have done you wrong, brought you to harm when we should have protected you."

Banhi's shoulders fell. "He knew we would, didn't he?"

Kholwa and Lesedi nodded. "And we did."

Alex took a breath, trying not to feel so much. They were blaming themselves. The weight of responsibility was too easily shared.

"There is much to learn," Banhi patted Alex's shoulder.

"You all know so much about, about, Yes-where," Alex borrowed Banhi's expression. When she said it, Banhi beamed while Kholwa gave her a dirty look. "No one ever told me about this. I don't know anyone who knows this place exists. How is that?"

Kholwa shrugged. "Look around, Alexandrea. Were there even a thousand women tonight? A billion sleep right now. That *is* no one."

Banhi winked at Alex. "That is statistics. One out of a million. Not good odds."

Concern grew on Alex like a casing of ice. "Why is everyone staying? I know they need to heal, but why not leave as soon as they can?"

Lesedi asked, "What do you mean? Where should they go? Look at this mess. It will not clean up by itself."

Alex was flabbergasted. "After what just happened? It's not safe here."

Kholwa remarked, "This market was frequented by my mother and her mother and hers. It is ours, to protect and rebuild. We do not run because one of us has a nightmare."

"Is it wrong to want to wake up," Alex tried not to be too sarcastic, "and roll over? Take an aspirin and go back to sleep knowing you're safe and alive?" She couldn't understand.

Banhi touched Alex's arm. "This has been a nightmare. Look at them. It traumatizes them. The shades are gone; you made us safe. We stay. Every one of us knows someone who will not be waking for the morning. When the sun comes, who will believe our grief? *It was a bad dream*, we will be told. Maybe, if the person lived nearby, a prophetic dream. Such speak may put us in more danger. If we say a person died, and that person is then dead, then maybe we are a witch and we killed them. But no one will listen to a woman crying about her dream. No one will hold her without wondering why she cries real tears for imaginary people."

"They should wake up." Alex wished she didn't keep expecting another shade crashing into the square. Every movement in the corner of her eye set her further on edge. She turned to the crowd and shouted, "Go and wake up!"

Lesedi ducked, as though by making herself smaller would show she was not with the screaming lunatic. "What are you doing?"

"It's me they're after," Alex warned.

Kholwa replied, "You are here. Where are they? Gone."

Banhi motioned with her arms again, throwing an imaginary spell. "Have you ever seen someone make real magic before?"

Kholwa conceded, "No." She eyeballed Alex with mocking suspicion.

Lesedi tapped Alex in the chest. "You are special. I knew you were to be special when we woke you like that sleeping beauty."

Banhi sighed, "Sleeping Beauty wakes with a kiss."

"I know it is different," Lesedi said, "but the same." She whispered to Alex, "Did the *Breath under the Bed* know we would ask you for help?"

"Maybe. Or punish you for helping me." Her mother's words haunted her, again.

Off to her right, she heard the lament of a group of women mourning the passing of a friend. Alex saw them, a group of eight, wailing over the body of a ninth.

She looked back at the triumvirate. They saw it, too.

"Poor woman," Lesedi breathed.

"It didn't need to be like this," Alex remarked.

"Never you mind the lives of others," Kholwa said. "You saved many lives today. You can't be known." She turned to ask Banhi to explain to Alex how dangerous it would be if everyone knew she had magic.

"What is she doing?" Lesedi tapped Alex's arm, "What are you doing?"

Alex's eyes were closed, deep in concentration. Everything was different here. She breathed deeply and did her best to feel calm. "Help me," she thought to the whispers.

All around her there was suffering. Pain. Loss. Some of this she couldn't take away. Some of this she had to.

Banhi asked, "Don't be foolish. Are you not thinking?"

Through her concentration, Alex replied, "What is the point of power if you don't use it to help?"

"Alex," Banhi scolded. It was too late.

Throughout the square women exclaimed in shock and surprise. Each woman was unique in Alex's thoughts as if she'd walked to them one at a time. As though she reached out a hand. To each one she felt, she touched, she healed. Bleeding clotted. Wounds became scabs, became scars.

Tears fell down her cheeks as she opened her eyes. These women didn't know her, but still suffered.

Women throughout the square gazed about to discover who had healed them.

One young woman approached Alex and asked, "You?"

"Mind your business," Kholwa chided, waving her off.

Others caught sight of Alex, by her clothes and skin, by her lack of thread, the stranger among them. Some pointed.

"What is she?"

"Is she the one who saved us?"

"I saw her destroy one of the shades!"

The surrounding mass pushed closer. Lesedi reached out to Alex. She and Kholwa and Banhi formed a guard around her.

"Go home," Alex shouted. "Why don't they go home?"

Hands reached past her guardians, trying to touch her, to caress her cheek, to pinch her arms and prove she was real.

Alex finally had everyone's attention, "Go home. Get everyone out of here. You're not safe here."

Lesedi looked in Alex's eyes. What she saw made her shout, "You must leave. All of us must go and awaken."

Chapter Seventy-Four

lex shouted at the crowd, "Go, get home. Run now!"

Banhi asked, "Are we not safe?"

Alex warned, "He knows I'm here."

Khowla chided, "I warned you not to heal—"

"It wasn't that," Alex defended, touching her glowing coins. Jeremiah set a perfect trap and she fell right into it.

The four of them spread the warning to the crowd.

Gradually, women headed off, following their threads, and disappearing down alleys and streets.

"We have done it," Banhi congratulated the others. "They are going."

Alex stared at each of her friends. "What are you waiting for?"

Lesedi pointed a slender finger at Alex. "I think the girl is right. Everyone needs to wake up." She motioned to the few groups that hadn't departed. "They feel safe because of you," she told Alex.

Kholwa cupped her hands around her mouth and shouted, "If you hear me, you must go. Go back, wake up. No one is safe here."

Lesedi eyeballed Kholwa and repeated, "*If you hear me*? What should they do if they do not hear you?"

Kholwa began to reply but laughter stopped her. The remaining women began departing. They were murmuring, talking, sharing their goodbyes and their sorrows. Perhaps wondering if they would ever come back. If they did, what would this place become? Would they ever feel safe here? Anywhere? Was this the end of their travels, of their dreams, of their life at night?

Some vanished right away, their threads emerging from nearby stalls and alleys, while others rushed down other roads.

"You should go, too," Alex told her friends.

Banhi took Alex in her arms. "You came when we called. The girl with no soul saved us."

Alex rubbed the older woman's shoulder. She watched Lesedi and Kholwa come together and embrace her as one group. "I'll see you again," she told them, "I know it."

Khowla asked, almost accusing, "Do you? For certain, you

know such a thing?"

"No," she told Lesedi. "I just mean that…."

Lesedi shushed her. "It's okay, child. We know."

The three women backed away. The square wasn't yet empty. Most searched the dead for those feared lost, but some rifled through clothes, trying to hide their act.

Alex would remain until her friends were safe. Her thoughts again went to Heather and Rose and Abby. Could this have been a diversion to separate her from them? Would Rose have the grace under pressure in the face of such danger to read from her Book? Alex believed so.

The earth trembled beneath. A fine dust rose from the ground.

The rumbling tossed Alex to the ground as though everything turned upside down.

Several buildings across the square crumbled in complete collapse. The fountain spire tipped precariously this way and that before it shattered, scattering mythological and chimeric creatures alike. As it collapsed, shards and fragments pulverized lower sections of the spire until the entire tower transformed into a race of dust hurtling to the ground. As the rubble crashed into the base, the moon-phase pool ruptured, and an explosion of water rushed into the square, pushing spilled chairs, and muddying the soil in a growing flood.

She saw that, although battered, her friends were okay. Righting themselves, they waved to show they were okay before continuing along the lengths of their threads. Then they stopped. They froze. They turned. They ran.

Crashing through the rubble; a single massive shade entered the square.

This one, however, was a towering giant of improper dimensions. Just the sight made Alex's legs quiver. Each thunderous footfall reverberated in her gut; all imagined existence trembled.

It raced towards Alex with an animalistic grace of a gorilla. She lost her breath, prescient as to what was about to happen, what could only happen next.

Alex screamed a warning that wouldn't save anyone. She began to cast a spell, to destroy this monster, to hurt it, to get it to focus on her, to confuse it, to slow it: To give Lesedi one extra second.

Chapter Seventy-Five

n her panic, Alex struggled to imagine a new fate for the beast. Alex turned air to ice, created a tornado, shot it with dozens of tiny shards of light. Despair shattered her creativity like a raccoon ransacking an attic. The horror reached into her chest and tore out her heart. Only it didn't touch her: Lesedi was in the shade's hands, screaming.

Echoing across the square, her bones shattered like dry leaves before it discarded her. Lesedi's body somersaulted like a ragdoll, crashing in an explosion of dust.

Alex cried out her anguish as disbelief.

The shadow ignored a cowering Kholwa. It focused on Alex.

Alex backpedaled, her eyes fixed. *Lesedi, please get up, please move. Show me you're alive!*

Banhi and Kholwa both raced to Lesedi.

Take care of her. Please let her be all right. I can heal her. I will. Alex turned and ran.

The delay diminished her lead. Peering over her shoulder, the gigantic shade had halved the distance between them. Each footstep covered several times what Alex was capable. She tried anything that came to mind. Fire, ice, splintered glass. Racing over piles of rubble, she showered it with light, encased it in darkness, flooded it with water. She turned down a street and tried to suck the air away, to shatter it, to crumple up the space it occupied and throw it away. The kitchen sink bonked off; perhaps had she thrown a thousand more. Nothing slowed it. Nothing worked. Each spell, each attempt, slowed Alex a step. Every spell left her hands a maelstrom and struck like a raindrop.

Alex's stomach churned. Her heart ached. She refused to believe Lesedi was dead. How could she face Banhi and Khowla if she'd failed them so? If she ever got back to them. *This is it.* As the rumbling steps were on top of her, her thoughts briefly drifted to Abby, Heather, and Rose, waiting for her in the attic. Were they safe? *I thought I'd be fine.* She anticipated the icy grasp of the shadow, the chilling, crushing clutch as it picked her up and squeezed the life from her. *What am I doing wrong? What am I missing?*

The creature was a shadow. It was as though she ran from percussive footsteps, the grinding of sand, the splintering of wood and cement and glass, as it stepped on the ruins Alex snaked around.

The shadow thrust its monstrous hand into the sand. A tidal wave of fine grains rolled from it. It looked like it would raise a mountain. Instead, it balled its fists, and like it pulled a tablecloth, it dragged the world closer. Alex had to remind herself she was in the realm of dreams.

As it pulled the fabric of this dreamed reality, made it askew, it seemed the whole universe groaned.

Alex remained in a crouch for only a moment. With a giant grasping hand rushing towards her, she leapt up, rocketing into the sky.

The hand came close enough to wash her in chilled air. She elongated her body, flying like a bullet. Once she was far enough away, above the clouds, perhaps, she would have distance to think. Distance to plan and plot. Distance to strike.

The shade reached after her. A swoosh of cold hands missed her; the turbulence spinning her about. She stretched to fly further away. The hands reached to her, fingers puncturing the sky. And then they pulled the universe violently closer; Alex with it. The universe groaned—like Abby's barn, on the verge of collapse. This world was coming apart and there was no waking from it.

Stabilizing herself from a spiraling freefall, Alex tried to figure out her next move. *If none of this is real, then maybe neither is the shadow.* She closed her eyes—every molecule in her body warning her against losing sight of it—to concentrate. *They dreamed this place, made the buildings, made it day. If everything is imagined, then can't I unmake it all? Unimagine every bit of it?*

The sudden, clamping, icy grip on her ankle revealed her mistake. As it squeezed tissue and bone, Alex knew she was lost.

My coin! If Charon can't see me, perhaps.... Alex snapped her coin dark.

Flailing in the air as the creature waved her body about, she now had no magic. *That was a mistake. One wrong choice is all it takes to die?* It seemed an unfair equation.

Flapped through the air like a doll, her eyesight tinted red by the blood flooding her head. Alex desperately fumbled at her coins.

Her body snapped like a whip. Were they not tethered to her body, she would have lost them.

She felt smothered, the icy-cold grip on her body preventing her from taking in more than a whistling sip of breath. Her insides squirmed as the shadowy fist compressed her. Her body grew numb, either cut off from blood flow or frostbitten by the bitter cold of shadow. Her hands lost dexterity; she could see that her fingers moved at her will, but the sense of control had left them.

The shade moved, an abrupt withdrawal. Its grip diminished long enough for her to take in a welcomed warm breath before clamping down again. Enough feeling returned to her fingertips to allow her to peel her coins apart. But then Alex saw why it had flinched.

The turbulent darkness they saw appeared flat and black, as though it was a hole punched into reality through which to peer into the void. It expanded; the soft, misty edges seething. Alex's eyes hurt to look at it, unable to focus or appreciate distance. It grew, coming closer, not growing larger. Its edges disrupted this reality, like waves of heat rising off sun-scorched blacktop on an oppressive August afternoon.

This thing killed Marta. Alex remembered falling into it, unsure how she survived the endless emptiness. *This is Matthew's weapon.*

Alex strained and struggled to get free. She understood the expression—between a rock and a hard place—unable to move to escape one menace to avoid another. She forgot her coins, trying instead to squeeze herself from the shade's grasp, like toothpaste from its hand, to avoid the fate that was certainly approaching.

The shade threatened Oblivion with a forward charge which ended timidly when the boiling darkness didn't flinch. She felt forgotten in its hand, but not forgotten enough to slip away.

She twisted to look up at the shade. "Do something," she shouted at it. Oblivion was growing larger. The darkness bothered her eyes to look at. It seemed flat, two-dimensional. It's increasing size meant it was moving closer. Moving so close it appeared to be swallowing eternity.

Tears welled in her eyes. She thrashed in the grasp, desperate to free herself. Matthew found her when she'd righted her coins and now—trapped by the shade—he would claim her. She feared there wouldn't be any escape this time.

The shade must have discovered her; the grip squeezed all the breath from her. She felt light-headed, felt herself slipping into another kind of darkness, not sure which of the three she was facing would inevitably claim her.

Blackness became all-consuming.

Chapter Seventy-Six

lex gently spun, lost in the dark vastness of endless emptiness. Without a horizon for orientation, no direction identified as up. Spinning left her sick and dizzy.

Holding her hand in front of her face, she inched it closer and closer until she smacked herself. *It's so dark here I can't see anything.* The notion had a deeper, more important meaning, but it was lost to her.

Is the shade here, too? If Oblivion touched it—and she had no reason to consider it hadn't—it suffered the same fate. *Can a shadow exist in darkness?*

After some unknown while, her eyes hallucinated neon-like distortions. They were all short-lived, vibrant, and not at all real.

Although in perfect darkness, she had a sense of the void's vastness. It wasn't like being blindfolded. Her eyes perceived inconceivable lightless distances. She was miniscule, not even a speck floating alone, lost. She wasn't dead—not yet—but did that matter? This was not life. This was not death. This was nothing. Would she die of hunger and dehydration? Would she know the difference when death overcame her? Her coin was dark, Charon would not claim her. Alex's heart pounded like a furious parent coming upstairs, echoing in her ears, throbbing in her temples. If this was to be her eternity, for once, Alex understood terror.

There were no whispers here. No voices. She was alone. *Where'd they go?* Alex believed they were dumbstruck by the emptiness; too in awe, too aware of their own insignificance to feel important enough to have a voice. She could sympathize.

The longer she drifted in the dark soup of nothingness, the more her thoughts drifted to the mundane. *What happens when I have to go to the bathroom? Can I sleep? How do I know my eyes are closed?*

Alex thought of Abby and Heather and Rose, back in her bedroom. She promised Heather she'd be back. *That was arrogant.* How many hours would have to pass before Heather lowered her head, before Rose said something smug, before they left Abby alone in the attic? How long before even Abby gave up? Would she? Could she?

She had magic only a few days and it ruined her. She longed for her old, ignorant life. Why did she have to have this curse? Where did it get her? Where did it get anyone who pursued it? Her mother, her father: both gone. Sacrificed for her; for what? For this? To have her languish, forever in the void?

She screamed, the void absorbing noise as it passed out of her mouth. She kicked and pinwheeled her limbs in fury and anger and disappointment and rage. Then she fell still.

Her ribcage contracted with a sob, and at once the tears came. She drew her knees to her chest and wrapped her arms about them. She could only feel them. She was alone, but at least she had contact with something.

Time seemed unknowable. She startled as if awakening but had no idea if she slept. No notion of the passage of anything except her beating heart. No idea whether she'd been here for days or just hours; time elongated by boredom.

What happens next? Will it be like this forever? Will there ever be a next?

"There will."

Who was that? Alex looked around. No one. Nothing. No breathing, no heartbeat, no sounds of skin bending, of joints creaking, of cloth moving, besides her own.

The darkness hadn't seemed to change, yet she saw her body. Felt firmness beneath her feet. A speck of light illuminated near her. Her coins were still dark. *I can make my own light.* She reached for them.

"I wouldn't do that. I think you're alive because they're dark."

"What?" She heard her own voice, louder than she'd intended.

"It senses the coins. Oblivion. It doesn't know you have one, so it just leaves you. When you vanished, I knew it was safe to send it."

Alex couldn't forget that voice. The gravel tone, pinched through a bent throat caused by a broken neck. The sinews in her limbs tightened like thick rope, preparing to fight. "What do you want, Matthew?"

Matthew stepped before her, emerging as though appearing from behind a curtain. *Was he there the whole time and I couldn't see him?*

She threw herself at him, like she'd been twisted too tight and just broke. "Where's Billy?" she cried through clenched teeth as she beat at him.

"I didn't come to fight," he pleaded. "I'll tell you," he offered. He snatched her wrists, freezing her attack.

She thrashed. Unable to break his grasp, she kicked at him with her knees. "Where's Billy?"

"Please," he urged. "I'll tell you. Just stop." His pleads drifted to the realm of demands.

"You better," she said as she pulled her hands from his grasp.

Letting her observe him, he took a step away. His crooked neck no straighter, his face aged, tired and drawn. Disheveled. His coin glowed, a thread extending into infinity.

He gave her a look, like asking permission, which she granted with a nod. He asked, "Does this remind you of anything?"

"This is like unimagined space."

"Very observant."

Alex began asking about Billy.

Matthew sighed. "I never wanted harm to come to you. I *need* you."

Alex scowled. All he'd ever done was harm her.

"I need you now. More than ever." His tone exuded sincerity. Alex wanted to argue, but what would she gain? She was at his mercy, now more than ever before.

Matthew eased himself down until he was sitting. He groaned as though succumbing to gravity exhausted his bones. She surveyed the blackness surrounding them. Darkness in every direction gave both a sense of the infinitesimal and the infinite. How far away could Alex see? Perhaps forever. Perhaps she could only see their two forms and was blind to anything else. The possibilities hurt Alex's head.

"This place is like a dream within a dream. Magic and imagination are inseparable." He looked away. "The void disturbs me." With a sweep of his hand, they were both seated on the top of a sloping grassy hillside. He looked around, proud of his accomplishment, and nodded in self-satisfaction.

He strained to observe Alex. "It's remarkable: Even in my own dream, I'm a broken man," he touched his neck, just above his glowing coin. "You'd think I'd imagine myself youthful. Or at least whole. But I guess the damage is too great."

Alex looked past Matthew. "Why should you be any different in the void?"

He didn't seem to notice the sarcasm in her tone. "We are each our own universe. Separate, unknowable from each other."

Alex wondered if he was answering her question or saying something because it was important. Like he'd planned to, but the opportune moment wasn't arriving. "You made the grass. Are you saying you can imagine yourself different than you are?"

"In dreams, you are how you perceive yourself. Apparently, I've come to know myself as an old, broken man." His tone, his wistful, disappointed gaze, almost made Alex feel sorry for him. He padded the grass. "Creation is not so unusual. Oblivion is unexplored. Unimagined. No one dreamed here until this moment."

Alex didn't want to agree, not with him, but her nod just happened. "So why do this? Why kill all those women when it's me you've *needed* all along?"

"That was Jeremiah. Adherents of his faith. They believe blindly until the truth runs them down. If it ever does. To them, he's deadly serious. But really, he's playing."

"Playing? That didn't feel like a game."

"No, he's seeing what makes you tick. Vivisecting you, to see what's inside while you're still alive."

"That's disgusting."

"If he wanted to kill you, you'd be dead. We're alive because he allows it."

"He sounds scary." She mocked. He didn't seem to notice.

"That's why he must be stopped. No one should have that much power. All those Books in his control."

Alex nodded. "Only you?"

Matthew laughed. "You think I'm after the power? *After all the magic?* It's the only way to stop him."

"Well, yeah."

Matthew offered a crooked grin. "Maybe it looks that way. It's not. I need to take away his magic."

"And you need me for that."

Matthew sighed. It seemed dramatic, almost orchestrated. "I didn't send the shade. Oblivion saved you. I did that. You don't seem to comprehend how important you are."

"What does that even mean?"

Matthew offered a grin. "I created you, you know."

Alex laughed. "Created me? Really, Matthew?" She wondered why she responded with sarcasm when verbally sparring with him.

"You wouldn't be who you are without me."

"It's done so much good. Everyone is so happy. Magic is great."

Matthew withheld his first response. "You're suffering. I understand. Greatness doesn't come without sacrifice. Without pain and loss."

"I never asked for this."

"You feel it was thrust upon you?"

"Um, yeah."

"That's fair. But I think it's not entirely true. If you search yourself, you might discover you want this. Or at the very least that you're unwilling to give it up."

Alex chose not to reply. If she could unload all her responsibility to another—Rose—would she? Alex hated that he was right.

"Deep inside, you like the responsibility of being special. You don't crave power. You don't flaunt your ability. All you care about is helping others. Like you've been given a noble quest."

Realizing she was proving his point, she added, "Where's Billy?"

He raised a finger as though making an important point. "I helped your parents make you. You have a purpose, by design. Your father was my student. I've had many over the years."

"You probably tricked him into helping you."

"No, Alex. *Your parents asked me.*"

Alex realized her mouth was open, whatever words she intended to utter abandoned her.

"They betrayed me, Alex. They used me. Giving you up was always part of the bargain. They accepted that from the onset."

"This surprises you? They wanted to protect me? You can lie better than that, Matthew."

"Every parent dies a little for the sake of their children. For you, they willingly sacrificed their lives. For me? They were... reluctant."

"Can you blame them? Look what it did to them."

Matthew nodded. "Peter was my best student. Better than I

ever was. I think his reasons were more abstract, more personal; he saw himself rebalancing the universe. The day Holly discovered she was pregnant his sense of commitment changed. He stopped seeing the bigger picture."

"And that was…?"

"You're the only one who can stop Jeremiah." Before she could say anything, he countered, "Be serious, Alexandrea. Look where we are. I took great risks to bring you here. To save you. Why lie to you now?"

"Fine. I'll humor you. How? How am I the only one?"

"I'm the last in a long line of men who sought the end of Jeremiah. No one has come closer than me, but I stand on the shoulders of giants. We've believed the Library is the source of Jeremiah's power, but we've never had a way to take it from him." Matthew looked at her, his awkward craned neck straining. "Think, Alexandrea." He snatched a fist in the air. "All those Books. You take away his Library and you take the source of all magic. He will be powerless."

"You make it sound so easy."

Matthew ignored her snark. "No one knows who he is, or if he even is a *who* anymore. Some say he made the first Book. Some say he's the devil. Others think he's God."

"It would explain the patriarchy of your friends."

"It would." Matthew resumed his analogy, "Some say he stole his powers from the Moon Goddess when he murdered her."

"You believe any of that? *Moon Goddess*?" She wiggled her fingers while she said the words, like she intended them to be spooky.

"I'm inclined to believe some part of each is true."

"Which parts?"

Matthew closed his eyes. "The part where he becomes god-like. Nearly omnipotent. Does that mean he killed a goddess? Perhaps that's just a metaphor, but then how do you explain the vastness of his powers?"

"Are his powers vast, or has he convinced people to believe they are?"

Matthew studied her. She worried from his look that he hadn't thought this through. He looked like an old man, struggling to find an elusive word hidden beneath a blanket of dementia.

"He didn't seem that scary when we met."

"He doesn't perceive you as a threat. We're play-things to him. At least, until we bite. Then he puts us down."

He had Alex's attention, but she couldn't let her demand alone. "This is all fascinating, but how do I get Billy back?"

"By stopping him. Jeremiah has him."

His words chilled her. Jeremiah's promises to return Billy replayed in her head. *Was he playing me the whole time?* "But I thought…." She lost her train of thought. "He and you, on Picnic Rock…."

Matthew shook his head. Softly, Matthew said, "Would I abandon you the moment I discovered you, unless something happened to me?" He squinted at her, rolling his body to maneuver his head for a better view. "Save Billy. Stop Jeremiah. These are the same now."

He had made his case and there was no arguing it. No matter how it reeked of a trap. Heather and Rose had searched. If Billy were anywhere but imprisoned by Jeremiah, they would have found him. "So, I take the Books and I'll get Billy?"

"Yes. Take all of them. Give them to me. I'll make a single Book. Only then will I have enough power to use his magic against him."

"Give them? Really? Is this the part where you lecture me about sacrifice? Do you look forward to breaking my fingers with your little hammer?" She blinked to hide the moisture brimming in her eyes.

His tone lowered. "In spite of what you've experienced, I don't look forward to hurting anyone."

"And if I don't?"

"Alexandrea, you and I are enemies of Jeremiah. Me through my deliberate betrayal. You simply by being a woman with magic. He has hoarded all the magic from the world into his Library by convincing his followers that unwritten magic—emotional magic—is dangerous. Your very existence risks damaging the foundations of faith." He took a breath. "You can sacrifice to stop him, or you can die in vain. And not just you. Everyone who loves you, who knows you, who has heard about you."

"Everyone?" Alex was once again haunted by her mother's words. "What if I don't give you the Books? Why can't I use them?"

Matthew stated matter-of-factly, "Women can't read from

Books." Alex bit down, severing her argument. Although she knew Rose had read from a Book, he didn't. She wasn't about to share that with him. "Emotions are fickle. By now you've noticed how insignificant things alter your spells. Books are magic pure. No woman stands the remotest chance. When you fail, then there will be no one powerful enough to stop him, perhaps ever again. Who would step forward knowing what he does to those who betray him?"

Alex shook her head. "You're so certain. You only see one way."

"I've been alive for lifetimes. Lifetimes. You're," he tapped his thumb against his fingertips, counting out the years in his head, "eighteen? You can't even comprehend a single life. I have knowledge of centuries. I've seen it all. No one powerful lives unchallenged. You or I would be but the latest in a long line of challengers. Generation after generation, built on shared knowledge, working to end his reign. And still, *he* remains."

Alex crossed her arms, "You're not answering my question. How will you be so much more powerful than me?"

"Because, young Alexandrea, you are an emotional creature. Because you wield your magic out of fear and anger. Because you would face Jeremiah, and when he showed you his true face, the one borne from millennia, older than time itself, the sight will turn you to ash."

He'll never change his mind. How can I argue? What experience do I have? What has life shown me that could help me face someone like Jeremiah? I've lived part of Sara's life, but that only taught me suffering.

"This isn't some trick. You won't give me the Books until you have Billy."

It felt like an afterthought he'd tacked to the plan for no other reason than to satisfy her requirement. "Whatever, Matthew. I'll do it. I'll get the Books. But it's up to you to take them. I will not give them willingly." She looked for his agreement, hoping he understood he'd have to take them by force. "I'm done talking about it." She looked past Matthew, her gaze following his silver thread. "How do I rescue Billy?"

"Go to the Library. Take out a Book. Take them all."

Rose said the same thing days ago. "How does that find Billy? Let me guess, he'll offer to trade Billy for the Books?"

"Jeremiah will threaten you with his well-being. In the end only you and the Books matter."

There was nothing about this Alex liked. She was being conned. She was already thinking next steps: Getting back, telling Heather, and then…. Alex hated having to admit this, "How do I get to the Library? I've only been there because George brought me. Should I ask George how to get back?"

"He'd like that. He has quite a thing for you." Matthew's smile was pleasant. Alex reminded herself how she hated him. "No. The Library is well hidden."

"That much I've figured out."

"Please permit me." He held out his hand. When she hesitated, he offered, "Do you still think I go through all this effort only to harm you now?" When Alex acquiesced, Matthew touched her right hand. He held it firmly between his two hands.

What Alex felt wasn't a headache. It was like a blister forming in her brain; a knot of information that hadn't been there moments before.

Suddenly her head felt swollen, her brain pressuring the extremes of her skull. It was like a flood entering with nowhere to go. Every here and there in the swirling waters there was some piece of debris, some glimpse of knowledge she hadn't possessed before that instantly swirled away in the turbulent water. He let go of her hand. "The Library," she muttered. Reality was like a shock. It was so close. "I know."

Matthew nodded. "Very good. Once I'm gone, walk to the edge of the grass," he pointed, "and Oblivion should release you." He paused, deciding whether to add something. "One more thing. In this game, people die. A lot more than have already."

"What are you saying?"

"Don't blame yourself for that woman."

The words confirming what Alex struggled to disbelieve felt like an attempt to wrench out her heart.

He continued, "For any of them. One day you'll learn death is always the end. Not even Jeremiah and all his power could save her. No matter how we like to believe, Charon takes a coin; if we're lucky enough." Matthew grunted, and as though he were ancient, his crooked body protested with pops and cracks as he climbed to his feet. "It's time. I've kept you away long enough."

"Matthew?"

He turned back. "Yes, dear?"

"If you're lying to me, I'll kill you."

"I know you don't want to believe me, but we're on the same side." He walked away, disappearing into the void, his thread and his coin vanishing into the distance like an afterimage.

Alex took a breath and looked around. The fake green field was beautiful. Without Matthew, she appreciated the silence.

"Damn," she cursed. "No wonder they couldn't find Billy." She hesitated, trying to decipher the discomfort in her skin. "I've got to get him back. What choice do I have but to walk right into this trap?"

She walked towards the unimagined edge of the field, and stepping into the void, spilled from Oblivion.

Chapter Seventy-Seven

lex stood in the ruins of the square. Dust swirling around her feet. Before her, Banhi and Kholwa knelt in the dirt, clutching Lesedi.

She's not dead. Alex raced towards them.

As she ran, she told herself lies about what she saw. *I can heal her. She's not dead. They don't realize it; I can heal her.*

The women looked up; Alex's grasp on hope slipped. She knew what they knew. She knew the shade killed Lesedi, but the shade was there because of her. In the equation that manifested in her mind, Alex might as well have committed the act herself.

Lesedi's body evidenced all the brutality of her death. Her skin, once so dark it looked almost tinged with purple, was now gray.

Not again. Not Lesedi. She collapsed beside Banhi and Kholwa and claimed Lesedi with her hands. "Let me try—"

"She's gone," Banhi pressed her hands on top of Alex's. "Sweetheart, she's gone."

Alex cried, "I can fix her."

"No girl," Kholwa said. "You don't want that. Look," she pointed at Lesedi's chest. "Her heart-star is gone out. Her thread is gone. Even if you could, there's no telling what comes back. It won't be her. That we know."

"Do you know?" Alex watched them both shrink in uncertainty. "You don't, do you?" She placed her hands on Lesedi, straightened her back. She wanted her body poised to help her feel strength.

"If you succeed and it's not Lesedi? Will you let her—if it is a her—go back to her life? You shouldn't play with these things."

"No, you don't understand," Alex pleaded, "it's Lesedi! She doesn't deserve this." She wasn't yet ready to admit that the death of the men in her house was her doing, yet she felt the full weight of responsibility for Lesedi.

"This," Kholwa motioned to the body, "isn't Lesedi. She is in her bed at home. Her loved ones will find her in the morning." Alex heard the epithet to that statement: *And believe she died peacefully in her sleep.*

Alex hesitated. "No," she didn't care what she sounded like. Tears filled her eyes. "No," she repeated, unable to make words out of what she was feeling. This felt so personal. Lesedi wouldn't have died had it not been for Alex. It wasn't action that caused this. Just her very existence. Alex looked on the still form and saw all the others. This wasn't just Lesedi. Wasn't just Banhi and Khowla. This was the Book Club. This was Heather and Abby. This was Rose.

Kholwa embraced Alex. "Shh, child. It's not okay, but it's what we have."

Alex collapsed into her. "It's not fair."

Kholwa softly asked, "Who said it has to be fair?"

"It's never fair," Alex cried. "But I'm supposed to change that."

Kholwa stroked her hair. "Dear girl. I'm sure you want to. I want you to. I want her back. I've known Lesedi nearly twenty years. I will tell you she is okay with this way."

"Listen to Kholwa," Banhi touched Alex's arm.

"When we left you, that first day when we met, we three were saying our goodbyes. Do you want to know what she said to me?"

Alex held her answer a moment. "What?"

Kholwa continued, "She said, *How many women have a whole life where they think this is all there is? Today we met her. Today we met the girl who changes everything. Isn't that exciting? We met her. We helped her. Her story is our story. We made our place in the story of the girl.*"

Sobs overwhelmed Alex. Her whispers mourned, too. Perhaps some of them knew Lesedi. Alex barely knew her, yet they felt like old friends.

After a few minutes, Banhi and Kholwa looked at her through tearful eyes. "Before, when you disappeared, where did you go? The darkness devoured you and we thought all was lost."

Alex didn't know how to answer Kholwa. She briefly explained Matthew and Oblivion.

"That's the Matthew you talked about. The one in the fight with...," Kholwa didn't finish; she didn't want to speak Jeremiah's name.

Alex confirmed, "He's the one."

"Oblivion?" Khowla looked inquisitively at Alex, "How did

you get out?"

Banhi shushed her, but Khowla explained, "One never knows if one will find herself in such things."

Alex pointed at her dark coin. "Matthew said it's because I don't have a coin. It's like with Charon. Charon doesn't pay attention to me when my coin is dark."

"I knew it," Banhi slapped her hands together. "When your heart-star is dark, everyone thinks you are dead."

Alex looked at Lesedi. Her eyes welled up again. *If only death were as easy as darkening my heart-star.*

"I've heard of such things," Banhi whispered.

"Stop your lies," Kholwa chided. "What things have you heard?"

Banhi made a face that was half-insulted, half-mocking. "Fine. I will not say it."

Kholwa rolled her eyes. "In front of Lesedi, no less."

"That's not fair," Banhi countered.

Kholwa shook her head.

Banhi rolled her eyes. "I once heard that each life creates a universe within this one. When a life is unlived, that is a universe of no thoughts, no dreams, no life."

Kholwa did not respond.

Isn't that what Matthew said? We are each a universe. Alex used the moment of silence to tell them about Matthew's plan and what she must do to rescue Billy. When she finished, they stared at her.

"You're not thinking of it, are you?" Banhi asked.

"Of course she is, Banhi," Kholwa remarked. "How else does she get her Billy back?"

"It's a trap," Banhi hissed. "Billy is bait. Why else would…," she wouldn't say the name, "would he hold him?"

"I know," Alex admitted. "What choice do I have?"

Banhi warned, "Don't go."

"I have to. There's no other way." Alex added, "He has Billy and it's time we get him back."

Banhi put her hands on her hips. "What if Billy is a distraction to keep you from the real goal?"

Kholwa scowled, "Banhi, how could you?"

The two fell silent. Alex understood why she had to go. No

one she loves will ever be safe. Even if she succeeds, Matthew will make his last Book. If all stories have to end in death, eventually she'd have to face it.

Alex looked about. When she arrived, the square was breathtaking. The entire market was awe inspiring. Now this place was a necropolis. It felt time to leave. She said so.

The other two looked on Lesedi. They touched her. "Goodbye friend," they each whispered.

Kholwa wiped her face. "What is to happen next? Were we supposed to live? Will he be angered that you saved us?"

Alex groaned. "I worry things have to get worse to get better. I don't know how any of us, least of all me, gets out of this alive." How many would she be willing to lose? Marta. Lesedi. Who would be next? Who would be the last?

Both women looked on her with concern. Banhi replied, "You? Die?" She gestured with her hands, her new sign for Alex's spells. "You are a special woman. Do not doubt yourself so. Without you, who do we have to believe in?"

Alex smiled slightly; it was all the joy she could muster. "Thanks. I'm not strong enough to face Jeremiah. Not alone."

"You are not alone." Banhi pointed at Alex's head, "There are many with you."

Was that a joke? Alex checked with Banhi for clarification.

"What I mean is you need to rely on those able to help."

Alex sighed. "Look around, Banhi. How many have to die because of me?"

Banhi tisked. "It's not an answer anyone likes, but perhaps to put an end to this evil, the answer is *all that are necessary.*"

Alex felt punched in the gut: What mattered more than the outcome? Alex groaned. "You're right. I don't like that answer."

"You know it's true," Kholwa agreed.

"I don't know anything, anymore." Alex caressed Lesedi's face. "If every loss hurts like this, how do I bear it all?"

Kholwa looked at Banhi. "You have an answer for that, Banhi?"

Banhi glared at Kholwa.

Kholwa laughed and replied, "Sweet child. The road ahead will be difficult. No one is like you. No one is like him. The rest of us are pawns. Protect yours. They all matter to you. He knows this. He can hurt you and never touch you. But you can never hurt him the same. He thinks nothing of sacrificing his pawns."

Alex nodded. She was answering reflexively when the weight of Khowla's statement fell on her like a mountain. Her heart ached at the notion of harm coming to Heather or Abby or Rose—or anyone she loved—for no other reason than someone sought to hurt her. The cruelty in it was profound and left her hurting preemptively.

There was nothing more to say. Alex looked back to Lesedi. "I will miss her. She made me smile."

Kholwa nodded. "She played daft well; always to make a smile." She tugged at Banhi. "We need to leave. Morning is nearly come."

Alex asked, "What do we do with Lesedi's body?"

"It's not her body," Kholwa answered. "What you see is there because you still wish to see it."

Banhi rubbed her eyes.

They stood and addressed one another with somber looks. They waited for Alex to stand with them.

"Goodbye, Alexandrea." They each used the same words. They each kissed Alex gently on each cheek.

Alex didn't want them to go. "Goodbye." She watched them turn. She watched them depart. She would wait here, standing beside Lesedi's body until they were safely away.

She knelt beside Lesedi. "Oh, Lesedi," Alex whispered. "I wish I could fix you." She rested her palms on the other's chest and closed her eyes.

Alex recalled something Lesedi once said. Today she left no coin, no Book. Lesedi worried about dying like this, disappearing without a legacy. Other women survived through servitude on paper and now exist inside of her; why not Lesedi? It was so unfair that the one way she most feared was the way she died.

Once Alex was alone, she screamed at the sky. She screamed until she no longer felt like screaming. She wasn't screaming for Lesedi, but for all the women who perished here. For Sara. For what she would soon lead her loved ones to. She resented that she was being forced to move those she loved into danger.

Alex could flip her coin and perform any sorts of magic to bury Lesedi or even rebuild the market. Instead, she piled pieces of debris on Lesedi's body.

There was nothing more for Alex here. Nothing except to forget this place ever existed and go home.

Chapter Seventy-Eight

ying on Alex's bed, her feet dangling to the floor, Abby slept. Alex stood where she appeared, shadow replaced evaporating mist. She took a deep breath, replacing the smells of upturned sand, destructed construction, and broken flesh with scents of home. Drying herbs hung from random locations throughout Heather's house, their delicate smells perfumed the air in powerful ways. Walking down a hallway, one might pass dusty blue sprigs of lavender followed by a tangle of peppermint. In her room, she was aware of mingling scents. The incongruity of smells from both places hurt her head, but she welcomed the pain. Smells of rosemary, heather, thyme, sage, and multitudinous other potpourri blotted and absorbed memories of destruction and pain; dulling the coarse edges which scraped at her insides as her mind flashed recent memories with wanton. It was as though punishing her through recollection was the only way to make the nightmarish images fade. There were so many.

Abby slept; a restless, light slumber. She wore jeans and her trademark sleeveless shirt. This one was black but faded to dark gray from washing. The shirt rode up, exposing a stripe of white stomach. The others had likely waited for a few minutes, perhaps as long as an hour, and growing bored or frustrated left the bedroom. Yet it was Abby, always Abby, who would wait for her, who refused to abandon her.

She didn't blame Heather or Rose for the wash of loneliness that swept over her. Comparing them to Abby would be unfair. Their leaving the bedroom wasn't abandoning her, but it was to Abby. She felt strongly for her Familiar . In the business of the day, she might not have been sufficiently aware to articulate it, but standing beside her, feeling the ebbing of her horrors, the immensity of her feelings for Abby swelled: Abby was her family. Alex could herself barely comprehend her dogged loyalty. Abby would never abandon her, doubt her, or dismiss her. As her Familiar, Abby willingly entered servitude, but Alex couldn't believe—refused to believe—that Abby waited here out of service. She didn't want to think anything from Abby was ingenuine.

Alex lay down beside Abby.

"You've been gone for hours. You okay?"

"You're awake?"

"Catnapping."

"Four hours?"

Abby looked confused, "Maybe. More."

Dreams happen so fast. Alex sometimes lived a lifetime in a dream and awoke to find a scant night had passed. How was it so different when she travelled there willingly, intentionally? Part of her expected to be back moments after she left, as though the dream sequestered consequences outside of time.

"How'd it go?"

Alex stalled twice before answering. "I know what comes next. It's about to get ugly."

"How do you know?"

"Because what happened there was horrible. Many people aren't waking up this morning."

"Not waking up?"

"Die there, die here."

"There?"

"The place you dream. Die there..."

"Oh." Abby seemed to be thinking. "You're not really okay, are you?"

"I'm, I mean, yeah, fine."

Abby half rolled over and put her arm around Alex. A simple hug. "Tell me about it if you want."

The muscle inside Abby's thick arm rested on her but not its full weight. Abby was holding her arm up but making it feel like it was at rest. Alex hoped that one day she'd be deserving of such acts. She didn't believe she earned them yet.

Alex wrapped her arm around Abby's. "Banhi brought me to this place. All these women meet in their dreams from time to time. It was amazing, the most beautiful place I've ever seen."

"It sounds unbelievable," Abby replied after Alex told her about the buildings roofed in flower petals or peacock feathers and whole buildings made of entirely of knots of ribbon or bundles of lace.

"The ideas, the creativity that gets shared in a place like that," Alex said, "I wish I saw it sooner."

"Go on."

Alex was looking into the square dormer over her bed. She glanced at Abby and saw she was doing the same. The sky was darkening as the sun set. Alex felt weight coming off as the light dimmed.

Alex told her about the attack. About what the shades did. "They did horrible things."

"Cowards," Abby shook her head. She studied Alex. "I feel like there's more you need to tell me."

Alex's eyes welled up. She couldn't find the words to tell Abby, as though saying the words would release the pain of Lesedi's death from her mid. She was so alive and then she wasn't. All this life, all this energy gone in a breath. She wasn't sleeping, she wasn't still; death removed something from her. If Matthew was to be believed, it was an entire universe. Is that why she couldn't just pretend that Lesedi was far away? Because she sensed the literal void her death left behind? All that remained was something in the form of Lesedi. It could have been any of them. *What is it like to suddenly not exist? Would I even know it happened? What is my universe like?*

Lesedi was just the one I knew. How many of those women's families didn't know she travelled in her dreams? Her family will mourn but be grateful she died peacefully, in her sleep. They'll never know the truth.

Alex could feel her eyes tearing, could feel her chest swelling and couldn't stave off the tears anymore. She shook her head and curled against Abby, holding her arm.

Abby didn't speak; she just held Alex as she cried.

*   *   *   *   *

Alex came into the kitchen, Heather smiled at her as Rose and Abby finished setting the table.

"I chose cutlets," Heather said, "because they're good cold. I'm glad you're back in time to eat them hot."

Alex looked at her aunt. She didn't know how to tell her about Billy. It felt like a false promise. She wanted so desperately to believe they were going to bring him home but couldn't trust anything Matthew said. Telling Heather that she knew where Billy was felt like validating his lies. And if his words weren't lies, what did that mean for her future? She knew all too well what it was like to be made into a Book. Meekly, she replied, "Me too." Alex tucked into a chair at the table. Rose saw her sit and shook her head, putting Alex's plate down noticeably further from the table edge than the others.

Rose asked, "Was it really so important?"

Alex bit her lip to hold back her gut response. Billy was still missing, and the perception was that she chose this strange, foreign woman over family. "Banhi took me to a place where thousands of women meet, like, every month."

"I didn't think Witch's Sabbaths were a thing anymore." Heather looked away.

"Isn't that where we went to ask about Billy?" Rose asked her mother.

Without looking at her, Heather replied, "It is similar. We went to a place where people go when they quit this life but aren't ready to die."

Rose grunted. "That's so creepy. I'm glad you didn't tell me before we went. Ugh."

How would Heather even know about a place like that? Alex explained, "With all those women in one place, it was easy for Jeremiah to have them all killed."

Heather gasped. Rose fell silent.

Heather gasped, "That woman, Banhi, she's dead?"

"No," Alex answered. "I was able to keep her safe. Her and a few others."

"A few?" Rose's eyes widened.

Alex tried to explain but only said, "Not enough." She didn't know their names, but she saw their bodies draped through the rubble. The vacant stares, the pain and injuries of the survivors.

Heather shook her head. "I'm so sorry, Alex. I didn't realize she was really in, you know, *real* danger."

"I know where Billy is." Alex then said, "Matthew told me."

All three of them turned to her. Rose spoke first, "Did you have to beat it out of him? You did something to him, didn't you?"

"He found me," Alex explained. "He saved me."

Heather mindlessly pushed cutlets in the bubbling oil with the spatula. "Saved you?"

Alex replied, "He needs me to defeat Jeremiah."

Rose grinned. "He *needs* you."

Alex looked from Rose to Heather. "Aunt Heather, Matthew and Peter worked together. When Peter untwinned me, he knew how because Matthew taught him."

Heather turned back to the cutlets, taking them out and placing them on a paper towel. "That's exactly what someone like Matthew would say. My brother was too good a man to work with him." Speaking through her concentration, Heather's words sounded hollow.

Alex watched Heather slowly walk to the table. *Why isn't she asking about Billy?* "And now we can get Billy back."

Heather strained to contain her emotions.

Rose gawked at her, waiting for her to proceed.

"How?" Heather finally asked.

"The Library is the key. I take the Books. Then all Jeremiah's magic is inside of me."

Rose glared at Alex. "You are not taking my Book."

"I'm not taking your Book, Rose," Alex said with exasperation. "Jeremiah has Billy. That's why you couldn't find him. That's why I have to go to the Library."

Heather fell into her seat. Her words barely had sound to them. "That's where he's been all this time?"

Alex nodded aggressively. Her eyes were brimming with tears of excitement.

"Billy's at the Library?" Heather's demeaner changed instantly.

Alex looked at Abby, and no one else. "To free Billy, I need to burn the Library down: take every Book away from Jeremiah. Then, Matthew wants to make his Book. Out of me." She could see the question in their eyes. They all knew how Books were made, but not one of them wanted to believe her sacrifice was part of saving Billy. No one spoke. Heather returned to the counter to bang her pans around. "That's the only way he'll be powerful enough to kill Jeremiah."

Rose argued, "You should do it. Didn't I tell you, take all the Books. Once you have all the magic, what chance does he have to take them from you?"

Heather threw the spatula down and spat a stream of epithets. "Let me guess," Heather said once she was done cursing, "women are too emotional? You aren't powerful enough because you can't control the spells?" Her tone was a biting critique on something she heard before. "Spells are pure when they're written down?" mockery painted her tone. "Emotions dull them?"

Alex didn't need to answer. Heather wasn't asking for confirmation.

Rose raced across the kitchen to take the plate from her mother, concerned Heather was angry enough to smash it. Heather turned to Alex. "Your father said that to me when we were teens. *You don't understand, Heather*, he'd say," her voice deepened in a mocking impression, which was all the more disconcerting because she reserved only reverence for Peter. "*Women should have magic, but the spells' power is weaker. For them to be written down, they have to be pure and perfect. Men can use them to fix problems women cannot.*" Heather looked around the room. "So, they're weaker. Imagine where this world would be if a single group of men didn't hold all this power. Most of the world doesn't even realize how they're being controlled. How much magic goes into making government work the way it does. Controlling people's minds. Men are false prophets...," she continued even as Rose tried to stop her.

"Mom, Mom," Rose pleaded before snapping at her mother, "You promised you'd stop talking like this." She looked at Alex and Abby and explained, "She got into all these conspiracy theories about witchcraft controlling the world. What was it, subjugating people by making them believe there wasn't any magic? It drove dad crazy."

"That's not why our marriage failed, Rosemary. Stop blaming me. One day you'll learn I'm right. It's not crazy-talk." Heather plopped down at the table, reiterating points under her breath.

Alex was grateful for the momentary silence, despite its awkwardness. She could see in each of their faces, the scales with Alex on one side and Billy on the other. Not one of them wanted to judge the balance. But Alex did. She could save Billy. She could end all of this. Maybe Matthew wouldn't kill her. Maybe she could find a way to cooperate. *All those women....* She'd freed them, or had she? They went from being trapped in a Book to being trapped in her head. Was that any better? Only to be returned to a Book. Was that it, then? Would she flaunt Matthew's certainty in the hopes of being able to save them all? All the women? Could she save them *and* Billy? Or would there be sacrifice involved that prevented both, like a cosmic *either-or*? Alex struggled unsuccessfully to grasp the enormity of what she was contemplating. And yet, she wasn't sure there was any other way.

"I never thought…," Heather mumbled. "I was so sure he was gone for good." She grabbed Alex's wrist—a little too forcefully—her eyes pierced Alex. "Are you sure about this?"

Alex wished she could be confident, but what she felt most was frightened. Very slowly, she nodded. "I am," she said with little emotion.

"The search is not over." Heather's eyes teared up. She wiped her face. Her words sounded tired, "What are we waiting for?"

Rose's eyes went wide, her words enthusiastic enough to make up for Heather's lack. "Are we playing cowboy, going in, guns blazing?" She looked at Alex, her grin bordered on maniacal. "Don't you dare suggest I stay behind to babysit these two again."

"Hey," Heather complained.

Alex tried not to look at Rose. She couldn't help but wonder what was in her heart. *Guns blazing? Doesn't she feel remorse, or anything, for Sara?* Alex couldn't help but think about the two men at her mother's house who died—even though they were intent on killing her and Abby. She'd seen enough death. It weighted on her with crushing pressure. Knowing there could be—would be—more didn't sit well with her, yet her cousin welcomed it. "I think it's better I—"

Heather interrupted, "Don't you dare say you're going alone."

Each time Alex tried to explain the danger, Heather interrupted her. "Tell me why it's safer for everyone to stay home."

Realization pushed Alex out of her seat. "Aunt Heather, please call the Book Club. Get them all to come over first thing tomorrow. If they don't want to or are busy, help them understand they're in danger. There are no safe places anymore. Jeremiah's people are hunting everyone who knows me."

"Okay," Heather said calmly. "And if they're not?"

Alex urged, "We'll have to help."

Heather stared blankly. "Okay. Then what?"

Alex hit the table with her hands, "Aunt Heather, look at me." She waited a half-second. "We're storming the Library. Do you understand what that means? We're attacking the dragon in its lair. Not I. We." She let that sink in. Rose made a fist and shook it in excitement. "The whole Coven."

Heather looked at her, "What good will I be?"

"I'm not going to burn *all* the Books." She nodded at Rose. "For this to work, I'll be handing some out."

Chapter Seventy-Nine

eather stared at Alex, slack-jawed. "But," she said after a moment. "But," she said a moment later, "Isn't that, I mean," she looked at Rose, "no offense, but isn't that," she turned to Alex, "sacrilegious or something?"

Alex sucked on her lower lip, trying to find the right words. "Heather, I've been to the Library once. They don't just store Books. They study them." She leaned forward. "Think about that, Heather. The Books are women. And they study them." She stood upright. "There are lots of men there. They'll use those Books to stop me. Last time, I took them by surprise. This time, they'll be ready. Why should they be the only ones to have magic? If I'm going to burn it to the ground, I need an army."

Heather made a face. "I don't know any spells. How am I going to, I mean, how is this even going to work…?"

Rose interrupted, "Mom, it's simple. You open a Book, and this thing happens. You'll just know you know. You'll turn a few pages and make something happen. You'll be freaking awesome." Rose glowed at the idea of her mother casting real spells.

Heather asked again, "You're giving us all magic?"

Abby spoke up, "I can't."

Alex raised her eyebrow, "Even with a Book…?"

Abby shook her head.

"How do you know? Have you ever…," Alex trailed off.

Abby held her hands out. "It's best that I stay away from magic. I'll be at your side. I'll protect you. But I will not so much as even try." Alex stared at her. Abby took a deep breath. "I need you to trust me on this."

"I won't ask again." Alex reached across the table and put her hand on Heather's arm. "Aunt Heather, we have a long day ahead of us. I could get to the Library myself. Because I've been there before. With everyone, we have to drive." *Just make the calls already.* Alex wondered if every decision would fall to scrutiny.

Abby looked at her, "We can drive to the Library? Where the hell is it?"

Alex grinned. "The Library is a real place. The way Matthew explains it, Jeremiah ripped it out of the world. He wanted to hide it someplace no one could find it. He hid it in the place Banhi calls the Between. He hid it in dreams."

"How do we get there?" Heather asked, "What's the point of driving if it's… in between?"

Alex understood what she was asking. "If you don't have magic, if it's your first time, if you're a guy who is being recruited, like Peter was, there has to be a way for you to get there. Without magic. That's how we're going."

Rose frowned. "You and I can use magic to get there. Can't they meet us?"

Alex looked at Rose. "We're going together. Matthew showed me. There are doors. Hundreds of doors, all over the world. The closest one is in New York City."

Rose pumped her fist again and sang, "I love New York."

Heather stared at her daughter, "What are you talking about? You've never been there."

Rose shrugged. "So?"

Heather shook her head. "Alex, that's five hours away. Without traffic. There's always traffic."

Before Alex could answer, Abby spoke up. "I'll start the calls."

"So that's that?" Heather looked around the table. "We're going? No further discussion?"

Rose groaned. "No, you're right Mom. Let's discuss it. That's a good use of time. What's *your* plan?"

Heather glared at her daughter. "I'm suggesting that before we all march off to certain doom, we should make sure everyone is prepared for what's going to happen." She looked at Alex, her expression suggesting she didn't want to say what she was about to, "After what happened last time, the Book Club will need some reassuring that this time will be different."

That was a promise Alex couldn't make.

Rose rolled her eyes. "First of all, I have magic, Mom. Second, we get Billy back tomorrow."

"I go where she goes." Abby motioned to Alex, "She's been to war, Heather. You heard what she said happened over there. This isn't the same woman in the field. She controls her voices now. I've seen her fight and she's amazing. That's why this will be different."

Heather stared at her half-eaten chicken cutlet. "I love these," she said to no one in particular, "but I can't eat anymore."

Rose reached to take it and Heather slapped her hand. "They're good cold," she protested. "I'll eat after my calls."

Heather clearly wanted to make the calls herself. She relieved Abby of any responsibility. Alex was thankful it was happening. "Make sure everyone is okay," she urged.

Listening to Heather on the phone over the next hour was, in Alex's mind, a master class in negotiation through any means: cajoling, guilt. At one point Heather spoke using only expletive-laden threats.

"What do you mean you're busy? What plans? My son is missing. Yes, yes, thank you, I appreciate your concern. I do. But let's be honest here, you've been coming to these fucking meetings for how many fucking years? That's right. It has been *that* long. Now I'm calling you and telling you we're actually going to do something real, something beyond your wildest imagination and you're what, washing your hair? I know you didn't say you were washing your hair, but trust me, washing your hair is so much better than what you said. Don't keep making excuses. You should have just said, *Oh, I'm sorry, Heather, I have bullshit to do*, and then I might still respect you. No, I meant that you should have said the word *bullshit*. Why? Because at least I'd know you were being honest with me. Really, and you don't think I'm afraid? At least *that's* honest. We've waited all our lives for this. To do something our mothers and grandmothers never imagined could be done. Are you saying you want to miss this? And what if because you don't come, it doesn't work? What if you were the last puzzle piece that makes this happen? Maybe you are in the Coven for a reason. Okay, thank you. No, I understand and can appreciate that. Yes, I know. I know you won't let us down. Good. See you tomorrow."

Heather looked up from the phone, the intensity suddenly broken, and saw the three of them, mouths agape, staring at her. She mouthed at them, "What?"

In spite of one hang-up, Heather secured the commitment of the entire Book Club.

Heather explained, "I told them ten. They'll be here by eleven. Someone will suggest we grab lunch. We'll be in our cars by one, assuming everyone gets gas first." She sighed. "You know Nancy will be here before anyone else, but she'll be running on fumes because she was rushing."

Abby laughed. "That's because all Nancy cares about is making sure she's present when needed. Donna will have no excuse for being late."

Heather stabbed at her cutlet. She said, "Betty said she has a friend with an apartment. We can use the bathroom, drink some courage." She mentioned where it was. Alex shrugged. One address sounded like another.

Alex inquired, "That sounds like it's not too far. Is Twenty-second far from Fortieth?"

Rose mocked her playfully, "Um, it's *eighteen....*"

Abby shrugged. "Eighteen blocks isn't a bad hike. How far east to west?"

Alex shrugged. The numbers didn't seem that far off, but one was East Twenty-second and the other was West Fortieth. She envisioned the Coven walking for hours. Although she really wanted to see the city, and see what all the fuss was about, she didn't want too many distractions.

Heather began working out logistics of getting everyone there. Hailing multiple cabs seemed it would be easier than she was making it out to be.

Heather finished her cutlet and put down her fork. She placed her hands flat on the table. "Tell me, Alex, what's the plan?"

Alex drew a deep breath. "I don't know how to make a plan for this. We go to the city, then we go to the Library. We'll go in. I'll give you each a Book." She hesitated, anticipating Heather voicing concern, but her aunt remained silent. "Then it's my turn. There's no way to be subtle about it and it'll attract a lot of attention. They'll hit back, hard. I need to focus on the Books. You'll lead our defense. Billy will be there somewhere. When we find him, you all get out while I finish my job."

"Sounds simple," Rose laughed.

Alex tried to mute the look she gave Rose, but Rose saw it.

"What, cowboy? Did I say something wrong?" Rose grinned. She held out her hands like she carried guns. "Guns blazing. Pew-pew! I like it."

Heather cut her disappointed glare at Rose short. "We're not leaving you." Before Alex could contradict her, she added, "We go in together. We come out together. Or we don't go at all."

There was no point in arguing. *Heather's never been to the Library. Once she has Billy, once he and Rose are in danger, she'll leave—with or without me.* The thought both settled and unsettled Alex. She wasn't sure if it was what she believed would happen or what she wanted to believe.

Heather cleared her throat, "Once you give me a Book, how do I cast spells?"

Rose spoke over Alex, "You'll just know. Once you look at the Book, it just makes you know."

"Makes?" Heather worried.

"It's more working together. You want to and then you do. It's so cool." Rose grinned.

Heather made a face. "Working together?"

"Don't overthink it." Then Rose sang, "You'll see."

Heather bit her lip; it was clear she couldn't admonish her daughter for something she was being asked to do. "I never expected it would come to this."

After a minute of silence, Abby asked, "So where exactly is the Library?"

They were really going. They were all committed. When it was just a plan, it was easier to think about. Knowing it was tomorrow made it real. It obscured everything that came afterwards. It was certainty and uncertainty at the same time. The worst kind of each.

Abby repeated her question. "Like I said," Alex answered, "it's a real place." She rapped the table with her knuckle. "Like real, from here. It was hidden in the dreamscape, on the Between."

Heather asked, "How does someone do that?"

Alex turned to Heather, "Powerful magic. And then some. The thing is, without a Book, without magic, you can't get there. The first time someone—a guy—goes to the Library, he doesn't have magic. He has to get there through... traditional means." She paused like she was waiting for the others to catch up. "So, there are these doors everywhere. New York City, Paris, London, Moscow.... I can't remember how many. When Matthew shared the location, there were hundreds; Europe, China, India. There's like even one in Antarctica. New York City is the closest, so that's the one I really remember. They're all here," she pointed at her head.

Heather nodded. "Okay, so we go into the city tomorrow. Will you be ready after driving for hours?"

Alex looked at her queerly. She'd never needed to sit in a car for even one hour before.

Abby half nodded. "Five hours in a car is exhausting. Even sitting. Will you be ready?"

Alex replied, "I guess if we're tired, maybe we take a quick nap or something."

Heather took a breath. "Alex, the women have high expectations of you. Most of them, anyway. When they ask you questions about your plan, you need to answer like you thought it through. You need to be confident, or they'll start testing you."

Rose looked between them, rolling her eyes.

Alex nodded thoughtfully. "What if it doesn't go the way I say?"

Heather responded, "That doesn't matter. They agreed to come. You want them on board with minimal apprehensions. When we broke your curse, all I knew was I had a spell to cast and something might happen. Peter prepared me only so far."

Alex remembered the way they questioned Heather.

Heather turned to Abby, "Abby filled in some of the details, so I wasn't totally freaking out thinking I was going to actually kill her." She turned to Alex, "I didn't know what happened next, so I shared everything I knew with the Coven. I got them excited. They knew they would be part of something important. I told them enough that they chose to believe I knew everything when in reality, I was winging it."

"Okay," Alex acknowledged, "We're going to drive to the city. We'll meet at Betty's friends place and rest up for an hour, nap, eat, pee, whatever. Then we'll take cabs," she looked to Heather to verify it was cabs and not some other term. "We'll take cabs to the street where the door is." She wished she could just get there already. Dread at getting to the door and returning to the Library was like an infection. The longer she had to wait the more it festered.

Heather spoke in the voice she used when quizzing their comprehension during class. "Perfect. What might we find on the other side of the door?"

Alex tried to hide her shrug. "What we find matters less than how we handle it. Rose and I will go in first."

Heather looked apprehensive. *I don't know what happens next. Does she want me to make something up?*

Rose looked at her mother, "Why are you acting like that surprises you? I already have a Book. Of course I'm going in first."

"I know," Heather breathed. "You're right. It makes sense; I just don't want to think about it that way. It'll be dangerous. I don't want you to get hurt when I can't protect you."

Rose frowned. "Mom, I'm at least as powerful as any of *them*. I'll be fine."

Abby leaned forward. "What she means, Heather, is she'll be busy protecting you."

Heather nodded, her face brave, her eyes wet.

Alex looked at everyone. "Let's not over-think this. We haven't even left the house yet."

Heather agreed, "Here I'm telling you how to marshal the troops. I'm not very good at this, am I?"

Abby soothed, "You did fine with Alex's curse."

Heather laughed. "Did I? I was freaking out inside. My kids just got out of the hospital. Matthew attacked you two in my house. I had to kill you, Abby. Even if it wasn't going to stick, I was sick to my stomach. And I had no idea what would happen to Alex." She shook her head. "No idea what came next. We get there, and the next thing I know we're debating salt."

Abby laughed. "That was hysterical. Same with the graduation gowns."

Alex looked at them. "You mean that wasn't part of the plan?"

Heather made a face. "No. That was Lydia's idea, all on her own."

Abby leaned forward. "Heather is detailing the process at one of the Book Club meetings, what, about eight months ago?" Heather agreed. "And she says that for the spell to work we have to be naked." Abby laughed. "There's no better way to turn believers into skeptics than tell them they have to undress in front of one another."

Heather was laughing, her eyes tearing up. "They started debating the degree of undress with me. What if we wear bathing suits? Nightgowns? Bathrobes?" Each time she said an items name, she and Abby cracked up.

"Finally," Abby said, catching her breath, "Heather gives in and gets them to agree to be naked under something loose fitting."

"I didn't know if naked meant only you," she motioned to Alex. "I told the Coven being naked makes it easier because I didn't know what else to say. Old witch lore talks about being naked, so it made some sense. You have to understand," Heather said, "Peter told me *he* would be naked."

Alex remembered. "Oh, you don't have to tell me, I know."

They started laughing together, Rose looking on, her face showing her growing annoyance. "Sounds like I missed all the fun."

Heather slapped the table as she laughed. The sharp bang still made Alex uneasy. "We're all out in the dark wearing nothing but graduation gowns. There's no support. They're drafty. Abby's dead and we're all trying to be serious and think we're real witches, and then Alex is like, *Okay, I'm back.* I'm sure we failed. Then Marta is doing CPR on Abby because she's not coming around and I'm beginning to realize I'm probably going to jail. Then Alex takes my Book and bursts into flames. She was *on fucking fire.* If I were wearing pants, I would've messed them. I mean," she arched her hands over her head as she shouted, "Whoosh!"

"And to think you left me home for this," Rose griped.

When they were done laughing, Alex placed her hand atop Rose's. "I need you most of all. You have the most experience with magic. When they get their Books, they'll look to you."

Rose pressed, "You can do magic now, right?"

Alex was contemplating how forceful her answer should be when Abby interjected, "Rose, there's nothing to worry about. This girl," she grabbed Alex by her elbow, "she is an unstoppable force."

"Really?" Both Rose and Heather responded.

Alex tried to smile graciously. Abby's compliment embarrassed her. She looked at Abby and said, "No bees this time, I promise."

Abby shook her head. "No way. Bees, cockroaches, whatever it takes, bring it all on."

Chapter Eighty

s they broke their kitchen-table meeting, Abby asked Alex if it was okay if she went home. "I want to feed Marty and Quest. I'd like to change my clothes."

Alex said, "You don't have to ask."

Abby nodded. "If you say so. I like knowing it's okay."

Alex gave Abby a hug. Heather saw her out. They spoke just outside the front door, but Alex couldn't make out more than an occasional word.

"You ready for tomorrow?"

Alex turned to Rose. "As ready as I'm gonna be."

Rose feigned surprise. "That's not the answer people want to hear."

Alex made a face.

Rose laughed. "I'm kidding, Alex. Geeze, you're so serious."

Alex couldn't find a reason not to be. *What's with her? Maybe she's just blowing off steam.*

Rose lowered her voice. "This is the closest we're going to get, isn't it? Bringing Billy home. It's down to this one chance."

Alex nodded. The sense that she wasn't coming back from this crept up from behind. She could feel its cold claws snatching at the base of her neck. It made sense that getting Billy back would involve a very dear exchange, a life for a life.

"Let's not fuck this up, okay?"

Alex glared. She didn't feel she owed anyone an apology for how hard this has been for her. Part of her hoped offering one to Rose might diffuse the tension between them. Yet, the more she spoke, the more it felt less like an apology. "No one told me what to do. I've had to figure it out on my own. I had to do a lot more than just read from some Book."

Rose looked deep in thought; Alex chose not to interrupt. Eventually, she said, "I thought you'd be better at it. You *have* magic. I *read mine* out of a Book. You just make yours."

Alex sighed. "They say the Books are pure. No emotion to interfere with the magic."

Rose squinted at her. "It's more powerful, too, isn't it?"

Alex struggled not to argue. She gave the win to Rose. "That's what they say."

"So," Rose offered, "what you're saying is that while you have more magic, mine is stronger and better?"

What? Alex felt attacked, but she stifled her knee-jerk reaction. *She's looking for affirmation.* "In a way, sure, yeah," Alex replied.

Rose had a half-grin on her face.

"What are you two up to?" Alex never heard Heather come in.

"Just talkin'," Rose answered.

Alex nodded in agreement.

Heather plopped into a chair beside them at the kitchen table. She threw herself back and groaned. She mouthed Billy's name three times but never said it aloud. Taking a breath, she placed her hands flat on the table. She looked at her two girls. "I need you to keep each other safe tomorrow."

Simultaneously, Rose replied, "I know," and Alex said, "We'll keep you safe, too."

Heather said, "Look out for each other. If I know you're both safe, I'll have nothing to worry about. Got it?"

Alex could tell Rose was growing upset. "Aunt Heather?"

"What?" Heather replied.

"I promise I'll watch out for Rose first," Alex confirmed. "But I'll also watch out for you and Abby. Maybe even everyone else."

"I'll be watching out for you, too, Mom." Rose said enthusiastically.

Heather pointed at each of them. "You," she said with a point, "two," with another, "first."

Both Alex and Rose nodded.

"Good." Heather twisted around in her seat to look at the clock. "It's getting late. You both need your sleep."

"Mom, it's not even ten o'clock," Rose protested.

Heather got up. "Then read in bed, Rose." She faced Alex. "You going to fight me, too?"

Alex sighed, "I'm exhausted."

Rose groaned. "I don't know when you two got so old."

Alex was particularly tired tonight. "It's been a really long few days," she whispered.

"I hope I sleep tonight," Heather said absently. "There's so much to think about."

Rose leapt to her feet, her squealing chair startling the other two. "Goodnight," she said as she retreated to the stairs.

Once Rose left, Heather touched Alex's hand and whispered, "I'm worried about her."

Alex wanted to disagree, to tell her aunt, *No, Rose is fine*; but she couldn't. "I know what you mean," Alex whispered instead. There was something in Heather's eyes that suggested she was worried about what was happening in Rose's mind. Alex waited a full five minutes, and when Heather had added nothing, she hugged her aunt and headed up to her attic bedroom.

Chapter Eighty-One

Morning came quickly. Alex found herself back at the table with Heather and Rose.

Conversation was light; only Rose seemed interested in normalcy. Alex assumed Heather—like her—was too focused on mental preparation. Breaks in their dialogue felt desolate. They'd share a somber grin before the conversation resumed. Sometimes Rose would laugh and suggest what she thought her brother would have said. For Rose—it seemed—Billy's return was inevitable.

Alex found herself staring at the counter. She could almost recall the disappointment when—nearly two weeks ago, and things seemed normal—Heather told her she couldn't go to college for another year. At the time it felt like her world might implode. Now, the inconsequence nearly tickled. *How could I know what was coming?* So much made sense now. The home classes, the overprotective parenting, never getting to go anywhere. *Heather's known for years. What was that like, anticipating each day?* Alex gasped, pretending to choke on her coffee: She'd heard Matthew ask that very question of her mother.

Watching her aunt and cousin, Alex wondered what they were thinking. *Rose is probably calm because she believes in her Book. But Heather?* Her serenity probably came from her faith in Alex. In spite of her failures, her aunt believed in her more now than ever. Alex wanted to live up to that faith. At the thought, her confidence strengthened, like Heather's faith became braces to bridge her doubt.

Her head became a swirl with thoughts of Matthew and Billy. And Jeremiah. And the Library. She couldn't know what was coming. There was a door somewhere in New York City, and the rest of her life lay behind it.

Am I being selfish not going alone? I don't want to. But it doesn't matter anymore. They're in danger either way. At least with me I can protect them. Right?

Alex had to be certain. One hundred percent committed. No doubts. No concerns for others—aside from the Book Club. At the Library, everyone else was the enemy. Could she be so cold-hearted?

She had to be. She feared the next breakfast at this table would be very different.

"You might want to keep the door locked," Abby said to Heather as she let herself in.

"Really? With these two here?" Heather chuckled.

Abby cackled.

Rose grinned devilishly, adding more hot sauce to her already pink omelet.

Heather offered Abby breakfast.

Abby grabbed a mug from the counter and poured herself coffee, "Thanks, but I had breakfast." She sat and nudged Alex. "Marty and Quest miss you. They howled half the night." Then she announced to the table, "I gassed up my truck on the way over. All four of us fit."

Heather offered, "I can drive, too."

"Aw, Mom," Rose whined, "can't we go with them?"

"I'd prefer if we were together, too," Alex interjected.

Heather sipped her coffee. "It's settled then." Her flat tone offered no insinuation, as Alex anticipated. Every time she stayed with Abby or rode in Abby's car, she worried she hurt Heather.

Nancy arrived first, just before a quarter to ten. At the door, she gave Heather a lingering hug. Dressed in jeans, a t-shirt, and sneakers, her long hair pulled into a ponytail instead of her usual bun. She had removed all her piercings and had on a trace of makeup, her cheeks rosy. Although she stood silently while everyone cleared the remnants of breakfast, she was a bundle of nerves.

She said hello to Rose and Abby, giving each of them a hug and exchanging a few polite words.

Nancy then approached Alex, giving her a massive hug. "It's so good to see you're better," she told Alex as she let her go.

It relieved Alex that Nancy said nothing to upset Rose. "Abby told me how you took care of me. I can't thank you enough."

Nancy was staring at her again. "Sorry," she said when she realized Alex's discomfort under the weight of her gaze. "It's just that I saw what happened to you four days ago and here you are, gearing up to do it again."

"It's a lot to think about, that's for sure," Alex said.

"I can't imagine," Nancy replied. "You're brave to go back so soon after, you know, things not working out so well."

Alex wanted to say, *Actually, I'm terrified.* Instead, she said, "Thanks."

"I'm so nervous. Couldn't sleep last night. I figured I'd eat breakfast and get out the door." Nancy played with her eyebrow, touching the spot that normally held a piercing. "Stan thinks I'm going to a book conference in the city with the Club. I hate lying to him, but what would he say if I told him the truth? *Hon, I'm a witch and I'm getting together with my Coven because this amazing witch needs us to watch her back when she fights this terrible man.* I must have said goodbye to him twenty times, you know, just in case. People at the hospital are worried about Marta. I know she's not coming back. They've already had the police check her house, but I can't say anything that makes me a suspect." She looked past Alex, "Is it almost time to go? The anticipation is killing me."

Heather recognized Alex's glare of desperation and intercepted them. She offered Nancy a seat and to make her breakfast.

Nancy accepted, "I'll take a cup of coffee"

Heather hesitated. "Maybe coffee isn't a good idea. Milk?"

"Sure." Nancy blew out a breath, "I'm sorry. I got here and saw Alex and she's so cool and calm and it got so real for me." She blew out another breath. "I don't know why I'm so freaked out. I deal with crisis all day at work."

Heather poured her a small glass of milk. "Here," she handed it over. "We're all a little numb."

Nancy took a sip. "Thanks." She made a face and took another sip. "Is this *cow* milk?"

Alex slipped out of the room. Rose followed and, in a whispered giggle, said, "That woman is nuts." In the other room, Heather did her best to calm Nancy. It wouldn't be long before Heather offered her something herbal. Alex wondered if Heather had already slipped them something to keep them so calm.

"She's scared," Alex defended. "We all should be."

"Nah," Rose smirked. "Not you and me."

"I hope magic is enough today."

Rose sneered like Alex called her inadequate.

Alex leaned forward and gave her cousin a hug. "I love you, Rose." She didn't know what else to say that wouldn't antagonize her cousin.

"I love you, too," Rose said, somewhat flatly; a reflexive

response.

The others arrived in fits and starts over the next half hour. Betty, Lydia, and Rachel arrived together. Alex vaguely remembered each of them. Betty was average height, her flaming red hair styled with at least a dozen blue plastic barrettes that didn't seem to have a purpose except to contrast with her hair. Her yellow shirt had an image of a cat with a mohawk, a nose ring, and spiked collar. Underneath it read, "Bad Kitty".

Lydia wore a white and blue polka-dot jumper. It looked like shorts or a skirt, whether you saw it from the front or the back. A wide blue belt synched at the waist, and filthy, old, canvas high-top sneakers.

Rachel was the shortest of the three, a little taller than Rose. She wore brown construction boots and camouflage shorts and t-shirt. The shorts were a mix of browns and greens while the shirt was pinks and blues with tiny pink bows on the trim at the sleeves. Her face was round, and her eyeliner thick. Her short, dark hair was unbrushed.

The three women no longer seemed as old as Alex initially thought. Late twenties, maybe early thirties. They said their hello's as they moved around the house, pointing and chittering to one another, saying gracious things, but remained a group.

Colette arrived next. Her dark, curly hair tied in a ball at the back of her head, same as last time. She was nearly as tall as Alex and carried herself with an elegance that Alex wished she could emulate. There was something about the way she held her long arms and positioned each finger that made her look like an ebony sculpture whenever she stilled, her fingernails flashing a spectacle of aqua. From a distance, she compared Colette's hands to her own. Hers looked inelegant and masculine.

Colette greeted the others politely. Alex noticed a formality, a politeness she hadn't observed before. It troubled Alex: these women weren't friends as she had once assumed.

Colette approached Alex with an immediate embrace. There was no formality here, and Alex was grateful for that. Colette made a fist for Alex to lightly punch, "We're doing this. *You're* doing this. I'm freaking out. Heather tells me you're okay. I was so worried I texted Heather like every five minutes until you were better."

June entered moments later. Her straight, dark hair parted in the center, pulled behind her ears. Even without makeup, her features were defined. She said her hellos to everyone. Then she rested her hand on Colette's shoulder and squeezed. Alex watched the eye movement between them. They were both in the field four days ago and had the best indication of what was coming. *That day damaged everyone.*

Several of them looked up when the motorcycle growled into the driveway and idled. Lydia and Rachel looked at one another and both said, "Carrie."

Alex liked Carrie, if for no other reason than Billy liked her. Carrie looked like an adult until a genuine smile broke the façade and turned her into a kid. Something about her fascinated Alex. Maybe it was all her tattoos or her tomboyish looks. Of the Book Club, Carrie was her favorite, so it bothered her even more when she overheard several of the others discussing Carrie.

We're car-pooling, so she takes a motorcycle? You wouldn't want her to drive; she's such a flake. She looks like she's trying to be a man. I heard she got another tattoo. Why does she do that to herself? She'd be so pretty if she took better care of herself. I heard she pierced her labia. Who does that? That's disgusting.

Carrie walked in, followed by Donna, the last to arrive. As soon as Carrie walked through the door, the whispering stopped. Colette and June greeted her. They made a point to inform Carrie that she was the topic of conversation. She waved the information away.

Carrie came in as a bundle of energy. Ripped jeans, leather boots with straps and rings, and a white tank top, her black bra showing through. More than one of her multitudinous tattoos were still scabby. She hugged Colette and June. She walked straight to Alex. The petite chef grabbed Alex by the wrist and with her thick outlined eyes glaring, sneered, "Good you're better." She threw herself at Alex in an embrace.

Donna, the oldest of the group, followed on Carrie's heels, walking with a noticeable limp. She greeted everyone by first name. To those who hadn't been with them in the field, she asked, "What's new? What have you been up to?"

Betty was unfortunate enough to inquire, "Donna, you're limping. Did you hurt yourself?"

Colette, June, and Carrie all turned. Carrie grinned and put her hands on her hips to watch.

Donna straightened up. "Oh, you didn't hear? Maybe, if you'd come when Heather needed you," she said loud enough to let everyone know she wasn't exclusively talking to Betty, "you'd know how I got this limp." Donna lowered her voice and over Betty's perfuse apologies, said, "What matters is you're here today."

The two stood there, like Betty was trying to find her next line and Donna was waiting for it. Finally, Betty said, "It won't happen again. We did the thing for Alex. It felt like we were done." She hesitated. "I'm sorry you got hurt, Donna. I'm sorry I wasn't there for you."

"Me too," Rachel added. "I'm sorry I wasn't here for everyone."

Alex was still with Carrie when Donna joined them. "Good morning, Alex. This is some improvement. Last time, well, you know."

"Thanks, Donna," Alex replied. "You're limp. Still hurts?" She asked with the implication that she would fix it.

Donna shrugged. "I have a bruise on my left butt-cheek that looks like a pomegranate. It's hard as a rock. I thought about bringing one of those chair-donuts for the car ride. At my age, I don't have many pleasures in life, and those bastards took sitting away from me."

Carrie laughed aloud. Alex wasn't sure whether Donna was being serious or sarcastic. Carrie said, "My legs are so bruised I look like I was running blindfolded in a furniture store."

Both Donna and Alex looked at her.

"You know," Carrie explained with a groan, "bumping into things?"

"You're not healing well?" Alex kept raising her arms slightly to hug them, but it felt rude not to ask first.

Carrie shrugged. "Usually faster than this." She looked at the scars covering her forearms, "My kitchen tattoos heal quick, and they're second and third degree."

Donna agreed. "I'm so glad you're having that problem, Carrie. I was trying to decide if they healed slower because they were magical or because I'm getting old. Everything is slowing down these days."

"Do you want me to, you know?" Alex spread her arms.

Carrie laughed. "I just put that together. Go for it."

Each embrace was short. Carrie took it better than Donna, who hissed at the discomfort healing caused.

"You think that's why we're so huggy? Healing one another?" Carrie mocked hugging one person after another, "Air heal, air heal."

Donna's eyes twinkled. "That sounds like something someone would write a paper on. *Senior thesis: Do witches hug more because they heal one another or is it unspoken sapphic tendencies?*"

Carrie bent over laughing. Alex smiled politely, not sure what was so funny. "You could argue that either way," Carrie snorted. "I've crushed on a few women here at one time or another."

This intrigued Alex. "Have you?"

Carrie grinned, her cheeks reddening. "Of course. I mean, sometimes one of them looks put together. You notice them one night and think about them until you see them again. Doesn't mean anything."

"Who would you notice today?" Donna asked as she scanned the room, intrigued. "Lydia?"

Carrie stared at Alex while she thought. Alex expected to feel uncomfortable, but she wasn't entirely sure how to feel about it. Turning away, Carrie snorted as she laughed. She lowered her voice, "Lydia? I mean, the girl is sweet enough and all, but not my type on a good day. All those dots hurt my eyes. Besides, what is that jumper thing about? How do you even pee without getting all undressed?" She waited for Alex and Donna to stop laughing. She gazed at Alex as she said, "Today, I'd have to say I'm liking Colette. Don't either of you say a word to her. I'm warning you."

Donna looked in Colette's direction. "What about her?"

"I keep seeing blue flashes. I guess today, fingernails are hot."

Alex studied Colette. "She is beautiful."

Carrie casually threw her arm around Alex's neck. "Good thing I like them tall, huh?" She caught Alex's eye and winked.

Alex wasn't sure if Carrie was flirting.

Donna studied Colette. "I see it. I don't disagree with Alex. Something elegant about her. When I met her years ago, I thought it was some put-on contrivance, but I think that's just how she moves." Donna tried to imitate the bend of Colette's hand in the air but couldn't mimic the grace. She said to Carrie, "Wasn't she married? I heard he died. I feel so bad for her. Anyway, I heard she's dating someone. Someone *male*."

Carrie put her hands on her hips. "So?"

"I don't understand," Donna said. "If she's dating a guy, then she wouldn't be, you know."

Carrie raised her eyebrows. She slipped her arm from Alex's shoulder. "It's more about my tastes than theirs."

Donna grinned. "I get you. Fantasy…."

"Exactly." Carrie grinned bashfully at Alex.

Alex was unsure why Carrie's fantasies would seem strange. She'd crushed on boys she saw on television. There was a boy she kissed once. As much as Rose made fun of her for it, there was something exciting about being that close to another person.

Donna tried to get Carrie to talk about some of the other women in the room. Carrie realized she said too much and crossed her arms, signaling she was done.

Indirectly dismissed from the conversation, Alex slipped away and found Heather and Rose. Abby wasn't far behind. Heather turned to Alex, "Should I get them organized?"

This was Heather's Coven. Alex was glad she wasn't being put upon. "I guess. Yes. Please."

Heather smiled and rubbed Alex's arm. "Can I have everyone's attention," Heather shouted, breaking the din of conversation. "Let's get going." Heather helped coordinate the drivers and the passengers. "Make sure everyone has a ride. Betty, give everyone your friend's address. Betty's friend offered to let us stop at her apartment to stretch our legs and pee."

Alex watched the party break into groups and smiled when June and Colette joined Donna and Carrie.

Chapter Eighty-Two

Alex spent most of the drive staring out the window. Thirty minutes in and she was farther than she'd ever been from home. Everything from here on out was new. She felt like an explorer, daring to sail out to sea, trying to remain confident the world wouldn't abruptly end with a waterfall dropping into eternity.

Abby was behind the wheel. Heather in the front passenger seat. Rose behind Abby. Alex behind Heather. It felt like a family. Alex wondered what it would be like when Billy was back. How would his experience change him? It seemed inevitable that the Billy they got back wouldn't be the one who leapt from Picnic Rock. Nothing was certain. Everything balanced on a pin.

Heather and Abby carried on one conversation while she and Rose had another. Each duo had history. *Will Rose and I talk like Heather and Abby one day? Will every conversation have all these comfortable references?* Alex had doubts. That future seemed impossibly distant; the road to get there dangerous. There was something Alex didn't recognize in Rose. Something changed. One possibility was magic. The other was murder. Her ear drifted from Rose to listen to Abby and Heather's conversation. They'd been to the city before, many years ago.

Cell phone texts bounced between the three cars; their arrival tones often followed by cackles. The subjects varied from needing to pee to joking about how slowly Donna drove. Heather considered Alex's reply suggestions. Rarely did she use any.

Crossing a bridge, Abby told them they were two hours from their destination.

"Two hours?" Alex studied the bridge supports. White guywires made triangular forms, like rigging diagrams of four sailboats in passing. She pointed at the bridge and told Rose, "Looks like sailboats."

Rose craned her neck to see out the window. "I see the spines of a dragon sleeping in the river."

Alex saw it, too. It reminded her of a stegosaurus. She had little interest in dinosaurs, but when he was younger, Billy was crazy about them. She hoped he still was. *He would have loved to see this.* Watching Rose stare out the window, Alex wondered if Rose was thinking the same thing.

"Two hours," Alex repeated. "I didn't think we were that far."

Abby replied, "We're close."

"Two hours? How's that close?" Alex retorted.

Abby cackled. "I forget you've never been." She glanced out the window. "Here, distance is measured in time, not miles. Remember we told you about traffic? On some roads, a mile can take an hour."

Heather groaned. "The BQE!"

Rose moaned. "A mile? Why wouldn't you just walk?" Before anyone answered, Rose added, "Can't we stop and stretch our legs?"

Heather turned around. "I told you half an hour ago that was the last stop."

"I thought that meant we were almost there," Rose moaned.

Abby muttered, "Are we there yet?"

Heather laughed. Abby asked again. "How about now?" They giggled like children.

Rose rolled her eyes. She looked at Alex and whispered, "You and me, we don't have to sit in this car for the whole ride. You know that, right?"

Alex nodded.

"You're choosing to?"

Alex nodded.

Rose let out an exasperated sigh and turned to her window.

Alex had seen photographs that suggested the city was nothing but towers and spires, a veritable Oz made of glass and concrete and steel. What she saw from the car was not as exciting as she hoped. Heather had told her that her first sight of the city took her breath away. *Maybe it was different back when Heather used to come. Maybe it's been so long the Empire State Building and the Chrysler Building aren't there anymore, like the Twin Towers.* Heather and Abby weren't looking around in any kind of awe, either. Alex looked across the river and tried to make conversation. "I thought there would be more to see."

"Where? What are you looking at?" Heather craned to look at Alex, who pointed out the window. Rose stretched to see over her. "Honey, that's Queens. The city is that way," she pointed to the wall of buildings that blocked their view of everything.

Alex felt robbed of the breathtaking views Heather and Abby mentioned.

Abby slowed the truck to allow Betty's car into the lead; it was her friend they were visiting. Abby followed Betty's silver Nissan onto the ramp and off the FDR Drive. As they snaked through the urban streets, moving sometimes just feet through cycles of traffic lights, Alex imagined they became part of a much larger caravan. It didn't seem possible that there could be so many places to visit that all these cars weren't going to the same one.

Rose groaned, "Why isn't anyone moving? Honk your horn. The light is green!"

Alex watched Abby's eyes shift to Heather. Heather replied, "It's the traffic."

Rose held out her hand. "The light is green, Mom. They're allowed to go."

Alex caught peeks of buildings she recognized and hundreds just as magnificent that she'd never seen in any book. Sunlight peeked to the sidewalks at obtuse angles, cut by the canyon of buildings surrounding them.

Alex had never seen so many people. Not even on the Between. There were so many it didn't seem possible for them all to be real. Some had to be extras—like in the movies—just background filler. She watched a woman hustling across the street in slacks and high heels, carrying a large flat bag holding a painting. *Did she have a job and a boyfriend and a dog and an apartment?* She lived in this whirling circle of life and yet Alex would only see her for this briefest moment and then never again. For Alex, she was just a curious bit of scenery. But she wondered if the woman was a universe, too. Crowds moved in rushing flows like blood in veins, pulsing down streets and pausing between the slow beats of the traffic lights. Each one was like the woman with the bag and the painting. Each of them—the hundreds of them—probably had never met any of the other people on the street before. Never even seen them before this moment. *How could there be so many people? So much life and emotion and thought?* Alex couldn't articulate what it was making her feel. It was like each one of them existed in their own universe, and, although she could see them all, they were actually as distant from one another as were the stars in the night sky.

More than the promise of seeing the towers of glass and steel, the humanity most intrigued her. *How do all these people fit into this space? Is every street this busy?* She imagined other avenues vacant; everyone surging only around them.

The sounds were overwhelming, the incessant honking, as though someone at the head of this parade was unaware the light had changed. Opened windows of cars sharing thumping bass—music that sounded foreign and exotic, sung in languages Alex never heard before—for the moment they paused beside the other passing car. The music invaded the sanctity of their truck and while Rose danced in her seat, Alex could almost imagine Abby throwing the truck in park, jumping out and screaming at whichever car had their stereo too loud. Alex liked the exotic intrusion. It thumped with life. It reminded her that there was so much more to the world—and the people in it—than she ever imagined.

On the corners, little stands sold all manner of foods and supplies, sunglasses and visors seemed as ubiquitous as carts that advertised Halal, their spicy and deliciously odors alien to Alex's nostrils. Large umbrellas with alternating primary colors shaded what Alex could only describe as small stainless-steel kitchens on wheels.

She found her thoughts getting lost, veering away from her task. She wanted nothing more than to be any of those other people, on their feet amidst the magical sights and sounds and smells that delighted and confused her. What she wouldn't give to be—for just a moment—that woman in the smart suit who was biting into some unusual meal wrapped in aluminum foil. Her mouth even moved, salivating wildly, as though sharing the bite. *The Library can wait a day.* She knew it wasn't true, but wished for a chance to live a life different from this one. She wondered how much life she'd missed. How much she would miss. *If I can, I'll come back here.*

"That smells disgusting," Rose said with the nasal tone of a pinched nose.

"It smells amazing," Alex contradicted, taking in a deep breath that elicited a fake gag from her cousin.

Abby turned back to Alex, "The traffic's bad enough that you could jump out, buy something, and get right back in the car before we moved more than a couple feet."

Heather was quick to correct. "Abby's kidding, Alex. She's exaggerating."

Alex challenged, "I'd be willing to try."

Rose pretended to dry heave. "What is that, anyway?"

Heather pointed out the window. "Mostly Middle-Eastern food, curries and spiced chicken or lamb." She turned to Abby. "Remember when we came here?"

Abby smacked her lips, "All they had was hot dogs in those days. What I wouldn't give for, what did they call it, a dirty water dog."

Both Alex and Rose groaned.

"That was a great day," Heather reminisced.

"It was," Abby confirmed. "Did Peter even have his license?"

Heather nodded. "Maybe a week."

Abby looked at Alex in the rearview. "The three of us came to the city for the day. We were what, seventeen?"

Heather nodded. "We had so much fun. Abby and I went to all the museums. Natural History and the Met. We ran through the exhibits to see everything."

"Do you remember when we got lost in Central Park?" Abby giggled.

Heather um-hummed.

Abby looked to the rearview. "Those museums are across the park from one another, so we figured we'd cut through. We got so lost."

Heather laughed.

Rose leaned forward. "What made you come here for a day?"

Heather twisted in her seat to explain. "It was Peter's idea to come. He was meeting a friend or something. He took off on his own."

"How'd he find us?" Abby kept peeking into the rearview to make eye contact with Alex when she spoke. "We didn't have cell phones. We didn't have a plan. I think Heather and I figured that when we ran out of things to do, we'd find our way back to the parking garage. We were so young and stupid. It's a miracle we got home."

Alex asked, "How did he find you?"

Abby's eyes widened. "I couldn't tell you. We, um, Heather, where were we?"

"At that point," Heather speculated, "I think we were trying to figure out how to take the subway to the Village."

Rose asked, "What Village?"

"It's a part of the city," Heather explained. "Way downtown.

It's supposed to be really cool. Live music and all sorts of things two underage girls shouldn't ever do."

"Anyhow," Abby continued, "we were on the platform, figuring out tokens, when Peter showed up with some friend." She turned to Heather, "I think he had a crush on you. He took one look at you and got all strange and left."

"I forgot all about that," Heather mused, drifting to a thoughtful distance. She snapped out, "No idea how he found us." Heather shrugged.

"Or how he lost his jacket," Abby uttered.

"Oh, yeah," Heather said. "He got in so much trouble for losing his jacket."

"I got in so much trouble," Abby recalled into the rearview. "We all lied to our parents about where we were going. We were too stupid to realize after the six-hour drive that driving back would take that long. By the time we decided to head home it was already late."

Heather cracked up. "We were so naïve. We started driving home at ten or something and it dawned on us we would never get home before midnight. I was sick to my stomach."

Rose asked, "What did you do?"

Heather sighed. "We didn't have cell phones. As usual, Peter saved the day. He found a rest stop. We took turns calling from a pay phone."

"What's that?" Rose joked.

Heather ignored her, "We all lied about why we'd be so late. We thought we were so smart."

Pointedly, Rose asked, "Did you get away with it?"

"No, Rose," Heather said, "I did not get away with lying to my parents. Neither did Peter. We were grounded for a week."

Rose grinned. "But you did it. It was worth being grounded, wasn't it?"

"Don't get any ideas, Rosemary. We couldn't do anything for a week," Heather warned.

Rose groaned, "You lived in Ashburn, Mom. What could you possibly miss? I bet it was so worth getting into trouble."

Heather sounded nostalgic, "It was." She turned to Alex as though remembering something. "When we get to Betty's friend's place, everyone will want to hear the plan."

Alex, her tone rising like a question, said, "I expected them to ask back at the house. It surprised me they didn't."

Heather nodded. "Me too. There might have been some tension today."

"Really?" Alex was sarcastic. "Some of them ragged on Carrie."

Heather looked at Abby. "That's actually normal. Carrie makes some of them nervous." Heather paused for a beat. "Most of these women wouldn't acknowledge one another on the street. At Book Club they behave, but they're not always kind."

"I didn't notice it last time," Alex said.

"Well, it was worse today," Heather explained. "It's like being at the field is a badge of courage. Those who missed it didn't want to ask what happened, and those who were there wanted to rub it in their faces."

Alex shook her head. "People are strange."

Heather and Abby said, "You have no idea."

"Getting back to what I was saying," Heather said with a sarcastic tone, "only give them one thing at a time. Tell them we're going to the Library. The door. Nothing specific. Nothing after that. If you tell them about giving them Books or casting spells, there'll be a lot of grumbling."

Alex remembered how Donna argued with Heather about Sara's Book when they removed her curse. That was Heather reading Peter's translation of the spell. They were about to read the Book itself.

"Got it," Alex replied after a moment. "No Book talk."

"You know what you're going to say?" Heather asked.

Alex almost replied to her aunt in the affirmative. Instead she said, "Look, I have a plan laid out in my head. First, we need to get into the Library. Once that's done, everything will become clear."

Heather was silent; Abby chuckled. Then Heather realized what Alex had done and replied, "Perfect."

Two minutes later, Abby followed the silver Nissan onto the sidewalk and down a steep ramp. When Alex realized it was just a parking lot in a basement, she felt silly for thinking something exciting was about to happen. It was reminiscent of the first time she got to sit in the car at the gas station carwash: So much anticipation, so little reward.

"Wow," Rose blurted out and pointed at a sign. "Fifty bucks

to park here. That's crazy. Look, there are monthly rates, too." She turned to Heather, "Don't these people know parking is free like, everywhere?"

Heather replied, "Things are a little different here."

Rose looked around, perhaps trying to see what made parking so expensive. She spoke in hushed tones, "I bet I could make the parking person forget to ask for money."

Abby pointed at her, "You'll do no such thing. I'll get parking. Don't you dare use magic to defraud someone."

Rose looked to Heather, perhaps hoping her mother would have a differing opinion. Heather was in staunch agreement with Abby.

Once they all got out of their cars and settled with the attendant—an activity not as smooth as getting out of a car would suggest—the eleven women followed Betty to the street and around the corner to a non-descript glass door and into the vestibule of an apartment building. Along the walk, Alex had never felt invisible before: people hustled past, never looking or making eye contact. She finally got to enter the city's lifeblood and didn't feel a part of it.

Betty scanned the resident list. It looked like a table of contents, a random list of names and apartment numbers like one might find at the start of a book. She pressed the button beside one name and waited. A raspy voice spoke through the popping speaker. "That you, Betty?"

"We're here, Susan," Betty replied, unable to hide the excitement in her voice.

Alex jumped at the clacking buzzer. Betty pushed the inner vestibule door, and they surged out of the constricting foyer and into the lobby.

They packed into the elevator. Alex and Rose made faces at one another about the unfamiliar odor.

When the elevator arrived on the tenth floor, they all stepped out.

At the end of the hall, an older woman leaned out an open door. "You must be Betty's friends," she stepped out into the hallway. "Come, I can't wait to meet you."

Chapter Eighty-Three

n Susan's apartment, after taking turns with the small bathroom, the women scattered to the couch and chairs, having forgotten that they'd already been sitting for hours. A platter of cheese and meats and crackers graced the coffee table. It looked delicious, but the thought of food made Alex sick. Instead, she looked out a window at the collection of buildings in her partial view. She grinned and pointed for Rose to see the Empire State Building.

"I thought it would be bigger," Rose dismissed the window, hoping Susan might mistakenly hand her a glass of wine she poured for her guests.

Donna joined Alex, sipping her white wine. "Reminds me of coming here during the holidays with my family when I was a kid."

"This was here when you were a kid?" Lydia joked, "Was it New Amsterdam back then?"

"Go fuck yourself," Donna laughed. "I'm not that old."

Rose managed to get a glass, although there was little more than a drop in hers.

"Can I get anyone anything to eat? Are you hungry? I could bring in some sandwiches or we could order pizzas?" Susan was a tiny woman, bouncing around the apartment with enthusiastic jubilation.

Alex waited a beat as the other women announced their toping choices; Heather didn't speak up. "We need to get going," she said.

The room quieted. All faces turned to Alex. "I'd love some pizza or whatever that was I smelled on the street coming here," Alex heard Rose make a retching sound to a few laughs, "but we can't get comfortable. We can't get distracted."

Lydia, her legs crossed as she sat, jammed against the armrest of the couch beside June, pulled on the hem of her polka-dot jumper, "Exactly what is our purpose? Heather asked for help to get Billy, and now we're in the City. What's next?"

Alex saw Heather nod to her. "Out there," Alex gestured to the window, "is a door. It seems ordinary and dozens of people walk by it every day. Except it's not ordinary. It leads somewhere none of you have ever been. We will open that door."

"A door? Really? We came all this way to open a door?" June said sarcastically.

Alex faced June. "There are hundreds of them around the world. This is the one closest for us. It's the entrance to the Library."

The group murmured, exchanging nervous glances.

June pulled her hair behind her ears. "Why do we need this door? Haven't you already been to the Library? Didn't you get there from Heather's house?" She took a sip of wine. "I'm not trying to be a jerk, Alex, but why'd we come to the city? Isn't there an easier way?"

"I can go to the Library. Probably Rose, too." Alex watched Rose beam. "How do you get there without magic? The first time a man goes, he comes through the door. They've been doing this for hundreds of years. That's why we came to the city. To use the door."

Heather offered the address.

Donna raised her hand like she was waiting for someone to call on her. "Hundreds of years? This part of the city isn't that old. I would have figured it would be below Wall Street, where the city started, where I grew up, in *New Amsterdam*." She jokingly glared at Lydia.

Alex shrugged. "The door is just a door. They made it go to the Library. They could have used any door."

"Are you sure? Couldn't they move it?" Carrie asked. "What I mean is, how do you know?"

That Carrie asked the confrontational question surprised Alex. "Because I know." Alex was surprised by the tone of her response.

"Hey," Carrie fidgeted in a chair taken from the dining room table. "I'm not trying to make trouble. We're here. Most of us will do what you tell us, no questions asked, but we're going to the Library. The viper den. Last time didn't go so well. It got scary. You almost died."

No questions asked? Who are they kidding?

Alex's extended silence brought more concern from the group. They started talking to one another, questioning what they were doing here, their safety, recalling Alex's collapse and the attack in the field. They even questioned Alex and Heather's justification for gathering them together again. *Is it safe? Are we asking for trouble?* Alex started towards the door. She thanked Susan for her hospitality and gave her host a warm embrace. "I hope to see you again soon," Alex told her.

She turned to the others in the room. "We're leaving now."

Lydia held up her wine glass and swirled the golden liquid. "I'm not done with my wine."

June pointed to a bottle. "Susan just opened this one. As soon as we finish, we'll go."

Alex almost let them win. They were the adults, and she was the kid they were indulging. "Why are you here?" Most of them looked up. "I mean, half of you didn't bother to come last time. Maybe I should go on my own. Go order your pizza." Alex almost let her lip snarl. Her resentment swirled like sand in a windstorm. Had her coins not been dark, she wondered what her emotions would have done. Alex watched a moment. Rose stood up.

No one said anything until Colette purposefully walked her glass to the kitchen. "Susan, can I help you clean up?"

Susan eyed Alex with a grin. "Go. I've got this." She pointed at Betty, "I'll stopper the bottle. It'll be waiting for when you get back."

As they made their way to the lobby, Alex felt they were punishing her with silence.

Stepping out into the street, Heather caught up to Alex, who was ahead of the group. "Do you want to take a cab?"

Alex blurted, "Walking is fine."

Heather nodded. "Because if you want to take a cab, we could call for two. We'll all fit in two. Maybe three."

"We will walk," Alex ordered. "I don't want to be in a car with any of them."

"You need to give them some leeway," Heather instructed.

"Do I?"

"They're just women. Not witches, not special. Just women who found one another because they believed something could make them special. They wanted to pretend magic was real. They made themselves believe in witchcraft." Heather glanced back, looking for her daughter, who was at the rear of the group. "I sort of promised them those things. I knew Abby would get Peter's Book for me. I knew one day I had to remove your curse. I prepared them. You could say I preyed on their desire to be special, so they'd help me." Heather took a deep breath. "You understand they're all jealous of you, don't you?"

Alex didn't care if her tone sounded like she mocked Heather,

"They want to be special. They want to be witches. When I give them the chance, why are they assholes about it?"

Heather winced at Alex's volume. "Nobody wants the right way to be hard, Alex. It's hard for them."

Alex took a deep breath as she walked. Rushing made her feel like she belonged here; her long legs made for long strides. Heather struggled to keep up. She said, under her breath but loud enough for Heather to hear, "Oh, and it's been easy for me?"

"You know what I mean, Alex."

"Maybe I don't, Heather." She glanced back, watching as several of them avoided eye contact with her. "Maybe you should spell it out in case I don't understand."

"I don't know how to talk to you when you get like this," Heather grumbled.

"Like what?"

"Like you're pouting."

Alex shook her head.

Heather, gasping, grabbed Alex's arm to slow her. "No one is saying you haven't had it hardest of all. It's just that we're following you, and you're leading us into the very world we want to be in, but you're the only one who belongs there. You have magic. Well," she hesitated, "you and Rose. You know what I mean. It's in you. The rest of us, well, it feels like lambs to slaughter. Most of us saw what happened to you last time. That was scary. So scary. We have no idea what waits on the opposite side of that door."

"Maybe I just don't understand. I need to be sure they'll be strong. I need to know they can protect me." She looked at Heather, "If they run at the first sign of trouble, there's no way we can pull this off. This isn't about me. It's about Billy."

"They won't run. They're just," she paused, "scared."

Alex paused for the crosswalk. "I get that," she said in hushed tones to her aunt. "You say that every time."

"It's true every time," Heather replied. "You're not going to make them brave. You need to take solace that they're all here. As scared as they are, they are all here for you."

When Alex didn't respond, Heather continued, "It's not you. You know that, don't you?"

Alex didn't. *How many times have I failed?* It felt like they were angry with her. Each time she looked back, not one of them didn't avert their gaze.

"They believe in you. They're scared. Heck, I'm scared, but I would give my life to know my kids are safe. That means you, too. They're here because of you, scared or not."

Alex glared at her. "You know I'm scared. Don't you?" She looked back on the others. "All of this falls on my shoulders. I didn't ask for this. If one of them gets hurt or dies—"

"That's not going to happen," Heather interrupted.

"You're kidding, right?" Alex's eyes welled up. "Do you know how many people—"

"Keep your voice down, Alex."

Alex lowered her voice. "Do you know how many people I've seen die in the past week? Do you?"

"I don't Alex." Heather's voice softened. She was getting upset.

"All because of me. People I cared about. So don't say it won't happen today. Don't you dare." When Heather didn't reply, she continued, "When you lie to me and it happens, you make it all my fault."

"That's not true," Heather protested.

Alex wiped her eyes. "But you do. You say no one should die, so when they do it's because I failed to protect them. Don't you see that?"

"I'm sorry, Alex. I didn't mean it that way."

"We're going to the Library. I don't want to go there. I didn't want to be there the first time. But I have to. I keep telling myself we're bringing Billy home. I'm going for *him*." She rubbed tears from her eyes. "I want to go and have food from one of those carts. I want to run around the museums with Rose like you and Abby did when you were my age. I want to do something fun." She pointed in the direction they were walking. "But I can't. Because as soon as I walk through that door, every man in the Library will try to kill me."

Heather looked at her feet. "I'm sorry, Alex."

"No, you're not. We're here to get Billy. Like you said, you'd die for your kids."

Heather stared at her through tearing eyes. "That was an expression, Alex. I don't want anyone to die. I don't want anyone to get hurt." She sobbed as she spoke, her mouth stringy. "Please understand me, Alex. I love my son. Bringing him home, though, it's a distant second to keeping you and Rose safe." She took a few deep breaths to stave off the flow of tears. "I love my son. He doesn't have to come home today—or ever—if it means losing one of you."

Alex tried to respond, but Heather stole the argument out from under her. She'd heard Heather's words, but their meaning was slower to arrive.

Heather squeezed Alex's arm. "Have faith in your Coven."

Alex nodded, sighing, "I prefer Book Club."

Chapter Eighty-Four

hey walked for nearly half an hour; the sun darting in and out of clouds on a windy late-June afternoon. It was warm in the sun, the afternoon light high in a blue sky. They stopped at the address, a three-story brownstone. Alex stood, reflecting the absurdity that behind this door, inside this small building, hid the immense Library.

"I expected it to be bigger," Donna judged the building.

Rose groaned, "It's not *actually* in there."

Donna looked at Rose but didn't respond. She turned to Lydia and shrugged. Alex heard her tell Lydia, "It can't be as big as she says if it fits in there."

They were on the west side, near 38th Street. The distant sound of traffic entering and leaving the Lincoln Tunnel was like the mechanical version of a babbling brook. In front of them, a set of stairs led up to a prestigious looking main entry. Below the concrete stoop, tucked amidst some unsightly garbage cans, lingered a battered six-panel wooden door, with a large brass knob and no place for a key. The deep red-brown paint cracked and peeled, revealing the colors beneath: hints of pea green and bubblegum pink peeking out from under the red and brown. The door stood a step down from ground level, and was tucked into the stairs that led to the front entry of the three-story building.

Alex opened the gate to the small fence that lined a miniscule courtyard that trapped the trashcans and protected the door. It swung free, despite the rust across the wrought iron bars and spikes. The cold knob was large, almost requiring two hands to grasp.

June asked, "Isn't this trespassing?"

Before Alex could glare, Heather hissed, "Just do what Alex says."

"Wait, before you open that door," Donna slipped to the front of the group, "tell us what we do next."

Alex stared at the mass of expectant faces. *Remember what Heather said. They're not questioning me. They're afraid. They want reassurance. Once they see, they'll do what I need. I just need to get them there.*

"I've never been through one of these doors," she began, "so I can't tell you what to expect."

"Tell them about the Library," Abby said beside her.

"You've never seen anything like it…." Alex explained the majesty of the place, trying not to oversell her recollection. She finished by explaining, "It's a beautiful place that houses horrible things."

Carrie opened her sack and started handing out small cans of pepper spray. "It's not much," Carrie said as the others took them, "but it's something."

Colette turned the can over in her hand, looking at the red nozzle. "Alex, do you think we'll need these?"

No. "I guess it doesn't hurt to have." She gave Rose a look to tell her to stop judging the others with her grin. "Ready?"

No one answered. The eleven women fanned out in a semi-circle around Alex, each waiting for someone else to reply.

"Go for it," Rose said at last.

Alex put her hands on the knob. It wouldn't budge. It wouldn't turn, and the door didn't give one iota as she pushed and pulled. It was sealed shut. Alex took a step back, stunned. She tried the door again with no change to the outcome. The weight of their glare on the back of her head made her perspire. She was frustrated and angry. *It should just open.*

"Maybe if we take the nails out?" Nancy pointed to the corners of the doors and the large bent nails, bleeding rust down the paint. Coarsely driven on an angle to join door to frame.

Alex studied the dozen nails. Matthew had shown her, and in her vision, the door opened. This door was here so men without magical Books could access the Library. *What good is a door that won't open?*

"Maybe they abandoned it," Donna said. "This might not be the door, anymore."

"This has to be it," Alex said. "This is the door he showed me."

"He?" Donna tipped her head. "Who's, *he?*"

Alex looked at Heather, who nodded. It was time. "I met Matthew yesterday."

The group of women didn't move, but Alex got the sense they wanted to recoil.

"We're here to get Billy." They reacted to Alex's words with the sort of surprise that suggested they'd already forgotten their cause.

"Wait, what?" June pointed, "Since when does Matthew want to help us?"

Betty asked with genuine concern, "This is the Matthew who tried to kill you, right?"

I'm losing them. One wrong word and they might walk away from me. "That's just it. Where Jeremiah is concerned, we're on the same side as Matthew."

Colette shook her head, her hair bouncing. "I am not on any side with Matthew."

Alex's chest tightened. She wanted to argue, to yell at them, *So, you know Matthew now? You have no idea what's happening. Except right now, Jeremiah is killing everyone who helps me.* Instead, she ignored them and turned back to the door that refused to open. If she didn't open it soon, they'd revolt. She couldn't keep them together if they continued to debate her. She pulled and tugged again.

Rose slipped alongside her. "Let me try." Before Alex said anything, Rose produced her Book. She opened it like a switchblade, snapping to a page. Rose uttered guttural words. The door creaked open.

"What was that?" Donna had her hands on her hips, her face twisted in disgust. "She's still got that… that thing?"

Rose's glare forced Donna to step back. "It's called a Book, Donna," Rose shouted. She motioned to the door. "Look what I did."

Rose slipped past Alex into the dusty room and stood, absorbing in the murk. She took a few steps, looking around. She turned to Alex. "It's just a filthy, stinky basement filled with junk." She picked up something she found, made a disgusted sound, and dropped it, scraping her hand against her jeans. She slammed the door closed behind her. "This isn't what we came for."

The group grumbled and Heather tried to reason with this or that one, telling them it didn't matter.

Rose disappeared her Book as she walked by. Alex was crushed. She had been so certain this was the way in. "Rose?"

Rose huffed. "It's not the door, Alex. It's not the right place. The Library isn't here." Rose looked away; her eyes welling. "We're not getting Billy back. Not today, not ever." She pointed at Alex. "I believed you this time. I was so sure we were gonna do this, side by side. I'm such an idiot; I'm done believing you."

Alex wasn't sure if she wanted to cry or explode. One was giving up and the other would level this building, if not the block.

This is the door. He showed me. What would be the point of tricking me? Humiliation? I know this is the door. I can feel it.

She wouldn't avert her gaze, even while hearing the others exiting the gate to the sidewalk to join Rose. With each step they got further from her, literally and figuratively, threatening to reach a critical point of dispersion when not even the gravity of their common purpose would keep them from their separate ways.

Fine. Go. Leave. I'll do this myself. I won't have you slowing me down, asking your stupid questions. I don't need this stupid door. We're here because all of you are pathetic and weak. You have no magic. I'd be better off with just Rose. We'd go in, guns blazing. We'd get Billy. Then, if Jeremiah didn't kill me, Matthew would. Rose would bring Billy out and everyone will be all, Where's Alex, *and Rose will tell them how amazing and brave I was, but because of them, because they gave up, I died. Serves them right.*

Alex vented her anger and frustration. She closed her eyes. She tried to steel herself, tried to convince herself that a successful death was better than constant disappointment and failure. *This is the door.*

This is the door for men who haven't been given a Book. Like my father. He probably came to this door and put his hands on this very knob.

The notion struck Alex. *That day they came to the city.* It made sense. *Why else?*

Alex took a deep breath. *Okay, let's say there's no secret knock, no special hidden button. I'm Peter and I'm here and the door won't open.* She turned to Abby, the only one waiting within the perimeter of the gate. "Was my father stubborn?"

Abby nodded profusely. "Once he set his mind to something, just suggesting he stop drove him crazy. He *had* to finish."

Heather agreed, "He could be obsessive." She gestured to Alex. "He let nothing stop him. He cursed you, untwinned you." She made a face, "Why?"

Alex walked to the door, looking it over for anything she might have missed.

He knew it would open. He knew and he wouldn't stop trying because he knew how much getting to the Library mattered.

She clasped the knob and started trying to turn it. She pushed and pulled, her body the only thing to move as she thrust herself back and forth. She didn't stop until she became damp with perspiration.

She stepped back. *What if I have to be a man? Could that be a thing? What if it won't open unless I have a dick?* She thought a moment. *Even if I could, I am* not *casting that spell.* She knew of no spell to do that, but the thought made her laugh.

"What's so funny?"

Alex ignored whoever asked. *Okay, he tried the door. He pushed and pulled. What would he do next?*

She threw her body against the door.

She groaned. *That was dumb. That'll bruise.*

"Let's wait at Susan's," she overheard someone say. "Rose opened the door. What's she trying to prove?"

Alex heard but refused to listen. *I'm thinking too aggressively. I have to be passive. This door is magical, it's protected, right? So how do I open it? How do I unlock it?*

She grasped the giant brass ball of a doorknob. It didn't turn, but she held it as though it might. She kept tension on the knob, her sweaty palms starting to slip, the metal warming in her hands.

Who would keep trying to open some random door unless they knew? What if it's not the door...? What if it's me? What if I'm the reason it won't open? What if my mindset is wrong?

She realized she'd been so concerned about opening the door, she never thought about what happened if someone was waiting for her right on the other side. *That'll be ironic. I open the door and some guy kills me before I know what happened.* She took the moment to flip her coins bright. *Now they can find me. Assuming they're still looking.* Alex hoped there was some surprise left in her plan.

She counted seconds off in her head—*I will open it—*expecting when she got to sixty—*I've got this, it will open this time—*she'd stop and try the other direction for one minute—*the door will open*—then stop and try something else. Maybe sixty and one seconds—*it's not me, it's the door*—just to be sure.

At fifteen—*open door, open*—the knob grew hot—*come on and open*—her hands sweaty—*no, no, no, no*—and she couldn't maintain her grip. Her hands slipped—*hold on a little longer*—sliding around the knob. She maintained tension—*just fucking open already*—but as she twisted her body to do so—*don't give up, it's not you, you can do this*—she realized she'd have to dry her hands and try again.

Is this a test? Did Matthew know I couldn't? Is he trying to show me there are some things a man has *to do*?

She was about to let go when she realized it wasn't her hands slipping: the knob turned.

The giant brass knob rotated slowly, as much the result of her efforts as it seemed to move on its own. The movement in her hands startled a yelp out of her. Just when her grip become tenuous, the twisting force threatening to make her contort in some inhuman way, the door slipped inwards.

Looking in, Alex understood she stood in one world, peering into another. This threshold bridged a vast distance.

Cool, dry air spilled out. Stale and musty, it smelled like old clothes. Alex's heart pounded. Her sweaty palms trembled. She'd done it. One step and she'd be in the Library.

Her heart fluttered with excitement: She opened the door, she overcame doubt, she proved she was right; this was *the door*.

She turned to shout for everyone to come back to look, but found them crowding around her, staring in. As she looked at their faces, their eyes returned her gaze, each one silently acknowledging they were ready to follow her wherever she led.

Chapter Eighty-Five

lex peered into the dim room.

It was cavernous.

The doorway before her was in a staircase that led to the house. This room far exceeded the volume of the staircase. The room wasn't actually under the staircase—it wasn't there at all—but the mismatched sizes still messed with her brain.

A series of ornate coatracks were lined in militant, even rows. The racks were long and wooden, strewn with hooks for the coats, a flat shelf littered with caps. Some coats were wool, still black or camel-colored and new. Layers of dust and moth-eaten decay covered others. Among them were caps, baseball hats, bowlers, fedoras, all sorts of brimmed and old-fashioned things, tri-foil hats she only ever saw in movies about the American revolution. Even some ragged fir things that looked like sleeping raccoons. Cobwebs covered the older ones like sheets, whitened by time and dust.

Beyond these, on far more distant racks, obscured under even thicker layers of dust, were coats in such a state of decay that they were coming apart, no longer capable of hanging whole on their hooks. Alex saw capes and dusters. Many were in tatters, littering the floor. Hats with plumes and ornate feathers tented in dust and cobwebs.

In one corner, a pair of metal gauntlets rusted away. Everywhere she looked were artifacts of eras long before the European founding of America, their purpose obfuscated by their own decay and obscured in dust.

Alex knew, among these remnants, was her father's lost jacket, not lost at all.

There was no one waiting for them. The realization lifted weight from her. Alex pointed at each of them as she spoke. "Rose, stick towards the back with Heather; Carrie and Donna, you two up front, behind Abby and me. Everyone else, just fall into line, two-by-two, okay?"

As the group scrambled like schoolchildren lining up for recess, Abby whispered, "Two-by-two?"

Alex shrugged. "Seemed reasonable enough."

Abby nodded. "Carrie and Donna?"

Alex couldn't help but blush. "They've seen magic before. They sort of know what to expect. And I blanked. Theirs were the names I remembered."

Abby peered in. Alex finished addressing the group, "Once we go in, Rose will close the door. We won't be coming out this way."

"What makes you so sure?" Donna half-raised her hand.

Alex acknowledged the racks of coats, "None of them did."

Alex turned and found her feet leaden. She wasn't just stepping over a threshold; she was crossing vast distances and entering an antechamber to the Library. Although no one attacked her when she'd opened the door, that didn't mean they weren't waiting in ambush. Was she leading them all into a trap? Would—whoever— wait for them all to enter so they had no place to run? Her heart raced. She had no idea what would happen.

She walked in. Nothing happened.

She didn't want to trouble the others with her concerns of ambush; what could they do without magic? She remained vigilant.

Crossing the threshold, the scent and taste of the air changed. It became dank. Her rubber-soled hiking boots ground grit into the stone floor. The air was thick and heavy and smelled of dust and decaying cloth. Behind her, the others stepped through.

At first they were silent; pure reverence. They stared, taking in the details, understanding that none of them had ever been someplace so old. Alex wasn't sure they understood they'd crossed such a distance, that they were no longer in New York City, much less America. This place might have originated in the real world but was now on the Between. They were on the other side. No one had to pay for passage.

Everyone was completely distracted by the garments on the racks. *No sense moving forward until this becomes a little common.* Alex waited.

The chatter began.

"What could we make selling these, even in this condition?" Donna slipped from her place in line to touch a coat. "These are authentic? I mean, this isn't for display, right, Alex?"

Alex ignored the question. She walked past the long rows of coat racks. At each aisle, her heart rose a little higher in her chest, like a trapeze artist on the upswing. She anticipated a trap but found no one hiding among the coats or in the corners. The chattering was growing louder; Alex wasn't sure how they hadn't attracted attention.

Around the room, small arches bled greenish light: a wall sconce carved into the wall. Iridescent green and glowing fluid pooled in each sconce. Towards the rear of the room was an archway. This was where they would venture next.

Several of the women were off, examining the articles. "Imagine some guy wearing this thing. How does this even go on?"

Donna pulled a tri-foil hat free of the cobwebs and shook it against her leg. She coughed at the billowing dust. She held it atop her head for a laugh, "Look, I'm a real daughter of the revolution!"

Lydia sniggered, "Didn't you have one when you were younger?"

Donna lowered the hat and joked, "You know I was never that young."

There seemed no end to their banter. Alex had hoped they'd be serious but was doubting they had the capacity. It was just like at the apartment. *They're scared.* However much she reminded herself, she still resented their reaction to fear.

"People," Alex uttered with exhaustion, "can we please be serious? We're not in New York City anymore. Danger could be anywhere. I can't promise we're safe."

Donna replaced the hat and trotted to her place in line, "Sorry," she said with exaggerated contrition. It was as though they each realized where they were. Fear drowned their fun. The line reformed.

"It's a coatroom. Men came and left their jackets and hats here." Alex hadn't looked for her father's jacket, nor would she, but knew it was here. "It's a passageway, and past that doorway," Alex pointed at an archway at the far end of the room, flanked by two glowing cut-outs, "could be another room. It could be the Library. Anything could happen next."

Lydia turned in place, "We're already lost? I thought you knew what you were doing."

Abby rankled at the remark.

Donna groused, "We're not lost; we just came in that door."

Nonchalantly, Alex said, "You're right, Lydia. Not a clue." Before anyone could say another word, Alex turned her back on them, walking toward the archway.

Behind her, the others made a disturbance. "What now?" She turned; everyone focused on Rose, who was at the entry. She had closed it after they entered, but it was open again.

"I just wanted to see," Rose stammered, motioning at the door. Alex asked, "What?"

Rose pointed. "That we still, you know, can get out."

"Well," Alex motioned with her hands, "we can, right?"

Rose motioned outside. "That's not where we came from." She closed the door again. "Watch," she opened the door onto a narrow cobble-stone street. Large gray blocks formed the wall that was just a half-dozen feet across from the door. Dawn-pink sunlight streamed down the street. "It changes every time I open it." Rose closed it again.

Rose was about to open it, when in a raised voice, Alex ordered, "Rose, stop it."

Rose released the door. She stepped back; her hands raised in defense. She showed her offense at being yelled at.

One of the other women—Alex thought it was Betty's voice—said, "This is better than a travel agent. Come through this door, visit another country. It's too bad we made plans today, huh?"

Alex rolled her eyes. *First, they try on the jackets and hats. Now they're planning excursions. Yes, I would love to explore everywhere the door opened to, but that isn't why I came. They don't understand the danger. Every one of those doors around the world is one door. Everyone comes to this same room. They're blowing off steam. They're realizing magic is real. They're here, testing me to make sure I'm the right leader. Making sure when they do something stupid, I'll correct them. Making sure I'll keep them safe.*

Alex leaned forward, "Next time you open that door, what if there's someone on the other side? Someone who knows we're not supposed to be here."

"How would they know?" Lydia asked.

Alex glared at her. She took a preparatory breath, but Rose answered, "Because none of us has a dick."

Heather hissed, "Rosemary!"

Rose giggled, her laughter echoing throughout the room. Realizing her volume, she sobered.

Even Rose gets how dangerous this is.

Alex paused inside the stone archway. If the first doorway

opened from multiple places, couldn't each doorway also change its exit? She wanted the group close. If something like that happened before they were all through, the group could split apart. Alex was grateful she wasn't alone in this creepy place, but her connection holding this fellowship together felt flimsy.

A semi-circle of dim green light of the last sconces spilled past the darkened archway. Blackness engulfed the way. Alex considered casting a spell but decided against it. *As soon as I use magic, they'll realize I'm here. If they don't already.* She touched Abby's charm.

"Alex, wait," Carrie said from behind her. After a second fiddling with her phone, she held it up as a flashlight. Immediately, eight other lights came on as anyone with a cell turned on their flashlight.

Heather put hers out, "We should use one or two at a time. To save batteries. Mine is searching for a signal. No bars down here."

Half the others turned off their lights. "Put them in airplane mode," Carrie offered, "that'll keep the batteries from running out too fast."

Rachel spoke up, "What if someone needs me? I won't get the call."

Carrie's tone made it unclear if she was mocking. "If you don't have a signal, how will you get a call?"

Colette added, "Rachel, don't you watch horror movies? You don't want your phone ringing here." Colette looked around, her face mimicking her concern, "This place is creepy as hell."

With a few nervous laughs, everyone toggled the setting on their phone. Carrie helped Donna set hers.

Alex brought Carrie closer to provide light. The tiny illumination from the cell penetrated the darkness only so far. The hallway appeared empty, but anything could lurk in the syrupy blackness. The stone walls cast odd shadows that lurched with the light. Alex didn't look back. She just started forward.

After only a few steps, complete blackness faded to softer gray. Their footsteps echoed in this narrow hallway; their silence uncomfortably clamorous. Underfoot, the floor smoothed; rounded stones set in perhaps concrete, and the walls, when washed by one of their lights, formed an arch of similar construction. Mineral deposits formed along the peak, dripping and making the walls appear wet, even when they—to the touch—weren't.

In the lightness ahead, a narrower archway choked the passage.

Alex hesitated, blind to whatever might be on the other side. They'd have to pass single-file. Anyone anticipating their arrival would be on the opposite side.

Alex concentrated. She thought about Matthew burning her. The searing pain of the flames. Watching her mother die. The fight in the field. Learning Sara was dead. It was like priming an engine: She had to ready her anger. She couldn't be frightened, or she could lose the ability to defend her Book Club. Once her heart pounded with indignation, she ducked through the archway.

The space beyond the constricting arch widened. Alex scanned the space before her. *Still no one.* She wasn't sure if this reassured or disappointed her. She so expected a trap; finding someone would at least confirm her suspicion. With each step, she feared her guard was lowering. She couldn't retain anger indefinitely, either. At what point wouldn't she feel the need to raise her hackles? Would that be the moment Jeremiah's men waited?

The floor transitioned to slabs of black granite. White streaks bled across the floor like water running down a window. The similar walls seemed to narrow ahead. Whatever ceiling existed, their cellular flashlights couldn't reach through the darkness. There was a noticeable absence of reverberation from above, as their echo was lost to the void. Alex had never realized how much sound her surroundings reflected until it didn't.

Ahead, the elongated hallway ended. Matthew's instructions gave the impression the Library shouldn't be difficult to reach. Silently, she cursed him, feeling lost and ill-prepared. *At what point did we go so far, we can't find our way back?*

It's okay; my father walked here. Peter passed here. She tried to imagine him. *What was he thinking? Was he nervous or excited? He knew where he was going, and it was thrilling.* She imagined Peter wearing the out-of-fashioned clothes he wore when—a few years later for him—he visited Sara. She found her hand holding her charm. It warmed her: Her father *was* with her.

She walked closer to what appeared to be a dead end. It seemed too unlikely to be what she initially thought she saw, but it was. A pile of bones. Judging by the skulls, this was a collection of at least four bodies that looked, by design, stacked by type. Femurs on the bottom, skulls on top of curling ribs. Pelvises and vertebrae formed a border. Alex's stomach dropped; this was not a good omen for their journey, not to mention how the others would react. She stopped just as Abby pointed at the skeletal pile. *What are these bones doing at a dead-end hallway?*

"Are those real?" Carrie peered around Alex. She made a noise to indicate her disapproval and disgust.

There was noise from the group, chatter and whispers in concerned tones. Abby had enough and said in a booming voice, "Who is stupid enough to die at the end of a hallway when the exit is twenty feet behind them?"

When Alex heard Rose and Heather gasp, she knew something was dreadfully wrong. She asked; Heather replied, "Where we came from is gone. I turned around, and well...."

Alex's insides went cold. *Another changing doorway.* She counted the group: Everyone was here. Blood drained from Alex's face: Instead of the chokepoint they passed through, the floor descended into the bowels of what, from their current position, appeared an endless labyrinth.

The space was immense. The cavernous walls and ceiling sparkled with mineral deposits, dripped stalactites, and returned an echo of her every breath. Below, the labyrinth was an endless intricate bewilderment.

Alex's mouth went dry. She swallowed several times to moisten it. *What did my father think when he saw this?* She turned back and, just past the Book Club, returning to the pile of bones. *Now I know why they died at the end of a hallway. Better than lost in the maze.*

Alex scanned the snarls, the dead ends, the tangles of corkscrews, hoping to spy a clear route, a simple path through the maze. She found none. It was an endless knot of squared twists and turns, choked dead ends, and relentless branching passages. She wasn't aware of the sensation of hope in her chest until it abandoned her, swirling like it disappeared down an open drain. She couldn't lead them into that. Going into the labyrinth was madness. No wonder unclaimed outerwear littered the antechamber. Who could find their way through this once, much less twice? The weight of the group's expectations piling on her back left her gasping for breath. They all counted on her, and she was so out of her depth that the sea she swam in might well not have a bottom.

The others took for granted that she was prepared to handle anything. She fought back jittery nerves, as they successfully breached her defenses. Overwhelmed by her complete lack of preparedness, she tried to imagine young Peter. Peter without a Book. *Was he prepared for this? Did he have a solution?* She clutched the charm, if only to have something to do with her hands. She wished she knew what to do. Go back to the pile of bones and look for a trick switch in the wall or enter the maze? Both seemed insane. *How did he know what to do? How do you give directions through this?* She kept thinking about her father. *He'd left Abby and Heather to visit a friend. He'd gone to the door and opened it and hung his jacket on a rack.* It was like she could hear his footfalls. *Did he look at the dead end? Did he panic when he saw the maze?* She could all but see him standing at the top of the ramp, wearing jeans and a powder blue button-down shirt, in sneakers, his hands on his hips, shaking his head. *Am I imagining this?* She could almost hear him say, "Well fuck me."

Behind her, Donna gasped, "That is one ginormous maze."

Abby whispered into Alex's ear, "Think first. What's the smart thing to do?"

Alex had no idea. "The smart thing is to use magic to send everyone home," she whispered into Abby's ear.

Abby half-smiled.

"I'm missing something obvious," Alex whispered. "Instructions need to be simple. A sentence. Easy to remember. What seems the most obvious thing to do next?"

Alex looked over the maze again. Her eyes blurred rather than seeing its vast unsolvable impossibility. *Going in is the easy part. Getting through. Getting out. Those are the hard parts. The impossible parts.*

If Matthew told Peter the way through, the instructions had to be simple. Like: Only make lefts. *Like:* It's like the door. Enter and turn around. The exit will appear there. She resented Matthew for sharing the location of the door and nothing else.

The others took turns standing beside her to gaze into the labyrinth. They each said something monosyllabic like, "Wow," before turning back and joining the group. Carrie rubbed Alex's shoulder. "There, huh," she whispered. Alex acknowledged with a sigh. "We have faith," Carrie told her before patting Alex's back and stepping away.

While the group was still in gaping awe, Donna stepped forward, "Do you think there's a minotaur?"

Rachel answered, "There's someone watching the maze?"

"A *minotaur*," Donna corrected, making finger-horns on the sides of her head, "not a monitor. A minotaur? Man body, bull head?"

Colette giggled, "Bull head? Like a typical guy who won't ask for directions?"

Alex watched. Nothing had happened yet, so they deemed it safe enough to joke and laugh out their fear and anxiety. It felt childish and immature to Alex, and yet, if it got them to move on, she let them have it.

Donna's face first flashed with annoyance at the disrespect of the mythology, but then got the joke. "I never thought of that," she said to Colette. "I wonder if that's where the expression comes from. Ha, I'll never say Bull-headed again without...," she trailed off, motioning with her arm.

Colette shrugged and in a deepened voice, with a dismissing wave of blue fingernails, "Naw, honey, I don't need to ask for directions, it's just left, left, right, straight, left, past the corpse, right, right. Or is it left at the corpse? Don't worry, honey, it's fine. We'll get there on time."

The others laughed nervously, but then Nancy asked, "Alex, this place is crazy. Really, a labyrinth? Who does that? You know the way, right?"

A cold sweat swelled from Alex's pores. Her stomach churned. *Can I go home if I throw up?* Anything Alex said to assuage their fears would be a lie. She said what she was thinking, "That doorway is for people who come to the Library for the first time. Men who don't have magic. How would you give them directions through this?"

Heather replied, "What are you saying?"

"I wish I knew," Alex muttered. Abby punched her arm. "I mean, how complicated could the route be? Directions would need to be simple. Maybe redundant. Or there are no directions. What if it's an illusion? Is it a way to dissuade people who find the door by accident?"

Betty laughed, "Who would open that door by accident?"

Rose took a few bounding steps closer to Alex. She pointed

into the maze. "I'm just guessing, but maybe the maze is for people who don't know the way." She looked back to the dead end and the pile of skeletons. "It's like a skull and crossbones saying, *Don't come this way*. Maybe that is the way. Maybe there's a hidden door or something."

Alex stared at Rose, dumbstruck. *She's right. The bones did that. We saw them and turned to the labyrinth.* To Rose she said, "Good call. Let's look."

Rose grinned.

There's Rose. Her expression had been missing the past few days. As soon as the others started into the hallway, the joy faded and Rose's new face, with the hardened expression, returned.

Alex watched the others grope the wall for an opening. She turned to Abby, "This doesn't make sense," she paused, wondering for not the first time if this was part of Matthew's plan: to trap her here. *No. That's stupid. I'm going to the Library. I'm missing something.*

Alex took a minute to think. This was all here from time immemorial. The directions wouldn't be written. Someone might drop them. *What did my dad do?*

Alex repeated her quandary to Abby. "What would you tell someone to do that no one would just think to do?"

Abby stared at her for a moment and then shouted to the others, "Move the bones!"

Donna turned around, disgusted, "I'm not touching the bones. There could be bacteria. Maybe they died of dysentery or the plague."

Alex was certain Abby was right.

Carrie asked, "You sure about this? Isn't it disrespecting the dead or something?"

Nancy pushed past. Ever the nurse, she said, "You can't disrespect the dead, only the living. The dead don't give a shit." With a sweep of her foot, she started kicking the bones to the corner.

Alex anticipated grinding granite would reveal an opening, like in the movies. Moving the bones, however, only resulted in the bones in another, less tidy pile.

Nancy seemed disgusted at the result. "That didn't do much."

June and Rachel faced the wall, caressing the surface.

"What are you doing?" Betty asked June.

June turned to look at her, "Maybe there's a secret panel.

Maybe a draft. Come on, you watch movies. There's always a secret panel to push or something."

Betty shook her head. Her flaming red hair darker in this light.

Donna pressed her hands against the wall. "Come on, let's all try."

One by one, the others started feeling their way around the wall. Only Alex, with Abby by her side, waited. Alex watched them working together. It seemed unlikely, but maybe they would find something.

"I searched there already," Donna complained to Colette.

Colette shrugged. "I'm taller; you searched up here?"

"Who would build a secret panel that high?" Donna asked.

"Who would build a secret panel period?" Collette retorted.

Their frustration was ready to boil over. They weren't searching because they believed, but out of desperation. The way back to the original door had been stolen by changing doorways. Even if they found the coatroom, would that door forever cycle to foreign lands? The only way was through. Once her hope couldn't fall any further, Alex peered to the entrance to the labyrinth. Ghostlike, her imagined father still waited.

"Alex," Colette said politely, "We're not finding anything."

Carrie agreed, "There's no way out. Not this way."

Donna glanced at Carrie, realization dawning, "You're thinking the maze is the way out?"

June stamped her foot, "I'm not going through that maze. It's impossible."

"It's probably not impossible," Carrie said.

June glared at Carrie. "What the hell do you know?"

Their confederacy was collapsing. *There isn't much time before there's no getting them back. Bringing them here was pointless.* Alex turned back to the maze. Her father waited, almost frozen.

She took her charm in her hands and looked at the dark center. *Daddy. Is this why he gave it to me? Is that why I see him?* She wondered if he was more than a vision. She approached him and whispered, "What did you do?"

Peter stepped down the ramp and disappeared at the first turn.

Alex nearly froze at the sight. She took an intentional breath and followed. She hesitated. Could she trust her eyes? Even if she could, could she trust her father? What if this was the trap? *This explains why the entry was unguarded.*

I just want to see where he went. Alex edged to the lip of the ramp.

"Come on, Alex," Betty screeched. "We're trapped. Do something."

Abby said threateningly, "Shut up, Betty. She's trying."

"Is she?" Betty made a face, daring Abby to prove her right.

"Stay here," Alex told them. Without waiting for confirmation, she entered the maze.

Descending the ramp, Alex's heartbeat reverberated off the rough-hewn black granite walls. The closer to the entrance, the deeper she descended, the taller the walls; until she no longer saw the maze. She looked upon the face of the wall that split the passageway into left and right routes. When she took that first turn, what would be there?

With each step the passageway revealed itself. With each step, it appeared empty. Alex refused to turn back. The last thing she wanted was to discover the entrance to the maze was no longer a viable exit. She didn't want to think about what that would mean to her or her Book Club if the way back disappeared.

She turned the first corner. And there Peter stood. Waiting.

He was so young. Younger than Alex. He looked like a child. Like he had his whole life ahead of him. He wouldn't visit Sara for another six years. The notion seized Alex's heart with icy hands: six years was all Peter had left when he came here.

From this view of her father, she saw the features of the man she'd known. Stoic silence his most recognizable feature. Adult Peter was in there, like the child was a chrysalis from which he was ready to emerge, pushing against the outer shell, blending the two forms. The next six years wouldn't be kind to him. How they would change him. This boy was not the man who summoned Sara.

Alex finally understood his sacrifice. Her sense of the future was riddled with impermanence. She once thought about going to college; like it was inevitable. Now she understood: the future promised nothing.

She edged closer; he offered no reaction. "Hey," she said softly. "Dad? Peter?" He didn't so much as blink.

Looking around for the ambush, she found herself very much alone. The sense was crushing. Instead of relief, she felt abandoned. This wasn't her father; not now. How was she doing this? Had her want been great enough to pull the memory from the stone walls? Magic? She fondled Abby's charm. "He's with me," she whispered aloud.

"So here we are, Dad. Together in the labyrinth. Then and now." She laughed to herself. "I know you can't hear me. You aren't actually here. You were, but years ago." She wiped her eyes. "What did you do? Why me? Did you know how you'd hurt me? The harm you'd cause?" She held out Abby's charm at the reach of the silver chain. "You cared enough to make sure I'd have this, but you didn't care about me. I was never real to you, was I? You never got to see me, your baby, and know how fragile I was. If you did, you'd never have let these things happen to me." She let the charm fall against her chest. In her head, Abby told her, *It's not that kind of charm.* Clearly not. Did it serve any purpose? Except for her to bear it around her neck like an albatross of her father's making.

Alex lowered her eyes to the floor and wiped tears from her cheeks. *I don't want to be here.*

She told her father as much, "You should know I don't want the responsibility you've given me. What do I know? I'm eighteen, Dad. What life have I had? What experiences have I lived?" She realized she had lived more than most. "That wasn't my life. I suffered with Sara. Because of you. You knew what happened to her and you made me go through it."

Alex closed her eyes. "What choice do I have? There's no way to go back." Only forward. It was exhausting. "The Library. All there is for me there is pain. I don't want it, but I'm going because I'm the only one who can. Matthew gave me no choice. You've been gone twenty years and are still working together. You thought you were so smart, but you did everything he needed you to do. It's like everything else was a lie. You lied to Sara. You lied to Mom. You didn't care about me at all. All you cared about was pleasing your master."

"Who are you talking to?"

Alex spun on her heels and saw Abby, Rose, and Heather leading the Book Club. Her heart reverberated like thunder in her chest. She thumbed to her father. "You don't see him?"

Abby made a face. "See who? Who's there?" As the others slowed out of fear, Abby sped up to be beside Alex.

Alex whispered, "It's my father."

Abby looked around. "Where?"

Alex pointed. Abby looked, then walked right through him. Alex startled at the sight, the two of them occupying the same space. It looked horrifically unnatural.

"I don't see anyone."

"Doesn't matter," Alex whispered. "You're here."

Abby nodded. "Where I'll always be; wherever you are."

Alex thanked her tearfully.

Abby hissed, "Is he still here?"

"Yeah." Alex paused. "He's not really here. He's here, but *then*, when he came. That day you and Heather told me about."

Abby nodded. "I know. I always knew. Heather didn't, but I did."

Alex didn't know what to say.

Abby looked deeper into the maze, to where this passage ended with more choices. "Are you following him?"

"I'm thinking about it."

"Good," Abby said. "That's the right decision."

"Why?"

"Because your father was the sort of person worth following. He cared about everyone."

Alex looked away from her. "No, he didn't."

Abby paused a beat. "You think he did this to you without contemplation? He agonized over it. It's the reason he accepted his fate, so you'd know he suffered, too."

Alex nearly argued on principle, but her mind superimposed this vision of her father—young, vibrant, waiting expectantly—with the vision she knew—zombie Peter. *Maybe Abby is right. Who'd do that, willingly?*

"Alex, I hate to interrupt," Heather edged forward, "but tell us if you're ready to try the maze."

"Try?" Alex asked.

Heather nodded. "It doesn't matter if you don't know. We came to follow you. No matter what. No matter where."

Heather didn't see Peter. She was ready to throw herself on the mercy of Alex's wits. They all were. Alex wasn't sure if she felt gratitude or pity.

Rose approached while her mother talked. "You should have seen Mom ripping into them when you left. Read them the riot act." She glanced back at the group, watching the huddled mass cowering together. "I just hope she never has to yell at me like that. It was amazing."

Heather rubbed her daughter's back. "Shut-up, Rose."

Rose grinned, "Whatever you say, Mom."

Alex glanced at Peter. She turned to the others. "Thank you for trusting me. I don't know what comes next. Maybe we go left or maybe right. It means a lot to know you'll be with me no matter what. Because I know one thing. I know we'll get to the Library."

Several women spoke simultaneously and stopped. Carrie started again uncontested. "You told us it would be dangerous. We're beginning to understand."

Colette added, "I didn't understand you actually meant life and death. It just never dawned on me, I guess."

Before anyone else spoke, Alex asked them, "Are you ready to try?"

They all nodded, most, timidly.

Alex wanted to ask again, to get them to shout with enthusiasm. Instead, she turned to Heather, Rose, and Abby, and asked them.

Rose responded first, "You better believe I'm ready."

Heather swung her arm, "Lead away."

Abby didn't respond. She didn't have to.

Alex looked to her father, frozen at his last step. He came to life and started down the hall. She chased after him, her long strides hiding her fear that he might turn a corner out of sight and be forever lost. Each time the cornering wall obscured her sight of him, her heart clawed into her throat, anticipating a vacancy. Each time she found him waiting. He seemed to pause whenever he got too far ahead. *Am I doing this, or did he leave this here for me?* She touched her charm. Her feelings were undecipherably complex. As grateful as she felt that he might have planned to leave behind this shadow, she couldn't help but acknowledge the acid in her belly that warned of her destination.

He disappeared around a corner to the right. She hop-stepped to nearly a jog not to lose him. He disappeared around a turn to the left. Her heart hammered as she chased him. No matter how fast she went, he moved just faster. He was always ahead, always disappearing around a turn.

She followed him left and then right. They passed straight through one intersection and turned left at the next. There appeared no rhyme or reason for any of Peter's decisions. She followed this memory, which walked without concern, without question.

Does he have any clue where he's going? At some point he got out. She couldn't keep the worry out of her mind that perhaps this vision was the trap. That he'd lead them on endlessly. Visions of exhaustion and thirst and hunger seeped into her mind.

"Alex? Alex?"

Alex paused with anxious hesitation. Peter froze.

Donna huffed. "Slow down, please," the older woman wheezed. "You don't even look the other way before turning," she held the wall as she caught her breath. "How do you know where you're going?"

Should I tell them the truth? Will they think less of me if they know I'm following my father?

Alex thought a moment. *What good does any answer do now?* "Do you trust me?"

"Yes, but—"

That was all the answer she needed. Alex turned and followed Peter.

Peter led her, never hesitating, never uncertain. It reminded Alex of the maddening order of Rose's dream-house, as turns switched back on themselves and Alex was sure they should have revisited intersections. After five tight, consecutive right turns, she half expected to stumble across Book Club stragglers crossing just ahead.

"Will this ever end?" one of them whimpered.

"We're gonna die here," warned another, faked laughter poorly sculpted fear into a joke.

"You're not going to die here," Abby scolded. "She knows where she's going."

Alex kept after Peter. *Is this ever going to end? How is he so damned confident?* The same nagging worry tugged at her stomach. This wasn't a trap; this was her father, showing her the way.

Despite grumbles and requests she slow up, Alex soldiered on. She was getting to the end of this. She was getting to the Library. She'd take the Books. She'd find Billy. Tonight he'd sleep in his own bed.

Turning a corner, Peter was gone. Ahead, the labyrinth concluded in another dead end. It was like the floor gave out under her. She nearly stumbled, her stomach spinning like she'd fallen.

"What's the matter? Why are you stopping? Is something wrong?" Questions asked from behind all hit Alex as pointed accusations.

Alex quickly realized that telling the Book Club that *She'd been following a ghost only she could see and it disappeared* was no way to inspire confidence.

In the distance, Alex spied four doors. Her heart stomped in her chest. She raced forward, perhaps this was the exit. The others raced behind her.

Alex practically skidded to a halt before the first doorway. In her excitement to find the doors, she had nearly forgotten the danger. With great caution, she approached the first opening with the stealth of the police she'd watched on television. Beyond the threshold, the Library was quiet and—insofar as she could see—empty.

"Alex, look," Rose pointed into the next doorway. "It's this way."

"The Library is through here," Alex pointed.

"And here," Rose answered.

"Here, too," Colette and Carrie motioned at the middle-right door. Donna and Betty said the same of the far-right door.

Abby asked, "Which one do we take?"

Alex wasn't sure. *Does it matter?* She examined each. "Look at the way the bookcases line up." Although the doors were but a few feet apart, through each, the angles of the bookcases appeared skewed.

Alex leaned into one door and Lydia into the next, facing one another. Once entering the Library, there was no other door with which to see one another. Lydia squealed, "Each one opens on a different part of the Library."

Donna peered through each of the doorways. "No Dewey Decimal here, I guess; misogynist jerk. Do you think we're in Reference or Fiction?" She alone laughed at her joke. She found it funny enough, apparently, to add, "We should look for section 133!" She looked about proudly, but no one inquired.

Colette answered, "This has definitely been a work of fiction. Come on, really, a maze? What the fuck is that about? Who thinks this crap up?" She shook her head. "I've been trying not to think about starving to death."

Carrie laughed. "Like one of those cartoons, I've been

thinking about who we'd eat first."

Colette rolled her eyes. "That is not even a little funny."

"No?" Carrie was grinning. "Not even now?" She pointed at the doorways out of the maze.

"Maybe a little now." Colette looked through another door. As she passed Carrie, she hissed, "Better not have been me."

Donna rubbed her chest. "This has been ridiculous, but we're here." She looked at Alex, and with a wave of her arm, said, "You got us this far. Lead the way."

Chapter Eighty-Six

lex entered the Library through the second door. Two bookcases crowded the opening. *This place has ends. I half expected to be let out in the center of an aisle.*

It was almost a week ago when George brought her here. She recalled her confusion, her discovery, realizing where she was. Today, these women arrived of their own free will, aware of what this place was. Alex tried to imagine it from their point of view. *What would my first time be like?* It was the most magnificent place she'd ever seen. And the most horrific.

They awed at the towering rows surrounding them, discovering the reality of Alex's explanation. The Bookcases were colossal. Disappearing overhead into the bright, diffuse light hiding whatever ceiling was up there. The rows repeated as far as they could see.

Alex found it amusing as they actively avoided looking at any one thing too long, as though ignoring it denied its presence. But the bookcases were exquisitely ornate, carved with a care and a precision without equal. Like Sirens, the cases and the Books called to them; too beautiful to ignore. Soon they could not help admiring the cases, and in time the Books upon them. The ancient bindings in this section of the Library were without equal. Some leather covers were dry and falling to crumbs, others looked well-oiled by the frequent grasp of human hands. It was easy to guess which Books languished unused.

Even Alex, for all her experience and understanding, found the appeal unavoidable. The Books were—for the most part—stunning; embossed, ornate designs, and stitched mosaics. Lush covers begged to be touched, examined, and read. She couldn't be certain if it was her whispers or the Books she heard, calling to her.

"These are exquisite," Donna ran her fingers over a shelf-front, carved to resemble a march of birds. Her fingers caressed each avian, standing upright in relief. "I wish these Books contained literature. I'd never leave." She surveyed in every direction. She shivered. "How many women suffered to make this place?"

Each had similar discoveries. They each wanted to share with one another the visual opulence. Looking up from a carving or an ornate Book, each clearly fought the desire to say, "Come look at this."

Is this place enchanting them? It was a disconcerting thought. There was power in these Books. So much magic, right at their fingertips. It was no wonder how Jeremiah found his power from the Library.

Alex abruptly pulled one random Book from a shelf. It slid out from between two others, the designs on their covers making soft snapping sounds as they brushed past one another. "Here," she handed the Book to Heather. She took another and handed it to Donna. She told the others, "Each of you, take a Book."

There was some confusion as everyone else reluctantly claimed a Book of their own. They each touched the top of the spine with a devotional fingertip. They slid their Book from its home on the shelf and into their arms, cradling it like a baby.

Donna stared at the thick tome in her hands, at the leatherwork and the faded embossing. She ran her hands over the cover as though seeing it weren't enough. Her head shook imperceptivity at first. "What do I do with this, Alex?"

One by one, the others looked up from their Books and wordlessly asked the same question of her. *It's time.* "Open it. Read."

Rose's voice sounded almost joyful, "None of it will make sense. Then it will."

"No," Colette stammered, and even those—Carrie and June and Betty—who raised the cover in compliance, stopped. "Women can't read from Books."

Rose answered before Alex found the words. There was no joy in her voice. "Who told you that? Where do you think that bullshit came from?"

Colette folded her arms. "Isn't it the law or something?"

Rose laughed for drama. "Man's law. So no, don't read the Book. Stay ignorant. Because that's what *they* told us. That's what *they* made us believe."

"Do you know what this is?" Donna shook the Book in Rose's and then Alex's face. "Do you understand what this is?"

This time Alex answered, "Do you, Donna? Because I have a much better idea than any of you."

"It's not right," Donna argued. "This is a woman's soul,

tortured out of her. I will not justify what they did to her by using it."

"Then her death was in vain," Alex countered.

Donna's eyes welled in anger. "Don't you get it? Some man took this magic from a witch."

They all waited for Alex's reply. She spoke to them all. "Then take it back."

Heather stepped beside Alex and Rose. She nodded to both before turning to face the Book Club. She raised the cover from her Book, the spine creaking with age. She waited. She glanced back at Alex. Her intent clear. Then she looked at her daughter. Alex had never seen this expression on Heather's face before. She was trying to be brave. Heather stared at her daughter. Rose had already done this; she was the bravest among them.

Rose placed her hand on Heather's shoulder.

Heather lowered her gaze and gasped at the glowing beauty of the intricate illuminations before her. Alex recalled how Peter had covered the pages of Sara's Book. In Heather's eyes, she saw that her aunt understood why he had, as the pages touched her in a way she didn't think possible.

Tears fell from her eyes as she looked up, "She's so beautiful." Heather's gaze dropped back to the open pages. She said to Rose, "I don't know what to do."

Heather took the first page and overturned the thick, stiff paper. Her breath seemed to escape her. "Each page is so beautiful, so different." She proffered the Book to Rose. "What should I be looking for? It's all gibberish. Is there a table of contents or something?"

Most of the others followed Heather. Books opened. Each of them taken by the beauty of their pages. Alex listened to their superlatives as they expressed their feelings, the Books overcoming them.

Rose delicately helped her mother to a random set of pages. "Just look at it, Mom. Read by looking into it."

Heather stared at the open pages. The others watched. She said with sadness, "It's just nonsense. These aren't even letters. They're shapes and symbols or something." Her voice slowed and trailed off, "Do they even mean something...." Her head tipping from side to side. Her eyes glazed. "I see," she said, "in the shapes, are those... more?"

"Let go, Mom," Rose stepped closer to Heather, rubbing her

back. "Keep looking. Inside each letter, there's a whole other Book. Keep going. Until you find the last one. The first one. Keep looking until you've read them all."

Heather collapsed against the bookcase. Rose helped ease her to the floor. "It's okay, Mom. You're falling. Just ride the flow, see the words within words. You go into it. It goes into you. Ride it all the way down."

"Oh Rose," Heather's disconnected tone sounded absent of thought, "I'm falling so deep, Rose. Does it ever end?"

"There's a bottom, Mom. You'll know you're there."

"Oh my baby Rose, you did this all alone?"

Rose watched Heather carefully. "Do you feel her? You'll feel her just before you get to the bottom."

"She's wonderful. Who are you?" Heather asked.

"She's not really there. Not alive until you need her. Until you ask her for magic. You'll feel her. You'll become a part of her, let her become a part of you."

"It's so complex, Rose, so many layers. Layers in layers."

"That's her, Mom, the layers are her."

A moment later, Heather's eyes welled up. "I feel her, Rose. Oh dear, oh sweet dear. I'm here. I know. You don't have to be scared or alone anymore. Be with me."

The others watched Heather in awe and terror. The fear of their approaching turn widened their eyes. Alex felt immense respect for Heather. A few days before, she was condemning Rose for using her Book. Now here she was, earning her own. And not just that, but she stepped before her Book Club to show them first. All because Alex said she needed her to.

Tears streamed down Heather's face. She touched her daughter's cheek. "I'm so sorry, Rose. I'm so sorry I doubted you." She looked to the others. "It's beautiful. I feel, how to describe it, like something I never knew I lacked is now a part of me."

"It *was* lacking, Mom. It's called magic," Rose grinned.

Rose helped her mother to her feet. Heather wiped her tears and hugged her daughter. She said, "Thank you, Alex. I never knew. You showed me the truth."

"Rose showed me the truth, Heather: Everything we believe about Books was a lie men told us." Alex continued, "We believed it and repeated it so much we all forgot the truth: Magic belongs to us."

Heather looked at the others. They stared back as if waiting for her head to explode or a penis to sprout somewhere, as if the Book would change or condemn her. "I had Peter's Book," she mused. "Could I have removed the curse myself?"

Alex and Rose both nodded.

"We could have avoided all this if only I'd—"

Alex interrupted Heather, "Known the truth? How could you? How else could you have known to be so brave?" She looked at Rose, who didn't acknowledge the compliment. *If Heather read from it first, what would have happened to Sara's magic? Could I have still taken it?* She felt that there were more complex machinations at play than she comprehended. *Peter did everything for a reason.*

Heather lovingly ran one hand over the cover. It seemed personal to her, a treasure she'd rediscovered after a lifelong separation. "Do you think Peter knew?" She paused, her voice quivering as she hissed, "Did he lie to me?"

Alex didn't respond.

"He did, didn't he?" Heather took a breath, steeling herself against betrayal. Her sainted brother was perhaps no better than any of them.

Alex touched Heather's arm, "I don't know, Heather. Maybe he had a reason, maybe he wanted to make sure you weren't alone when we figured this out."

"He should have shared that with me."

"Maybe he didn't know. I wonder if *any of them* do."

Heather looked over the Coven. She touched her Book again. "I wish I had at least tried."

Alex didn't answer.

Heather looked at Abby. "I miss my brother so much, but if he were alive, I'd kill him." Abby laughed bitterly. Heather turned back to Alex, her eyes wet, and hissed, "He betrayed us all. He hid the truth and made us think we were inadequate."

"He sacrificed everything, Heather," Abby reassured her. "I refuse to believe he'd hurt you or Alex on purpose. He gave everything to our cause."

"We're all here now," Alex said softly, "because whether he lied or not, we did everything the way he intended. And now instead of just one of us with magic, we'll all have it."

Heather turned to the others, her eyes red and irritated. They stood in silence, their Books in their arms like children on the first day of class. They all stared at her. Some with pity, others with wonder, a few with suspicion. "What are you waiting for? I'm fine; family drama. Open your damn Books."

Carrie was the first, opening it without further question. Donna followed her. The rest didn't wait to see who among them would be the last.

One at a time they collapsed to the floor, dizzied by the descent into their texts.

Rose pulled a Book off the shelf and after a momentary perusal, returned it. When she saw Alex watching her, she posed like she carried two pistols. "I thought maybe I could do two." She made a face, lowering her hands in disappointment. "I guess once you're connected with a Book, you can't get another."

Heather turned to Rose as the others swooned. "Was it like this for you? Out in the field?"

Rose nodded, "Yeah, only I didn't fall down."

Heather petting her daughter's head. "Of course not. How did you know what to do?"

"I did what made sense."

"I meant how did you know how to use the Book?"

Rose shrugged. "Turn the page until it feels right. You'll see." Heather nodded, still uncertain. "It tells you, Mom. The Book knows what you need and helps you find it."

After several minutes, each of them was standing.

Alex watched several fingering through their Books. They showed one another a page or two, more enamored over the artistry than the undecipherable nonsense on the page.

Carrie tilted her Book forward. "Rose, you mean we'll just know how to use these?"

Rose suddenly found herself the center of everyone's attention. For the briefest of moments, Alex felt the sour tinge of jealousy. Suddenly everyone had magic and she was no longer special. More than that, she'd never read magic from a Book. Her magic didn't come easy. It required so much anguish and mental gymnastics to craft her emotional state. And unlike them, she couldn't just keep reading. Once the emotion was exhausted, the magic was gone.

"None of this makes sense," Nancy looked over one page in her Book. The illumination was a mix of metallic gold, blue and red, with black text. "How do I cast a spell?"

Rose turned back to Alex, smiling. Alex was happy for her. For a change, only Rose had the answers. Alex always felt she was guessing. Yet, there was something gloating about Rose's smile. Alex dismissed the thought, worried she was painting with jealousy. They could get their answers from another. She wasn't sure how she felt about that.

Rose stepped among the group and explained, "Let the Book guide you to the page. You'll feel when you find it. To cast the spell, stare at the first symbol; it's the one in the big, fancy box. Your mouth will, how do I say it, it'll kinda go," Rose cocked her mouth open to demonstrate. She looked like she was mocking someone for being stupid. "When you look to the next symbols, your mouth will move for each one. You only have to breathe, and the Book does the speaking for you."

Colette edged forward, "Is that why they're always carrying the Books? They have to read them every time?"

Rose thumbed back at Alex, "She's the only one here with real magic. The rest of us get it from the Books."

"Oh," Nancy asked, "how do they make them appear and disappear like that?"

"Yeah," Betty added, "how do you do it, Rose?"

"Like this?" Rose grinned fiendishly. She twisted her hand through a wisp of mist as though reaching in and pulled out her Book.

The group tittered with excitement.

"Show us that," Lydia clapped her hands.

Alex cringed at the noise the group make. She didn't want them attracting unwanted attention. *Maybe if Rose shows them, it'll make them more confident.*

"I have no idea how I do that," Rose confessed.

The group diminished.

There goes that idea.

Rose looked smaller than usual under the disappointed gaze of the group. "It's like I had to know the Book before it showed me how to hide it away."

Rachel asked, "Where do you put it?"

"Hell if I know," Rose answered. "It's always right about there," she waved the Book in the air near her hip. "I'm sure you'll figure it out."

They admired Rose. *They never look at me that way. I bet now that they have magic, they'll be different. Maybe it's the Books. Maybe that will make them feel like a team. A real Coven.* Alex wondered how she'd fit in.

"Are we," Colette asked, "real witches now?"

"Yup," Rose responded proudly.

Alex added, "You always were, you know."

"Well," Colette argued politely, "it's different now that we have magic." Had her grin grown any wider, the top of her head risked falling off. She looked at the others. "Magic!"

Rather than reply, Alex stepped back.

Betty played with her bright red hair. "What's next?"

They turned to Rose. Rose shook her head adamantly, "Don't look at me." She pointed at Alex.

Alex suddenly found herself not liking the attention. *What comes next won't be fun.* "You'll find Billy." Before anyone could ask *How*, she continued. "I'll take care of the Library. Do you think burning this place to the ground will be enough of a diversion for you to find him?" She waited a beat. "First, I have to read a Book."

"But I thought you don't have to read to have magic." Donna looked confused.

Alex knew what was coming. The pain. It would be intense and insanely personal. The brutality in each Book would be hers to endure. "You remember the flames?"

Donna nodded, her eyes wide. "Oh. That. Again?"

Alex nodded. She looked from one to another, their returned gaze falling away when met with hers. *Are they afraid? Jealous? Of what?* She realized they didn't understand what it was like for her. The pain was half of it. The other half was comprehending the depravity of the human condition. Understanding the truest nature of cruelty. The whispers in her head told her another side of that horror. What she would soon suffer through wasn't her suffering. She was freeing the last remaining remnants of those tortured women. Alex would emancipate all those women; acknowledge their suffering and end it.

Her hand might have been weighed down by thousands of pounds of lead for all the effort it took to collect a Book. Randomly, her hand fell on an oversized tome. She slid it from the shelf. The grain of the leather cover pressed against her palm.

This is why we came. But I don't want this. One Book was painful. A whole bookcase was excruciating. She knew. Their pain. Their humiliation. She'd rage at the injustice. Disgust would boil her blood. She would revile the men who cared so little they wantonly abused and tortured and slaughtered these women. Laughed at their suffering, spat on their dying bodies, all the while believing they were doing good work. Believing the resulting Book to be a sacred artifact. Sacred, but made by their own selfish hands. *I am here to burn them all.*

Chapter Eighty-Seven

"Hey, oh, wow. I'm sorry, I didn't know anyone was back here."

Alex found herself surrounded by ten women with Books drawn, ready to cast spells to attack an unprepared and unsuspecting interloper.

Drawn to the focus of their ire, Alex found the intruder. He looked no older than Alex, who tried to decide if his presence endangered them. Inquisitive brown eyes poked out beneath a mop of straight, dark hair. In spite of his confusion, a broad smile hadn't left his round face.

His voice cracked, "They, ah, let women in? I mean, I didn't know. Cool. Since when?"

"We just got here," Alex said. She was reminded of Rose's gunslinger's comment, her hands tingling. She wasn't sure what emotion she could easily summon if he was a threat. An enormous Book was tucked awkwardly under his arm, but he made no motion to access it. Everyone watched her for guidance. He seemed harmless, and that unnerved her most.

"Oh. Alright. Neat. Welcome." He looked around Alex at the others. "Welcome," he repeated as he acknowledged each of them. "I was thinking, since you're new here and all, maybe I could help you. Um, what section are you looking for? Or are you thinking more specific than section?"

"What section is this? Is it a section?" Rose examined a shelf in case an answer was there.

He looked at Rose, his mouth opening and closing like a fish as he tried to answer her. He looked to Alex, but his eyes twitched once more to Rose, as though magnetically attracted to the pretty girl. "It's, um, older Books. Um, compilations, you know, scrolls and such that were made into Books."

"Alex?" Heather said.

"That's good to know," Alex indulged him, ignoring her aunt. "So older magic?" Was she suddenly curious that there might be some order to this place or postponing her tribulation? Each moment they came closer to being discovered. *What if he's here to stall us?*

"Um, yeah. Really older," he grinned. "Like ancient. Ancienter than ancient, if that's even a word. These are the earliest Books."

"Interesting." Alex smiled. It didn't feel like he was stalling. More importantly, he seemed knowledgeable about the Library. *He could prove useful.* Alex checked the bookcases, as though they might have left. Immediately, her heart wrenched in expectation. The price to take magic back was just as great as losing it. She recognized she was the one stalling. "I'm Alex," she offered her hand. "It's short for Alexandrea."

He grinned and accepted her handshake. "Caleb. It's short for Caleb." Alex laughed politely. He looked like a nice boy, maybe in college. She couldn't remember the last time she'd met a boy her age. Mark White, maybe, but Caleb was cuter.

"What are you studying?" He looked at the group, perhaps noticing the disparity in their ages. "Are you guys like a study group?"

Is he honestly this naïve? Alex recalled the clamor when she came with George. The Library was perfectly quiet.

From behind Alex, Heather cleared her voice. "We're more a *Women's Studies* study group."

Caleb nodded thoughtfully. "That's really cool. Well, this is the place to learn about women, I guess." He nodded again, as though absorbing what Heather said. Then he explained, "So, like, I'm working on this really interesting project. I mean, I'm studying links between older spells, like from the middle ages, um, twelfth century, say," Caleb said like someone requested clarification, "and really ancient spells, like five or ten thousand years ago... earlier... ago."

"Links?" Donna, ever the teacher, queried from behind Alex. "What do you expect to learn from that?"

Someone hissed at her.

Caleb nervously motioned with his hand. *He's adorable.* He replied, "Well, spells represent a well of knowledge from people of a set time. The older the period, especially from long ago, you know, like, really long, the stronger the magic. But more limited."

"Alex?" Betty urged.

Alex turned and said, "It's okay. We'll just be a minute."

Rose inquired next. "Really? Limited? How?" Alex couldn't tell if Rose was asking because she was curious, flirting, or competing.

"Well, if you think about it, if the person casting a spell has no idea about concepts from a more modern era, they can't cast spells that reflect that understanding. Imagination, understanding of natural phenomenon, that sort of thing kept magic primitive. You get it? Magic can only do what they believed it could do. As time went by," he continued, unaware he already bored most of the others, "and people understood more, magic wasn't as strong, but they did more with it. Like it was diluted by knowledge or something." He held up a finger; he was about to make his point, "But what if the same spell did different things with different understanding? What if it truly was limited by the caster's knowledge? If that's true, and I believe it may be, then what can we do with really old spells that seem to have no purpose anymore? I mean, does anyone care about mesmerizing earthworms?" Caleb's eyes bulged in excitement, "I mean, I can't even rationalize what someone would have done with that six thousand years ago, but who knows what that spell could accomplish now with a more modern understanding. It could, like, maybe create tunnels or mine gold or something even cooler."

Heather interrupted once Caleb paused, "Diluted, you said? Spells got weaker?"

"Um-hum," Caleb acknowledged. "I really can't figure out why, though."

Heather's tone transformed. She started with clear patronizing sarcasm and switched to accusation, "Maybe it was genocide. Ever consider that? The slaughter of millions of women."

Caleb looked taken aback. "What are you talking about?"

"Mom," Rose defended, "I don't think he knows."

Heather snapped, "He knows. He's a man. He sure as hell knows."

"Knows what?" Caleb asked. Heather frightened him, but when his eyes fell to Rose, he smiled, thinking perhaps she defended him.

"Those Books," Heather pointed at the Book under his arm and waved at the surrounding shelves. "All these Books came from women. Torture a witch long enough, and you render the spells out of her."

Caleb imperceptibly shook his head. "No. What? No." He half-laughed, "That's, um, oh, are you making a joke?"

The other women fell into line behind Heather. They all shook their heads at once.

"Is that why it feels…? When you, you know, read…? Oh." His voice barely above a whisper.

Again, they nodded at him.

Alex pitied this kid. "You don't know where these Books come from, do you?"

Caleb looked away, upset. "No. That's…. Please tell me you're kidding."

Alex said, "It's true, Caleb. Every Book here; every one was a woman who had her magic stolen. A man took it by causing her excruciating pain." She now knew where she'd find the necessary emotion. His ignorance infuriated her. That he would use Books and never consider their inception.

For a moment, emotions wrestled across his face. He didn't move. He seemed just there, incapable of action. Like he was a collection of features: Large brown eyes and dark, straight hair, jeans, a light blue shirt, and red headphones resting on his collarbone. He blinked, life returning to his face. "You're not scholars, are you?"

As Alex shook her head, she was sure all the others were doing the same. What they must have looked like to this frightened boy.

"You're not a women's study study group; or whatever that lady said?"

Alex shook her head.

"What are you doing here, then?"

What did he decide? However much he looked the part of a lost puppy, her emotions felt raw. How many Books had he used? How much did he ask of the women trapped in them and never once come to realize where the magic came from? Alex was ready for their conversation to end, one way or another. "I've come to take it all back."

"You can do that?" He looked terrified. "I mean, sure you can. Why not. But, I mean, how?"

Heather edged forward. A finger in her Book holding her place. Her tone reminded Alex of those times she'd been screaming at Rose and Billy and then answered the phone, oozing charm through gritted teeth. "Caleb, you should see her do that. It's amazing to watch."

Caleb nodded with uncertainty. He looked at Alex and then at the others, coming back to Alex. He would stare at her, but his eyes were always distracted, flashing off to Rose. *What's she doing to distract him?* She turned. Rose was smiling, mischievously. *He can't keep his eyes off her.* Alex couldn't help but grin. *Perfect.*

"I didn't know," he practically squeaked. Clearing his throat, he continued, "It's horrible. I mean, I guess, I just, I mean, no one told me. I didn't know it as fact." He paused, looking at the Book in his hands. "I've been told so many things. They weren't lies, but they weren't truths either." He slowly shook his head. "I'm sorry. It's so horrible."

"You should go," Alex instructed him.

Donna hissed, "You're letting him go?"

Rachel asked, "What else can she do?"

Donna said firmly, "*Not* let him go."

"When you said *Take it back*, before, you didn't mean *steal*, right?" Caleb asked.

"No, I did not mean steal. I free the magic from the Books." Alex stated.

He offered Alex his Book. "Start with this one," he said, "it's the oldest I've ever found."

Alex replaced hers on a shelf. She accepted Caleb's. Thick, heavy, large; it smelled earthen. The dry leather cover sucked the moisture from her skin. It felt unusually heavy for its size. "It doesn't look that old," she said, nodding to other tomes that looked far older.

"The Book isn't that old. What's in it, though, is ancient." Caleb said.

"You might want to get out of here," Alex reiterated.

Caleb shook his head. "I study magic, Alex. I've only ever wanted to learn about it so we could use it to make the world better. Look, I know not everyone here is an academic or whatever, but for many of us, some of us, whatever, these Books are sacred." He quickly looked around, seeing Rose before coming back to Alex. "It's like finding out your museum has plundered treasure, and even though it means a lot to you, you have to repatriate it, you know?"

Alex had heard about that in the news.

"I want to watch it happen." He half-smiled. "I want to see what you do for, what's the word, *posterity*."

"You're sure?" Alex questioned.

Caleb nodded. "It's the right thing to do, isn't it?"

"You should stand there, with them." Alex motioned to the

Coven. "Once I start, it's going to get ugly."

"Ugly? You?" Caleb blushed as one of the women groaned. Again, his eyes flickered to Rose. "I know what you mean. They're going to try to stop you."

Alex nodded. "They will try."

"You should know, there are a lot of us who might agree with you. Especially, you know, once they understand the truth."

"I appreciate that, Caleb," Alex told him. She kept checking the aisle. It may not have been his intention, but he was doing a phenomenal job of stalling them, and she let it happen. "If you stay, they'll try to kill you, too."

"Really? Well," Caleb gulped, "I still want to watch."

She followed the flash of his eyes again. "Here," she said, taking his hand and guiding him. "Stand with Rose." To Rose, in an exaggerated tone she said, "You'll take care of Caleb, right?"

Rose grinned. "Sure, I'll keep him safe." She turned to Caleb and took his hand to shake. "I'm Rose. It's short for Rosemary."

Alex was unsure if Rose was mocking her or him.

As Caleb and Rose became acquainted, Alex retreated to the intersecting aisle. The others were impatient, afraid to spend a moment longer than they needed to. Most didn't trust Caleb, but some, Rose in particular, adored the cute boy.

Alex took a deep breath. *It's like diving from the high board. Just leap. The water will always be hard and cold at first.*

She looked back at the group and awaited their acknowledgement. They were ready. She looked at Caleb. He and Rose were already holding hands. Alex examined Caleb's Book. Respectfully, she touched the edge of the cover. Slowly, she pulled it open. It creaked the entire way, as though no one had opened it in a thousand years. The vellum pages crinkled, the spine groaned, the entire book changing shape as it spread open to her.

With one more very deep breath, Alex looked down upon the first page.

Chapter Eighty-Eight

rittle with age, Alex's touch caused the edges of the pages to fall away like snow. The designs on the page hardly seemed as ancient as Caleb suggested, and for a moment, she doubted his sincerity. *What if Jeremiah sent him with a Book I can't burn? What if it's not a real Book, made from a woman, but to do me harm?* She glanced at the boy. He'd already abandoned himself to Rose's eyes.

Returning to the Book, Alex's eyes followed a design around the page; an artist's representation of braided hair. One braid was brown, another blonde, and the other, light auburn. Small, awkwardly line-drawn animals lurked and hid about the braid; what appeared to be an owl—two circles, a V for a beak, and stick-feet—peeked from one corner. Crude looking mice—little more than triangles with tails—scurried along the length of the page. One chased by what had to be an S-tailed cat. She saw butterflies and bees and dragonflies. There were flowers and beehives. The more she looked, the more the page revealed. It was beautiful in its simplicity, a spiderweb at one corner dripping dew, as though the page was a walk through a field of wildflowers.

Struck by the beauty, Alex searched for the text. The more she searched, turning a page and then another, the more the animals and creatures returned her inquisitive gaze. She chose not to ask Caleb how this Book was supposed to be read. Instead of allowing impatience to frustrate her, she kept at it. She could almost see the tall wildflowers—little more than sticks with cups on the end—sway in the breeze. In the corner of her eye, a round bumblebee was visiting flowers. As the Book revealed its secret to her, she understood. In other Books, she assumed the symbols were letters and words. Here, the symbols were the very plants and creatures. The field became clear. Wild roses and violets, hummingbirds and snakes, were not the design, but the spell itself. Within the thin strokes of ink that designated the hummingbird, lurked an entire aviary. More than a field filled with flora and fauna, this book was an entire catalogue of life itself.

Within one mouse, a small triangle with three whiskers and a looped tail, scurried a multitude of rodents. Chipmunks and squirrels and groundhogs hid in the ink.

The cat chasing the mouse hid lions and tigers and pumas. *This is such a strange Book.*

Alex placed her hand on the page. The oils from her skin stained the page. The Book tried to suck her in, the dizzying sensation was different this time; she fell amidst an entire field. Her fingers, instead of gripping the animal skin, dug into dirt. Her fingertips curled into moist, rich soil. She pulled, tugging the page from the binding; the soil gave. Roots snapped. Worms and ants wriggled and scurried from her. Caleb winced as the pages tore.

She expected, as had always happened before, to see the shapes spill from the page. But Caleb hadn't lied; this was magic older than any she ever come across. At first flower petals, red and purple and orange and yellow, fluttered and twirled to the floor. The line drawings tumbled away, saturated with their ink. The startled beating of a bird made her heart leap and the others around her cry out in surprise as a blood-red cardinal took flight. Birds and insects fluttered away, flowers and leaves wafted to the Library floor, while animals as small as earthworms and bees and mantids and ants wriggled and fluttered away. The mice scurried, their little claws scratching the pages as they leapt away. One raced up Alex's arm, over her shoulder and down her back; an orange and black calico cat lunged from the Book, a yelp punctuated its landing. It caught sight of the mice and careened down the aisle, pouncing from sight. The animals seemed to gain weight; the Book bouncing in her arms as creatures emerged and leapt, freed from the Book after a written eternity.

The others gasped in wonder at the sight. They offered oohs and aahs at the cuter ones and disgust at the multi-legged bugs and rodents, or at the insects that only got so far before being crunched or devoured. Caleb was shushed even as he tried to explain, "The oldest magic was nature".

Something changed.

Shovels cut into her. Pikes and picks dislodged small bits. Rocks overturned, split. Trees cut. Forests denuded. Fields burned. Rivers damned, flooding plains. Forests cleared; soil stripped to bedrock. Explosions enlarged holes. Minerals evacuated from mines dug deep into her meat. The ground she believed lay dormant under her feet cried with her voice. She willingly gave, but her children only knew to take. They twisted her, covered her with sores and pocks that never healed, burned her flesh and scraped her to the bone, picking at every scrap. They replaced her with versions of their own. Built large, dead forests in which they lived like parasites. They chose what could grow and poisoned the rest. Alex writhed as she was stripped raw and remade into something she no longer recognized.

Is this, she thought when she could, when that pain subsided enough to allow words to form, *magic so old that it's the magic of the world?*

The pain was not pain, not precisely. Pain was how her mind interpreted what she was meant to feel, but it was not. It was a separation of life, a dissection of stone from soil, and then stone to block, to wall. Wood from tree, stripped and honed, joined and remade as structure. She understood she was not feeling this directly, but as a translation, an interpretation. Nature wanted her children to have these gifts, offered them up as her sacrifice, but that didn't mean they were taken painlessly. She felt each scratch of obsidian as a log was honed, each curl of wood falling to the ground. It was a part of her, which through time and rot she would reclaim. Fruits and vegetables, plucked from her hair, cooked, chewed, swallowed, returned to her. It wasn't pain, it wasn't sadness; she had so much to give, she did not feel depleted. Not at first. She felt taken for granted, as though the recipients of her gifts assumed the things she produced would happen with or without her will.

This was not pain. This was love. Flesh cut from her body nourished others who gave back to her in other ways. She gave herself willingly.

Then she felt something she hadn't before. A tickle. On her flesh, in a small alcove carved over millennia by the dripping of a clear, cold spring. She felt that magic, once eternal, now being locked away: painted onto a cave wall.

She felt that magic scraped away and fed to a woman to become carved into rock to be fed to a woman to become engraved in clay tablets to be fed to a woman to become painted on the hide of a wildebeest to be fed to a woman to become inked onto a curl of papyrus to be fed to a woman to become written into a scroll to be fed to a woman. Alex followed her magic across the epochs, given and taken, sometimes lost, but always found. Taken and given like the coming and going of the tide, until at last, one woman provided her captors with this Book, a compilation of thousands of ancient spells, hundreds of years ago.

Alex's eyes welled at the pain, the indignity, the betrayal of it all. This was not theirs to take.

This is what Matthew proposed to me: consume the Library and make one tome. Magic reunited. One Book. His to master.

Her tears dried in anger. What Matthew proposed was to take the pain suffered by every witch, everywhere, forever, and channel it through her. Make hers the burden of understanding, and then murder her. She hoped all the creatures were free from this Book, because something deep inside was awakening: It was not rage or anger. It was wrath.

Alex clawed at the page, her nails digging deeper into dark, black-brown soil; heat rising around her like a nearby furnace door thrown open. She roared, lifting her head and screaming her disgust and vengeance. Her voice came not as a cry, but a fiery crackle. The Book responded, crying out to her in a giant whoosh of hot, curling flame. It disturbed her long hair in its flickering tendrils as it expanded like an unfolding explosion to the unseeable Library ceiling; spreading, hiding the soft glow in a yellow-red display.

Alex no longer knew her corporeal self. Her body was a thing of fire. Each curl, each spark, each twist of flame was like a finger on a dexterous hand. She clutched the Library covetously.

Hundreds of thousands of Books, more, their pages curled and discolored in heat, their designs spilled onto shelves from between closed pages. Their vitality surrendered, the tomes fell against one another, collapsing to ash.

Anguish twisted her. Her body writhed in agony, wrapping around herself as she danced. She nearly withdrew in the pain from a thousand hammers, knives, tortures, shattering her bones, cutting away her flesh, twisting and shattering her limbs. Instead, she suffered to crave more. Reaching, claiming another shelf, then another bookcase. Her body was ripped apart anew with each page, but like holding her arm in a flame, it took every ounce of will to not succumb to reflex and pull away. Those women cried out for her salvation. They sobbed thankfully when she claimed them, releasing them from their paper prisons. Her lack of corporal form saved her from the base reactions, the sweats, the dry heaves, the tears, the hurt. She didn't resent the Books. She caressed them with fiery appendages. She embraced their covers. Pressed their spines against—into—her body. Slipped her fingers into their pages. Pried them apart. Wider, wider. Her heat filling them, they cried out as she pulled the women inside herself. Their anguish became hers as she relieved them from their endless torment. They entered her, became a part of her, the weight of their punishment evaporating. They grew lighter, freer, disappearing but not lost. They whispered to her.

*   *   *   *   *

Rose watched Alex with careful enthusiasm. Her expectation actively shifted wildly from excitement to disappointment. She'd heard Alex's tales of what happened when she read from a Book, and Rose found herself buzzing with excitement at finally seeing the spectacle. Her cousins' fingers tore at the page as her face twisted with an ecstatic agony. Rose's heart rattled with expectation; she half expected nothing to happen, like when her mother's yellow car refused to turn over. The gigantic Book in Alex's hand released a puff of smoke. Rose wondered if that was the extent of the show when the page browned and curled. A single flame—like a candle—popped into existence, before her mouth fell agog as the flames wrapped, like vines, up into Alex's hair and around her head like a crown.

Alex's body grew to eight, then twelve, then twenty feet tall, transmuting from flesh to light and flame. Rose's heart pounded in her throat as she told herself she didn't just watch Alex die in the flames; the fire growing like a pillar and spreading across the distant, invisible ceiling like a nuclear explosion. It was like being bathed in heat. Then, the raging flames momentarily stilled. What looked not unlike a fiery appendage reached out, smoldering Books before it even touched them. At contact, fire raced Book to Book like they'd been doused with gasoline, engulfing the entire massive wooden structure with near instantaneity. Then the flames reached to another and another.

Rose mopped sweat from her burning eyes, still unable to look away from the conflagration. Her mind fought to remember this was Alex; it wanted her to panic, to run from the danger of uncontrolled flames rapidly consuming everything around her.

"Rose? Rosemary!"

Rose startled, realizing her mother hadn't just spoken her name for the first time. The women of the Book Club were gathered close by Heather, their sweaty faces illuminated by the thrashing firelight. Heather's expression was one Rose couldn't quite grasp. She was purposeful as she opened her Book and shouted to the group, "While Alex burns the place down, let's get my son," but also sad.

"Are you okay?" Caleb shakily asked her. "That was quite a thing." It was only then she realized his grasp on her arm had relieved her hand of feeling. She told him she was fine, while politely prying his fingers from hers.

Carrie asked, "You want to be up with your mom or stay back here?" She kept looking at the flames. Rose anticipated her saying something—they were all talking about Alex and the fire—but Carrie only added, "You've done magic before, so I'm staying wherever you go."

Books drawn, Heather lead them charging down the burning aisle.

Rose liked the idea of taking up the rear. It allowed her to keep an eye on the whole group, but also be in the front if someone surprised them from behind. Caleb followed her like a well-trained puppy, at her heel. First Rachel joined her and Carrie. Then Betty and June. A gap formed as several women hung back to be closer to Rose. *Did my mother tell them to watch out for me?* When everyone but Donna and Lydia ran with her, she realized that no, this wasn't her mother's instruction. They felt safer with her than with Heather.

The heat was excruciating. The roaring flames reminded her ears of the same unknowable language they spoke summoning magic from their Books. A bubble of cooler air formed around them. The edge swirled with heat and smoke, like it couldn't cross the invisible barrier. She looked at the flames and could almost sense them looking back. Like Alex was protecting them. *Do your thing. We'll be fine.*

Heather slowed, "Don't fall behind, keep up!" She was nearly panting, her hair sticking to her face. As much as Alex's bubble surrounded them, it was still brutally hot. "These aisles are so fucking long."

"Do you even know where he is?" Donna challenged.

Rose glared at Donna for asking the question. "Of course she doesn't," Rose snapped back. She expected Heather's expression to admonish her tone, but her mother's face offered only appreciation.

They raced forward, through the hellscape of the burning Library. It was like everything burned; the Books, the bookcases, the granite floor, the air. Around them, Books collapsed into piles of ash on blackened, red-glowing alligator-skinned wood. Like a freight train roaring around them, Alex's fire expanded in all directions.

Heather reached an intersection, and as she took the corner, her backpedaling feet lost traction. She slammed to the floor amidst a shower of sparking bolts. Rose's chest tightened and her hands balled to fists as her mother screamed in pain. Rose only needed to look—like she communicated telepathically or imbued her will on the others with her eyes—and Carrie, Abby, and June were kneeling at Heathers' side, pulling her back to safety. Leaving Caleb, Rose leapt into the aisle, her Book opened, and glared down the crowd of twelve to fifteen men cowering in the inferno.

Some fired their bolts, while others created showers of water to vainly douse the flames. With a glance at her Book, Rose's jaw set. She exhaled, her eyes skimming the bizarre shapes and symbols, her clenching stomach nearly belching air from her lungs to give voice to the spells.

The energy surged through her. It was like her whole body expanded from the pressure of the energy which raced down her arms, emerging from her fingertips. Had it moved any slower, it might have been unbearable. But the buildup and release, even in rapid succession, was rapturous.

Bolts shot from her fingertips, exploding granite and wood where they missed. The wind was knocked from her by a strike, the electricity feeling like an eel thrashing under her skin for a moment. Yet, she didn't drop her Book or miss more than a syllable. She was enthralled, her hands trembling in excitement.

Betty was at her side a moment later, her flaming red hair plastered to her scalp. When she fired her first bolts—barely sparks—she laughed, "This is so cool!"

Donna joined them, an odd preciseness to her guttural pronunciation. Her bolts looked more controlled, like someone had groomed the static fuzz from the streak.

Rose repeated the spell, playing with her breath, shifting her mouth as the Book allowed. Her bolts struck like bullets, knocking their targets prone, leaving glowing spots, like little molten pools of electricity.

Carrie, June, Rachel, and Colette were soon at her side as well. With a glance, Rose confirmed that Abby and Nancy were caring for Heather while Caleb watched. Rose started forward, her words coming as shouts, the bolts emerging not as sparks, but as full-fledged strikes of lightning. She saw the panicked expressions on the men as she closed on them. Their panic fed her as she rushed forward, drunk with excitement.

Donna warned, "Don't get too close." All Rose could think was, *Don't waste your breath with words.*

Another strike spun one of the men into the air, his Book fluttering into the flames where it hit the ground as a splash of ash. This was too much for them; some men abandoning their Books. One even threw his at Rose. They grabbed their fallen comrades and raced away. Rose lowered her Book, disappointed. The fight had been thrilling. She winced from the burns on her leg and abdomen where she'd been struck. She hadn't felt them until she gave them attention. Over the roar of the fire, she could barely hear the others celebrating their victory.

It was all Rose could do to not give chase. Her back was slapped repeatedly. "That was amazing." "Did you see their faces?" Heather emerged from the aisle and aggressively grabbed Rose in a hug. Rose initially thought Heather was trying to throw her to the ground, but her mother spoke into her ear, "Rosemary Hawthorne, I am so proud of you."

The others added to the accolades. "Did you see her?" "I wish I could do magic like her." "She was amazing!"

I was pretty amazing. Better than Alex ever could be.

"Rose, I don't know if we're going to find Billy," Heather said. "Maybe it's too dangerous." She looked at the flames around them. "There could be many more here."

"Did you ever want to find him?" Rose snapped. Heather looked like the words came with knives. "You wouldn't stop looking if it were Alex, would you?"

The others looked startled by Rose's directness and gave them space, like they were creating a sparring ring. Donna started saying something about Rose respecting her mother, but several of the others hushed her.

"It's not that simple, Rose. Giving up on Billy isn't something

I want to do. I think maybe it's something we have to do."

Rose nearly slapped her. She was furious. "How dare you?" She'd barely gotten the words out when her mother collapsed against her like she'd been shoved, her face twisted in surprise and pain.

Men emerged a few aisles down. Eight of them, showering them in sparks and bolts. Her Book was open, and she was reading before she even thought to do it. Sparks flew all around her; the others cried out as they were struck. Rose shouted the words as she marched forward. Lightning burst from her fingers, hitting several of them at once. They convulsed and dropped to their knees. It took one strike for the men to disperse. This time, she gave them chase.

Rose ran, reading and firing. One of the men stopped and turned to face her. "What are you doing here?"

The tone of his voice startled Rose, like he knew she was a child and that somehow mattered. His face was sweaty and filthy, smeared with char. Shadows shifted wildly around him as he read, as she read. Rose's heart raced like a train bearing down on her.

"You're just a kid," he said, lowering his Book. Rose seethed. She wasn't just a *kid*. She was a *witch*. He continued, "I've got a girl your age." His face softened. "Why would you be here? Who would bring a *girl*, here?"

Rose's chest was like a drumroll. Her hands trembled. *I'm not a kid.* Yet, there was that part of her brain that told her not to fight because he was an adult. Because he was pretending to care for her. Because he'd trick her into lowering her guard before he snatched away her Book and left her defenseless. Then they'd call her a *kid*, and a *girl*, and she'd have no way to prove otherwise. No way to shove their words down their fucking throats.

Her eyes snapped down to her Book. She fired again and again, before he could find his place. She stepped closer, firing as he abandoned his Book to the flames and raised his hands in defense. Lightning burst from her fingers. She placed her hand on the man's chest. His heart pounded rapidly. His chest expanded and fell. "Please don't," he begged, but she kept reading.

The wind was like a tornado bursting into the Library. The flames swirled into the aisles and in many places, flickered out. Rose's sweaty body shivered in the sudden chill. Her eyes fell from the page before the last symbol, and her hand dropped from the man's chest.

Wood and Books crackled and popped as they cooled.

Bookcases collapsed, creating billowing clouds of ash. *Did Alex finish?* She grinned like her ears each caught a corner of her mouth and pulled. She regarded the sobbing man. His eyes looked away from her. He kept whimpering, "Please don't. Please don't."

Rose looked at the entirety of the destruction around her: an apocalyptic landscape of burned forms. "I can't believe it. She did it," she said aloud. "Alex consumed the Library." She felt a measure of disappointment creep across her chest. The man crawled away. She had no reason to make more magic. No reason to fight. She felt like something glorious had been snatched from her.

It was then she realized she was alone. She could hear the cries of celebration. *They realize it too.* They were celebrating Alex's achievement. She wanted to be a part of the triumph. She disappeared her Book and ran towards where she'd left the others. It was at that moment she realized they weren't celebrating. Those were screams of pain.

Chapter Eighty-Nine

lex hadn't strength to cry or sob or ask *What is happening* or *Why me* or *When will it stop*. Alex had burned and returned from her flames before. Perhaps she had spread herself too thin? Grown too large? Too fast? The last she remembered, she was desperately searching for a wall, for proof there was another end to the Library. Her fiery body was immense, reaching, growing. And then it wasn't. The fire choked. Her body snapped to her usual proportions in an agonizing instant, as though she awoke to find herself knotted and twisted and broken in a million places.

At first, the pain was too all-consuming even to scream. Like she'd been torn apart, the tiny pieces still connected by raw nerves which screamed horrifically at her predicament. She was aware of nothing else. If she could, she'd have accepted anything to have it end, even if that defeat was her death. Anything to put an end to her suffering.

Her pain choked the meaning from the words being spoken, but she recognized the voice.

Even as the pain subsided, its echoes raked her body. Touching hands gave her no comfort. Her skin might as well have been sliced to streamers and doused with salt.

"It'll be okay, Alex," Abby chanted. "It'll be okay."

Her Coven knelt around her, touching her, their faces wet with tears, contorted with disgust over her anguish, all witnesses of the churning transformation she endured. None of them offered words, mute with grief and sickened by shock. Caleb separated himself, stepping away to be neither with nor apart from them.

"Rosemary!" Heather screamed.

Racing around the corner, Rose crashed to her knees beside her mother. "What happened?" Her tone was overstuffed with accusation and disappointment. Heather's answer escaped her in a gasp.

Her Coven clotted into clinging groups. They barely breathed, waiting to see what would happen next—to see who had done this to Alex.

Abby's face was wet with tears, her teeth bared in anguish and rage. Alex followed the flash of Abby's expression, but Alex's eyes wouldn't focus. She made out an approaching shape. She strained to move; agonizing pain stabbing every sinew. All this time she feared the trap and now, at her most vulnerable, they were here.

Blinking away her anguish, she resolved a bald man, symbolic tattoos painting nearly every inch of his flesh; her memory returning to a mind consumed with the present. Whispers cried their fear to her. Told her they saw him die, flayed him when he forced their touch. Watched Jeremiah turn him to ash.

"Book?" The word came out as though her first ever: Slow, crude, unpracticed, and malformed.

He made a face. "Master won't waste his time until you're able to talk."

Alex wondered if perhaps he spoke to someone else, but besides her Coven, he was alone amidst the smoldering ruins of the Library. The air stunk of burned paper and firewood. There were heaps of charred wood and ash as far as she saw, the once shiny granite floor now a dull, shattered, gray.

"Jeremiah?" Saying the name felt akin to calling on him. She opened the door uncertain if she was ready. The truth revealed itself in the shivers her own voice shot through her body.

"Master," he confirmed.

"He turned you to ash," she said.

"Wasn't me," he responded, proudly. He was a placeholder; his presence was a knife to her throat. Jeremiah was coming. He was the slicing hand.

Under the embracing touch of her entire Coven, Alex's pain subsided, although agonies of chilling aches haunted her body like wandering spirits. Her body feared movement; sick after what she endured.

"You're not ready for him, yet," he uttered.

Abby warned him, "Just leave her alone. You want to bother someone, come see me about it."

He ignored her. He rested his hand on the ground, nearly touching Alex's arm. "Soon."

"Please don't touch me," Alex begged, fearful that he might provoke her to flame again.

He said, "I've seen what you've done to the other Books."

Something about his tone made her ask, "Other?"

"Exactly. Master took me from a shelf, gave me life."

"Life?" Memories of the field were chaotic, like flash cards thrown into the air during a tantrum. His words assigned meaning to those memories she didn't want to believe could be real.

He unbuttoned the top of his gray shirt and pulled the collar aside, exposing half his chest. The ink in his skin was chaotic; there didn't seem to be any reason to the size or direction of the designs, they spiraled and then ran in intertwining lines, overwriting themselves. "I'm a Golem, a servant of magic. I do what I'm told. So long as," he referenced his flesh, "it's written here."

Alex asked, "You're here to kill me?"

He laughed. "You? No."

The threat in his denial was as though he'd said *yes*. Beside her, the women stirred.

"Not them, either. I'm waiting until you're ready." He glanced down the aisle. "He's a busy man. Man? Yes, that's fair."

Tension released her limbs like someone turned a key and unlocked them from the bondage of her fear.

"Who are you?" Alex asked.

His face changed. "You mean, like my name?"

"Alex, why are you talking to him? Can you move? We'll protect you." It was Heather.

What am I thinking? Jeremiah is coming. She felt like she was standing in cement under a grand piano, the rope bearing it, fraying rapidly. The last time she faced him it was Sara's intervention that saved her. She had intellectualized that being at the Library meant encountering him, yet fear of him—of what had been done to her— kept the realization away. Until now. She consciously tried to catch her runaway breath. *What am I going to do? Am I ready?* She looked at her disquieted Coven. *Are they?* Her whispers had before been a sea of voices, but was now a roar. *That's why Jeremiah is coming; to take them back.*

Alex tried not to hear the Coven discuss the fool's errand of how they would protect her.

Heather asked, "Can you move?"

Agreement was easier than contradiction.

"Show me."

She righted herself, leaning her torso on trembling arms. They responded like she'd never before used them. "Help me," she asked the others. Once upright, although unsteady, she stood on her own.

Without a word, Book turned away, feet crunching the ash. Distance made him smaller and smaller until she lost him in the rubble.

"You've made quite a mess." The startling voice approached from the opposite direction. Book stepped from behind a wrecked mound of ash, but it wasn't his voice she'd heard. Behind Book, wearing poorly matched tan slacks and tweed jacket, Jeremiah approached. Alex's gut turned icy. She feared that what was coming would be worse than anything so far.

"They're just Books. Each one catalogued. They'll all return. It's happened before. Nothing is new. Everything you've done, this grand act of defiance, is temporary." Jeremiah grinned. "Everything is temporary, if you have long enough to wait."

Is this an act? Is he hiding his rage? His indifference chilled her.

Heather threatened Jeremiah, "Leave her alone."

He ignored Heather. Jeremiah's eyes narrowed, looking at Caleb. "What are you doing with them?" His actions seemed a little too rehearsed, as though to suggest he didn't know everything. "It's Cody, no, Caleb."

"I, um, I know what's happening. Here. Now," Caleb's voice quivered.

"Is that right?"

Caleb nodded frantically. "These Books, they're not ours to take."

Jeremiah's face twisted in disappointment. "This is not the time for philosophical discussions."

"When?" Caleb sounded as defiant as a five-year-old.

Jeremiah turned to Book. "Accompany him to the Farm."

Rose stepped between Caleb and Book.

"It's okay," Jeremiah condescended. "My Farm is a fine place. Men aren't allowed, but I make exceptions for naughty boys."

Caleb asked, "What about Alex and them?"

Jeremiah's eyes flashed: It almost seemed he liked that Caleb knew her name. "They aren't your concern. I haven't come to harm anyone. Only to shine light on a grave misunderstanding. I'm certain Alexandrea will soon understand none of this was necessary."

Caleb joined Book. "Don't go," Rose warned.

Caleb looked back at her, then at Alex, looking for her confirmation. He seemed resigned to do as he'd been told. Whether that was from fear or obligation, she couldn't discern. Which didn't matter; Alex couldn't offer any objective advice.

Jeremiah tapped his foot. "You're welcome to stay with them, Caleb. Just consider what happens next. They leave the Library. They go home. Do you go with them to live happily ever after? How will you earn a living? You won't be welcome here again. Your work is important. Is a misunderstanding worth your future?"

"You're not going to hurt them?" Caleb asked.

Jeremiah reassured, "Not one hair on their pretty heads." Alex wanted so desperately to believe him.

Pity lined Caleb's face. "I'm sorry, Alex," he said. With an uplift of his right hand, he added, "I hope the next time, you know, it's different. Not here."

Alex replied, "Me too."

He looked past Alex. "Bye Rose. You're amazing."

Jeremiah mocked him with a sigh.

Caleb's face flushed. Book was waiting. Together they departed, Caleb pausing several times to peer back until he was lost amidst the sea of ruin. He walked like a man heading for the gallows.

"Why not just kill him here? Do you get off on giving him hope?"

Jeremiah frowned. "Why does everyone assume that my first reaction is to kill?" His laugh suggested he might or might not be kidding.

Alex looked back at her Coven. Abby sighed when their eyes made contact. Heather looked down. Rose motioned to her closed Book, her finger holding a place. Alex shook her head, wondering if Rose was crazy enough to think they stood a chance. Inside, Alex felt Jeremiah's presence exerting something on her, diminishing her. Silencing her whispers. Behind them, Carrie and Donna stood the middle ground, Nancy just behind them. The others edged away, separating themselves from Alex and her family. Colette, June, Betty, and Rachel created their own cluster. Rose motioned with her hand again, perhaps thinking Alex didn't notice the Book or her finger tucked into its pages. Alex hissed, "No."

Rose sneered.

"Do something," Heather pleaded, watching her daughter opening her Book. Colette and June grabbed at Rose. Alex tried to release her rage, but everything inside her fizzled like damp fireworks.

"I wouldn't do that," Jeremiah hissed.

Rose struggled as Carrie and Rachel joined in. She held her Book, dangling from her fingers and started reading sideways.

"Please, Rose," Heather begged. "Someone help."

Betty appeared her Book. She snapped it open and with intense eyes scouring the page, her mouth snapped to position. She took two steps beside Rose and read.

With a disappointed shake of his head, Jeremiah motioned at Betty. She cried out her surprise as the pages ignited to flame. She discarded the Book when the flames embraced her face and singed her fire-colored hair. Even once the Book fell from her hands and burned on the floor, her writhing dance continued. She twisted and contorted to the extremes of her body, her joints snapping. She fell back over herself, her head cracking against the ground.

Abby grabbed Alex, imprisoning her in a protective embrace. Even had she been free, she was helpless but to watch. Her concern felt muted, as though it waded around her brain in knee-deep mud.

Betty screamed, but she might as well have accused Alex of murder. Alex brought her here and her stomach bubbled with responsibility. Responsibility that weighed on her shoulders heavily enough to buckle her knees, her arms trembling from the weight of watching another suffer for her deeds.

The others ran to Betty, trying to comfort, trying to hold, trying to heal her.

Nancy screamed: Betty's coin burned in her chest.

Book scooped Betty's smoldering Book from the floor.

"No," Jeremiah ordered his servant. "Let it finish."

Alex begged him to stop, but Book blew across the page, turning glowing embers back to flame. Betty cried out, her coin flaring.

"Stop," Alex begged. "Please. You're killing her." Nothing felt real. How could this be happening?

"I haven't touched her. I'm destroying her Book, lest she use it again."

Alex forced herself to look away. Where she expected to find her anger building, was empty. Unable to summon her magic, she broke from Abby and rushed at Jeremiah.

He stopped her with a word. "Let it finish or I'll take another."

Alex's eyes welled with anger. Behind her, Betty's body ticked and jerked. The others cried. "No, Betty, no. Not like this." "I told you, we shouldn't touch those Books." "You're really going to *I told you so* now?" "Betty, please, I'm so sorry."

"You said you weren't going to hurt them," Alex whimpered.

The corners of his mouth curled upwards. "I haven't touched her."

"She's dying because of you." Alex looked at her, at the others lamenting over her, at the coin disintegrating to ash in her chest. Alex's chest ached. She recalled Lesedi. *This is not the way anyone should die.* Her whispers swirled and chattered with increasing agitation. *At least as a Book they might live again.*

Jeremiah looked to Book, "Clean up that mess." To Alex, he added, "Do you like my Golem? Let me explain how to make one."

Alex didn't want to hear. Although she felt the sting of tears in her eyes, she refused to cry. Not now. There'd be time enough for that eventually. The others cowered with Betty's body. They stifled their grief. Carrie and Colette still restrained Rose, who was no longer trying to use her Book.

Jeremiah tapped his fingertips together. His face plain and serious. "You take a Book, I know you know the kind I mean, and you take a woman, who still has her spells."

"I don't want to know," Alex whimpered.

"Oh, but you should." He looked around Alex at the others. "They all should. How else will they know when it's about to happen?" He looked at the Coven. "When their glowing soul—I believe you call them coins or heart-stars," he said with contempt, "is placed between the pages of a Book, something remarkable happens. Just the desire to live is enough for those little words to disappear. In one breath, the Book empties onto the coin." He pantomimed taking a coin from a Book he just opened. "The coin is returned to the woman. Then a miracle happens. The coin consumes her. Transforms her. Like a butterfly emerging from a chrysalis, the Golem is born."

Alex trembled. "That's even worse than making a Book."

Jeremiah's face reddened. "Is it? Is it Alexandra? Are you sure? Because you need to tell me if you'd prefer that I extract a Book or make a Golem. I will do whichever you prefer."

"I don't care what you do with me," Alex answered.

"I wasn't asking about you, dear." Jeremiah turned towards Book but never took his eyes from her. "Fetch the Polka-dots and the dark one with the ridiculous fingernails."

His threat snatched hope from her heart. She couldn't believe someone could be so cruel. Even Matthew with his hammer had purpose she could comprehend. "They didn't do anything. They followed me. I did all of this. Not them. Please." Tears of grief overwhelmed her. She couldn't hold them back any longer.

Jeremiah mocked concern, "*All of what* did you do? *This*?" He touched a charred piece of lumber and rubbed his fingertips together. "This was a small part of my collection, dear child. You seem worried about consequences. For doing what? It's not like you broke a lamp. This," he dismissed, "is nothing."

Another Book emerged from down the aisle, joining Jeremiah. Only by noticing differences in their tattoos could they be told apart. *How many are there?*

The women tightened their group, but it was clear Jeremiah was culling those who strayed furthest from Alex. Carrie and Heather put themselves between Jeremiah and the others.

"You see, Alexandrea," Jeremiah said as Book walked past her, skirting the distance to stay out of her reach, "there is a price to pay for every action, great and small."

Book pointed at Colette and Lydia, his glare ordering their compliance. He knelt to scoop Betty from the floor.

"Don't touch her!" As soon as Heather screamed the words and saw Jeremiah's eyes darken in reproach, she shrunk back, her eyes darting to her daughter.

Jeremiah took a step towards Heather. Perhaps his concentration faltered. Perhaps what Alex believed he was about to do to her aunt was greater than whatever machinations restrained her emotions. Like floodgates catastrophically failing, Alex's anger erupted volcanically. The force of her rage was startling, like someone had opened a can of warm soda, unaware it had been shaken. Her head roared. The whispers found their voices. The immense, blinding flashes of lightning cracked like panes of glass shattering in quick succession. Almost startled by her own power, Alex aimed it all at Jeremiah.

Rose's Book was out in an instant. She spat the words like they soiled her tongue.

Jeremiah writhed in the midst of the electrical cage Alex put him in, electricity coursing through him. Rose's bolts struck him. Carrie and June and Colette appeared their Books and joined in. Heather, Nancy, and Rachel aimed their strikes at Book, driving him from Betty's body.

Donna fumbled her Book in her panic. It spun across the floor, striking Alex's feet.

Anger poured out of Alex. She kept looking at Betty to replenish the well. The Book striking her shoe, Donna apologizing and excusing herself, Jeremiah's grin—as though he were enjoying the performance—quenched her anger. Absent her rage, not even the sight of Betty's body could fill her void fast enough to prevent uncertainty from seeping in.

Jeremiah started to say, "Impressi—" when struck by Rose's next attack. With a wave of his hand, she slammed to the floor like she'd been hoisted up and body-slammed.

Before Heather could even check on Rose, Donna squealed. She'd reclaimed her Book but now stood arms reach from Jeremiah. Before Donna realized it was gone, he'd snatched the coin from her chest.

He held it tauntingly before them. Donna realized her predicament. She turned to Alex. "No, no, no, no," she whispered her desperation.

"Don't," Alex begged. "Please." This was worse even than the outcome she'd dreaded. She had no reason to expect he'd leave her and kill the others. How many before he was satisfied that he'd taught her his lesson? She looked at her Book Club, cowering and fearful. By opening that door, she had marched them to their deaths. Not even Heather or Rose was safe. "I'll do anything."

Colette stepped forward. "I'll go with the Book-man." Lydia stood beside her.

He flinched when Alex nearly touched him. She was ready to plead, willing to do anything to stop whatever was coming next. *Not again, not another lost forever.* For a moment, she hated Billy for being the reason she'd come.

The coin spun and twisted in the air, hanging by its thread. He looked up at it, his mouth opening. Alex lunged as it dropped. Like brushing crumbs from his sleeve, he batted Alex to the ground.

The thread sparking at his lips disappeared like a lighted fuse in a sparkle of dust.

Donna's face slackened. Alex cried in horror. She recognized Donna's expression: she'd seen it every day on her father's face. Someone squealed. Another gasped. One cried out. Rose let out a curse directed at Jeremiah. He didn't hear it or acted like he hadn't. Carrie clutched at Donna, the agitation making Donna sway.

Bile crept up Alex's throat where she tasted it on her breath. *I did this.*

"I said I'd go," Colette screamed.

Lydia looked at Colette then Betty then Donna and collapsed to the floor, sobbing, "I don't wanna die."

Alex fought to her feet. "Stop," she begged. "Please. No more. Not again." She was sure he smelled her fear. She knew she stunk of it.

Heather softly whimpered, "Please, bring her back."

He looked at Donna. "That's no way to live," Jeremiah's false compassion stung. Without the aid of a Book, he whispered, his sounds chopped and throaty.

Nancy and Carrie looked at one another in horror. Carrie held a hand up to her nose. "I'm going to be sick."

Lydia asked, "What's that smell? Is that… barbeque?" Carrie bent over and vomited.

Donna's eyes widened, her mouth becoming a horrific scream of steam. Her skin darkened in mottled patches. She crackled like a fistful of chips. Her clothing sparked. Plastic buttons melted and dropped from her blouse. Her skin became the color of coal. Then all at once, her form collapsed like a bundle of blackened feathers, billowing across the floor.

Several of them screamed. Most stepped from the chalky cloud. Alex cried as the warm, dark cloud swelled around her ankles. Heather sobbed and sheltered Rose, whose eyes snatched closed. Nancy helped Carrie to her feet, wiping vomit from her face with her bare hands as Carrie's body wracked with sobs.

Alex heard their whimpers, their cries. "We're all gonna die here." "We had no business taking those Books." "What were we thinking?" "We're fools, not witches." "What's he going to do next?" "We're all dead."

Jeremiah focused on the others. "If you would follow this…

person looking thing," he motioned to Book, who was now carrying Betty. "Polka-dots. Fingernails. If you please."

Colette stepped forward. Carrie hissed, "Don't Colette," but Colette shook her head as she joined Book. She wiped her face and tried to present herself with dignity, but her emotions overwhelmed her, sending her back to tears.

Lydia slipped from June's touch. She took Colette's hand. Lydia's eyes were ringed in black, striped with tears.

The two of them looked at their feet, holding one another, trying to find comfort where neither had to give. Alex hoped one might look at her. She wanted to see their resentment. She wanted to feel their blame. She deserved their hatred and wanted to feel it, to know they blamed her, too. She was helpless. Alex wished she could birth some emotion, anything besides grief. Even if she could, she feared the repercussion. Who would he murder to punish that transgression? Would losing Heather or Rose—or any of them—be worth the scratch she might make? *I killed them. This is all my fault.* She hadn't consumed nearly enough of the Library. Billy was still missing. *I might as well have murdered Donna and Betty myself.*

As Book led Colette and Lydia away, only Alex and Jeremiah watched them. Alex wondered if by not watching them, the others were denying culpability. She'd sentenced her Coven, her friends, to death. She saw no path through this. Putting an end to this was her responsibility alone. She knew there was rage beneath the surface, lurking there like black crude, waiting to gush when tapped. But it eluded her.

Deep within her head, all her women cried out. None of them were telling her what to do, vying for control, whispering suggestions. They were frightened, just like Alex.

Jeremiah approached her. "You try so hard," he whispered. "What will it take for you to learn? I am a man of my word."

"You said you wouldn't hurt—"

Jeremiah interrupted her, "For what obligation do I owe you my honesty?"

Alex was ashamed at how desperately she had wanted to believe him.

He gestured at the burned ruins surrounding them, "Just because I didn't turn your bodies inside out doesn't mean I can't. It's not my fault you confused courtesy with kindness."

"I won't do that again."

"How optimistic of you. After all this, you're still hopeful." Jeremiah stepped back. The distance, the release of tension at being out of immediate reach brought tears to her eyes. She wanted to turn to Abby and Heather and Rose but feared he'd see and didn't want to give him reason to take any of them.

"Help me understand. What compelled you to try burning my Library? What was your desire, your want? What had you hoped to achieve?"

Alex whimpered, "Billy. To bring Billy home." She wiped her running nose.

"I remember hearing about him the last time you and I met." He dramatically looked around. "Was there something here you needed to bring him home? You could have just asked."

"He's not here?" Alex asked, the question serving also as the answer.

Behind her, Rose cried out, "What? How long did you know?"

Alex's voice weakened, "Matthew told me Billy was here."

"Matthew told you he was *here*?" Jeremiah seemed genuinely surprised.

Alex didn't want to keep playing his game. But Jeremiah's eyes were sharp. He didn't need words to threaten her silence. She nodded.

A spark lit in Jeremiah's eyes. "For—what has it been—three hundred years? Matthew's friend Laurent planted this crazy idea in his meager skull—that the Books are the source of my power."

Alex agreed with her eyes.

"What Matthew is too young, too infantile to comprehend, is that my power doesn't come from Books."

"Why should I believe you?" Alex asked. "For what obligation do you owe me your honesty?"

For the second time, Jeremiah's surprise appeared genuine. "Well played." Thoughts twisted his face and widened his grin.

Like some concepts too great to be comprehended, Alex didn't understand what else could provide Jeremiah with such power. Yet, even if she couldn't explain why, part of her knew. She saw it in Caleb's Book. It wasn't the Books, it was the earth, the natural world, the entire universe; from its grandest scale to the smallest energy that held atoms together, giving the universe mass and weight that was magic. And all of that magic was contained here, within the Library.

"I am the source of magic," Jeremiah said. "Take every Book and give them to Matthew, and I still control it. Why can't you cast a spell?" When Alex heard his next words, she heard her mother's warning, and she mourned hope abandoning her, "Mine is the dark heart of all the universe. Without me, there is no magic.

"I think you regret coming here." Jeremiah explained, "Matthew and his people were harmless little crickets, singing in the night, hiding under moist rot and decay. Today he scratched me." He walked a circle around Alex, driving the others—even Abby—back with his presence, separating her from her Coven, her pack. "You will earn your escape. Who better to conclude Matthew's misguided game than the child he helped create?"

"I came here for Billy." Alex felt the danger of her contradiction as the words emerged, barbed. Behind her, Heather whimpered something about Billy never coming home and Rose warned her never to say those words again. "I came to find Billy. I don't regret trying." She shook her head, uncertain if that was true. Was Billy's life worth Donna's and Betty's and maybe even Colette and Lydia's? "Let them go. I'll stay. I'll pay for what I've done. I'll take care of Matthew. If that's what you want from me."

Behind her, no one argued. No one told her they wouldn't leave her side.

He approached Alex, his eyes trading callousness for sympathy. "I forget what it's like to be mortal. It's been so long for me, Alexandrea, since I feared death. It once bothered me, losing friends and lovers, experiencing them grow old and decay." He shook his head. "People are like puppies or kittens. Sometimes they play with toys and sometimes they chew the furniture and crap the carpet. Sometimes they do wondrous things, and sometimes they make little girls burn Books."

Alex winced. "What are you saying?"

"You have my attention. You're the first to surprise me, since, well, ever. And a *woman*. Look what you've done. Matthew couldn't do this. Many tried. I am impressed. I will know you better."

Alex couldn't hide her disgust at the notion.

"Don't touch her," Abby and Heather shouted in unison.

"You feel hurt by me, but someone else dared you to put your hand in my cage. Matthew knows how sharp my teeth are. He knows

I bite. He murdered your friends by sending you here. He hurt you today. Remember that. You will pay him back the hurt he's caused. Destroy him. Then live out your life pretending not to remember any of this."

"You're letting me go?"

He grinned. "Go? Where can you go that I can't find you? What can you do that I won't know about? I want to learn what you will do. I want to learn so the next one—there will be a next one—is extinguished before he even starts. You're walking away from my Library, but you'll still be as trapped as ever."

"What about the Books?"

"You only *think* you took them. If I blink too long, you'll grow old and die and everything you think you took will return to me."

The reality of Jeremiah's immortality struck like a speeding truck. Her life was like a minute in his world; a single rotation of the second hand would take more casualties than she feared he might. To defeat her, he need only wait. That was why he was letting her go. From his perspective, it was only a short while until she had grown old and was moldering in a grave.

Alex took a long, slow breath. She looked at what remained of her Coven, of her family. Her chest was carved out and raw to see their hollow eyes staring back at her. Rose didn't look at her with broken pity; Rose glared at her with disappointment and anger. *I deserve that stare.* She wished the others would look at her the same. *I don't deserve their pity.*

"Once you let them go, I'll do it. I'll kill Matthew. I'll even bring you his head."

Heather gasped, "We're not leaving without you!"

Alex tried ordering her, "You have to."

Heather shook her head.

"I don't need his head to know." Jeremiah spat back.

Alex dreaded asking for confirmation; just saying the words gave him opportunity to invalidate her hope. "They can go?"

"Once I show you how you'll defeat Matthew." He pointed at Rose and curled his finger. "You! Come here."

Alex's heart cracked, as if breaking in two. Before she could step between them, the threat from Jeremiah's eyes withered her intent.

Rose scowled defiantly. Her Book hung in her hand,

unforgotten. She marched forward, her Book rising to be read.

Heather threw herself before Rose. "Not my daughter," she wailed. "Take me. Don't hurt her."

"Get out of the way, Mom." Rose sneered, "I've got this."

"No." Heather held her arms out. "Not you. I've already lost my son. I can't bear it." Heather turned to Jeremiah, her eyes red. She never looked so angry, so tired, or so scared. While Rose protested, Heather demanded, "Don't touch my daughter."

Jeremiah thoughtfully nodded, "You've tasted magic. Not like her," he referred to Alex. "But you'll do."

"Jeremiah, please," Alex begged.

"Mom, let me go," Rose demanded, slapping her Book against her thigh in frustration.

"It's okay, Rose. I know. I've always known," Heather whimpered. "Promise you'll let them go." Tears ran down her ruddy face.

Jeremiah approached Heather. Then he turned abruptly to Alex.

Rose wailed, "Mommy!" She held Heather, sobbing into her mother's hair, touching her mother's face.

Jeremiah threw Abby aside like she was a leaf. His fingers clamped on Alex's face, twisting her head back. He came so close that when he spoke, their lips brushed one another.

There was something electrifying about his touch, his physical contact, skin to skin. Alex's bowels twisted, his touch radiating through her. She tried seeing what happened to Heather; why Rose was crying, but his grasp was ironclad.

"You think you can come here without consequence. You're a child. You haven't lived a single lifetime. I offer you one chance. Will you take it?"

Alex strained against his grasp to nod.

"Do this, when you find Matthew."

Out the corner of her eye, Alex saw Rose, Heather collapsed in her arms. Rose wiped shiny drool from her mother's mouth.

Obscuring her view with his fist, Jeremiah's hand opened. Blinding her with the pure white light of Heather's coin.

His fingers were in her mouth, pushing Heather's coin between her teeth. He forced it into the back of her throat, gagging her. "Swallow Matthew's coin."

She fought the weight of the warm disk in her throat. She wanted to spit it up, wanted to vomit, die, anything but swallow it. Her eyes glared. Her lungs burned, her chest and diaphragm heaved and spasmed for breath. She felt it, a lump lodged at the back of her throat. She gagged, she choked at it. She wanted to be sick everywhere to have it out of her. He wouldn't let her. He kept it there, forcing her to swallow Heather's coin.

Betraying her, her throat clenched. Heather's coin slipped down her throat. She choked, trying to cough it up, sick with despair, but it kept going down.

Chapter Ninety

The coin strained down her throat. Inch by agonizing inch. Even her retching dry heaves couldn't slow it. It kept moving, this unwanted bulge, testing the limits of her throat, uncomfortable inside her. Alex's body was coated in a slick sweat; this was Heather's coin Jeremiah fed her.

And then it stilled.

It spread. It grew. It threatened to burst her chest from the inside. It changed. It diffused. It became something different.

Wave after wave of warmth, almost heat, radiated through her. Filling her chest, penetrating deep into her tissues and bones. Reaching into her arms and down into her groin and into her legs. It tingled in her fingers and toes until she couldn't tell it apart from herself.

She noticed a presence. Becoming part of her, another person dissolved away. *Is this Heather?*

Alex sensed the despair, the fear. Heather knew what was happening.

Heather's anxious fear joined her own twisting gut. Although she had no choice in the matter, it was a betrayal of her aunt. Like Alex had smothered Heather herself. Except Heather was becoming a part of her. If this Heather had limbs, had a voice, Alex was certain it would grab hold of her for comfort and cry out for her help; her sympathy, asking—no, begging—Alex to do something, anything. This thing inside her wasn't vanishing. It was becoming Alex. Alex could sense, in those last desperate twinges of terror thrashing at her insides, that even though she knew it was Alex, Heather fought against becoming someone else.

And then she was gone. Alex knew Heather wasn't really gone. Some part of her, however small, would always be with Alex.

Jeremiah released her.

Instantly, like an avalanche in her head, she found herself recalling experiences, having memories that didn't belong to her. It was like opening a curio cabinet and discovering a treasured collection she never knew existed. Distant memories, forgotten moments, became apparent. Heather's memories burrowed their way into Alex's mind. Suddenly, she understood Heather in only the way Heather understood herself.

This was not another whisper. These were now her memories.

The strongest, most important memories muscled their way to the fore. She reminisced in the joy, the sorrow, the guilt, the regret of all that used to be known only to Heather. It was like rummaging through a drawer that was accidentally left unlocked and discovering the secret treasures Heather hid away. Except these weren't all treasures. Joy, heartbreak, anger, love, disappointment, embarrassment. Alex didn't want to know the things Heather chose never to share. Knowing, understanding her aunt thusly, felt an even greater betrayal than if she'd willingly swallowed her coin. Because knowing these things meant she knew the parts of Heather that Heather had even hidden away from herself.

For a moment, she might have forgotten she was Alex. The sensation that was Heather became so strong, felt so real, Alex nearly mistook it for herself.

Chapter Ninety-One

itting. Feet playing in the scratched-out trough of soil, hands holding the thick chains suspending the curved rubber strap on which she sits. A playground.

A chain-link fence corralled patch of foot-worn grass and sandpits. A metal slide, swings, monkey bars, and a contraption for climbing that resembles a spaceship. Long wooden teeter-totters. Three giant concrete tubes. A wooden merry-go-round.

Peter. Sitting atop a concrete tube. His red parka unzipped. His pockets bulging with gloves. It barely fits him anyway; he is so tall.

Abby. Beside Peter. Her thick flannel jacket bunched and tied about her waist; her mittens fallen to the ground.

Both teens. Young and pimply and innocent. Talking about nothing so important they couldn't talk about anything else.

Inside, Heather feels a twinge.

The way her brother—her twin—talks to Abby, sits beside Abby, makes Abby laugh. His jokes are the same stupid jokes he's told Heather so many times she can't understand how Abby laughs.

Abby. There are no reservations, no insecurities when she is with Peter. Abby laughs and makes wide-eyed faces when the jokes are dirty. She grins at Heather. Her eyes say, *I know why you love him.*

I don't love him, Heather thinks. He's my brother. I *have to* love him. Everyone loves Peter. Peter is the charming one. The smart one. The kind one. All I am is the pretty one: Peter's sister.

She doesn't feel resentment. She *makes* herself feel it. She watches Peter's animated arms entertain another. She feels she is losing her brother. Her twin.

What does he like about her? Abby is her friend, too. They played together and shared secrets and talked about boys. Mostly Heather talked about boys. Abby had little use for them and pointed out overlooked flaws.

Abby is fat. Fat and ugly. Fat and stupid. Heather doesn't mean it. Thinking it doesn't make her feel better. Only worse. She loves Abby. Like a sister. Except she is a new addition to her family. But that isn't it. She feels excluded. Left out. As though Peter needs something from Abby and doesn't want Heather to know. Before Abby, they were Peter and Heather, Heather and Peter. One word. PeterandHeather, HeatherandPeter. Now Peter, Heather, and Abby, or Peter, Abby, and Heather. Do they fit together? In some ways it is better. Different. It is okay when Abby is her friend. When she and Abby are together, alone, without Peter. But when she is with him, it feels wrong. Like her brother doesn't want her there.

Peter makes and keeps his promises. Is he making promises to Abby? Is she that important to him?

Come here! Peter waves her over. Abby smiles and waves. *Come 'ere*, she says. Cold mist leaves their mouths, like cartoon speech bubbles. Heather shakes her head. *I don't want to.* Peter makes a face. His whole body asks, Why not?

Heather puts her hands on her belly. *My stomach doesn't feel well.*

Peter looks over, *Are you okay*?

Heather replies, *I want to go home.*

Peter makes a serious face. Abby looks at him and then her as he asks, *Are you okay to walk home by yourself? Do you want us to come?*

I'm fine, Heather snaps. She thinks, Walk home by yourself? Is he serious? Is fat Abby so much better than me that he can't just come?

She stands. The swing undulates. Stray hairs caught in the chains yank from her scalp as she walks away. Punishment for her thoughts.

She can't hear what Peter is saying, but Abby laughs. Probably jokes about me. She turns and they wave.

Feel better, Peter says.

We'll come with you, Abby says.

No, she tells them. *I'm fine.*

Peter checks, *I thought you said your stomach hurts.*

She puts her hands over her stomach and walks away.

Once the playground is lost from sight, Heather cries. Her stomach doesn't hurt, just her heart. Peter chose Abby over her. She could have asked him to walk her home, but that felt like asking for his love. She hates herself for being alone. She hates herself for hating Abby. She hates herself for feeling jealous.

*   *   *   *   *

Heather is looking out a misty car window. The moisture fogging the glass forms drops that run, leaving clear stripes. Her body buzzes. The black, impenetrable woods beyond them are alive; crickets, owls, cicadas and a whole cacophony of life singing out, calling for partners and prey. She chooses a solitary lightning bug from the multitudes she sees and makes a wish. Their yellow-greenish glows look like stars that haven't yet fallen to the ground. Her mother once told her they listen to your wishes because they only live one summer. Stars are so old they forgot how to listen long ago.

The leaves dance with the warm breeze. Like fabric rustling, like ball gowns swaying. Here, she's just another animal in the night.

The engine is off. They are so removed from human life, it seems, that she might as well be alone in the world. She thinks about what might happen next. She is nervous and excited and terrified and thrilled.

The boy in the seat next to her, Eric, leans over to kiss her.

Their lips not in sync, his kisses misplaced: more on her face than her lipsticked lips. They'd kissed many times before. Never with this urgency, never with this intent. She opens her mouth a little. His lips fall into place. His tongue touches her lips, her teeth, her tongue.

His hand touches her leg at the knee. His other hand, the small of her back.

His hand slides up her leg, not reaching, not at first. Exploring, gently understanding the contours of her thigh.

Their lips come apart. He withdraws enough to look at her. He looks wild, half-starved. He terrifies her, excites her. She wonders how hungrily she is staring back.

He leans forward, the warmth of this face on her neck, his kisses moist, punctuated by his tongue. His breath hot. The hand on her thigh slides higher, resting near her hip, hesitating. The hand on her back slides around, pausing below her breast. Waiting.

Her heart pounds; her hands tingle. Her body begs for more, terrified that once she gives her consent, she cannot ever take it back.

She presses her hands against his chest. He is young and skinny, his chest all ribs and muscle, sinewy and firm. She pushes a little, senses the panic in his hands, in his mouth, as she separates him from his feast.

She looks at his eyes, and leans forward to kiss his neck, to touch his chest, to touch his thigh.

His hand cups her breast. He squeezes, but little else. She feels high; she feels drugged; she has such excitement; this can't possibly be her she is experiencing. This is someone else, someone who knows what they are doing, someone with confidence, willing to dive without ever checking if there is water in the pool.

As his hand comes around her hip, following the lower seam of her underwear, she pushes him back again.

He arches his back, puffing his chest. He stares at her, his eyes darting from her eyes to her mouth to her breasts. He leans forward. She almost lets him, almost gives him one final okay. Instead, she holds him back, pushes harder.

What? Are you okay? His voice is soft, not accusatory. He is asking if she is okay, not why she doesn't want to have sex. She nods. His hands slip from her body. *Then what?* Now he's asking about sex.

She is uncertain what to say. She's heard songs about this moment. If it wasn't meant to happen, something would interfere, like a sign or something, she believes. Nothing happening is permission to continue. It still doesn't seem like it is her here. She'd have more sense. She has to say something. *I think I want to,* she finally says, *I mean, I really think I do, but I need to know what you're thinking right now.*

His eyes dart again from her face to her breasts to her exposed underwear, back to her face. *I'm thinking that you're the most beautiful girl I've ever seen.* He smiles. *You're so pretty; so sexy.*

Heather takes a breath. She feels undressed. The humidity in the car feels, for the first time, damp. *That's not what I mean,* she protests, increasing the distance between them. *That's not what you're thinking, that's what you're feeling. What are you thinking?*

He is quiet. Maybe he doesn't understand what she wants to hear. She needs to know their sex isn't just about how pretty or how willing she is. That could happen with anyone. She needs to know why he wants it with her. She doesn't know how to ask that won't sound weak or needy or pathetic.

He looks out the windshield. Deep breaths. After two false starts, he says, *I'm thinking I'm really scared because I've never done this before. I mean, I know what to do, but I'm not sure how to do it right. I want it to be special for you. I want you to like it. I heard it's supposed to hurt and maybe make you bleed, and I don't want to hurt you.*

Still sex, she thinks. This isn't what she means.

He keeps talking, *I'm thinking that I really like you, maybe even love you.* He looks at her when he says that, looking vulnerable, looking for her reply. She holds back. Once she answers him, the conversation is over, and he hasn't said what she needs to decide if she goes home or stays.

If we do this now, tonight, I don't know what will happen next year when I go to college. I mean, it's so far away, but it's a big deal. Couples break up over college all the time and, he hesitates. *What I mean is, I'm thinking that I want to know you better than this. I mean, I want to know every inch of your body; I want to know where you like to be touched. I want to touch your arm a certain way when we pass in school and you'll know I mean something more by it.*

Still sex, she thinks.

I want our connection to go deeper than this. I want to know your hopes and dreams so I can help make them come true. I want to know your worries and fears so I can protect you from them. He looks at her. His hunger is gone.

I want you to know that I believe in what you said, about women and their magic, and I swear, if we become something more, together, you know, get married, have kids, whatever, I will make sure that our daughter knows that truth.

Heather watches him. He deflates slightly. He looks at her. Stares at her. *Anyway, that's what I'm thinking.*

Heather kisses him, tears at his clothes. She is the aggressor, the hunter. She kisses his body; she undresses them both. She loves him more passionately, more deeply than she ever does again.

*   *   *   *   *

Heather is home. She has a bond with this house. She was born in this house. Now she is an adult. Tenants had occupied it for the past ten years, people she feared would one day buy the house from her parents. They tried. When Heather's mother signed the house over to her, they refused to move out. Eventually, after failing to pay rent for three months, they disappeared over a weekend.

The house feels empty. She is alone. Eric works a second job at night, trying to keep them afloat during their second year of marriage. She doesn't sleep well when he is away. She isn't sure if it's guilt because he works so hard or his absence from their bed. She hasn't slept most of the night. She tosses and turns, more anxious than usual. *If I can't sleep*, she whispers to the dark, *why shouldn't I just get up and do something?*

The sleepless night casts a heavy weight on her, makes her feel like she is an anchor at the bottom of the ocean, dragging through the sand. Although the sun is just coming up, she doesn't feel ready to greet the day. She doesn't understand why she feels this way. She isn't prone to depression. Not like Eric's mother, who sometimes didn't get out of bed for days on end. She can't understand why her heart is so heavy today, why her restless sleep has been dreamless.

She abandons the bed and parts the curtains—bed linens folded over the ornate bars the previous tenants left behind. Why didn't they leave the curtains? Heather guesses spite. She hated their dramatic window treatments. Out here, in the middle of nowhere, she wants her windows to always show her the outside. For now, anyway, the bedsheets give Eric the darkness he needs to hide from daylight to sleep.

The phone rings. Heather hopes against reality that her school might call at this odd hour. She snatches it and says, *Heather Hawthorne, how can I help you?* She hadn't taken Eric's last name professionally, a decision that caused tension for a time. *It's on my diploma*, she told him. *I don't want to have to explain why my names don't match.* That wasn't the truth, and she was sure he knew it. Peter's name was Hawthorne, and Peter was her twin, and that would be forever. Eric would only be her husband so long as both of them wanted: the relationship was dissolvable, impermanent.

Sobbing on the line. Heather's stomach sours at the whimpering. The voice, familiar but drowned with tears, says, *It's done, Heather. Peter did it. He's gone now. You should know.*

Heather understands how the house felt before they moved in, empty, abandoned of contents. Everything left her.

There is silence on the line; Heather worries Holly had hung up until she hears her sobbing again. *Holly*, she sympathizes, *I'm so sorry, Holly. I, um,* she stutters, realization washing over her like a cold wave. Peter's gone? Peter her twin, no more? *Peter, oh Holly, I'm,* she finds herself undone by emotion and unable to continue. Her brother, the boy who always had the answers, who would always protect her: gone? She finds an unfillable void open in her heart, a hole exceeding the thing that held it. She listens to Holly breathing on the phone, uses it to catch her own breath.

Why—when Peter brought Holly to meet her—hadn't she had jealousy toward the woman who took her brother away? And why did she feel it now? Is Holly more entitled to grief? She hates herself for suggesting Holly's five years of marriage shouldn't trump their nearly thirty shared years of life.

You should know, Heather, Holly says at last, *it worked. I'm pregnant with a baby girl. Only a girl.* Heather hears the conflict of joy and grief in Holly's voice. *I should be so happy, Heather. We did it. We actually did it. All that talk, all that anticipation, and it's over. It's over, Heather. Didn't he realize he'll never see her grow up? Why didn't I understand that yesterday? It's like he told me what would happen, but the words meant different things then. He'll never know if he was right; if she becomes a real witch. I miss him so much, Heather.* Holly sniffles and apologizes for blowing her nose. *I'm sick thinking we made a terrible mistake. What if it's like this because it shouldn't be tampered with? What if this is the beginning of bad things we made happen?*

Heather waits for Holly to continue, but she is silent, save for her sobs. *It worked?* Heather isn't so much asking as repeating. She doesn't know what else to say. Doesn't know how to say it. Doesn't know how to convey sympathy to someone when her own heart is breaking. *Oh, Holly,* she says, *that's wonderful.* The words come out, and she hears the cruelty and regrets them. She realizes what she meant to say and tries to drag those words out, *I mean, I know, believe me, I know, but that's what Peter wanted. That's all he's ever wanted.*

It's not all he wanted, Holly corrects, *but what he wanted most.*

He did it. You have a daughter. You know he succeeded. He got everything he wanted.

Holly interrupts, *I'm sorry, Heather, I just can't, I, I can't keep talking about it. You had to know. I've been putting off calling you since Abby brought him home a few hours ago. I've been up with him all night, hoping he'd snap out of it; wake up and be Peter again, but he's gone. I wanted to tell you. I thought you should—*

Heather interrupts, *Abby? Brought him home? You said he was gone.* Heather holds the spark of hope that feeds on anger that Holly is exaggerating.

His body is here, Holly whimpers, *but there's no light. He's empty. There's nothing. He's nothing. I'm sorry. I can't. I'm sorry. I have to go.* Holly hangs up the phone.

Heather returns the receiver. She is standing in her nightgown. When had she gotten up? The phone rings again. Is Holly calling her back? Was she mistaken or was Peter playing one of his jokes where he pretends a little too long? The school with a job? It disgusts Heather she is even thinking this when she answers the phone. *Hel-lo?* She tries to answer cheerfully, but the sing-song melancholia is unmistakable.

You heard, the voice on the other end says. It is Abby. She is so in tune, Heather thinks, she heard it in one word. A moment of silence. *I wanted to tell you if you didn't know. I'm sorry, Heather. If you want me to come by so you're not alone, or if you want someone to talk to.... I know how much you love Peter. I figured maybe we could just sit and not be alone today.*

Heather takes a breath. Abby is all she has left of Peter, of their childhood. How was I ever jealous of Abby? she wonders. Abby was the third wheel no one could do without. She was the soul of their childhood, the outsider who brought her closer to Peter even while being blamed for moving them apart. Every precious memory she had with Peter, every photograph of his smile, every memory of his over-loud laugh, Abby is in. It is almost as though Peter became alive when Abby came to them. Abby's presence confirmed all her memories were real. They weren't memories without Abby, and Heather is fine with that, because as long as she has Abby, she'd have Peter, too.

I would like that very much, Heather tells her.

*   *   *   *   *

Heather comes home, parking her new yellow car in the driveway. She lets herself in the unlocked front door. Eric is in the kitchen, looking through the fridge for something to eat, leftovers that hadn't yet gone bad. *Hey hon*, he calls out. *How was work?*

Heather stands in the doorway to the kitchen and watches him rummaging through the refrigerator. She isn't sure how to act, how to stand. She'd brought the pregnancy test with her to work, stole off to the bathroom during her free period. Now she isn't sure how to tell him. Isn't sure how he'll react. Normally, she'd lean against the doorframe, trying to pose coquettishly, playfully seducing him with her eyes. She was sure she looked ridiculous. Despite her exhaustion, she made sure not a day went by that they didn't try to get pregnant. To hell with cycles and temperatures and science. Just plain, old-fashioned perseverance. It was un-sexy and exhausting. It was not the sort of thing she expected sex and marriage to be like. It was like coming home and making dinner. And then making dinner when they were done.

She doesn't know why he doesn't sense her distress, why he doesn't stop what he is doing and be there for her. He looks up as if surprised by her presence. *Oh, I didn't see you there.* He has to know; by now they'd be going through the motions of undressing one another and seeing how far up the stairs or into the bedroom they could get. Is he just as bored with it as she is? Wouldn't this be good news, then?

I asked you how was work? He points to the open fridge. *I figured I'd reheat some leftovers to celebrate Friday, you know, so you could have a night off. That's hot, right?* He stands up and tries to look sexy. He looks sleepy, like he's had a stroke.

I'm pregnant. The words just fall out. She thinks about producing the little white wand with its small window and symbols, wrapped in toilet paper and tucked in her purse. It seemed a good idea at the time, but gross now: she'd peed on it. *Twins.* She watches emotions play thoughts on his face. Surprise and joy, confusion, diminishing to frustration.

His tone is accusatory, *How do you know twins? Does it test for twins?*

Heather worries she'd said too much: She doesn't know. There is no way to know, not for weeks, months. *I just do. It's always twins.*

Eric doesn't respond. She watches his face perform again. Then his eyes widen. *We're going to be parents? We're having babies? Little witchy babies?* He dances across the kitchen to pick her up and spin her in the air. All she feels is close to the ceiling, unbound from the floor. They hug, they kiss, they celebrate on the kitchen counter.

When they finish, pulling their clothes back into place and wiping away their perspiration, Heather excuses herself to clean up and have a few minutes.

Eric nods, *I'll have dinner hot enough to eat in ten minutes.*

Heather climbs the stairs, disappearing behind the closed bedroom door. For the first time in years she doesn't look at the bedroom across the hall.

She sits on the edge of the bed, trying to think. She lays down and curls up and cries. All this time, all this work, and she is finally pregnant. She is going to be a mother. Only, she realizes she doesn't want kids. Which is to say she does want kids, just not the ones she carries. She is in love with the idea of children, the notion of two healthy, happy babies she will raise, not a girl who would never achieve the ability to have magic and a boy she resents because his very existence hinders his sister. She thinks about Holly and the beautiful child she has, the mop of red hair, freckles, and bright blue eyes. When Alexandrea was born, Heather was in the delivery room. She was holding the child, all tiny and stinky. She would always remember looking down and seeing her face snuggled in the blanket, topped with her filthy red hair. It was twirled into a cowlick, styled by the fingers of a nurse, giving it a twist, like cream settling in coffee. It reminded Heather of the bud of a perfect *rose*.

*　　*　　*　　*　　*

Heather and Eric decorate their Christmas tree, or as Heather likes to joke, next year's Yule log. Her stomach had popped three weeks earlier, the first time she felt pregnant as opposed to just bloated, and Eric is drinking both their shares of spiked eggnog. Heather doesn't mind, she is happy being with him, tying cinnamon sticks and stringing popcorn on floss to make ornaments and garland. Dinner was finished an hour ago, and Heather is waiting for Abby to call. When the call comes, she climbs the stairs to their bedroom to take it in private.

Hi Abby, Heather says as she answers the phone.

Hey, Abby replies, *happy Yule.*

Heather grins. She loves the way Abby subverts the holiday, *To you, too. Are you seeing Holly and Alexandrea for the Eve?*

Yes, Abby confirms. *I'll be with you for the Day. What time do you want me there?*

Heather hesitates to contemplate timeframes, *We can start noshing around two. Dinner at five?*

Sounds good, Abby replies. Then there is silence, like they are each waiting for the other to say their goodbyes first. They aren't winding down the call; Heather knows Abby is waiting for her to say something.

Finally, she does. *Abby, Eric and I have stopped fighting about, you know, the thing. He wants absolutely no part in it. Not after what it did to Peter. He promised me he would, Abby, but now he's saying there's no way to know if it worked or not. He doesn't believe Alexandrea is special. He said he promises that when we know more, he'd be there, but this is too uncertain for him. What good will it do once they're born? Can you imagine that?*

Abby takes an audible breath. *I can*, she hisses. *There's no guarantee what Peter did worked. No one knows if Alexandrea is special.*

But, she contradicts, *that hasn't stopped you. You watch over Alexandrea.*

Abby groans. *You know why, Heather. I made a blood oath. I'm her Familiar. Now and forever, as long as we both live.*

Heather shakes her head even though Abby can't see. *I can't understand how you can have so much passion for a two-year-old. She's a child. A bay-bee. That oath made you her servant. Like you exist to make her happy. It drives Holly crazy; you know?*

Heather hears Abby ruffle over the phone. *It's part of the oath, I think. I get pleasure from her. The older she's growing, the more we're together, it's becoming all I ever want. I know Holly's not happy about it. She warned me last month that I'm spoiling her. I guess not every whim and desire a child has should be indulged.*

Heather can't understand how they are still talking about it. Didn't Abby just invalidate her own argument? *If it gives you, as you say, pleasure, then how do you stop?*

I don't know, Heather. I guess I need to stay away. Watch her from afar. It'll hurt. Not being near her hurts. But if that's what's best for her, I'll work through it. I'll rationalize I'm doing good for her and that will counterbalance the, you know, negative. Heather waits for her to add something, she can feel this is her moment, as long as Abby says nothing else.

Heather says, *If you can't be there for Alexandrea just yet, maybe you can for me.*

There is silence on the phone. When Abby at last speaks, her tone loses all joy, *You know I can't do that, Heather. I'm Alexandrea's Familiar. I can't moonlight. It doesn't work that way, much as I'd like to, it doesn't let me choose other loyalties. Even temporarily.*

But, Heather says, *just help me. I'm not asking you to do anything extreme. Together, we can do this and Eric doesn't have to know. I think I figured out how to do it without the same consequences, you know, so no one else gets hurt. I think—*

Abby interrupts, *You know I can't do that. A Familiar can't perform any magic, Heather. That's not a little, that's none. Absolutely none. It's forbidden.*

Heather pleads, *But—*

Abby doesn't let her speak, *No, Heather, magic breaks the Oath. One spell, and that girl is on her own. She's only two. A bay-bee,* she mocks back. *I made Peter a promise. What if without the Oath, what if I hate her? I promised I would protect her no matter what. That I would obey her, no matter what. I can't help you, Heather. I won't. Please don't hate me. You know I'd do it if I could.*

Heather is sure Abby is crying.

She doesn't know why Aunt Abby loves her so much. Please, Heather. If I accidently broke the Oath, how would I find that devotion? It would stop. If I made it to Peter, then maybe, but I didn't. What would that child think when Aunt Abby doesn't love her anymore? What would happen to her? Do you want to be responsible for that?

I understand, she tells Abby. *I had to ask.*

Heather is glad to be off the topic until Abby asks, *Besides, you're what, six, seven months pregnant?*

Six, Heather replies.

Abby lowers her voice, *Heather, Holly wasn't even pregnant one month. You don't know what it could do to you now.*

Heather takes a breath. *I know,* Heather says. *I owe it to my girl to try. It's not fair that Peter's daughter has this chance and mine doesn't. Just because she was first-born, it's not fair that she gets to be the only special one.*

Abby is silent.

Don't judge me, Heather begs. *My daughter should have the same opportunity as his, don't you think?*

Abby tells her, *Believe me, I get how unfair it is. Maybe Peter really knew more about what he was doing. Maybe we're all here to serve her. Maybe, oh, I just don't know. I'm making shit up to make you feel better because I don't know what else to say. I'm sorry, Heather. I can't. Please, don't ever, ever ask me again.*

I understand, Heather tells her. *It was selfish of me to ask. I'm sorry I put you in that spot.*

I love you, Heather.

Heather never heard Abby sound so broken, so manically defensive and it troubles her. Her devotion to a baby is mind-blowing.

Who was she going to find to sacrifice themselves to her daughter? It was always Peter, always the male. He did everything first; he got all the best of everything and left nothing for his sister except his feminist platitudes.

Finally, Heather responds, *I love you, too, Abby. See you in two days?* There is a moment of silence during which Heather wonders if Abby is still on the line.

I still don't understand why you don't come to Holly's tomorrow. She'd love to have you.

I know, Heather replies. *But Holidays are supposed to be happy, and I can see the pain in Holly's eyes when she looks at me.*

You really think looking at you makes her think of Peter that much?

I know it does, Heather confesses. *Because that's what seeing Holly does to me.*

Abby is quiet. Finally, she says, *I'll see you.*

Heather finds a smile: Abby the reliable one. Alexandrea is so lucky to have her. It wasn't luck. It was planning and plotting. Peter figured everything out and left everyone behind to try to make something of his mess. They say their goodbyes and Heather places the phone down. She sits on the bed and cries. It isn't fair. Peter got to have the special daughter. Why not me? Why never me?

When Heather returns downstairs, she worries Eric can tell something was wrong. She tries to keep everything inside and knows she sucks at that. Everything is always written on her face. Eric always knows.

Everything okay? he asks.

Just Abby-talk, you know, reminiscing about my brother at the holidays. It can be hard.

Eric's brow furrows. He takes a deep breath and tips his head, *Reminiscing... or talking about the thing?*

Heather tries to make her dismissive laugh sound authentic. It sounds so phony it hurts her ears. *We were talking about being kids. You know, the stuff you'll endure when she comes for Christmas dinner.*

Eric nods, either satisfied with her answer or humoring her. Heather can't tell. Eric approaches her and rubs her hip. *You say dinner; I think dessert,* Eric growls, a weak attempt at seduction. *Whaddya say? Huh? Huh?* He repeats his monosyllabic question as though that's all it takes to make her wet.

Heather groans. *I feel enormous tonight,* she tells Eric, rubbing her belly. *I'm fat and emotional and exhausted. The last thing you need is for me to start crying in the middle of sex.*

Eric backs away a solitary step.

Disappointment, she thinks, his other tool. She is too spent to play this game tonight. If she stays, he'd eventually triumph. *You know,* she says, trying to sound tired, *I'm exhausted, and the next two days are such a to-do; I'm going to bed. You okay if I turn in?*

Eric doesn't hide his disappointment when he replies, *You want me to come up with you?*

Heather adamantly shakes her head, *No. I'm processing a lot and wouldn't mind some alone time. I need to sleep. Are you okay with that?*

Eric looks at the tree and at all the decorations that have yet to find their place. He is putting on his brave face, the one that made him look like a child and usually melted her heart: he is playing hard-ball tonight. *As long as you don't mind my male aesthetic,* he jokes, sweeping his hand across the tree, *you know, everything jammed in at eye-level?*

Her laugh is genuine. So is her exhaustion, *Don't make it so I have to fix it in the morning.* She embraces and kisses him goodnight. *I love you Eric. Always know that, no matter what.*

Eric grins. *I love you too, babe. You sure you're okay?*

Is he asking or plying another tactic? Getting her to prove she is okay? She shrugs. *Just feeling a little down around the holiday this year. Having* twins *has me thinking about my brother a lot.* Before he can say anything about *the thing*, she adds, *I just miss him so much.* She kisses him again and heads upstairs. She closes and locks the bedroom door.

Once in bed, Heather relaxes. She remembers the first time she saw her mother make her coin glow. Told her about where she went. It was a forgotten secret, something everyone knew once, long, long ago when nights were long and sleep plentiful enough women could spend hours travelling and congregating.

Lying still with her eyes closed, the blankets covering her clavicle, she can tell the moment her coin glows; she rises from the bed. Looks back at her sleeping self. Leaves through the mist: Tonight is another witch's sabbath, the fourth one she's attended this month. She has gotten word of one woman who might help, but unless she found someone—anyone—willing to help her, this will be her last dream-walk for this purpose.

She wanders through the streets of this little market. It is still early; most women she encounters are from Western Europe; their voices lilting in such romantic ways, a faint accent giving away the language they speak. Heather marvels at how cultural differences from the Old World create subtle changes in the architecture around each city of dreams. One building made of feathers and soap bubbles had mansard roofs, another replicated Stonehenge, the horizontal lintels becoming countertops lined with small bottles with handwritten labels, describing what each potion could cure or cause.

Heather asks around. *Has anyone seen.... Does anyone know.... Could you help me find....*

Most shake their head, but she knows when they are being honest and when they know what her request means by the horror on their face. It frightens her that they are so disgusted they lie and say they don't when their faces cry to her, *Are you so desperate?* Time is growing late; Eric was bound to come up the stairs and find the door locked and bring her back with knocking and accusation.

Please, she begs one elderly woman who stares in shock. *Please tell me where I can find her. I am desperate. There's no one else who'll help me.*

The woman raises her hand and points. *Outside the gate.*

Outcast. No one goes to her. She is a killer. She spits on the ground in disgust.

Heather nods. *Thank you. Thank you,* she prostrates. *I need her. Thank you.*

Leaving the market, walking past the old stone and mortar wall, she comes upon one tent separated from the others by a moat of vacancy. The tent is windswept, black faded gray, and covered with so many holes and patches Heather wonders if there is any original tent remaining. Is there significance to such a collection of holes?

She waits outside; the fabric billowing and snapping against itself in the breeze. She found the place. The search is over. Now all she has to do is walk inside. Part of her wants to leave, to go home and be sleepy when Eric comes to bed, to apologize to him for her state before and make love to him. That's all she has to do; walk away.

Going in is no guarantee she'll go through with it, Heather muses. She can learn what it involves and decide then, taking each trepidatious step until she has gone far enough. She can, can't she? If she enters the tent, will she ever be able to stop? Heather looks back at her sparkling thread waving off into the distance. Has she come all this way just to turn back? Isn't it some sign that she found this woman at all? Proof that it is meant to happen, proof that her daughter is destined to be special, too?

Heather enters, expecting to see some grand hall that belies the outer dimensions of the tatty canvas, but enters a disused tent smelling of soot and rotting food and body odor. The old woman squints up at Heather. She is old and sunbaked brown. Her milky eyes examine Heather as she licks her cracked lips and inflamed gums, her tongue covered in yellow scum. She points at Heather with filthy fingernails. Yellow scale covers one foot, the toenails thick and brittle. This woman's appearance sickens Heather. This woman is disgusting.

Hard to look at me?

Her voice rattles Heather. Startled, she replies with obvious dishonesty, *Oh, no. Not at all.*

The old woman snorts and spits into the smoky ashes between them. The spittle sizzles. *This is my dream-self. This is what I've become because of my deeds. This is not who I am when I wake, but who I will be when I die. If,* she punctuates with a gnarled finger, *they don't take my coin first. Which, believe me, would be merciful.* She nods several times as though confirming deeper and deeper thoughts.

Then, without looking up, *What do you want?*

Heather tells her story from the beginning. She speaks of being born twins and of Abby joining them and of Peter and his studies. The old woman snorts harder this time and spits, *No one comes to me because they want something easy to talk about. You want a loved-one put to an end? You need revenge or to send a warning? You need drugs or guns or something more dangerous? These things I do. Love potions,* the woman spits again, mindless to the large spot on her own draped clothing where her yellow spittle lands.

No, Heather says, trying to remain calm. *I didn't come for those things.*

The old woman nods. *Then tell me. Not the story. I could give a shit why. Tell me what you want accomplished. Tell me the unwritten ending you seek.*

Heather wants to turn around and run. She experiences the desire to leave, the pull on her thread probably imagined. This is proof, she thinks, that I'm doing the right thing. Still, saying the words without the narrative justification feels so wrong. *I, I,* she stutters, *I need one of my twins removed.*

The old woman rubs her gums together, finally asking, *One?*

Heather nods. *Yes, the boy, I mean the male twin.* Heather hates when she slips, words making the thing in her belly a child. It isn't real. It isn't anything until all hope at removing it is lost.

The old woman nods. *I have heard whispers of such things. You've come to me because you want me to do it?*

Heather nods.

No, the old woman spits. *Even I won't dirty my hands with such a thing. I've heard rumors about this, the abominations that result. The stories you've heard, the tales where it works, that's what they are: Tales. Lies. People grasping for hope that magic isn't gone away.* The old woman shakes her head. *It's gone. It's a lie that you can bring it back. It's a trap to do away with all those who think such thoughts.* She shakes her head again. *I won't lie to you and take your money, and believe me, if I thought it could be done, I'd be rich.* She nods again, then lowers her head dismissively.

Heather is desperate. She's not going to argue and tell this woman her brother did it. That's a secret she'll never share. This is her last option. *Okay, I understand. You won't do it, but, but,* Heather searches for anything to keep the witch engaged, *would you help me so I can do it?*

The old woman looks up, her face aghast. *Haven't you been listening to me? What so horrible happened to you that you would take that chance?*

Heather's eyes well up. *I want her to be special… more than I want either child.*

The old woman grins, her smile all gums. *You're a fool*, the old woman says. *It'll probably kill all three of you.*

She said probably, Heather thinks. That's not no. Heather wipes her eyes. *I don't care*, she says, tears falling down her cheeks. *I have to try. I'll die for this.*

The old woman eyeballs her. She uses her pinky to scrape the inside of a nostril. *Really?* she asks, *willing to die?*

Heather nods timidly, then confidently.

The old woman grabs her feet, examines the fungal infection on her toes before placing them flat on the ground. She grunts and hauls herself upright. *So be it*, she huffs, and begins collecting bottles she clinks together as she groups them on the floor, giving each a firm twist, driving it into the sand.

After a few minutes she holds out a flask of cloudy purple fluid. Heather reaches for it and the old woman withdraws her offering like a snake striking in reverse. *We haven't discussed cost*, she whispers.

Heather takes a long, slow, deep breath and asks, *What do you want?*

A gummy smile greets Heather's reply. *How much will you offer me?*

Heather reaches for the flask and says, *It's already made. If you ask too much and I walk away, what'll you do with it? I asked you what you want. If you're not fair with me….*

Not desperate anymore?

I'm not, Heather starts to reply, recognizing her lie in the old woman's face. Heather feels trapped, so she relies on honesty. *I'll agree to anything. Please don't take advantage of me. I don't have a lot to give.*

The old woman closes her mouth and smiles. *If you had anything, including sense, you would never have come to me. I'm the provider of last resort.* She thinks a moment, shaking the glass, stirring the liquids that are separating. *This will likely kill you. So here's what I want from you. I know what should happen if a woman is untwinned.* She squints. *Everyone who has ever tried has died. If you succeed, this,* she hesitates and produces a scrap of paper, *is the address where my daughter lives.*

Heather takes the scrap and asks, *How much do I send her?*

The old woman shakes her head as she proffers Heather the glass. *Write her a letter. Tell her you came to me. Tell her I was kind to you. That I helped you. That I'm a good person. That I love her.* The old woman isn't looking at Heather any longer. *Tell her I am an old wretch who only ever comes home to feed my body because my life there is so horrible. Tell her I am sorry I wasn't a better mother. Tell her—*

Heather interrupts, *Why don't you tell her?*

I would, the old woman cries, *if she'd listen to me. When you're a mother, you'll understand how difficult it can be, mother to daughter. I'm not the only one who pays for my mistakes. Sometimes sorry is never enough.* She shakes the glass enough that the contents threaten to overflow. *Say you will. Swear to it.*

Heather composes herself. *I will send a letter to your daughter, and I swear I will tell her you were a kind woman who helped me when I was desperate, and I will make absolutely clear that the only thing you asked for in return was that I tell her this truth.*

The old woman coughs back her tears and hands Heather the glass. *Drink this. Every drop.* Heather accepts the glass and sniffs it. It smells repulsive. She gags on the scent of decay and wet animal. She turns the glass three times looking for a clean spot to place her lips. Heather puts her mouth on the lip of the filthy vessel. She can feel—and taste—the unclean glass, but she tips it back and swallows hard, trying not to think about how the flavor makes her want to vomit. She gasps for air and hands the glass back. The woman chuckles.

Heather asks, *What?*

The old woman sheepishly replies, *I'll make the potion now.*

Heather points at the glass. *What the hell did I just drink?*

The old woman doubles over in laughter. *No, no, I'm kidding with you. That was it.*

After a moment of repeated laughter, the old woman composes herself, but still finds her joke amusing. *It's time,* she tells Heather. *Go home. Go to your body. Do your business.* Heather nods. *If you die,* the old woman warns, *they'll find you in your bed. They'll say you died in your sleep. You,* she points a finger at Heather, *will be gone. No afterlife. You understand? You'll no longer exist.*

Heather nods. *I understand.* Before anything else can be said, she leaves.

Heather finds herself standing in her bedroom, staring at her sleeping self. It feels wrong. Like every photograph feels wrong. She settles on the bed, her silver thread just a few feet in length, pulling on her. She touches her body. Normally, her hand slips through, but this time she feels solid. Her body groans. Heather can feel her own hand touching herself. It is a strange feedback loop, her hand touching a body that is also her.

She touches this separate version of herself for nearly twenty minutes, trying to work up her nerve. She closes her eyes. The potion makes her head spin when her eyes are closed. Opening them helps, but it takes time for the rotations to stop. She presses and feels pressure in her abdomen. She presses harder. It becomes uncomfortable; unbearable. She closes her eyes again, preferring the way the room lurches. She finds her resolve. Pressure makes her sick. She wants to throw up. She opens her eyes to see her hand has disappeared up to her wrist. She is aware of the warm, wet viscera. She dry-wretches, fighting to keep dinner down. What would happen if she threw up? Would her body throw up? She doesn't know how much longer she can tolerate the sensation. It is an intrusion in her body, an inward pressure threatening to explode her. She pushes. She finds her womb. She can feel them: her babies. They are soft and fragile and tiny and aware of her touch. They move inside and against her hand. They move and they touch and they push and they kick. They are in separate sacks in her womb. She feels one and then the other. She isn't sure which is the boy. She touches one and then the other again.

There is something about the way she feels, about the way it feels when she touches them; she believes she knows which is the boy. She holds it, squeamish what might happen if she is not gentle enough. She squeezes. Holding first the child and eventually his coin. When coin is all she holds, her fist clenches and pulls. She can feel the resistance, not just in her hand, but in her abdomen. The sensation is not unlike what she imagines pulling out her own spine would feel like. Discomfort twists her. She catches her breath. She tries again. With each subsequent attempt, her tolerance diminishes. She tries again. And again. Pulling gently. Pulling sharply. She can't bear it. The pain is so intense, it feels like she's trying to drive a truck out her belly button. She is in tears, in agony, sick from attempting to tear her insides out. Sick to have come so far. To be right here, and yet, to fail.

She tries again; collapsing, trying to catch her breath.

She sees a thread, silvery, sparking. It's barely a loop extending from her body. *Maybe....* She gives one final tug. The thread reaches outward, like the coin has already travelled somewhere. Then it disappears, leaving only a brief shadow on her vision. The spasming agony forces her hand open.

Biting down on her free hand stifles her screams.

She has failed.

Failed herself, failed her daughter.

Gently, she repositions the child where she first touched it. Its tiny hand clutches at her pinky. Heather bites her lip and pulls her hand away, crying as her hand slides from her abdomen, empty. She looks at her sleeping form. She wishes she had died; at least then she wouldn't have to live with the fact that she wasn't strong enough. She crawls and lays down. The elixir hasn't worn off, but Heather still sinks into herself. She experiences the dichotomy of body and soul as she lay there, momentarily doubled, as the last effects eventually wear off.

When Heather wakes, the pain hasn't faded. She is soon bent in half, howling. Eric thunders up the steps and finds the door locked.

Heather? Heather! He shouts as he pushes on the door, forcing it open, the strike plate and doorframe coming apart.

My babies, she cries, *something happened to my babies.*

He kneels at the edge of the bed and takes her hand. *Tell me—*

She screams, *We're dying, Eric. Help us.*

He scoops her out of bed and in a minute, they are in his car, racing to the hospital. Her body burns, her stomach on fire, flames tearing through her flesh, turning her insides to hardened char. She looks out the window into the cold winter night, despondent, inconsolable. Holiday lights everywhere. The pain is endless. What has she done? She was so desperate to make her daughter special, like Alexandrea; did she kill her in the process? She punishes herself with expectation. The bitter irony that she killed her daughter and would birth only a son.

*   *   *   *   *

Heather lays in the hospital bed. Days have passed since her admission. She feels fine—physically at least—save for the throbbing pain where her IV stuck her arm. She hasn't bent her elbow for fear the needle would carve her to the bone. The whole joint aches.

Her doctor told her she'd go home in a day or two. Incompetent cervix. Deep vein thrombosis. The diagnoses varied. Each spoken with certainty, no matter how uncertain the doctor was. Heather knew it was none of those. Once they told her the babies were fine, she didn't care about the pain, which subsided over several days.

She was convinced her doctor hated her. Hated may be too strong a word, but the first time she told him she was having a home birth, a wet birth, his face told her everything: He despised women like her, women who cling to nature. He preferred bringing children into the world in a sterile hospital room, taking them straight from their mother's womb to a strange nurse who would clean them and wrap them in blankets, weigh them, test them, prick them, swab them, practically sterilize them before they were clean enough to rest in a plastic incubator. He probably recommended formula over breast-feeding. She couldn't wait to be home and was sure her doctor couldn't wait either.

Holly visited her from time to time and told Heather's nurses they were family. Her daytime nurse was a young woman who, when the ward was quiet and everyone had their lunches and few people had complaints beyond *The turkey sandwich is bland*, or *Can I have chocolate pudding instead of tapioca*, would spend time in her room. Heather enjoyed her conversations with Marta. Marta was about her age, a kind woman, recently divorced because she realized she liked women more than men, who said goodbye at the end of her day and told her the night nurse's name.

The first days they talked about pleasantries. Heather found her so easy to talk to; she told Marta first about her gardens and then about her conspiracy theories. *Women were always supposed to have magic, but men took it.* Even the crazier ones. *Of course the President knows. How do you think he got to power?* Eventually Marta broaches the subject. She said she sensed it the moment she came into Heather's room. She asked Heather if she practiced Wicca. Heather told her, *No,*

I'm just a witch.

With Heather preparing to be released, she and Marta made the most of their time together. Holly came twice most days at the start and end of her shift. Eric visited occasionally, but two jobs kept him exhausted. Some days he didn't come at all. Marta resented Eric but wouldn't say so. Instead, she changed the subject any time Heather brought him up. But Heather understood what that meant. She didn't intend to tell anyone, but she found herself telling Marta her secret; the only secret she held from everyone, the secret that brought her to the hospital.

Heather, there's this guy here to see you, Marta says as she lingers in the doorway, her blue and white scrubs looking as tired and overworked as her expression.

Who is it? Heather can't imagine who would visit that Marta hadn't already met. She'd met Alexandrea. Even Abby.

That's just it, Marta says, her face twisting with concern, *he said who but I can't believe.... It's just... you're gonna think I'm cra-aazy.*

Heather pushes herself upright in bed. Her stomach feels full and more comfortable reclined, but she wants to be engaged with Marta. *What's he say?*

Hear me out, Heather. I should send him away. There's no way he is who he says. Yet, well, I think I believe him. He knows.

Heather lets silence ask Marta to continue.

I don't want to say it. It'll sound crazy coming out of my mouth, but when he says it... She holds up her hands and shakes her head. *Don't get me wrong, I'm not an idiot. I told him to go, but he knew, Heather. He knew my name; he knew how you and I met. He knew things about me I don't think I've told you. He knew about, you know, how you got here.* Her voice lowers to a whisper, *He knows what you did.*

Heather is uneasy. *Is he Matthew?*

Marta gives her a *how did you know that* look and says, *He knew you'd say that. Oh, Heather, this is freaking me the fuck out. He said that's not who he is.*

Heather is trapped in this little hospital room and whoever was there, whoever knew her intimate details, is coming for her. Her heart feels like it's beating so much faster than the monitor reports. *What should I do, Marta?*

I think you should see him. Marta is quiet for several moments. *I'll be right here in the hall. I think whatever he has to say you should hear. He knows too much.*

Heather nods hesitantly. *Okay. If you say so, Marta. Who is he?*

Marta steps backwards as she leaves the room. *I'll go get him, Heather. He says his name is William. He says he's your son.*

As dramatic as Marta's parting words, all Heather's suspense and anticipation vanish like a toilet flush. She's more curious how some nut convinced Marta of this lie.

A short minute later, he steps into the doorway. He is on the taller side, thin and gaunt. His clothes hang off his body, like they were loose when he bought them, and then lost significant weight. He grasps the doorframe, waiting there.

Hey, he says softly, *it's so good to see you again. It's been,* he pauses, *a really long time.*

Heather aches at the sadness in his voice. *Marta said your name is William.*

He nods. *Yeah. You let Eric name me. You once said he hated his name because he could only ever have one. He wanted me to have as many nicknames as I wanted. You called me Billy when I was a kid.*

Heather heard Eric complain about his name more than once. *At least it's short,* she'd say. *Heather has no nicknames, either. You don't hear me whining about it.* She thought Eric wanted to name the boy because he feared she'd name him Foxglove or Chris, short for Chrysanthemum.

William sighs. *I think I would have been okay with Chris, though. I was always jealous of Rose's name.*

Heather's heart is pounding. *Rose?*

William nods. *Rosemary. It's what you're naming my sister.*

Heather hisses at him, *How the fuck do you know that?*

William looks around the room. *Is it okay if I come in? Just out of the doorway?*

Heather wants to say no but nods. He is so familiar it scares her. William takes three steps forward and pauses at the foot of the bed. *You did it, Mom.*

The name doesn't feel directed at her, but she knows it is. *Did what?*

He touches his own belly, *When you, you know, the thing.*

Heather pushes back, *What thing?*

When you reached into your womb and grabbed my coin. Two days before Christmas. You thought you failed. You pulled and pulled, and it hurt, and you couldn't do it. He pauses, waiting for his words to sink in. *But it worked.*

Heather is sweaty and shaking. She hadn't been so detailed when she told Marta. *If I succeed, how is he here? How does he know?*

William continues, *You damaged my coin, Mom. Bruised it. Tarnished it. Ever so slightly. I'll seem normal, but never quite right. I'll make stupid decisions. I'll do things you hate. Everything, whether you know it, whether I know it, leads to what happens tonight.*

The incongruity snaps Heather's concentration. *Tonight? What are you talking about?*

William places a knee on the end of the bed. *My coin is broken in time, Mom. I'm twenty-eight years old and I haven't been born yet and I haven't seen you since I was….*

This is important, why is he stopping? She asks, *Since you were what?*

He shakes his head. *I can't tell you, Mom. Shouldn't. If I tell you, you'll make it so it can't. It has to, Mom. Just like Peter had to.*

Heather interrupts his speech, *Don't you dare talk about Peter. You don't know him.*

William grins. *I do, Mom. Maybe even better than you. I helped him. I helped him hide Alexandrea. I helped him figure out how to let you cast the spell to end her curse. You haven't done that yet.* He smiles at her. *It works, you know. You do it.*

She pushes herself upright, her stomach resting on her lap. How does he know about the spell? That was her secret with Peter.

And Rose, he says, *she's amazing. You keep thinking Alexandrea is special. Wait until you see Rose. She will do amazing things, Mom. She's the key. Only,* he hesitates.

What? Tell me, William.

He looks conflicted, like he doesn't know if he should say it. Slowly, hesitantly, he says, *It's that Book.* He looks at her. *It's going to be trouble for her. And you.*

Heather whispers, *Book?* She is so confused. Peter told her about the Book, hidden away, waiting for Alexandrea to tell her to remove the curse. She asks if that's what he means.

William looks around. *It's funny,* he says, *that happens right here, in this hospital. Just not yet.*

Heather's mind spins with confusion. *What are you talking about? Nothing you're saying makes sense.*

It will. In time. For you, tomorrow is the future. But my past. I'm not born yet, but I lived most of my life before today. It's still linear for me, confusing to describe things that haven't happened yet. Hard to tell you enough, but not so much that you do anything different. Because you can't. Everything you have yet to do has already been done for me, but it can't happen until you do it.

Heather stares. His rambling seems more and more confused. It makes her want to chalk everything he's said to insanity, yet the more she wants to disprove, the more she sees the clues. The glimpses of her and Eric, the hints of Peter and her parents, all tucked away inside the way he moves and the way he speaks, his mannerisms, and his expressions. *What happens next? When will I see you again?*

The question saddens him.

When I'm born, he tells her.

Heather holds out her hand, *I mean you, see you again.*

William's face shows he understood. *You won't, Mom. We both die before we see one another again.*

She gasps.

He sighs at her shock. *You'll know, but when it's time, follow Rose. She'll want to look for me. You'll know she won't find me. Don't stop until she stops. You'll be looking for me then and I'll be here, talking to you right now. And after right now,* he takes a breath, *I don't know. Everything else is in my future, and while I've been able to see all the places I've been before I went back to them, I can't see past tonight.*

Heather asks, *Tonight?*

William nods. *Tonight. Alex comes to rescue me. I'll die. Death comes for her, too.*

Heather is confused, *Who's Alex?*

William grins, *Alexandrea. You'll see. She'll come to live with us. You think everything started with Peter, but that's the real beginning.*

Heather tries to wrap her head around that. *Why does she live with us? She's just a baby. Where's Holly?*

Mom, William says stiffly, *if I tell you, you'll try to fix it all.*

She asks, *Shouldn't I?*

William shakes his head. *It's all in motion, Mom. You did it. I'm telling you so you know you can't fail. You can face anything and know you'll succeed. You must be so strong, Mom.*

But, Heather says, *why do you have to die?*

William laughs. *You know, Mom, you always told me I make really stupid decisions. It's like a shorthand between us because sometimes they're not really my decisions. I just see where I need to be and I go. I can't help myself. Alex is coming to save me. I've got to be there. It's the only way, and I've got to die for it to finish. If I don't go, everything falls apart.*

Heather nods. *I think I understand.* Tears swell in her eyes. *You're really my son?*

William puts his hand on his chest. *I swear.*

Heather reaches out and William comes around the bed to hug her. As they separate, he touches her stomach. *I can't believe I'm in there, too*, he says. *Watch.* He closes his eyes. Heather can feel her stomach warming.

What are you doing?

William doesn't answer. His coin glows in his chest and stretching out from him are a dozen strings, a web, each stretched in a different direction including to her belly. She gasps and he smiles. *Pretty cool, huh? Everywhere I've been.* He backs from the bed. *Waddya say, I'll see you in a few months?* He points at her stomach. *Time to go. Destiny, and all that.*

Heather doesn't mean to sob. *Can't you stay a little longer, maybe tell me a little about yourself?*

He shakes his head. *Those things are best learned for yourself. I love you. I'll see you.*

Heather smears her tears across her face. *I'll see you, Billy.*

Before he clears the door, he pauses. *Oh*, he turns, *I almost forgot. You don't have to remember, but I have a message for Alex.*

If I don't remember, Heather starts to say.

William interrupts tearfully. *Alex*, he says, *I know I contributed to everything you've been through. I'm so sorry. You never asked for this, and it's far from over. I know you want to rest. You're so tired. There's so much I want to tell you. I hope one day you can forgive me. I don't deserve the sacrifice you must make.*

What does that mean? She's a baby. When do I tell her?

William shakes his head. *It's nothing. Something I needed to get off my chest. When it's time, you'll tell her.* He turns and disappears down the hall.

After he leaves, her room feels empty. The electricity of his presence lingers, a sensation as though he doesn't belong to this world. She sits in bed, rubbing her stomach, and for the first time since she could remember, speaks to her unborn children. *Hello Billy, hello Rose. I can't wait to meet you.*

Am I interrupting? Marta appears in the doorway.

Heather shakes her head.

I was out in the hall, like I said. I heard everything. Marta pauses. *You okay?*

Heather nods.

Good, Marta says, *because it sounds crazy.*

Heather nods.

But it's true?

Heather nods again. *I think so. I really do. Yes.*

Marta steps back. *I'm late. I've got to make my rounds.*

Wait, Heather calls after her. *I need help. I mean, if this is all true, I'm gonna need a few women to help me.* She looks at Marta. *Do you know any other women who feel or think the way you do? You know, who believe?*

Marta shrugs. *I'll see who I can think of. I don't just want anyone. I want to be certain.*

Heather smiles. *Good. Thank you, Marta.*

You really need my help?

Heather nods.

Marta twitches with excitement. *I always knew it wasn't just a feeling.* She leaves the room. *I'll come see you before my shift is up, okay?*

Heather watches Marta leave, look back and excitedly wave before disappearing down the hall.

*   *   *   *   *

Heather is in the bath; the water bloody and stinking. Across the room, Abby and Holly towel-off her babies. Eric kneels at the side of the tub, holding Heather's hand. *I did it,* Heather says, her body limp and energized now that the birth is over. Everything hurts. She never felt anything so horrible and hoped never to again.

The water's getting cold, she says, splashing the surface with her hand. *And it's disgusting. I can't believe I'm still sitting in this. I pooped.*

Eric pulls the plug and grabs the shower handle. After setting the temperature, he washes her down, her hands holding the sides of the tub as the last of the bloody water sucks into the drain. He shuts the water and dries her with a towel. Then he wraps her in a robe. Her legs are wobbly and unsteady; he brings her to bed.

I'll bring Rosemary in as soon as they're done with her, he tells her.

She smiles, she can't wait to feel their squirmy, squishy warm bodies on her chest, to feel them feeding. *And William*, she says. Every time she says the name, she wonders how he was. Did he die that night? She just gave birth to him and her heart aches, missing him already.

Eric goes still. *I don't know I can trust you with him.*

What are you talking about?

Eric lowers his voice. He can't look her in the eye. *Heather, I know what you did. That night I rushed you to the hospital. I knew the moment you cried out. I said I wouldn't, so you tried it yourself. You almost lost both babies, and I almost lost you.* He rubs his face. *How do I know you're past all that? What guarantee do I have that you won't try to harm him again?*

Heather breaks down. She can't stop the flood of tears. How can anyone accuse her of this, now? In that other room there is the little man who visited her in the hospital, who she will lose too soon to the past. How can she ever harm him? *I didn't do it*, she hollers at him, the tears and the snot making her voice sound choked and otherworldly. Her body hurts. *I couldn't. That's the guarantee: I had his tiny body in my hand and couldn't do it. I love him. I love them both so much. They're both perfect and special and, and, and....*

Eric kneels beside the bed and strokes her face, wiping her tears.

I had to know. I've worried for the past three months. I never knew how to say it.

She looks at him, her voice calms, *I'd never hurt them. They're my babies. They're, oh, after all of this, they're a part of me. I'll die* *before anything hurts the*m.

Eric kisses her cheek, then stands and leaves the room. When he returns, he carries a baby in each arm. Heather opens her robe. He lays a naked baby on each side of her chest. Heather feels them squirm and fuss, clutching hands scratching at her skin, their tiny mouths like little fishes sucking, looking for a nipple. She knew she would love nothing like she loves these two.

*   *   *   *   *

A thousand memories followed; they blurred and blended, moments of firsts, moments of joy and sorrow, as Billy and Rose became toddlers, children, pre-teens. She often looked at Billy and thought of William, wondered if that were not a dream. It gave her confidence, allowed her to believe in her own success, helped her see the truths behind the realities.

At first, Eric tolerated the way she'd talk, the conspiracies about witchcraft as the driving power behind wealthy men, behind governments, behind every political decision. Her answer for every controversial decision was always magic. She was blind to Eric's rolled eyes or how he left the room or half-joked that she was sounding crazy or begged her to stop. She was blind to the growing animosity between them, believing it was his problem, his shortcoming.

One evening, they are back at home, fighting about something she said at dinner in front of others; he accuses her of being drunk. She tells him how she feels, *Just because you weren't man enough and left it to me doesn't mean you get to not hear the truth.*

Eric flies into a rage. She fears he might strike her, but he directs all his anger at her words, at her thoughts; never at her.

I can't, he says when he calms down. *I just can't anymore.*

He moved out of the bedroom.

A week later, out of the house.

He still came for dinner, to see the kids on the weekends. They were still a family. Only, *mommy and daddy just needed some space from each other.*

She remembered Eric leaving them. Standing in the house, the divorce finalized, feeling empty and alone. She mourned her marriage.

She buried the hopes and dreams they had borne and nurtured, but hadn't yet reached maturity. The future was unknown, and yet, she held onto the distant remembrance of a crazy man telling her secrets from a hospital doorway. A crazy man who was looking more and more like her son.

Billy and Rose are becoming teens. Peeking out of their precious child-faces she starts seeing adults. It disarms her, these are her babies, they are not allowed to be adults so soon. Billy growing up means he will leave, disappear, and die. She can't let that happen.

There is a knock at the door. Heather opens it.

Standing outside is a soiled teenager, trembling in fright.

Heather doesn't recognize Alexandrea at first, not without Holly, not standing outside alone. Her stomach thrashes, but she still has to ask, *What happened?*

The child doesn't know, she barely shrugs.

Are you okay?

Another shrug.

Heather looks. Danger likely followed her here, and while she should let Alexandrea in and protect her, she turns to her own children, still in the kitchen: Her children, not Peter's.

Heather wonders what will happen if she closes the door, and pretends she never saw Alexandrea there.

She looks back and forth between Alexandrea and her children as if this is an either-or commitment.

If Heather lets her in, how can she keep her family safe?

Holly hasn't. Or why else is Alexandrea here? The realization of what that means sends her head into a dizzying spin: Holly is dead.

Although spoken twelve years ago, she can still hear William tell her that this moment is when it all begins.

Sweetheart, Heather says, *did the men who came to your house have magic?* Alexandrea clutches her head and squeals. Heather knows about the curse, saw first-hand what it does to the girl, but needs to keep her family safe. Alexandrea wouldn't tell. Peter locked the truth out of her. It is her responsibility now. Everything that came before this moment, her children being born, Peter sacrificing himself, William coming to her, all lead up to this. She'd never known responsibility this intense. What she does next bares the weight of those decisions.

Why don't you come in? Alexandrea crosses the threshold and turns to Heather, her eyes shedding tears. Heather has to say something. Alexandrea is looking around. She's been here many times before to play with her cousins, but never without Holly. Is she looking for Holly now?

Aunt Heather, she cries, *why am I here?*

Sweetheart, Heather whispers, saying to Alexandrea the only thing she can hear, *there's been a horrible car accident. Your Mommy and your Dad; they're gone now.*

Alexandrea shakes her head and clutches her aunt as she sobs. Heather doesn't know what else to say, so she embellishes the lie. *Abby dropped you off. Remember waving goodbye when she left? You've come to live with us now.* Heather looks to the kitchen at her children. When she answered the door, they were twelve, nearly teenagers. Now, they appear as children. Babies. They are so innocent, so helpless. Although the same age, Rose always seemed older than Billy. How will Rose take to an older sister? Will she see it as a good thing, or will she feel relegated to middle-child-hood? She looks at Alexandrea, who at fourteen is awkward and lonely. How will she fit into their family? Their broken family is just beginning to heal, to feel whole as a triumvirate. Alexandrea will return them to four. Heather can see Peter in her eyes, and as soon as she sees him there, she knows Alexandrea will be her child forevermore.

She looks back at Rose and whispers, *Please forgive me.*

*   *   *   *   *

At the hospital, Billy is in a private room in the ER. Rose sits on the side of the bed.

Heather's hands are shaking. She wants to vomit and curl up in a corner and let other people deal with this: Her niece, her Alexandrea, just told her about her nightmare, the trigger warning: Matthew found her. None of them are safe any longer. She anticipated this day for the past four years; thinking she'd pick up and run, but now, two children at the hospital, wherever could she run?

William warned her. She knew the moment the kids were late from their hike. She knew one of them was going to the hospital.

It happens here, he had told her.

Heather takes a deep breath and thinks about what to do next. How will she keep two of her three children safe? They are unprotectable in the hospital. Abby is the answer that keeps coming into her head: Abby is Alex's protector; Abby will die for Alex. Maybe her children in the hospital is a blessing in disguise; she can send Alex and Abby off, separating the danger from her children, keeping them safe until the danger makes itself known and they can figure how to react to it.

She must call the Coven. She hopes they will understand that all these years, the meetings and the fun, was in preparation for this moment. She hopes they won't come expecting pizza and wine. She has her doubts. *Marta*, she calls out, *it's time.*

*   *   *   *   *

Heather holds Peter's Book, her reverence for the tome; through these accursed pages, she is connecting with her brother one last time. Her stomach disagrees, however. Abby is dead. Heather has never cast a spell. Peter coached her for years, but it was William who gave her the confidence that all but left her the moment she looked down at the notes in Peter's handwriting. What is this garbage, she thinks: *Feel afraid, feel loss*? That's the spell? No one will believe this. They'll throw me in jail for murder and take my kids away. Eric is going to be on television, and he'll say she always thought she was a witch but she's just insane. At least she'd wind up in an asylum, and not executed, which would be à propos of her situation: a witch put to death.

Despite her deepest doubts, not one of them questions her. Not one doubts her. This makes Heather question their sanity.

You do it, William had told her.

She thought he was crazy, a madman pretending to be her son, but he was right about *everything*. He told her she would succeed. That also means he will soon be gone. But he isn't, not yet. For now, all she has to do is try. She tells them what Peter had written. They don't say a word. They don't question how crazy it sounds. They cast their spell and believe for the first time they are all real witches.

*   *   *   *   *

Heather is in a field. She lost sight of Rose. She can see Alex, lying in the tall grasses, her body convulsing, her mouth foaming. Around them fires blaze high into the sky, swirling flames blasting out heat. She fears the men encircling them, their Books held confidently, sparks flying from their hands, hitting this diminished group of women like electrical rocks. She races to Alex. She realizes, when she thinks this is the end, her end—that she will die here—she hasn't thought of Billy this whole time, even though he was the reason they came. Why did she bother to keep looking when she knew it was fruitless? Because he told her to? That was insane. She looks around, because thinking of Billy couldn't happen without thinking of Rose. She finds Rose. For a moment, she thinks Rose will die watching her mother attend to Alex. But Rose isn't dying. Yards away, her daughter stares into a Book. What is she doing? William warned her that a Book would cause Rose trouble. Heather is terrified the Book will overpower and obliterate her daughter, disappearing her from the face of the earth in a puff of smoke. Instead, her daughter returns fire, throwing lightning bolts with her fingers like some Norse god. Heather stares at Rose and in that moment realizes that tucked beneath the swelling pride hides a welt of jealousy. How amazing it is to see: a real witch in action.

William is right; Rose is the key. While Alex, the girl they all had their hopes pegged on lay unconscious, it is Rose who turns out to be the powerful one. Rose was the strong one controlling the elements and saving them all, using a power Heather wishes she could know, could understand, could feel for herself. She loves Rose; she watches her daughter force the men back, controlling the fires that Alex started, and telling these grown women what to do. Who is this girl? Is this really her child? What, she fears—because nothing good can come from a Book—is to be the consequence of this? Will she lose Rose? Will Rose no longer need her? Will the Book still destroy her? Why hadn't William told her more?

As Heather helps them evacuate Alex to the car, she swears to herself that no matter how useful it is, the Book is too dangerous for anyone—especially Rose, who is just a child—to use.

*   *   *   *   *

Standing in the Library, Rose beside her, a Book in each of their hands. Jeremiah calls Rose forward. The bottom drops from Heather's world. This is it. This is the end. There are two ways out of here: watch her daughter die, which will surely kill her, or offer herself.

She thinks of William one last time. Her son had been missing and yet is with her through all of this.

We both die, he had told her. *My day is today*. The words leave her lips. Jeremiah's eyes change. From certainty to surprise, to amusement, back to certainty. He hadn't anticipated this; he expected they'd be too frightened to argue. He assumed they'd go like lambs to slaughter. Feeling demoralized and powerless. He hadn't expected her to be this strong. She sees what he has done to Alex and then to Betty and then to Donna. If they fight, how many more of them will die? In choosing self-sacrifice she found a chink in Jeremiah's armor.

He gives her not a second. A tug at her chest, the familiar sensation of something being yanked out that was never intended to leave, like her spine being wrenched away. She recalls the last time she felt this. Where once she was ashamed of what she'd done, she is proud now: *You did it Mom. It worked.*

She is going to save them all. Her daughters, Rosemary and Alexandrea would live through the day because of her. All sensation around her fades. She feels like she is becoming faint, but the spiral into which she falls will be eternal.

She understands what William meant when he said she didn't have to remember what he needed Alex to know.

"Alex," she begins.

Alex was aware she was present, standing in Heather's memory.

"Listen to me."

Alex nods.

"If he's taking my life to feed yours, you'll know everything there is to know about me. You'll know my thoughts. Listen."

"Okay, Aunt—" Alex replied before realizing Heather was speaking at her in a memory, unaware she was there: Heather understood she was dying and made one final effort to give up her secrets.

"I've made mistakes. I tried to protect you. I tried to make you feel like you were my child. Your parents chose this destiny for you, and that was unfair. All this time, I used you to bring Billy home when I knew we never would, when I should have just set you free. He's gone. You're going where he is. You'll find him there and he will die.

"Not for his sake, Alexandrea, but for yours: Don't go. Stay away. He's never coming home, no matter what you do, and I know that now. Rose is all I have left. You and Rose. Take her, go with Abby, go someplace far, far away. Flip your coins and hide. Live a life free from all this, find happiness. The pursuit of magic has given me nothing but pain. Don't let that happen to you. Live, Alex, love freely, wildly, and find happiness everywhere you can."

Heather fell silent for a moment as Jeremiah clutched Alex's face, shoving the coin in her mouth.

"Of course," she said as she saw this happening, "if they don't let you, if they come after you, if they don't give you peace, then give Rose her Book and together, hunt these bastards down. Destroy every last one of them."

The warmth that is Heather dissipated throughout Alex's body, and she is alone.

Chapter Ninety-Two

eremiah's hands were just slipping from her face. In less than a second, forty years of Heather's life plowed through her brain like a steam locomotive. There should have been greater solace in her heart, but Heather being gone was a planet-sized hole torn in Alex's chest. She at once felt too numb to feel anything and overwhelmed by loss. It was like simultaneously being on a mountain and buried under it.

The agony was gone nearly as fast as it had come. The memories were at once fresh and old. They instantly faded to tatters; keeping Heather in her mind was like holding smoke in her fists.

She didn't need to see the dazed expression to know Heather was gone.

Heather was a part of her now. *Why did Heather lie to me? Why not tell me the truth about Peter, about Abby, about Witches' Covens? Had Heather told me about Billy—William—I would have known it was him, that day at my parent's house, pushing the Book to me.*

Emotions swirled around her like a tornado. She felt betrayed. She felt loss. She felt love. Heather was too complicated for her to swallow in one sitting. Instead, she felt torn apart, ripped open, rendered, and stuffed haphazardly back together. She wanted to collapse, to wail out the pain that tore her up inside. But she couldn't. She would never get that opportunity for the same reason she wanted it: Jeremiah.

Rose retched as she heaved and cried, clutching at her mother's husk, calling out to her, begging her to come back. Rose's chest heaved like she might vomit from the exertion. Alex's heart shattered to atoms, feeling Rose through Heather's eyes.

From behind Rose, Nancy and Carrie tried comforting her, tried to soothe her pain. "Oh Rose," they said before their words failed them.

Rachel, and June stood, frozen, desperate, and terrified. They were now seven—not counting Heather—from twelve. Besides her aunt, two were dead. Two others were likely not long for any world.

This seven were all who remained.

Heather wasn't Heather; oblivious to her daughter's pain, unaware of her cries, abandoned of her humanity. Alex saw in Heather her own father, possessed by only the dimmest spark of life: Twins to the very end.

"How do you feel?" Jeremiah interrupted the moment; Alex's heart sank. He spoke like nothing had happened, like there was no reason for Alex to feel any different. His head tipped a little as he studied her.

The question clawed at her for an answer. Her body tensed and tightened. Her sinews groaned and strained. She wanted to scream at him. Call him a murderer. He'd violated her with Heather. Yet, when her lips parted her gritting teeth, her intended answer didn't carry enough truth to pass. Yes, her chest burned with molten lead. Her cousin, her best friend, pulled her own hair, broken—perhaps beyond repair. Alex should have collapsed to the floor, the weight of the past week like an anvil dropped from space. Instead, she felt stronger. Her body buzzed. The tolls of the day fell away like confetti. For the first time, perhaps ever, she was certain there was nothing she couldn't do.

"You've never felt so good before, have you?" He didn't wait for an answer. His forefinger and thumb made a circle. He said, "That small disk is the key to everything. Without it," he motioned towards Heather. "Men used to symbolically eat the hearts and brains of defeated warriors to take their power. They didn't understand. This was your first; I doubt your last."

The fact that she felt so good was her greatest betrayal. She'd never felt such guilt. Like she danced on Heather's coffin at her wake. She couldn't speak. She felt nothing and everything. It was dizzying. She wished she could collapse and sob and allow the pain to take its toll.

"For you to stand a chance against Matthew, you'll need everything I gave you."

"I don't care," Alex's voice was hushed. She wanted this torment over. She would fight and die right here to have the pain in her heart extinguished. That pain was for Rose, not for Heather. She knew where Heather was.

"I understand," Jeremiah replied. "You want to kill Matthew. Find your cousin. Billy? But then you want to come back here, free the women I've taken. Avenge the ones I've killed. Then kill me."

Alex seethed, hot tears falling from her eyes. Part of her wanted those things. But part of her wanted to walk away. To wake up from this nightmare and be happy when Heather tells her she can't go to college for another year.

"Except this is how your story ends. The fatalism of Alexandrea, dying in the most unfair fight. Unable to avenge the losses she loved. You've known, though. You've known since the very beginning. Death waits for you."

She wasn't sure what prevented her from casting a spell. Did her fear of him—the idea of his power—make her impotent? Like with Sara, or at the house: men coming to take a witch's power cast spells to protect themselves. Or did he control magic, and by extension, her ability to use it? Did it matter? What more could he do that was worse than this? When would the loss be too great? When he fed her Rose's coin? Would Alex stand fast until everyone she loved was dead? Could she? Alex knew she didn't have the strength.

Had she known since the beginning she would die? Or was Jeremiah planting the seed that would become a self-fulfilling prophecy?

Alex looked back on the others. They comforted Rose, who collapsed to the floor with Heather's Book   not acknowledging anyone. If she were safe…. "Send them home." She turned back to Jeremiah. "I need to know they're safe before I go."

Jeremiah said, "You don't get to lose and call the shots, Alexandrea. You leave not knowing which of them live or die."

Alex smoldered.

"That's good," he said of her rage. "Bring that to Matthew."

Alex never hated anyone this way before. She had hatred for Matthew. But Jeremiah; she wanted him dead, no matter the cost, no matter the sacrifice. She hadn't realized her passion before, the depth of her vitriol. If she had to trust him for the wellbeing of all those around her, then they were all expendable. Her anger grew like a vibration. She bore the immense weight of her Coven's lives. Knowing they weren't safe freed her. Once Alex realized she had no control over their safety, the chains that imprisoned her crumbled to dust.

She looked from Jeremiah to her cousin, to her aunt. She felt like an empty cup placed just below the surface of a pool; all the water rushing into it. Everyone suffering because of Jeremiah. What felt like a lonely flicker of candleflame suddenly roared with the swirling eddies of a fiery hurricane.

Jeremiah was talking. Saying something about it being time. Alex heard nothing.

"You may pick one of them to accompany you."

A storm of emotion rose inside Alex; hate, rage, heartache; aware that in a short time the realizations of the day would wash over her like a wave of rusty nails. She wanted to hurt someone for the sake of her own pain. She wanted to rip out her hair as the weight of anguish crushed her. She desired to destroy Jeremiah. She despised his smugness, loathed his mannerisms. She wanted to punch him in the face every time he finished a sentence and the corners of his mouth momentarily curled. If she were alone, if there was no one to protect, she would risk extinction. She would unleash everything she could muster, no matter the futility, if just to nick or bruise him, even if it forced him to destroy her, swiftly or slowly. Except she knew all she'd accomplish was having him murder another of her friends.

Alex dug deep. Donna and Betty, dead or consumed by Jeremiah. Heather, a living corpse, consumed by her. Rose, tortured by the pain of her mother's torment. Abby, struggling to comply with Alex's demand and her own forced desire to serve her. Colette and Lydia missing. Caleb. Billy. Sara. Matthew tricking her to come here. Lesedi. All the women in the market. The pain in those Books. Hundreds of thousands of voices. Millions. The cry of hatred rose inside her like boiling magma on its way to eruption. And then: Heather. Her aunt who took her in. Who became her mother. Who knew for years that Billy would go missing. Who spent her life looking into the abyss that awaited her and never hesitated to smile. She thought losing Heather would empty out a part of her too big to ever refill. She thought the only way to dull the pain would be to spend the rest of her life avoiding every thought about Heather. But it became clear: Heather was the final catalyst she needed.

She expected ordinary lightning.

Jagged arching bolts of electricity sprung from her hands. The blinding light cast fierce, piercing shadows everywhere. This wasn't some branching tree of energy. From her hands erupted immense, crackling power. These streaming pulses of light snarled and snapped and struck at Jeremiah. They pierced him like spears and entangled him in a web which snaked and sparked and crackled across his body.

Terrified that he'd shrug off her attack and then murder Rose or Abby, Alex reached into her rage. It was like plunging her hands into boiling oil. She had one chance, and she'd be made to regret not putting everything into it.

The granite floor trembled. Huge slabs of stone upended as the floors twisted upon themselves, shards broke apart and in the raising gusts of wind, boulders sprung from the floor to batter Jeremiah.

She'd never seen this much energy released by anyone before. Jeremiah suffered the battery. She needed to kill him. Of all the things she desired—freedom for her friends, escape, Heather restored to life—her desire to murder Jeremiah was greater. She didn't want to contemplate what would happen if he survived.

Alex screamed every ounce of emotion she possessed, hatred and fear, anger and rage and disgust. It never felt so good before, and that frightened her, but it also strengthened her. Inside, her voices rose in chorus, roaring as they joined her, contributed to and strengthening her.

As an encore performance, her mind replayed memories. Except this time, the experience was from both sides. She didn't just earn Heather's smile: she felt Heather's pride. Booming thunderous explosions upended the floor surrounding Jeremiah, throwing stony shrapnel into the air. She came down to breakfast and felt Heather's heart warm from her slight similarities with Peter—shards of rock careened at his body like thrown knives, slicing through him. She listened to Heather talk about her divorce, and felt Heather's trust for her with her secrets—flames exploded around him, torturing his flesh, blackening him. Alex understood Heather's mental acrobatics every time they spoke, choosing words that wouldn't trigger her head. The heat raged, the stone floor glowing red until the sharp broken edges began to ooze. Alex was all she had left of Peter, and she loved Alex just as much as she had her brother. Sometimes when she'd had too much to drink, she would pretend Alex was Peter and she could unload her heart—Jeremiah's burned body stilled.

Alex had never felt so overwhelmed by a sense of love before, a love that was now gone. Telling Heather they were heading out on their hike. Heather's apprehension. Heather's faith in her as she let them go. Even Heather's feelings for Rose. The unspoken apologies. The missed *I love you*'s. At least Alex knew now. Rose would never understand how adored she was. How regretful Heather was. How she hoped Rose would be strong enough, smart enough, ready for the day her cousin became a witch. Alex shared this love with her whispers. She sustained them with everything Heather gave her. It was the first love most of them had experienced in centuries. And Heather had enough for everyone. And they took it. And they understood what the world lost. And they hated the man who had taken her away. And they punished him with their wrath.

Rose, her face ruddy and mucus-smeared, stood beside Alex. She uttered in the guttural tongue from her Book. She fired sparks at Jeremiah. Then Carrie and Nancy and Rachel and June each joined. They stood shoulder to shoulder, the first witches ever to set foot in this Library, and they made Jeremiah burn.

Wind swirled, blowing ash, the remains of the bookcases scouring away. Lightning crackled in the air, the scent of ozone soon overwhelming the odor of burned wood and paper. The Library quaked. Fire burned ravenously and rocks pelted the charring corpse, flaying flesh from bone, searing and separating, breaking him down, turning Jeremiah to charcoal.

Alex would burn Jeremiah's atoms away if she had the stamina. Maintaining the emotion was exhausting. As much as she tried to hold onto the anger and the pain, the intensity of her power greedily devoured this fuel. Even with the help of all her screaming whispers, she was spent. She pushed, like squeezing the last bit of herself out the tube, like trying to scream with no air left in her lungs.

She knew she should still hurt. She should still be angry. But she'd turned those sensations into something else and used them all up. It didn't leave her happy. It didn't leave her empty. It just left her.

The lightning and the flames died, like she shut a spigot. Taking their cue, sparks ceased from the others. The man-sized lump of char crackled as it still burned, glowing and groaning as it cooled.

Rose stammered, "Is he…?"

Alex turned to Rose. "I don't know."

"Come on, look," Carrie antagonized the smoking lump, "he's burned to a crisp. There's nothing left of that piece of shit."

The sounds it made, cracking and groaning were disarming. Each time the black mass fissured to reveal a glowing seam, they startled. Alex spoke slowly, "I can't trust what I see."

"No, Alex, he's gone. We did it. We freaking did it!" Carrie shouted.

Alex wished she shared Carrie's enthusiasm.

Rose stepped forward, still holding her two Books. "Let's be sure!"

Carrie stomped past Rose. The closer she approached, the more she recoiled from the heat.

"Carrie, don't do what you're thinking," Nancy shouted.

Rachel and June confirmed their concern. "Come back here, Carrie," one said, then the other, "It's not safe."

Abby got closer to Alex. "You beat him."

Alex ignored Abby.

Carrie kicked at the lump of char. It smoldered and cracked. She kicked it again, fragments sheared off and pulverized as they crashed to the ground. She kicked it repeatedly, shouting as she did, and again, a sixth time, a seventh, and then the hunk of coal fissured and fell away, crumbling to the ground. The crash made everyone jump, made them all step back.

June asked Carrie, who likely added another burn to her collection of kitchen tattoos, "Are you okay?"

Upright in the center of the pile of rubble remained a desiccated pile of black, bony, charred matter, shaped like a man bent and cowering in self-defense.

Carrie looked at the others and laughed out her nervous fear. She kicked at it again.

Before she made contact, the desiccated man snatched Carrie's throat. Her legs kicking as her petite form lost the ground, as she struggled to breathe.

The whole world grew cold as Alex realized Jeremiah wasn't yet defeated.

The form turned to Alex; what she thought were eyes, glowing pits in the skull, burned at her. The mouth creaked open and the voice that emerged roared of heat and char and reeked of sulfuric death.

"Look on me, Alexandrea. See me for what I am."

She replied, "You're nothing. Burned flesh and bone."

"I am eternal," it protested. "I am whatever I choose for you to see."

"Let Carrie go!" Rose shouted. She raised her Book and read.

The thing didn't flinch when struck by Rose's sparks. It discarded Carrie. Her body crumpled at Alex's feet. With a dry, gritty, flick of his wrist, Rose screamed, pinwheeling and rolling like a rag doll.

Alex crouched to touched Carrie, making sure she was okay. Carrie nodded as she wheezed and choked, scrambling out of the way. June and Nancy went to Rose.

Abby called, "Watch, Alex, it's getting closer."

"Stay with them," Alex ordered Abby.

"You think I was some old man. Flesh and blood to destroy with fire," it said. "The body I was born into long ago decayed."

Alex feared one of them was about to become the new Jeremiah. The ultimate failure: to become your enemy. "So, you take a new one from someone else?"

"Only the weak have to take."

The charred figure wiped its face, smearing char and soot from flesh. The skin it revealed was not that of the old man.

"I've underestimated you, Alexandrea."

The new Jeremiah emerged from the ash like a butterfly emerging from a charcoal chrysalis. This Jeremiah stretched as blood and flesh filled and engorged his limbs as he emerged, naked, young, and tall.

He stepped closer, the stone still radiating uncomfortable waves of heat, edges and broken cracks still glowing. Their bodies nearly touched. He rested a hand on her cheek. He looked at Abby. "You should step away." Abby didn't argue. Try as she might, she couldn't help but withdraw from Alex.

"Alexandrea," he whispered to her, "Look."

She didn't want to. She wanted to cover her eyes. He placed his other hand on her other cheek. He forced her head slowly back; she hadn't the strength to prevent it. Her eyes met with his.

If she didn't hate him so, this Jeremiah would have been handsome. Fiercely featured, chiseled, strong and tall; just taller than her. His hair was a deep curly blonde, his eyes a sea of green. His skin, still growing taught over his muscular frame, was tan and flawless.

Alex stared, unable to look away. She gave everything to her attack, and he endured it. She was empty. All she felt was his heat, unabashed in his nudity. *What is he doing? Is he trying to seduce me, fuck me, or humiliate me?*

Kill me, she told him. *Let the others go. Do whatever you want with me. Accept my sacrifice, my last act to protect my loved ones. It's a fair trade.* She felt the words but did not hear them. They came from her mouth, but she made no sound.

Jeremiah grinned. She heard his words, battering inside her brain. *I am the second child and only son of Time and Destiny.*

Around Alex, stars began shimmering. With his words, Jeremiah created vast networks of matter and dust, stretching between expanding balls of glowing gasses. She stared in awe and wonder, trembling in fear as she understood the vastness of which Jeremiah spoke. He was explaining his universe to her. To prove her insignificance, to break her spirit as she discovered how puny and irrelevant she was. She had been to Oblivion. It prepared her for this truth. Rather than fight it, rather than try to argue that she mattered, she understood that the universe saw her as an inconsequential speck. She gave herself to the vastness. She abandoned herself to it.

That's when she heard choking.

Chapter Ninety-Three

he woman was perfection. Alex's eyes hurt to linger too long. She radiated beauty. Everything in her proximity, rather than paling by comparison, became that much more magnificent. It was like a spotlight surrounded her and everything within it looked lush and fertile. Even the hands, the perfect hands, strong, veined, powerful, crushing her throat.

The woman reached at the young man, struck at him, tried to make him release his grasp. Tall, handsome, clothed with crude leather tied about his waist, imperfectly covering his genitals. His teeth clenched; his wide, beautiful eyes cried sparkling tears as he knelt, his hands around the goddess's throat.

She collapsed, her beautiful, naked body folding upon itself as she kneeled and bent over and back, stretching her whole form onto the ground, her body picking up speckles of dirt like dark glitter. Her eyes opened wide. Her beauty was so bewildering that Alex could not help but envy her.

The woman's arms grew tired and heavy. How could such perfect and mocha and slender and muscular and unblemished arms be so cumbersome? Alex didn't comprehend until she saw her eyes spinning, mouth puckering like an infant, her tongue jutting between perfect blue lips.

Why are you here? This isn't for you to know.

In the goddesses' chest, a coin glowed. Pure and white, it was so bright that Alex, even staring at this memory, shaded her eyes. It seemed to wash color from everything, leaving the world pure white with only the occasional black shadows.

Beside her, a child appeared. Young and cherubic, Alex recognized Charon. The folds of fabric it wore perhaps only numbered five. It held out its hand, and seeing the beautiful woman, gasped. Its hand recoiled; covering its mouth. Its large, dark round eyes grew wider as it gazed upon the fallen beauty.

The young man claimed her coin. He held it aloft and contemplated, squinting into the gleaming spectacle. Charon held out its hand. The young man was placing it in the child's palm until he had second thoughts. Charon face became a twist of anguish as it tore from the emerging skeletal horror. It was too late; shadow consumed light as the coin disappeared into the young man's mouth.

She took me as a lover, Jeremiah explained sullenly. *I was a boy and did not understand what that truly meant. She was, well, you saw her. Beauty wishes to be beautiful. I believed she was just a magnificent woman who desired a plaything. I could not conceive her a goddess: the goddess. No concept she was eternal. Her soul was the least of her. She was not of flesh and blood, not like you and me. She became human so we could love one another. She was magic, the origin of it all. She was the beating heart of all creation, and I took her life. Consuming all she was.*

Do you understand what that did to me? How that felt? One moment I was a child, barely a man. If counting had been invented, I might say I was perhaps fifteen, a stupid, ignorant primitive. The next, my heartbeat powered the universe. Magic, each spell, pulled like a thread from my flesh. I was a fraying scrap, a supplicant of another power that now belonged only to me.

Alex eyed Jeremiah, no longer in his memory, but before him in the Library: his touch withdrawn. "That's what you believe? You killed her and thought you deserved this?" She motioned at the Library.

"You've tasted one soul from a very flawed, weak—"

Alex interrupted, "Don't you ever talk about my aunt again."

Jeremiah didn't argue. "I don't know why you saw that. I've never shared that truth with anyone. I hadn't intended to, not with you."

Alex paused, his words resonating. *Is he being truthful? Did I take the memory from him when we touched? Did I hurt him?* "I don't believe it."

"You witnessed my memory." He appeared upset she didn't believe his story.

"That's what you've made yourself believe. It's what you tell yourself." Alex wasn't fearful any longer. He was not all the things he said he was. He was a murderer. An imposter. His power didn't belong to him. In the subtle expression of his face, she understood: he knew she knew. Somewhere in that truth, they both recognized, existed weakness.

"It's time for you to face Matthew."

Alex said, "Let the others leave."

"You've not been to Matthew's home. You can't send yourself there. I will give one of you that knowledge for her magic. Two of you may go. But first, choose."

"Send the others home first." *Why two of us? What is he hiding? Why not just send me, unless, what if the magic connects us? Is that even a thing?*

"You fear I'll do something horrible to them once you've departed. Alexandrea, I am not an evil man. I use cruelty to punish. Who would I be punishing if I waited until you were gone before I harmed the remains of your family?" He laughed out those last three words. "Choose now, or I *will* punish you. I will take the pretty girl."

The others quieted behind Alex. Rose was no longer crying but clawing her way forward. In each hand she clutched a Book: hers and Heathers. Her face was ruddy and wet, her chest still heaved, but her eyes appeared to be aflame.

Alex had no choice. She had nothing left with which to fight. Jeremiah was unstoppable. Immortal. She couldn't trust him, but she also couldn't keep fighting. This was no losing battle; it was a slaughterhouse.

"Rose, you will never forgive me for this. But I need you to protect them." She turned to Jeremiah. Heather's memories informed her decision. With no small sense of defeat, she said, "I choose Abby."

Rose lunged at her, her eyes tearing, teeth clenched, screaming, her Books abandoned to the floor. Several hands grasped and restrained Rose, who thrashed and threatened and attempted to break free. "Let me go," she cried and swore at Carrie and Rachel and Nancy and June.

Abby's face was awash in betrayal. She looked as though slapped. "I can't," she whimpered. "I told you, don't ever ask me to use magic."

"I know what you said."

"Then why?" Abby's eyes teared. "Are you angry at me?" Abby snorted as she wiped her nose, tears wetting her cheeks. "I can't serve you and serve magic."

Alex steeled herself. Rose collected her Books. Alex hurt saying this to Abby, seeing how much pain she was causing. "You don't know what you want. Not since the day you took your oath." Alex lowered her voice. "It's what you think you want, but you can't possibly know anymore.”

Abby grabbed fistfuls of Alex's shirt. “Don't make me do it. Please don't.”

“Before we get carried away,” Jeremiah interrupted as though nothing transpired, “let me give Abby her spell.”

Alex placed a hand on Abby's cheek, “Do this one last thing for me. We don't get out of here any other way.” It was like apologizing while still twisting the knife. She wondered how any of them would get out of here.

“Can't you understand how much it hurts?” Abby balled the chest of her shirt with her fist.

“I want you to be free, Abby. I want to know every decision you make comes from your heart and not from me.” The pain on Abby's face was torturous. Just the expectation was causing incredible discomfort. Alex was harming Abby. She hoped releasing Abby was the right decision to make. It had to be.

Jeremiah handed Abby a Book. She repulsively took it, as though while they both touched the same Book, by extension they touched one another. The Book in her hands, she stroked the cover nervously. Her eyes darted from Alex to Jeremiah.

Alex ordered, “Open it, Abby. I'm asking you. Please open the Book. For me.” The words hurt coming out, like they scraped past her heart. She didn't want Abby to read from the Book. She wanted Abby to be free from her oath. She wanted to know that Abby's choices were her own.

Abby opened but refused to look at it, her eyes crying betrayal. Alex had never seen such an expression from Abby directed at her. It stung. It gave her doubt. She'd never been so uncertain before. But she couldn't go back on her word. Not now. Not here. “Read the Book, Abby.”

Behind them, Rose interjected, “Alex, you could—”

“No, Rose,” Alex hissed, “I won't. You will protect them. You will get them home.”

Rose boiled away, June and Rachel trying to comfort her. Alex regarded Abby again.

“I'm begging you, Alex.” Veins bulged at Abby's temple and her throat. She would do anything to protect their bond, but she was also being told to break it. “Please don't make me.”

“Read the Book.” Alex hated herself for the cruelty she was

dispensing. Even as she told herself *It's for the best*, she questioned her motives.

Abby closed her eyes and lowered her head, spilling tears. Gradually her eyes opened. She stared at the offending pages. She said not a word, just staring, unwavering, unmoving. She barely breathed. She barely blinked. But she cried. She stared until at once, her eyes looked up at Alex. In them, for the first time, Alex understood uncertainty. "I'll do my best to see you through this, Alex."

"No more promises, Abby. I'm asking one more thing. Take me to Matthew. Then you're free."

Abby nodded, a little confused.

Jeremiah gestured to Abby. "The spell is writ. Cast it on Alexandrea."

"What about…," Alex started, distracted by Abby's trembling hand searching the Book.

Abby turned the pages, searching. She settled on one page and squinted, perhaps uncertain. She glanced at Jeremiah, who approved.

Alex finished, "… them?"

Abby looked at the Book. Her eyes settling on the first symbol. Her jaw looked misshapen as it waited for her breath.

"Send them home," Alex begged.

"Soon," Jeramiah said coolly.

Abby spoke the ugly, guttural words.

Jeremiah waited until Abby was nearly finished with the spell. "Once you realize what has been done to you, you will forever resent the girl."

Before Abby could reply, the air snapped as it rushed to fill the void where she and Alex once stood.

Chapter Ninety-Four

isplacing the emptiness when Alex and Abby disappeared, air rushed past Rose. The disconnect in her senses caused her to startle, and that gave her troubled emotions momentary reprieve.

Nancy tended to Carrie, bruises blooming across her throat, her breathing raspy and painful.

A step behind her, Rachel sobbed. "They left us," she muttered. "We never should have come. It's over." June tried comforting her, looking like she wasn't far from similar conclusions.

To Rose's side, Heather stared at the smoky ruins. She looked at Rose, and for a moment Rose's heart nearly exploded, but Heather's regard was empty, and she turned away.

Rose peered at the six of them remaining: Nancy, Carrie, June, Rachel, Heather, and herself. They walked in twelve. All this for her brother? A loss of half these women who came offering help. *Alex should have known. Matthew tricked her to get everything he needed, and now she is being fed right back to him. Serves her right for being so stupid.* Rose wasn't ashamed by her confidence that she wouldn't ever see Alex again. Soon, she'd be tortured to make Matthew's Book. What troubled Rose was she wasn't sure she cared. Too numb to tell, her heart broken when Jeremiah shoved her mother's coin into Alex's mouth. *Alex. Always Alex. Why does everyone think she's so special? What has she done? What has she done right?* Rose had wanted to intercept Heather's coin. Instead, she watched it, like a dropped car key disappearing into a storm drain. Except it wasn't a car key, it was her mother.

What was she even thinking? She didn't fight. She didn't try to push it away or spit it out. Of course not. She swallowed it right down. It made her glow. Her posture changed, her eyes brightened, everything about her became more. *Alex didn't fight because she probably wanted it. How selfish that of all of us, Alex got to be the one.*

Was she being unfair to Alex? Blaming her for everything that happened here? *Maybe. But isn't it her fault? We followed her. We did everything she said, and now look at us*. Rose wanted to tell herself it wasn't Alex's fault—that it was Jeremiah's—but it was simpler to blame her absent cousin.

"Rosemary Hawthorne, daughter of Heather Hawthorne. The youngest woman here, and the one they will look to for guidance. How does that make you feel?" Jeramiah taunted.

Rose felt mocked, as though she was missing the hidden meaning in his words and didn't understand why they were demeaning.

"Leave her alone," Carrie croaked. "She's just a kid."

Carrie was struggling to her feet with Nancy's assist. Jeremiah grinned. "You're clearly the muscle. Interesting. You protect someone else without regard for your own safety. Unlike Abby, no oath motivates you. Just unrequited lust."

"What do you want? If you're not going to let us go, at least be decent about killing us." Nancy said, getting Carrie to her feet, and pushing the others towards Rose.

"The healer. This is coming together for me. And you?" He turned to June. "Why are you here?"

June tried to look calm, unable to hide her trembling hands. "I thought it would be fun. What a fucking shit-show."

Jeremiah nodded. "What a disappointment this must be."

June tried to nod, trying to maintain the illusion of fearlessness.

"And you," he addressed Rachel, "what's your purpose?"

Rachel took a half-step backwards. She stammered, "I only wanted m-magic. To be a real w-witch. To see it and know it was real."

Jeremiah grinned. "And now that you've seen magic, what have you learned?"

Softly the answer came, "I never want to see it again."

"Good," Jeremiah almost whispered. "You've all served your purpose. Alexandrea will die at Matthew's hand, and he will realize he's failed." He paused, as though thinking something through. "She was the only one who mattered. You've each taken all the magic you can. There's no further purpose you serve. Perhaps I send you all to the Farm."

Rose struggled to shout, tears choking her voice, "Stop fucking with us. Let us go or kill us already." Blinded by tears of anger; her voice lost momentum. *What am I doing?* She half-expected Heather to grab her from behind and chide her for being so brazen. *Don't antagonize him*, she'd say.

Jeremiah didn't hide his grin. "They don't understand you. Perhaps they never will."

Carrie said, "Of course we do. She's a kid. Leave her alone."

Jeremiah's eyes dismissed Carrie with enough force she stepped back. He addressed Rose again. "They didn't see you coming." He chortled. "You, Rosemary, must be set loose." He laughed. For the first time it was genuine. He turned and took a step away. Without turning back, he said, "Go. Be on your way."

Rose took a deep breath, "I don't know how to get through that maze."

"Idiots," Jeremiah shouted at them. "You have a Book. They have magic. You can go anyplace you've already been."

"What about my mother?"

Jeremiah continued on his way. "Hope she wants to go someplace you'll be able to find her." He disappeared in the ruins.

Rose turned to the others. "I wanna go home."

"I go where you go," Carrie said.

Rachel shook her head, "Anywhere but here."

Rose wished her mother could tell her what to do. "Let's go to right outside that door. We all know that place."

Nancy rushed to Rose and gestured to the others. "Go. We'll meet you right outside that stupid little gate."

Carrie spoke but stopped, touched her neck, rubbing the hand-shaped purple bruise. "Shouldn't we help Alex?"

Rose looked at Heather and shook her head. Rachel disappeared through a small breath of mist first. *Chickenshit.* June held her Book open, waiting for Rose's okay. The moment she nodded, June read and disappeared.

Nancy touched Heather's arm. "What about her?"

Rose's eyes welled. "I can send her wherever she wants to go. If there's want in her." She looked at Carrie and Nancy. "Go. I'll be right behind you."

Carrie asked, "You shou—"

"Go!"

"Okay," Carrie defended, backing away, and opening her Book. She and Nancy avoided crashing into one another by simultaneously stepping through puffs of mist.

Once Rose was alone, she wrapped Heather in a hug and sobbed. After a minute, she stepped back, rubbing her face against her sleeve. "What should I do, Mom?"

She watched Heather's face, and answered for her, "*Go.*" "But what about you, Mom?" Rose spoke for each of them. She said, "If I try to send you somewhere but you're not thinking of going anywhere, then what happens?" "*At least I won't be here.*"

Rose put on a brave face, but tears kept spoiling her. "We're going to the door, Mom. The brownish, reddish door we came in through. Please think of that door." She opened her Book, holding the other under her arm. She stared at the page, and just before she locked onto the first large symbol, she whispered, "Goodbye, Mom. I love you."

Chapter Ninety-Five

 ose found herself on the street, the night air cooler than that afternoon. Her body shivered, but not from the temperature. She looked around in a sudden panic. The streetlights lined the street, each door was lit, some by multiple fixtures. The darkness of the night sky in the city was a miserable gray that made Rose ache for home: there was not a single discernable star.

Footfalls raced towards her. Turning to confront them, Carrie, Nancy, June, and Rachel seemed to appear from darkness as they stepped into the glare of a streetlight.

"We didn't think you were coming," Carrie rubbed her arms. "We've been waiting. We worried something happened. We were deciding if we should go back."

Rose couldn't believe what she was hearing. Her heart felt withered and empty yet bursting. "You would go back there for me?"

Nancy replied, "She said we were thinking about it. She didn't say we were crazy." She winked as Carrie cackled, then winced. Each one of them still had the wherewithal to laugh, but the cavernous loss they felt took it from them prematurely.

There was something about standing on the sidewalk on a city street. It was easy to dismiss what had happened as some sort of hallucination. It was easy to feel like they'd go home and find ruin turned right. Except they all knew it wasn't a hallucination. What they'd experienced made it difficult to celebrate their survival.

Rose asked, "Mom?" Just the sound of the word made her lonely, ready to cry.

Carrie and Nancy both shook their heads. "You sure you sent her here?" They both scanned the street.

Rose nodded.

June touched Rose's arm. "She never came out."

Rose's heart broke again. "I don't know where she went. She could be anywhere."

The other four were silent. They looked at Rose and then couldn't any longer. Nancy said, "At least she's not there. Wherever she is, it's where she wanted to go, right? Maybe, she's, you know, home."

Rose nodded. *Maybe she's not.* The idea that her mother could be anywhere unsettled her further. Would she be one of those people she saw on the way here, filthy, catatonic, and homeless? *How many of those people are like that because someone fed on their soul?*

"We'll find her, Rose," Rachel whispered.

Nancy nodded. "We will. We're out. We made it out. We fucking made it out." She sighed and whispered, "Why us and not them?"

Rose nodded, wiping her face. Being alive wasn't enough. "It doesn't feel good. Just the five of us."

Rachel anxiously looked at the door. "Should we get going?" She didn't say the words, but Rose could tell that being near the door was freaking her out. She wasn't alone. At every sound, every random dog-walker or bicycle bell brought their eyes back to the door, expecting it to open and for Jeremiah to emerge, giving chase.

Rose turned to the door. *What I wouldn't give to do this day over. When I opened the door and found the basement, we should have given up and left. But no. Alex had to keep trying. She had to get the door open. That door didn't lead to Billy; it led to hell.*

Nancy tugged on her shoulder. "What's done is done, Rose," Nancy whispered. "You can't change it."

Rose responded, "I was wondering what I could do to make sure no one goes through that door again."

"You heard what Alex said," Carrie added, "destroy this door and they'll just put it somewhere else."

Rose pointed at the door. Her voice quivered, "I went through that door today. I thought I was an adult. I had this Book, and I was going to kick ass." She looked at the others. "Everyone I love is dead. I'm all alone. What's next? I don't know how to get home or what to do tomorrow. How didn't I know this would happen? Shouldn't I have? Something this big can't just sneak up. There had to be clues or signs to see it coming."

Nancy rushed forward and embraced her. "You couldn't, Rose. No one asks for tragedy. No one expects it. People leave for work and never come home. They go on vacation, or they go to a party, or they go to sleep. No one asks for it, and no one can prevent it. We have to pick up our pieces and decide what it means now. And every morning we wake up and we pick up our pieces all over again and decide what it means now. Day after day, until we get used to doing it."

"No one can replace your family," Carrie told Rose. "Until you say otherwise, I'll be your family. I'll make sure the house isn't empty."

"Me too," Nancy told her. "I'll be your family."

"Me too," June nodded. "When I'm not travelling, at least." She laughed at herself and then wiped her nose.

"Me too," Rachel added. "We're all we have now. We're all who knows the truth."

We're all who have magic. Rose looked at the four women, tears blurring her vision. She feared they were saying this only because it's what she needed to hear. She couldn't bear being alone, not tonight, not tomorrow, not for a very, very long time.

They were each poised to walk, hesitating until Rose joined them. They walked, slowly at first, towards Susan's apartment. "We could just send ourselves," Nancy said. "If it weren't for the cars, we could go straight home."

Carrie shook her head. "I've had enough magic for one day, thanks."

June cackled. "One day?" She waved her hands. "I'm okay if I never know magic again. I'm done with that shit."

Nancy and Rachel laughed. The weight of the day shortened and darkened their laughter, as though nothing was funny.

Rose watched her feet on the sidewalk, the way the streetlights made her shadow slowly spin around her as she walked. *Magic is all I have now.*

When they were two or three blocks away, the streets were much busier than by the door. Rose asked, "Why are we going to Susan's? What are we going to tell her?"

Nancy rubbed her forehead. "I've been trying to decide what to say the whole way. I can't tell her Betty's dead." The words gave them all pause. Hearing someone speak of the finality gave each of them chills.

Carrie looked around self-consciously as she let out an inappropriate laugh. "I mean, what would happen? She calls the cops and we take them to the door?"

Rachel looked at them both. "What if we opened it for them? You know, opened it, opened it."

Carrie rubbed her hands together. "Could you imagine a SWAT team going in there? Would they even stand a chance?"

June shook her head. "They'd get one look of the maze and be all, *Nothing to see here, everyone out.*"

Carrie laughed, "It is New York. They'd probably be all, *This again?*"

"What if the cops know?" Rose asked softly. "What if we get to the door and even one of them knows? Don't you think they'd protect their secret?"

"That's an unsettling thought," Nancy said. "Let's get far away from here."

"Straight home?" Carrie asked, "Get our cars and go?"

"Carrie, I'm exhausted. I can't make the drive," Nancy warned.

"Then we take turns, or we stop at a motel. Let's just go. Please," Carrie begged.

Rachel nodded emphatically. "I need to be away from here."

June agreed.

"She's right," Rose decided. "We need to leave."

A few minutes later, they were at the parking garage, exchanging tickets for cars. Rose and Carrie climbed in Nancy's car, and Rachel in June's. Slowly pulling out onto the road, they were on their way.

Chapter Ninety-Six

The drive from New York City was excruciating and silent. They reached the house well before dawn. As Carrie—who drove the final leg—pulled into Rose's driveway, Rose's heart jumped at the sight of Heather's car. Then she remembered they took Abby's truck.

Behind them, June's car flashed its headlights as it drove past. Rose couldn't blame them for not stopping. Her whole body hurt.

Once Carrie parked and shut the engine, they sat in the car, unspeaking, for almost a full five minutes. Opening the doors to get out—the door chime, the locks clacking—tore into the mournful silence of night. They tried to minimize their sounds by gently closing the doors before walking to the house.

Dew covered two other cars and the motorcycle in the driveway. Rose knew those cars belonged to people who weren't coming back. She didn't want to think about what that meant or how they'd deal with it.

Rose wanted being home to feel better than it did. Instead, it prodded her wounds. This building wasn't only her home, but the place she shared with people she loved. All of whom were gone. Although nothing about the house changed while they were away, everything about it was now different. It was now *her* house. How could something belong to the dead?

Carrie and Nancy whispered. As Rose started for the door, Nancy said, "If you don't mind, we'd like to crash here."

Carrie added, "I don't think anyone wants to be alone tonight."

Rose froze at the front door. Hot tears dropped down her cheeks. The pre-dawn air lingered, damp and cold. With a deep breath, Rose opened the door. Scents of the house bombarded her; tumbling out of the doorway. Drying herbs and life permeated the air. Every sight, every smell, held memories. She wanted to want to breathe in everything, to take in this potent reminder of yesterdays. She instead resented the smells, like they mocked her pain. Like they taunted her by announcing Heather was gone. Alex is gone. Billy is gone. Yesterday is gone.

She turned on the lights, inviting her new family inside.

Nancy screamed. They startled at the figure waiting for them. Rose appeared her Books, ready to strike at Matthew or Jeremiah, or whoever was violating the sanctity of her mother's memory.

"Sorry," Nancy apologized. "I just saw and," she caught her breath. "My mind just," she couldn't get out the words.

Dolly meowed; glowering at Rose and hissing. Rose disappeared her Books. Dolly stretched and again curled into Heather's lap. Heather sat on the couch in the living room, looking tired but at peace, Dolly protecting her.

Rose let out a singular, joyful laugh, and broke into tears. "Home," she said to no one, "she wanted to go home." She ran and hugged her mother.

*   *   *   *   *

Already experienced sleeping on the couch, Nancy claimed it, once they placed Heather in her own bed. Rose offered Carrie her brother's bed.

Lying in her own bed, staring at the ceiling, Rose listened as Carrie snored, asleep in seconds. Rose found herself lost, her thoughts like an impenetrable forest. Surrounded by trees, there seemed no way through. No way forward. The thought ashamed her, but was her mother really here? No. Her mother, her cousin, her brother: all gone.

She wished she could feel them, to know they were alive. She tried imagining them in another room, in another house. It wasn't the same. Was belief the source of her heartache, or could she actually feel the rift their departure tore in the universe? She wasn't aware her thoughts gave way to sleep until she awoke to the sounds of breakfast.

Her heart shrieked. She bounded out of bed, eager to prove she'd had a nightmare. Her mother was making breakfast. Everything was fine and normal, and life could still be happy. Then, at her bedroom door, Rose heard Carrie ask Nancy to pass the butter. She collapsed back onto the bed. It was nearly noon.

Rose pulled on clean clothes, washed her face, then wandered into the hallway. Heather lay in bed, staring at the ceiling, Dolly curled up beside her. *Was Dolly at her side all night? Dolly was my cat. Why is Dolly suddenly so attached to her?* From the hallway, Rose heard purring.

Downstairs, Carrie was making omelets. Nancy made a pot of coffee, and she and Carrie were deep in conversation when Rose entered the room.

"Morning," Rose forced a brief smile. Before she sat, Nancy and Carrie took turns embracing her. Nancy stroked her hair and tried to utter something but welled up instead.

Carrie returned to the stove. Rose had never seen half the pans Carrie had taken out. She felt the urge to yell, to make them stop touching her mother's things, to stop moving things from where Heather left them. As if each time something was moved a remnant of Heather evaporated, until there would be nothing left of her. She remained silent.

Carrie moved expertly and fluidly at the stove, never rushing. With her right hand she cracked eggs into the pan and scrambled them as they cooked. By comparison, she made it look like Heather had never known how to use the stove.

Carrie plated and served. Then she and Nancy joined Rose at the table.

"I've been thinking," Nancy began, her voice lower than usual, as though speaking at a funeral, "my schedule gives me a few days off each week. For a while I can stay with you." She watched Rose for a reaction. "I could help with Heather. Help cook and clean. Would that work?"

Rose shrugged. She pushed her food around. She hadn't the will to eat. Worse, it tasted better than anything her mom ever made; the feeling of food in her mouth made her nauseous.

Carrie looked between Nancy and Rose. "I work… mostly evenings and weekends. I could cook… a few meals, make things to freeze." She paused, resting her hand on Rose's, "I don't mean to be rushing you. My lease expires in August. I can help, you know, financially, too. I'll pay you rent." Before Rose could reply, she added, "But we have time before that's even a decision. You know, give you a chance to get used to, you know."

They worked out their scheduling. Rachel would come by when she could. Every two weeks, when she wasn't travelling, June would stop by. It seemed like they accounted for every minute of every day.

Rose was overwhelmed. She was trying to cope with what happened to her mom. And Alex. And Billy. And yesterday. And now these women—friends of her mother but veritable strangers to her—were moving in. And taking over.

Rose pulled her hand from Carrie, swollen tears threatening to jump from her eyes, and with the scrape of chair legs, turned to run from the kitchen. Blocking her way to the stairs, Heather swayed from their collision. Rose startled at the vacant eyes, at the open mouth, the saliva-shiny lips, the mussed hair, the slept-in clothes. This wasn't Heather.

They stood, face to face. Rose covered her nose, gagging, "What's that smell?"

Nancy jumped to her feet and grabbed Heather's arm, putting a hand around her waist. She guided Heather up the stairs to the bathroom as though she'd done this before.

Rose followed Nancy and Heather, sickened by the trailing stench that stained the air. Nancy helped Heather into the hall bathroom and eased her into the tub.

Nancy delicately removed Heather's clothes. As Nancy thoughtfully stripped her down mother, she talked Heather through it. "I'm going to take off your shirt now. Watch your ears. Very good, Heather. I'm going to lift your legs so we can take off your pants. Will you let me do that?"

Rose watched Nancy wash Heather, rinsing the soil from her body. She started to realize she needed more help than she originally thought.

While she toweled Heather down, Nancy said, "I'll grab a stack of adult diapers from work. I'll make sure you never have to do this yourself."

Rose felt obligated to stay until Nancy finished. But she couldn't watch her mother like this. As she left the bathroom, Nancy said, "Good idea, get clothes. Maybe sweats. Something comfortable and easy."

Rose rummaged through Heather's closet and dresser. Everything smelled of her mom. Everything reminded Rose of something Heather did when she wore this blouse or that.

On top of the dresser was a small photo frame of Heather and Peter as children. Rose bundled the clothes as she stared at it. "Uncle Peter," she mouthed. She never thought about Alex having to do anything more than watch him wandering about. In the hall, she heard Nancy helping her naked mother out of the tub. She wondered if hidden in all of Alex's talk of helping around the house was hours of washing shit off her father's back.

Once Heather was dressed in black-faded-to-gray sweatpants and sweatshirt, she started for the hallway. She tapped shoulders with Nancy as she pushed past, bumping into Rose, who couldn't get out of the way fast enough. Heather bounced off and bumped Rose a second time.

"Hey," Rose pushed her mother out the door. Nancy washed her hands in the sink, her forehead soaked with perspiration. Rose started to leave but stopped. "Nancy?"

"Yeah?"

"Thanks." It didn't feel enough. She was drowning in fear of being alone with Heather and just being alone in general. Her voice quivered, "Really. Thank you. That was," she fought not to cry, "amazing. I never…."

Nancy smiled at her. "Everyone thinks nurses have glamourous jobs. Seducing rich doctors and sexy patients. This is what I do. Heather was… is my friend. She deserves to be cared for."

Rose nodded, crying again. "I'm going to go to bed," she whimpered.

Nancy dried her hands and folded the towel, placing it squarely on the vanity. She gave Rose a hug. "I'm sure it feels like you're all alone. I will never tell you how to feel, but we're here for you. Until you want us to leave, you'll never truly be alone."

Chapter Ninety-Seven

ays blended. Days when Rose felt numb were an improvement. Anything triggered tears. But she wasn't alone. She frequently caught Carrie or Nancy crying. *Heather isn't even their mother.* If they cried, why did she feel so ashamed when she did?

She hadn't thought of Alex in days. For all she knew, Alex and Billy were together, having a grand old time. Or dead. She sometimes heard the others talking about Alex, but with each day that passed, any hope they voiced withered. Lately, they wondered whether they'd ever find out what happened to her.

It was Sunday; Heather had been a zombie for three days. For the first time, no one was available for the evening.

"I'm so sorry," Carrie repeated for the third time as she stood half out the front doorway. "I tried to get my shift covered, but…. I'll be back around midnight. That's," she looked for a clock, "eight hours."

Rose nodded. "I think I could use a little time alone."

"You sure?"

Rose shrugged. "I haven't been alone since…. I'll be okay." She wasn't sure she was being truthful, but Carrie half-leaving was more painful than being alone.

"See ya in a bit," Carrie closed the door. Rose listened to Carrie's motorcycle rev and pull away.

Rose peered at the empty house. Just two weeks ago, life filled the house. Alex and Billy and Heather and her. It was as though the house itself died.

Carrie had left them dinner, so Rose went looking for Heather.

She found Heather, Dolly at her feet, in the upstairs hallway, looking at where the attic stairs used to be. Rose folded and closed them two days ago. Seeing Rose, Dolly, as per usual, hissed and ran off.

"It's been three days, Mom. She's not coming back."

Heather didn't move.

Rose wished it wasn't true, wished she didn't believe her own words. There was such finality to them: *Alex is dead.*

Rose stared at her mother, her slovenly sweat-clothes. Her greasy hair combed flat to her scalp. No makeup, no care for appearance. Heather was unkempt. This woman, her mouth wet with drool, wasn't her mother. Rose's heart felt like a spring popped from the mechanism. Seeing her like this, gaunt, vapid, sickly; it was like her mother was replaced with an inferior model, a broken prototype; and instead of being the center of the universe, the heart of the house, she was a broken chore, a surface always in need of dusting, a carpet stained and dented by furniture they no longer owned.

Rose guided her mother by the arm down to the kitchen and placed her into a seat. Carrie left the plates set, as always, perfectly. The golden-brown chicken breast with a thick comma of gravy dusted with diced herbs to one side, with a perfect half-circle of rice—she used an ice-cream scoop—and small salad to the other. Carrie always carried the plates to the table with a rag in her hand. As she put them down, she spun the plate and wiped the rim.

Carrie had already diced the chicken on Heather's plate into baby-bite-sized morsels and skipped the rice.

After Rose finished eating, she slid her chair closer to Heather's. Using her fingers, she loaded a teaspoon with chicken-bits.

"Open wide." With no spark of recognition, with no sign of intent, Heather's mouth opened in proximity to the spoon.

She watched Heather chew, disgusted by the parted lips and the little bits that fell out.

Rose cleared the table. She looked guiltily at the dishes in the sink. She scraped them off and placed them in the dishwasher. Carrie would clean them without comment, but that wasn't fair to her, either.

Heather had already wandered from the kitchen. She followed her mother, used a dishrag to wipe her face, and taking her by the elbow, guided her upstairs.

Rose pulled back the covers and eased Heather into bed. She pulled the sheet and blanket over her mother, tucking it at her chest, her arms resting at her sides. She sat on the bed beside her mother and looked at the woman who lay there, staring at the ceiling. She touched her mother's cheek, caressed it, and couldn't help but cry.

Satisfied that there was nothing more to do, Rose stood to leave. She turned back. "This isn't fair," she said aloud. "It's not fair to you, and not to me."

Heather didn't respond, mouth-breathing at the ceiling.

Rose kissed Heather's cheek, then raised her mother's head enough to extricate the pillow from under it. She hugged it to her chest before placing it over her mother's face and pressed down with all her weight.

Heather's body was compliant, like she was okay with this. Rose kept pressing. A flinch of an arm, a tick of the leg. Rose made sure the pillow was tight.

A hand raised into the air. It didn't reach for Rose, who half-expected it to grab and push at her. Fingers opened and clasped. It didn't mean Heather didn't want this. Then the other hand, in a gentle arc, collided with Rose's arm, gently following her contour to her shoulder, her neck, her face, where the warm back of her mother's hand rested on her cheek. Rose's tears darkened spots on the pillow.

Rose threw the pillow to the floor and threw her body onto her mother's, digging her hands under her mother's back, feeling her mother's arms descend into a half-hearted embrace.

"I can't, Mommy," Rose cried, tears and mucus smeared between their faces. "You shouldn't have to be like this. It should'a been me. He asked for me. I wouldn't know. I wouldn't feel anything. It'd be okay, Mommy. I can't. Not like this. Not anymore."

Rose lay until Dolly wandered in. Dolly, as per her new routine, jumped on the bed and curled up beside Heather's head. Rose stared at the fluffy tuxedo cat and pet her. Dolly whined and tucked in tighter against Heather.

Rose fled the room. She washed her face. She changed her clothes. She appeared her Book and vanished.

Chapter Ninety-Eight

ose waited outside the trailer door, the dark ruins of her father's house in the distance. This trailer was larger than Abby's, and newer. For the longest time, she listened to the sounds within. These people were oblivious to the suffering in her life. They were a family of four, her father's family, and that didn't include her. Not yet.

Rose climbed the simple wood landing. She made a fist. She knocked. Inside, the sounds of activity, of family, stopped. The television kept chattering mindlessly. Questions, statements; *Someone's at the door….*

Someone fumbled with the latch. She recalled from Abby's trailer that the door was a screen and a solid door put together, and if she opened the wrong latch, she only opened part of the door.

The door opened. Her father wore sweatpants and a t-shirt stretched around his belly. "Rose," he asked, "what are you doing here?"

"Who's there?"

Eric turned inside and answered Jennifer, his wife, "It's Rosemary."

"What does she want? Everything okay?"

Eric turned to Rose, "What do you want?"

Rose felt herself boiling away, waiting to explode. Each time she opened her mouth to speak, she feared erupting into a fit of hysteric tears. She didn't answer, however she tried.

"Where's your mom?" Eric scanned the street-light lit road. He called out, "Heather?"

"Dad," Rose said at last, "I need help." *Let me in. Please let me in. Stop treating me like a stranger. I'm your daughter. You're my only parent.*

"Where's your mom?" he asked again.

"What does she want? Eric," Jennifer came to the door in sweatpants. Her t-shirt was neon pink, "are you going to let her in?"

Eric backed from the door. "Did Heather drop you off? You two have a fight?"

Rose wrapped her arms around her father's middle. "Mommy's gone." Tears wetted his shirt.

Eric closed the door. "What do you mean, *gone*? Where? Did she tell you to come live with me?"

"Eric, look at her. Give her a moment." Jennifer turned, "Hunter, Caitlyn, go to your room."

"Mom," Caitlyn whined, "we're watching—"

"What did I say?"

There was silence until the door closed, her children away. Jennifer stroked Rose's back. "Sweetheart, what happened? Where's Heather?"

Rose whimpered and released her father from her bearhug. She wiped her tear-soaked face. Her cheeks flushed red with embarrassment. She cycled through the words in her head, her body trembling.

"Rosemary," Jennifer stroked Rose's cheek, "it's okay. Start from the beginning and just tell me the story. Tell me what happened to Rosey today. You woke up *and....*"

Rose felt nauseous. She couldn't open her mouth.

"Come on Rose," Eric's tone wasn't as soothing as his wife's.

Rose finally took a breath. "Billy, Heather, Alex, Abby." *I got their names out. Now I only have to say the words*, "All dead."

Neither Eric nor Jennifer said anything.

Rose started crying again, hot tears streaking down her face as her body trembled. She snorted and coughed. "Alex got her magic."

Jennifer looked shocked and stared at Eric. She placed a hand on his arm, but he shrugged it off.

"She said she knew how to get Billy back. It was horrible. This man killed Mommy's friends."

Jennifer gasped.

Eric whimpered, "It worked? Alex...andrea has—had magic?"

Jennifer scowled at Eric. To Rose, she soothed, "Go on, sweetheart. I know this isn't easy but keep going."

Rose nodded. "The man took Mommy's...," she hesitated. *Do they know the word? Has Jennifer even seen a coin?* With her hands, she formed a circle over her chest and continued, "... soul. He made Alex swallow it."

Jennifer looked confused. Eric's face was reddening, his

bottom lip playing in his bushy moustache. "What did that do to her? Did that kill Heather?"

Rose shook her head and nodded.

Jennifer sighed. "So, Heather's not dead. Oh, thank God."

Rose shook her head and to her father said, "It made her like Peter."

Eric slammed his fist on the table. "I fucking told her."

Jennifer chided him, "Eric, now's not the time. Was Peter the one you told me about?" She whispered the word, so Rose mightn't hear, "Zombie?"

"Yup," Eric confirmed. "That's the one."

Rose continued, "Then he made Abby break her oath to Alex and sent them to…. He said Matthew will kill them."

"Wait, what?" Eric looked shocked. "How in hell do you break a Familiar's oath?"

Jennifer turned to her husband, "What are you talking about?"

Eric explained a Familiar to Jennifer. "It's all true, Jenn. I told you she was crazy, but apparently it was all true." He looked at Rose. "Am I right? Tell her you've seen it. Tell her magic is real."

Jennifer smiled like she was trying to get the joke rather than be the butt of it. "Stop being an asshole, Eric. Rose, how did you get here tonight?"

"Magic is real, Jennifer. I've done it." Rose confirmed.

Eric froze. After an excruciating minute, he asked, "Done?" He glanced at Jennifer, who was faking a polite laugh. To Rose, his tone deep and depressive, he added, "Heather did the thing? Heather gave you magic too?"

"No." She appeared her Book. The suddenness of its appearance startled both Jennifer and Eric.

Jennifer grasped her chest in shock, "What the fuck?"

"Take that out of my house, Rose," Eric demanded.

Jennifer looked between them. "Where did that book come from?"

Eric pointed at it. "It's cursed. They're magic. Spellbooks."

"What are you talking about, Eric? Are you saying Heather was… not crazy?"

"Oh, she was crazy all right." He addressed Rose, "Take that thing and get out."

Rose whimpered, "And go where?"

Jennifer placed a cautioning hand on Eric's arm. "Don't send her away. She has no one else." She looked at Rose, "Honey, do you need to stay with us?"

Before Rose answered, Eric commanded, "You cannot not stay here with that Book."

"But Dad," Rose tried to explain, tried to tell him the Book wasn't dangerous, but Eric snatched it from her hands.

"No fucking Book comes into my house," he threatened.

"Give it back, Dad," Rose pleaded.

"No good has ever come to our family from the pursuit of magic." Eric warned, "These things are evil."

"What are you talking about, Eric?" Jennifer asked, "What's in that book?"

"Give it back, Dad," Rose lunged for it, falling short as Eric stepped back, opening the Book.

"You're welcome to stay with us, Rose. You're my daughter. You're family, but not with this. If you stay, you must never talk about magic again. One word and you're out. I will not have magic ruin my family ever again," Eric said bluntly.

Eric grabbed the pages that stood upright from the open Book and ripped them out.

To Rose, the paper tearing sounded like trees falling, like a rocket engine, like a seam opening in the earth and separating wider and wider. Her chest burned. It hurt like a dagger pushed, slowly, so it broke her skin, nicked its way through her breastbone, and slid into her heart. All she could do was scream at the pain.

Jennifer looked from the Book to Rose, to Eric and back. "What is," she jabbed the air at the glowing coin in Rose's chest. "Are you doing that?" she tried to ask over Rose's anguish. "Peter, stop it, you're hurting her."

Eric crumpled the severed pages and threw them to the ground. He grabbed the book, half in each hand and wrenched, his face hellish, trying to rip the Book into two.

Rose fell to her knees, her fingers clawing at her chest, drawing blood. She roared in agony, squealing and crying and choking on dry heaves.

They all heard it, saw the specks of dust bursting into the air as the Book's spine separated. It tore a little, a little more. Threads stitching pages together snapped, one than another.

Rose fell prostrate, the pain leaving her little control beyond writhing in it. Her bladder emptied as she convulsed.

Jennifer screamed, "Stop it, Eric," and grabbed the Book, prying it from his hands and throwing it to the ground. When he glared at her, she screamed, "Do you even see what you're doing to her?"

As though seeing Rose for the first time, Eric dropped to his knees. "Oh my God, Rose, I'm so sorry." He placed his hand on her cheek, shocked at how hot she felt. His words came out in a gradually slowing frenzy. "I didn't mean to. Rose, I'm sorry. It's just, you know, your mom and magic. I was angry, I didn't realize it was doing anything to you. I thought you were shouting. I thought you were angry."

Rose reached past her father and collected the Book and the crumpled pages, drawing them into her chest. She glared at her father, her eyes fiery and bloodshot, speckled with burst blood vessels.

As Rose struggled to stand, her jeans stinking of urine, Jennifer helped her, "I'll get you something to change into. Maybe you should just sit. I'll pour you a glass. Water okay? Something stronger? I think brandy would be okay, considering…."

Rose shook her head violently. "It's not your fault, Jennifer." Her voice was ruined from screaming, almost husky. It tasted of blood. "You made promises, Dad. You were supposed to do to me what Peter did to Alex."

Jennifer spoke under Rose's words, "What is she talking about, Eric?"

"Instead, I had to take magic for myself. I had to steal it from a man and use a Book." Her coin was still glowing. There was a dark crack in its edge, like a sizeable quarter of it shattered off. The ragged edge and web of cracks warned the entire disk might fail at any moment. "You did this to me. You're a coward. You're a liar." She started for the door. "Heather may be barely alive, but at least she's there. You walked away. You left me. You're dead. You understand? You're dead to me. If I ever see you again, you will be."

She opened the door, having no trouble with the dual doors. She stood in the doorway, reeling from the lingering pain. Everything hurt, and it wasn't subsiding.

"Eric, please tell me *what the fuck* is going on," Jennifer shouted. "Sweetheart," she said softly to Rose, "you don't have to leave. Just take a few deep breaths. We'll sort this out, I promise. Stay,

I'll give you a change of clothes, you can take a shower. I want to understand. I want to help you."

Rose turned to her. "I need to get back. My mother needs me." She took a breath and in a softer tone, added, "Thank you, Jenn, for trying. I'll remember you were kind to me."

"Do you need a ride, sweetie? I can drive you home," Jennifer offered.

Eric did his best to moderate his tone, "Please, Rose. Listen to Jennifer. I'm sorry."

Rose opened her book and vanished.

Chapter Ninety-Nine

or the past three days, since attempting to reconnect with her father, Rose told no one what happened in the hours Carrie was at work. She desired to unload the burden, but didn't feel capable of discussing it. It wasn't ambivalence that stopped her: she felt nothing. She wondered what Alex would do in the same situation. How she would handle it. She doubted Alex would have had the strength to ease Heather's suffering, either.

Dolly remained at Heather's side. Any time Rose came across her mother, Dolly was there, winding between and around Heather's legs, sitting in Heather's lap, sleeping on Heather's chest. Rose assumed the cat was being protective, but more likely missed the regularity with which Heather once fed her.

She barely thought on her father. It was too painful. Recalling his angry words, his ignorant anger at magic, also meant feeling her coin cracking, breaking, crumbling. She carried her Book covetously now, determined to protect it at all costs.

She tried repairing her Book. She hoped to fuse the pages back into place, to mend the broken spine, but no spells within the covers or skill she possessed could heal the inanimate thing. She relied on clear tape and glue. The Book remained askew; it sat awkwardly, flipping open wide, always to the same page, showing the broken and fraying guts of string that held them in place. It felt fragile; it felt betrayed.

Rose did think about Betty. Rose never paid her much heed to begin with. She was an older woman, maybe in her mid-twenties or thirties, and on first notice, Rose thought she was ridiculous. Flaming red hair stifled with bright blue barrettes—the type Rose forbid her mother from putting in her hair once she was old enough to see how stupid the fake molded bows looked—and her silly cat t-shirts. At the Library, Betty had been the bravest among them. Betty could have cowered with the rest of them, with Alex, but chose instead to attack. She did not get in line and walk to her death. She went out fighting. It was a blaze of glory. Jeremiah lit her Book on fire, just as her father had tried to tear hers apart. Rose couldn't help but replay the death over and over again, Betty's coin burning up in her chest. Rose felt Betty a compatriot: Jeremiah killed Betty, offering a warning Rose wouldn't understand until her own father tried to kill her too. Inadvertently or otherwise.

For the past three days she hadn't uttered a word about it. She wasn't sure if she felt bad for what she'd tried to do or weak because she'd failed. Not that Heather could forgive her, but her apology was caring for her mother. She'd even showered her once without assistance.

In these three days, Carrie and Nancy handled the two abandoned cars in the driveway. Rose never asked. The cars were just gone.

Rose wondered why no one ever came to the house looking for Betty or Donna or Colette or Lydia, or Marta or Abby, for that matter. It was as though they were just gone, and the fact they existed at all vanished with them. It made Rose wonder about Nancy and June and Carrie and Rachel; why were they always here? Why didn't they have families to go home to? Rose pitied them, and yet, it made her feel closer, like they were all part of a newly formed club of orphans.

Carrie and Nancy spent the most time at the house. Followed by Rachel. When she wasn't travelling, June would stop by for a day or two. She spent so much time living in hotel beds her nights not travelling had to be spent in her own. Sometimes she brought Rose small airport gifts and trinkets from the cities she'd visited or connected through. It was her way of reminding Rose that even apart, she thought about her. It sounded sweet but felt hollow.

She appreciated the constant help. There were so many things Heather did that Rose didn't have to do, like dust and vacuum and cook and clean up afterwards. There were many other things that Heather did that no one looked after. Six days was enough for weeds to infiltrate Heather's garden. There was never a ceramic tub of warm milk thickening to yogurt on the counter. The herbs hanging from the ceiling began to vanish as Carrie used them to season her food. The transformation was underway: Heather's house was becoming hers.

Not once in three days did Rose waste time thinking about Alex. Her cousin might pop into her head, but Rose would banish her. Alex was bad luck. Alex was cursed. Alex was responsible for all her pain. If not for Alex, her mother would still be normal. If not for Alex, her brother would still be here. If not for Alex, she wouldn't have had to play second fiddle to an older sister after so many years as the eldest. If not for Alex, her parents would still be together. If not for Alex, her life would be perfect. If not for Alex, she wouldn't have so much pain and rage bottled up inside.

On this third day, six days since returning from the Library, almost three weeks since Billy leapt from Sacrifice Stone, Rose sat on the couch in the living room. Carrie paced the kitchen. Dinner made, she was late for work. Rachel was running behind, and Carrie didn't want to leave Rose unattended.

"It's okay, Carrie," Rose shouted from the couch, where she played with Heather's Book. "I can be alone for a half hour."

Carrie said, "It's just, you know, Rachel should be more responsible."

Rose opened the cover and pinched the pages, so they flapped by, teasing their symbols in a blur. "I'm not her responsibility. I'm not yours, either." Rose realized how that sounded when Carrie didn't reply. "I appreciate everything you do. I just worry you're, what's the word my mom used all the time, neglect, I worry you're neglecting your own lives."

Carrie came out of the kitchen. She hadn't gelled her short, dark hair into a spiky mess, but let it fall naturally. It looked messy and uneven but took an edge off Carrie and rounded her face. She looked younger, even kind of cute. She wore her rubber clogs and white drawstring chefs' pants, a white t-shirt with a blue sports bra showing through.

She gave Rose a look that Rose didn't quite understand. *Does she know what happened?* Rose felt a little spark of worry: if accused, what would they force her to do?

"There wasn't much of a life before, to be honest," Carrie still made the face. "You see the hours I keep. When I had friends, they went out without me. So what if I don't go out? My liver could use the break."

Rose imagined Carrie partying and drunk, probably doing drugs and having sex all the time. "I guess I just don't want to make you late. I mean, if you hafta go to work…." She didn't want to bring up Sunday. She didn't want to use it as the example.

Dolly slunk into the room. Heather wouldn't be far behind.

Carrie turned on her heels. Her tone changed. Everything about her changed, "I left you alone Sunday," Carrie began.

Here it comes. Oh, crap.

Heather wandered in, shuffling to her chair.

"Something happened."

"Nothing happened."

"Come on, your eyes were all bloody. What happened? You can tell me."

Is she testing me, or doesn't she know?

Heather sat. Dolly leapt onto her lap. Dolly began kneading when something caught her eye.

"Come on, Rose. I noticed right away. You can trust me. I was there, too."

Rose fought to get the words out, "I don't know what you're talking about."

As though stalking prey, Dolly slunk off Heather's lap, her body tight and crouched. She leapt from the chair to the coffee table to the end table, where she tucked her feet in, fitting her whole body on Heather's Book.

Typical cat. Rose glared at Dolly. *Glad I was done with that.*

Carrie put one hand on her hip, gesturing with the other. "I get it, Rose. Sometimes it's hard to understand what you're feeling. Especially at your age."

Dolly called out. It was half meow, half yowl.

"What's that supposed to mean?"

Carrie fought the urge to reply in kind. Instead her tone was soothing, "What it means is that I promise I'll make sure you never have to feel left alone again. It's not fair. It was too soon. I'm so sorry, Rose."

Rose was about to say okay when Dolly yowled again, a startling shriek like her tail had been stepped on. Rose brushed her hand to shoo the cat from the Book, but Dolly hissed and swatted, scratching skin that would bleed after a moment.

"Shut up, Dolly," Rose shouted at the cat, who was making so much noise they couldn't hear one another speaking.

Carrie's shoulders lowered. She muttered, "Fuck, Rachel. I'm going to be late." She looked at Rose. "You sure you're… okay? If I leave you won't do anything stupid?"

Rose realized she couldn't reply too enthusiastically. Everything felt like a confession. "I promise," she said between Dolly's growing growl.

Carrie was talking herself into leaving. She collected her things and swung her purse over her arm. She opened the door and froze.

"Carrie?"

Carrie looked at Rose, her face pale with fright.

Sparks flew past her; one struck the ceiling. Dust and sheetrock rained down. Dolly hissed. Rose leapt to her feet. Jeremiah had found them.

Carrie shouted at Rose, "Get…," she couldn't figure out where to tell Rose to hide. They simultaneously appeared their Books.

Dolly yowled again, louder than before, as though Heather's Book was hurting her. There was nothing Rose could do, not now: Someone was racing in.

From the look of the muscle shirt and the thick bruise-covered arms, Abby had been fighting quite some while. A Book in her hands, she fired out the door as she and Marta retreated inside.

"Quick," Abby cried, "I need a Book. Anyone have a spare?"

Rose glared at Abby. "You already have a Book."

Carrie called to Rose, "Rose, the Book on the table. Give her that."

Rose grabbed the edge of the Heather's Book and tipped a begrudging Dolly from the cover. *Not Mom's Book.* Dolly stalked back to Heather's lap.

Marta took it from her. Rose tried to hold onto it but was too shocked to do anything. She let it slip from her fingers. "You died."

More sparks flew in from outside. Abby returned fire.

"Yes. No." Marta delicately opened the Book.

Dolly yowled again. She was kneading Heather's lap, meowing non-stop. *What is wrong with her?*

More sparking bolts, more accurate this time. Abby dropped to her knee, groaning. Carrie was too close to the door and struck off her feet. Spilling to the ground, her Book spun from her hand, pages turning wildly on their own.

"Rose," Marta seemed too calm for the panic of the situation. "This Book is empty."

"What?"

"All the pages are blank, Rose." Marta held the Book open to Rose: the pages unwritten. Oxidation around the edges, finger smudges and stains still dotted the page, but not a single illuminated symbol remained. "Where'd the spells go?"

Rose had just been looking at that Book. *It was fine. It was normal. And then Dolly sat on it. Is that why she's been so weird since I got my Book? She took the spells? What the hell does a cat need with magic?*

She looked at Dolly, as though the cat might confess. Dolly purred unusually loudly on Heather's lap, seemingly contently oblivious to the chaos.

The light changed as a figure stepped into the doorway. A Book in his hand, he fired sparks. Twice at Abby, knocking her off her feet as she squealed and cried in pain. Once at Marta and once at Rose.

Rose convulsed at the strike. It felt like knives stabbing clear through her flesh. She raised her Book into her line of sight and returned fire. Her lightning was red, ragged and fiery. Her bolts shot through the air, nearly a dozen of them. The doorway exploded in a shower of sparks as some missed their mark, but the others knocked his body about, driving him backwards onto the porch.

Rose didn't realize how much she enjoyed the action, the power surging through her body. She started forward when she heard a familiar cry.

"Help me up, Rose."

Rose looked around the room. Everyone else, clawing their way to their feet, paused—they heard it, too.

"I need your help, Rose."

More sparks left burning cinders on the walls. Some of these came from behind the man in the doorway, who turned from them and, shouting from his Book, fired at the other man who was returning fire.

Heather sat expectantly, Dolly in her lap.

Rose touched the cat. Her fur, electric and loaded with static, discharged like a slap. Dolly hissed at her, and in a fit of spinning claws and fur, bolted away.

"Rosemary!"

Rose saw the shadow re-enter the doorway. She grabbed her mother's arm and yanked Heather to her feet. Rose was struck twice before she turned around. Her legs gave out under her. She dropped hard to her knees.

"Rose," Heather cried, the concern on her face overwritten with anger. Still holding Rose's shoulder for support, Heather raised her hand. Bolts of electricity shot from her fingertips. Rose couldn't take her eyes off her mother: Heather held no Book.

Rose climbed to her feet. Even at this distance, Rose recognized the second man on the lawn: George.

Sparks flew from Carrie, Abby, Rose, and Heather. Marta crawled behind the couch.

George fired, but not at them.

The man grunted, firing twice more before dropping to his knees. He glanced back at George, taking multiple strikes in the instant his head was turned.

The man, hit from all around, clawed at the doorframe, his hands convulsed and couldn't secure purchase. His Book tumbled from his grasp. He dropped like deadweight.

As George stepped over the dropped man, he discarded his Book. Stepping to one side, he dropped to his knees, his hands raised in surrender.

Abby threatened him into a chair.

"Mom?" Rose looked up at her mother, eyes wide.

"I'm here, baby," Heather breathed. She collapsed back into the couch, her hands trembling from fatigue. She closed her eyes.

Rose rushed to embrace her mother. Heather could barely hold her.

Carrie's eyes were wide with amazement. Her clothes smoked where the sparks left charred stains. She raised her shirt to examine her wounds. Her flesh was equally charred and raw where hit. She winced, "Heather? Abby? Marta?"

"Watch him, watch him," George warned from his chair. The other man was coming around.

Rose raced across the room and took his Book. "How's this feel?" She ripped out pages and tugged, twisting, and separating pages from the cover.

Abby asked, "What the hell are you doing?"

Rose motioned to the man, but he wasn't in agony. He wasn't struggling. He stared at the crazy girl who tore up a Book. Rose studied the mess in her hands as he started crawling out the door.

Rose was furious. *Why doesn't the same fucking rules apply to them? Why didn't tearing up the Book kill him?* She threw down his Book, cover and pages separating like feathers after a pillow fight. She snared him by the back of the neck and cradled her Book in her other hand. The words she spoke dripped with her disgust. She wanted to tear him to pieces and only destroyed a Book. She cast her spell, firing lightning into his skull. He convulsed, sparks racing across his body. She wouldn't let go, even as his flesh charred against her palm. She kept rereading the last line, firing again and again.

He opened his mouth as if screaming a billow of steam. Rose kept firing, his body jerking with each strike like it hurt, and as long as he reacted, she wanted him to be in pain.

"Easy, Rose," Carrie cried out. "He's dead. You can stop."

Rose wasn't so sure. His feet kicked. His skin twitched. She kept firing and firing, her guttural words spoken in staccato, her eyes whizzing over the page as fast as her twitching mouth could keep up.

Marta collected the damaged Book and its scattered innards. "Maybe she's okay."

Rose hesitated. Knowing she'd only hurt whoever languished in that Book refreshed her vitriol. She returned to her Book. She continued her attack even though the man no longer moved. Even though his skin was browning.

Heather wrapped her arms around Rose and pulled her away. Rose immediately felt the shift of weight as Heather went from pulling on her to leaning against her, as though getting up and crossing the room exhausted Heather's energy. She shushed her daughter. "It's okay, Rose. We're safe now. The bad man is gone. I'm here. I'm back. Dolly brought me back."

"Back from where?" Rose pulled from her mother. *But Dolly erased the Book.* Unsupported, Heather crumpled to the ground.

"Momma," Rose asked, picking her up and holding her steady, "how?"

Carrie looked from Marta to Abby to Heather and asked them all, "What happened? We thought you were dead. Is Alex okay?" Carrie checked the door, as if expecting Alex to walk in.

Rose bristled. She pointed at George, sitting in the living room. He winced at the sting of her fingertip. "What about that?"

Heather held onto Rose, trembling from the effort of standing. Rose walked her mother over and eased her into the couch.

Abby lifted George's Book from the floor. She raised it slightly like it was the conch that let her speak. "Alex and I were at Matthew's apartment. George shows up. He brought Billy. Like they were friends." Her mouth looks like she has more to say but nothing comes out until she looked at George. "He helped us."

Rose only heard one part. Her heart felt like a spring overwound by anticipation. *George brought Billy? Why isn't he here? Where's my brother?* There were two possibilities that danced through Rose's mind. She latched on to hope, asking, "Did Billy stay with Alex?"

George shook his head. He dropped his face into his palms.

Abby pushed him. "Why help us?"

George looked up, tears streaking his ruddy face. "Sara told me to. When she was…," he hesitated. "Sara was in Alex. When I was here, before. You knew that?" Abby nodded. "She sent me to save Billy. To help Alex. I," he shook his head, "didn't think it would turn out like that."

Abby turned from him.

"I tried. I didn't know—" George stammered.

Rose heard their exchange and watched their reactions. The way their eyes cast down, the way they couldn't look at one another. She knew what that meant, and that so disagreed with her she could only assume she misunderstood. "What happened to Billy?" Rose looked at Abby and then at George. "What happened to my brother?"

"Your brother died," Heather told her. When Rose contradicted her, Heather explained, "I've always known."

Rose wished she'd been stronger with the pillow the other night. "How could you have known? You're a fucking liar!"

"He's gone," Abby said, tugging on her shirt. She groaned, "Ugh, I'm never wearing a stupid muscle-shirt again."

Carrie said, "That's all you wear."

Rose couldn't understand why no one was answering her. "What the fuck are you talking about?"

"These shirts are all Alex. Maybe I wore one once, and she made the association. *Abby wears muscle tees.* She made me obsessed with them."

Rose shouted slowly, like she was trying to have her lips read, "Where is Billy?"

Carrie added, "And Alex. Where is she?"

Rose cast Carrie a caustic glance. *Always Alex. Fuck Alex.*

"Sit down, Rosemary." Heather patted the cushion at her right. She lovingly pet Dolly, who was sleeping, curled up on her lap.

Rose snapped at Abby, "What the fuck happened?"

Tears spilled from Abby's eyes. The large woman took Rose into a bearhug. "I'm so sorry, Rose. I'm so sorry."

Whatever Abby was trying to tell her was too big for the narrow opening Rose allowed. It just stood outside muted, unable to come in. "Sorry for what?"

Abby held Rose at arm's length. "Matthew murdered your brother. Alex tried…, she did everything to save him."

The words hit her like speeding trucks. She tried making sense of them. Alex tried? Alex always tries but never succeeds. "She clearly didn't try very hard." Rose was still talking about Alex's track record of failure when Abby broke in, her voice as tearful and ruddy as her face, "Alex died protecting your brother."

The breath left Rose. A punch to her gut wouldn't have knocked the wind from her as thoroughly. "They're dead?" The words sounded pitiful and small. They didn't get far from her, just hung in the room, both question and answer.

Carrie sat beside Heather in the place she asked Rose to sit. "Are you okay Heather?"

"Rose," Heather's tone was serene. She seemed unphased by the news. "You have to understand, Rose. A lot of things happened to your brother since he disappeared."

"What are you talking about? You can't know what happened to him." Rose couldn't slow her heart. It was galloping away in her chest, like it already knew something she didn't. "You've been all distraught. Everything was *I've got to find Billy. Billy is missing. You can't go, Rose, because Billy is missing.*"

Heather said matter-of-factly, "I've known for a very long time he wasn't coming back. He told me, before you were even born." Rose shouted, "What the fuck are you even talking about?" while Heather asked, "You remember that night, Marta?"

Marta nodded.

Carrie looked stunned as she tried to slide as far away from Heather as the couch would allow. "You knew? You were both dead." She looked at Marta and back at Heather. "How is that even… well, apparently everything is fucking possible." She looked at her lap and softly added, "Except for Alex. We really lost her?" She looked at Abby. "How'd she die?"

Abby took a long breath. "Death came for Billy." Abby's eyes welled up. "It saw Alex and…," she swallowed, tears running down her face. "It *recognized* her. Death recognized Alex and… it became the Reaper."

Heather looked into her lap and whimpered.

"What's the Reaper?" Rose cast her gaze around the room for answers.

Heather looked up, her face wet with tears. "Sweetheart, the Reaper comes for you when you resist death. There's no escaping it."

Abby nodded. "Alex was *amazing*. I've never seen anything like that. She was keeping Billy alive with one hand and fighting the Reaper with the other." She sobbed, "It was too powerful. Nothing she did mattered."

Rose crossed her arms. "Nothing Alex does ever matters."

Heather, Abby, and Carrie gasped at her remark. Heather chided her, "Do not talk about Alex like that again."

Rose raised her chin, "Why not?"

Heather pursed her lips before speaking sternly. "Because I can forgive you for a lot of things. Even things you did because you were in too much pain while I was gone. But I cannot forgive you for disparaging Alex."

Rose's heart skipped several beats. *She knows I tried smothering her?* The words came out so tiny, "You know?"

"And I forgive you, Rose."

"For what?" Carrie looked at them both.

Rose wouldn't say. Heather placed her hand on Carrie's knee and softly replied, "For things between a mother and her daughter."

Rose was quiet. Everyone stared at her. She wanted to change the focus. She turned to Abby, "Then what happened?" She was waiting for the part where Alex failed to save her brother so she could point it out to her mother. So she could rub it in Heather's face. *See, Alex didn't try that hard.*

Abby pointed at the charred body. "This schmuck shows up. In the middle of everything that's going on and he attacks me and Marta." She pointed at George. "He started fighting on our side. It was like the world was ending. The Reaper is killing Alex. We're outgunned. The last thing Alex did was cast the spell that got us out of there. She sent us here."

Abby collapsed into a pile on the floor, pulling on her muscle shirt like she was trying to rend her clothes. "I miss her so much. Being without her hurts." She sobbed.

Marta knelt at her side, soothing her. "I know, Abby. Alex saved us all."

The words escaped Rose's mouth, unbidden, "She didn't save my brother."

Abby looked up at Rose with an expression that begged Rose to stop. Like Rose's comments were causing her harm. "No one survives the Reaper, Rose. No one cheats death."

Rose couldn't believe the words. She didn't want to. For all her resentment, she realized she didn't want to lose Alex. She pointed at Marta and Heather. "But they came back, couldn't Alex...."

Heather shook her head. "That's different, sweetheart." She petted Dolly. "I read from a Book. Dolly found me in it and brought me back." She laughed. "All this time. Sitting on my newspapers. Witches and their cats. Makes sense now." She scratched Dolly's chin. "You save witches from Books. You saved me. Yes. You did."

Marta added, "And I was in Oblivion. Alex gave me one of her coins." She looked at Heather apologetically. "Had she kept it, maybe she'd still be alive."

Heather soothed, "It's not your fault, Marta. She would do anything to save the two of you."

Rose didn't want to believe it. She didn't want to believe any of it. *If Billy were really dead, I'd feel it.* There was no gaping hole. Just her savage resentment for these women telling stories that couldn't be true. She wanted to pull out her Book and use it to burn down the house. She wanted to punch holes in the walls and pull the whole thing to the ground with her bare hands. She wanted to scream and rage and strike these women for telling her lies.

Then she realized what she needed to do. The plan left her mouth as soon as she formed the thought, "I'm going to destroy Matthew. I'll find Billy. You'll see. I'll even find Alex. I'll bring them both home."

Acknowledgements

Following the enthusiastic reception of The Book Club (From the Books of Alexandrea series), I was excited to get this second story into fighting shape. A lot goes into getting a book into the world, and while independent press is largely do-it-yourself, I am helped by countless people from alpha and beta readers to the fans of the book who eagerly await the next installment. I owe you all debts of gratitude.

Laura, my alpha reader. The initial draft of The Between was unfortunately flawed. I was struggling through a difficult period, discovering just how extensive my anxieties were, and you were at my side as I worked my way to the other side. You recognized how my frame of mind tainted the story and convinced me that there was nothing I couldn't fix, myself included. Thank you.

Julie Perry, my editor. You cannot imagine how grateful I am that you became a member of the Book Club! Your edits were invaluable for their polish and clarity. I so enjoyed our video sessions, debating punctuation and prose. You took one of the most arduous processes and made it as fun as game night!

Leila Kim. What circumstances bring two people together to become friends. Your enthusiasm has touched me so deeply I truly don't have words. You are my very own Annie Wilkes (minus the sledgehammer). Keep selling those flutes!

Alex Baxter. You've been on this journey with me nearly from the beginning. Helping me take the steps to fix myself, to become the person I knew was in there. Thank you for being my friend as well as my therapist.

Peter Aperlo. Your first note to me was "Most writing is rewriting". I learned to love rewriting. Again, thank you for the generosity of your time and wisdom. Your notes pushed me to write at a whole new level.

The Book Club. My beta readers. You took the time to not just read this book before it was ready, but to answer my many questions about it. Your contributions made this a better book.

In no particular order:

Tiffany Wesley, Nicole DiGiose, Jackie Gallo, and Joseph Morris.

My friends and family. Your enthusiastic support through the process has been so important. Whether you merely asked how the book was coming or ventured out in the aftermath of a blizzard to come to my first signing.

I've been fortunate to have the friendship and support of several local businesses. Some have hosted signings, others announced and displayed the book: Sparkling Pointe Winery, McCall Vineyards, and Peconic Bay Vineyards. Thank you Mike, Brewster, and Evan.

And finally you, Dear Reader. Being an independent author is difficult work. The enthusiasm with which so many of you have expressed your enjoyment of and eagerness to continue reading my work has touched me. I believe a book is completed twice: First by the author, then again by each reader. Thank you for helping me tell Alexandrea's story.

Find me on social media: @jhnadler
Please consider leaving a review.

About the Author

JH Nadler

This is Jason's second novel.
A former volunteer firefighter, when he's not writing, he works as a project manager.
He founded North-Forks, a blog of wineries and breweries of the North Fork of Long Island, where he lives with his wife and two insanely co-dependent cats.
You can find him at jhnadler.com and across social media @jhnadler.

Alexandrea Hawthorne's story continues:

The Books of Alexandrea
Book 3: The Library

Coming in 2023.